THE ROCKER WHO BETRAYS ME

OTHERWORLD

USA TODAY BEST SELLING AUTHOR

TERRI ANNE BROWNING

The Rocker Who Betrays Me (The Rocker Series, Book 11)
1st Edition Published October 2015
Published by Terri Anne Browning
Written By Terri Anne Browning
Editor Lorelei Logsdon
Cover Design and Picture by Sara Eirew
Models Carolyn Seguin and Stef Prince
Formatting by M.L. Pahl of IndieVention Designs

ISBN-13: 978-1517493608
ISBN-10: 1517493609

10 9 8 7 6 5 4 3 2 1

Dedication

To the man who loved his Annabelle first.
Rest in peace, dear man.
I hope your Annabelle would have made you proud.

Acknowledgements

Normally this is the point where I say thank you to all the people who have made The Rocker Series such a success over the last few years. I think they know how much they mean to me and how much I appreciate everything they do, not just with helping with these kick-ass books, but in my everyday life as well. You all know who you are and I love you to the moon and back.

Right now I want to prepare you for what you are about to read. *The Rocker Who Betrays Me* is full of angst — heartbreaking, ugly-crying angst. There were times during the writing process where I just had to close my Mac and walk away from a scene for a few hours before I was able to finish certain parts. Out of all the rockers I have given you, Zander has always been the elusive one for me. I started this book six different times and ended up deleting it every single time before I was truly happy with where he was taking me. For once, my bad-ass rocker didn't know how to talk to me and we stumbled a few times along the way. Yet as soon as we got to where we understood each other, the book turned into one that became so much longer than the other books in this series. Z's story needed to start from the beginning, meaning OtherWorld's beginning as well.

Now kick back, relax, and enjoy *The Rocker Who Betrays Me*.

Happy reading.

TABLE OF CONTENTS

Prologue

Annabelle

My heart was beating so hard it was a wonder that no one noticed how badly my chest was shaking. Even though I was trying to deny it to myself, I knew it had nothing to do with the fact that my biggest client was fighting for her life just down the hall in the ICU ward. My subconscious was trying to make itself known loud and clear as to what I was really feeling, what I was really thinking.

For the first time in more than seventeen years, I was in the same room as Zander Brockman. I'd imagined this moment for every damn one of those seventeen years and each time I'd always come up with a different scenario of how I would handle myself should that ever happen. I've imagined myself as calm and collected, broken and weeping, raging mad with my fists flying toward his sexy-as-sin face, and every emotion in between.

I hadn't taken into account how my heart would break a little more from just seeing his face, or how my body would respond to his nearness. It only pissed me off. How could I betray myself like that? How could I let him affect me in either of those ways after what he'd done?

I sat on one of the uncomfortable chairs, waiting on Emmie to finish up her calls before we went downstairs for the scheduled press conference that we'd set up. My mind should have been on the job-at-hand and the fact that my biggest client was fighting for her life after risking it to save Mia Armstrong. Instead all I could do was sit there and sneak glances at the rocker standing with his best friend and Natalie Stevenson across the room.

Fuck. Time had been good to Zander. There were even more tattoos on him now than there had been the last time I'd set eyes on him in the flesh.

His hair was a little longer now, curling like it always did; his face even more defined, making me want to trace each angle with my fingertips. He was even sexier now than he had been at eighteen, making it nearly impossible for me not to react to him. It wasn't fair that he had only gotten better-looking with age while I'd been fighting back the hands of time from the day he'd left me.

His head started to turn and I quickly looked away before he caught me staring. How embarrassing would that be to get caught gawking at the man who had made it abundantly clear seventeen years before that he was through with me?

Disgusted with myself, I lowered my eyes to my phone and realized I had a text.

R U Ok?

My heart melted at the sight of those three words from the only person who had ever cared enough to put me first. I swallowed hard and swiped my thumb over his name before lifting the phone to my ear. It had barely rung on the other end when I heard his voice.

"Annabelle," my brother said, sounding relieved.

"Hi," I choked out. "Everything okay?"

"I was going to ask *you* that," he said with a small, deep laugh that quickly faded. "You didn't respond to my text. Are you okay?"

Noah knew how difficult this was for me. I always avoided anything that had to do with OtherWorld. It was one of the reasons I hadn't been at the festival with Gabriella and her band when she'd been shot. Being here now, surrounded by people from my past, was bringing back memories that were both bittersweet and painful.

Grimacing, I forced myself to lift my head and straightened my shoulders. "I'm fine, Noah. Honestly." It wasn't the first time I'd lied to my brother, but it had been a long time since I'd had to, and I hoped he would forgive me for it. "I'm just busy. Things are crazy here. Emmie and I are going to be doing a press conference in a few so I need to go."

"Okay, I understand. I'm just worried about you, honey. Chelsea and Mieke are worried too." I tightened my hold on the phone and stood, making sure my back was to the three people standing across the room so they couldn't see my expression right then. "We'll watch the conference."

"Don't," I whispered. "Don't let them watch it. I don't want Chelsea and Mieke upset when they see me."

I heard the deep breath that Noah blew out, and I clenched my fingers even tighter around the phone, making my entire hand ache. "Annabelle—"

"I have to go, Noah. I love you."

"Damn it, Annabelle." I heard his growl but didn't wait for the explosion that was about to erupt from my brother. I hated that he was upset with me, but I couldn't let them see me right then. Not when my emotions were so close to the surface. Not when everything was churning inside of me like a hurricane.

I quickly disconnected and put my phone away. Turning, I refused to let my gaze travel across the room. Thankfully Emmie was walking toward me, immediately distracting me from my inner chaos. The little redhead with those big green eyes didn't smile as she approached, but I doubted she would smile again anytime soon. I could understand what she was going through, having nearly lost her daughter less than twenty-four hours before. My heart clenched in sympathy for her.

"Ready?" Emmie demanded in a hard-as-steel tone.

I gave her a firm nod and turned toward the ICU's waiting-room door. Opening it for her, I waited as she exited before following her. Only when the door was firmly closed behind us and we were about to step onto the elevator where two guards stood at attention, did I relax a little. Damn, I was exhausted.

Just being in the same room with Zander had been enough to drain me of all my physical and emotional strength.

How the hell was I going to keep this up for however long it took before this shit was over?

17 years ago
Annabelle

The sound of something breaking jerked me awake. With a gasp, I sat up in bed and strained my ears as I tried to listen for what had awoken me.

"I don't know why I ever married you, you worthless piece of shit!"

When I heard Mom's screech I jumped out of bed and grabbed my backpack. She was drinking—again. When she drank, she got mean, and lately that was more often than not. If she was yelling, then she was yelling at Jacob, and that never ended well. *At least not for me.* She would take out her rage on her husband, and he would take his out on me if I didn't leave now.

It didn't matter that I was only in a pair of pajama shorts and a tank top without a bra. My backpack was like my survival pack. I always kept what I needed in there for when this happened. I had a change of clothes as well as a few Pop-Tarts and a bottle of water in there along with my schoolbooks.

My bare feet landed on the damp grass outside my bedroom window and I moved quickly toward the darkened window of the house next door. Recently this had become an almost nightly habit, and I knew that if he wasn't home, his window would still be unlocked for me. If by some chance it wasn't, then I had one other option. That was the good thing about having friends that were also your next-door neighbors.

I tapped my fingernails on the window, silently counting to myself until I reached fourteen. It would drive him crazy if I didn't wait to get to fourteen and he was in there. I held my breath, hoping that he was home. It wasn't that he had to be home for me to hide out in his room, but that I *needed* him to be there.

Before I could draw another breath, the curtains flickered and the window opened enough for me to climb in. The bed was right under the window and I dropped down onto it, tossing my backpack on the floor before wrapping my arms around Zander's waist and burying my face in his chest.

Strong fingers tangled in my hair, holding me against him as I tried to contain my broken sob. Fear was still racing through me and I kept wondering what would have happened if I hadn't heard my mother, if she hadn't woken me up. How long would it have been before Jacob had been in my room?

"Are you hurt?" His voice was rough with sleep but full of dangerous promises if I told him I was.

"No," I whispered, my voice quivering.

He released a relieved sigh. "It's okay, Anna. You're okay. I've got you." Zander kept whispering those words over and over again against my ear and slowly I began to relax.

He was right. I was safe here with him holding me. I knew that Jacob wouldn't dare come here. Not only did he not want Zander's grandparents to know why I was hiding from him in their grandson's room, but he also wouldn't risk the hell storm that would fall on him if he dared to upset Zander.

My tears started to dry and I closed my eyes as I soaked up the feeling of security that being in Zander's arms gave me. Before long my breathing began to even out and I fell into a dreamless sleep.

Safe. I was safe here...

Sunlight streaming through the open window woke me the next morning. I stretched and smiled when I came into contact with the hard body still lying beside me. My heart melted at the sight of the guy who had become my hero over the last few months.

I'd known Zander all my life. He and his mom had lived with his grandparents in the house beside mine before I'd even been born. Best friends with my brother, I'd grown up loving the boy who was two years older than me just as much as my own brother. We'd been playmates, friends, and each other's shoulder to cry on from the time I could walk. I was the one he'd sought out when his mother had been diagnosed with breast cancer. He was the one I'd wanted holding my hand when we'd said goodbye to my dad after his accident. The day his mother joined my dad in Heaven, I'd held onto him just as tightly as he'd held onto me, offering him all the love and support I could give.

Out of all of my brother's friends, out of all the people I knew I could turn to, it was Zander that I'd gone to when things had started getting ugly at home over the summer. The first night I'd knocked on his window, he'd been ready to slay the dragon that was my stepfather for me.

There was a reason why Zander only had a handful of friends. For the most part he was just the guy who got into trouble for pulling harmless pranks with my brother and their friends. He was full of humor, and his ability to make me smile even at the lowest of times had always melted my heart. It was what came when his hazel eyes turned green that made people keep their distance from him. He had a temper, and while it took a lot to get him riled up, once he was, it could get dangerous if someone wasn't careful.

I'd heard the whispers, the ones from people who thought his mind was broken because of his OCD. Just as I'd heard the whispers about how they knew he was going to hurt me one day with his violent temper. I wanted to laugh in their faces. Neither of those things were true. He wasn't broken, far from it. Although he doubted himself, I knew that Zander was the least broken person in the world. As for hurting me, I knew that he would never do that. Zander would have killed for me, but he would never touch me with anything that resembled violence.

Jacob was a different story, however. After what had happened that first night, after seeing the bruises from where my stepfather had woken me by dragging me out of my bed and beating me, I'd had to beg Zander not to do anything to him. We'd stayed in his room together that entire weekend before I trusted him not to rip Jacob apart. But I knew that he must have said something to my stepfather, because Jacob kept a wide berth when he was around Zander these days.

I pushed myself up onto my elbow so I could look down at Zander better. Sometime over the last few months my feelings for him had changed dramatically. When I looked at him I didn't see the boy I'd grown up loving as much as my own brother; I now saw the man who was sexy as sin and held my heart in an entirely different way.

If you took one look at Zander you would forgive me for wanting him so desperately. His eyes were more often hazel than not, and were always full of amusement. There were already smile lines around those eyes I adored so much because he laughed every day. His face wasn't beautiful, like Liam Bryant's was, but that was a good thing. He had a strong jaw, a wide mouth with a full bottom lip that I'd been daydreaming of tasting more and more lately. His dark hair was cut short, but when it grew out even a little bit it started to curl. Right then his jaw was dark with stubble and I couldn't help wondering how he would look with a beard. His bare chest was already starting to get covered in ink, as well as his left arm and both hands.

His grandmother had prayed for his soul the first time she'd seen the tattoos, but it was the first time I'd ever looked at Zander as anything but a brotherly figure. It had opened my eyes to just how I really felt about this boy/man.

I'd fallen in love with Zander Brockman at some point over the summer.

It was a dangerous, stupid thing to do. What was it about a bad boy that made girls flock to them? I wasn't sure if it was because of his reputation of being dangerous or if it was because he and my brother had started a band with their friends two years ago. Either way, he had girls chasing after him like savage dogs in heat. He probably didn't even consider me as anything more than a sister.

Sighing, I glanced at the clock beside his bed and realized I was going to be late for school if I didn't hurry. I climbed out of bed, grabbed my backpack, and quietly crossed to his connecting bathroom. I didn't shower because I knew that would draw attention from his grandparents.

Opening my backpack, I pulled out the fresh clothes and my toothbrush. Using Zander's toothpaste, I brushed my teeth before washing my face and changing into the cutoff jean shorts and T-shirt. My boobs weren't much to get excited about so I didn't need a bra. I finger-combed my hair into a ponytail and then pulled my flip-flops out of the backpack. I'd have to start packing tennis shoes soon because the weather would be getting colder before long.

Dressed, I cleaned up my mess and zipped up the backpack before going back into the bedroom. Zander was still asleep, but he didn't have to be at work for another hour or so. I bit my lip. In the past I hadn't really thought about if I liked school or not. Now that I was in my junior year, without my brother and his friends, I was starting to realize that I really hated it.

Noah and his friends had made high school so much easier. I'd had someone to sit with every day at lunch and no one had dared to mess with me. Noah, Zander, Devlin Cutter, and Liam Bryant had been there to protect me. Without them there to run interference, I was starting to realize that most girls were catty and all-out bitches, while guys were either sick, twisted assholes or creeps who tried to get me to notice them.

I slipped my backpack on and tried to climb over Zander's sleeping body. The bed sank in as I opened the window a little more, and two strong arms wrapped around my waist. I sucked in a deep breath, secretly loving having him hold me like that, but didn't melt against him as I ached to do.

Zander pulled me down onto the bed and pulled me against him. "Sneaking out without so much as a goodbye? I'm hurt, Annabelle. You're breaking my heart, babe."

I snorted. "Yeah. I can tell." I grinned up at his smiling face, loving how his hazel eyes looked with the morning sun shining behind him. His eyes really were like windows to his soul. Most of the time they were full of amusement, but even when he was pissed and his temper was ready to go supernova, his eyes let you know what he was thinking. They turned more green than hazel, with gold flecks flashing like flames in his eyes. No matter which they happened to be, hazel or green, I always loved looking into them like I was doing right then.

"Do you have to work after school today?"

I nodded. During summer vacation I'd worked at my family's garage every day. Since school had started a month before, I'd been working after school Wednesday through Friday and all day on Saturdays, because those tended to be our busiest days. It was Friday, and I would be closing the garage as I usually did.

"I'll pick you up and we can get a burger before we come home." His eyes started to turn more green than hazel as he spoke. "I don't think you should even go home tonight, babe. Just sleep here."

I lifted a brow at him, trying to make light of the whole thing because I knew he could go full-on green and gold in a heartbeat if I didn't. "You sure you want to pick me up? I mean, won't I be cramping your style, rocker boy? Don't you and the guys have to play at Floyd's Bar and slut yourselves out to the groupies?"

The green disappeared and hazel eyes laughed down at me as he smirked. "If I didn't know better I'd say you were jealous, babe." He tickled me just under my ribs before I could lie by denying it. I bit back a laugh as he tickled me again before releasing me. "We're playing early at Floyd's, so I'll be able to pick you up."

"Oh, okay. If you don't mind, then I'd like that." I sat up and Zander fell back onto the bed, smiling up at me like he always did.

Looking down at him like that, being assaulted with how perfect he was, I couldn't resist touching him. I lowered my head and quickly kissed his cheek. "Bye, Z," I called over my shoulder as I climbed out the window.

I might have gotten a little bold by kissing his cheek like that, but there was no way I was going to stick around and see his reaction. If he laughed at my innocent peck on his cheek I was pretty sure my heart would have broken. My feet were on the ground and I was about to turn and head for the street so I could catch the bus when he leaned out the window and caught my wrist.

His eyes were green again, and those damn flecks of gold were shooting flames at me, but he was smiling. "See you tonight, babe."

Zander

My shirt was soaked in sweat when I walked into my grandparents' house that evening. Spending all day in the sun had become my way of life since graduation. Devlin Cutter and I had been working for the county from practically the start of summer and we both knew that it would be our career if OtherWorld didn't take off like we hoped.

I'd spent the day patching potholes on a back road with Devlin and two other guys for most of the day. The September heat had beat on me all day and I'd be lying if I said I wasn't ready for the cooler weather that fall promised. I couldn't complain too much, though. My job paid well, and I had benefits, plus evenings and weekends off, so our Friday-night gigs at Floyd's Bar were still possible.

Bending, I unlaced my steel-toed boots and kicked them off before entering the kitchen. I could smell Gram's cornbread baking and my stomach grumbled in protest. It seemed like lunchtime had been days ago instead of just hours, and I was starving. Glancing at my watch, I figured I had time to take a quick shower before we sat down to eat.

"Zander?" Gram called out as she left the pantry with a can of peas in her hand. Seeing me in her kitchen, her eyes softened and she smiled at me. "I thought you were going to be late."

I smirked at her as I dropped a kiss on her wrinkled cheek. "Nah, Gram. You know I would never be late for your supper."

17

She patted me on the shoulder and then grimaced when her hand came away covered in sweat. "I don't know how you can stand being in the sun all day, honey. Your poor face is going to get as wrinkled as Gramps is before long if you keep it up. Did you wear sunblock?"

I shook my head at the little old lady who had basically raised me. "I put some on, but it sweated off after about an hour. We were so busy I didn't bother putting more on."

She made a disapproving noise in the back of her throat and I quickly excused myself to go take a shower before she used one of her wooden spoons to tan my hide for not listening to her. She was always worrying about me. If I'd thought that my graduating from high school and getting a real job would have made her stop, I'd been wrong. Not that I would admit it out loud, but I liked that she still worried about me.

In the shower, I let out a relieved groan as I let the lukewarm water wash away the sweat and grime of the day. I took my time washing, since it was a Friday and we had our usual gig that night. We were going on earlier than usual that night because I'd requested it, so I didn't have much time after supper to get out to Floyd's Bar.

The reasons for my request had gotten all of my band-brothers pissed off. Not because we were going to be in and out of the bar sooner than usual—meaning our pay wasn't going to be nearly as good—but because they wouldn't get the pussy that came with the later show. My jaw clenched and I leaned back against the shower wall as I thought about Annabelle.

I didn't mind her coming to me every night. I knew as long as she was in my room, she was safe. It was how scared she was every time she came to me that messed with my fucked-up head. Jacob Malcolm was a hair's breath away from getting buried in one of the potholes on one of the back roads that I had to fix every day. It took all my willpower not to fuck that bastard up, but I'd refrained from doing so because Annabelle had begged me not to do anything that would land me in trouble.

Blowing out a frustrated breath, I raked my hands through my dripping hair, pulling on the ends like the mad man I was. All my life I'd fought with my OCD, but I knew it was more than that. My mind was broken and there was nothing I could do to fix it. But when Annabelle was around, when I had her to smile at me and flash those damn blue eyes up at me, I felt like I wasn't nearly as broken.

That the one person who brought me peace was scared to even sleep in her own bed was not helping my sanity any.

Muttering a curse, I beat my fist on the shower wall, imagining Jacob's face as I destroyed it. It was only when my hand started to ache that I turned off the water and reached for a towel. My knuckles were swollen, but at least I hadn't busted them open. It was going to be a bitch playing later, but I'd deal with that. I'd rather play hurt than have my rage for that fucker so close to the surface.

I was still distracted from thinking about Annabelle, though. So much so that Gram kept asking me if I was alright during supper. I knew I was worrying her, but couldn't manage to reassure her. She knew that if I wasn't laughing and joking around that something was wrong, but Annabelle had pleaded with me not to tell my grandparents about what was going on in the house next door.

"You gettin' sick, boy?" Gramps asked as he swallowed a bite of the apple pie Gram had made for dessert.

I forced a smile for the old man. He was the only father figure I'd ever known, and I knew I could have done a hell of a lot worse when it came to having a male role model to show me how to be a man. Gramps was a gruff man, who rarely showed any emotion, but he'd always treated Gram like she was a queen. That was good enough for me.

"Nah, Gramps. Just tired. Been a long week."

Having worked his entire life for the county before retiring ten years before, Gramps understood just how tiring it could be. With a nod, Gramps went back to eating his pie and I hurried to finish my own so I could get out the door. Devlin was already waiting in his driveway two houses over when I called a 'goodnight' to Grams.

Seeing me headed toward the old truck I'd bought with my first paycheck that summer, he came over and climbed in beside me. He had his own truck, but it was a waste of gas for us both to drive when we were going to the same place.

Normally Devlin and I would have been joking the whole way to Floyd's Bar, but neither of us was in a laughing mood that night. I'd told him that Annabelle had climbed through my window again the night before and he'd been brooding about it all day just as much as I had been.

We knew what was going to happen if things didn't change for Annabelle at home. Her brother had moved out at the beginning of the summer to live in the apartment above the garage his family owned—the only real garage in West Bridge Tennessee. He knew what was going on at home, but I don't think he really understood the real danger his sister was in. Annabelle hadn't told him everything. Once he did, once *I* told him all of it, things were going to change for all of us.

Noah and Annabelle were closer than any siblings I'd ever known. He would want to protect her even more than I did. My jaw clenched and I shook my head as I stopped at the only stop sign in the county. Maybe *more* than I did. Maybe. I wasn't sure if that was possible, but what-the-fuck-ever. Noah would put Annabelle first. He would want to get his sister as far away from their mother and stepfather as possible. I knew he would quit OtherWorld.

My gut clenched at that thought. Not just because I would miss Noah, who was like a brother to me, but because I would miss Annabelle.

So fucking much.

I would miss her climbing through my window every night. I'd miss her burying her face against my chest and holding on to me until she fell asleep. I'd miss the way her soft little body felt against my own. And I'd miss waking up beside her every morning.

For fifteen years I'd thought of Annabelle as a sister and one of my closest friends. But two years ago those feelings had shifted and I'd started looking at my friend in an entirely differently light. Annabelle wasn't just a friend any longer. She was a hot chick who I wanted. Bad.

Mostly I'd been able to keep a leash on my feelings for her, but that was getting harder and harder to do now. I'd been fighting with myself since that first damn night she'd tapped on my window. My fucked-up head didn't understand that wanting Annabelle Cassidy was a bad thing. Not only was it wrong to want my best friend's little sister, but she was two years younger than I was.

Two years might not seem like that much of a difference, but when you were nearly nineteen and the girl wouldn't be seventeen for a few more weeks, things got tricky. I was considered an adult while she was still technically a baby. Jailbait was what Liam had called her one night.

Yeah. She was definitely jailbait.

"You gonna go, bro?"

I blinked, realizing I'd been stopped at the stop sign for several minutes. Letting a few curse words loose, I pressed on the gas and drove through the intersection. Devlin chuckled for the first time that day and I felt a little of my own tension ease slightly at the sound of my friend's laughter.

By the time we got to Floyd's Bar, I was relaxed enough that I didn't feel like a homicidal maniac. I played like shit when I was pissed and didn't want to mess the night up even more than I already suspected it would be. Finding a parking spot, I jumped out of the truck and spotted the trailer that Wroth and Liam pulled with Wroth's Ford. We kept our stuff in the trailer and since Wroth was always so worried about his guitar getting fucked up, he was the only one who pulled it.

And since the fucker scared the shit out of me, I didn't protest. Seriously, not much in the world scared me, but Wroth Niall was at the top of that short list. *Second only to my fear of something happening to Annabelle.*

Noah, Liam and Wroth were already carrying our gear inside so Devlin and I jumped in to help. Mostly I played bass, but because my Gram had been forcing me to play the piano since I was three, I had some skills with the keyboard as well. Of course her version of skills was playing Mozart whereas mine was learning to play Metallica and actually making it sound good while being played on a cheap-ass keyboard.

Because I loved my Gram so much, I'd learned to do both, but she didn't need to know about the Metallica part. It would probably break the old lady's heart and that would only lead to my broken mind getting that much more fucked up.

Once everything was set up, we had half an hour before we had to start our set. We sat in the back office of the bar drinking the beers that Floyd slipped us. Wroth was the only one who was legal to drink, so if we wanted to drink we had to do it in the office.

I lifted a beer to my lips and swallowed half before blowing out a long breath and finally turning my gaze to the guy sitting on the shabby old couch to my right. "We gotta talk, man."

Noah's light blue eyes were so much like his sister's that my gut twisted when he lifted them to meet mine. "What's up?"

I clenched my jaw and glanced around at the other guys in the room. Liam was off in the bathroom and I could only guess what he was doing. Since he'd started dating Tawny, his whole personality had changed and he'd been getting deep into the drug scene. Devlin sat on the rolling chair across from me and Wroth was staring off into space like he usually did. The dude was scary as hell without those demons flashing in his unfocused dark eyes; when they did, he looked like he was fucking possessed.

"It's about Annabelle," Devlin cut in.

Even from the few feet separating us on the couch I could feel the way Noah tensed up. "What about her?" he gritted out. "Is she okay?"

I tipped my beer up and swallowed the rest in one gulp before speaking again. "She's been spending the night with me every night for the last few weeks, man. She's scared shitless of Jacob."

Light blue eyes narrowed. "What the fuck are you talking about?" Noah snarled. "She's been spending the night with you? How the fuck has she been spending the night with you?"

"Dude, relax," Devlin cut in. "It's not like that. She's just been sleeping there. Nothing else. Z wouldn't do that, man."

I didn't speak, because I wasn't sure if I would do *that* or not. I wanted to, so damn bad. So far I'd been able to keep from crossing that line, but it kept getting harder and harder with each passing night.

Noah's shoulders dropped with something that looked like relief crossing his face. "Okay, then what the fuck is going on? Why is Annabelle sleeping in your room?"

"Because things are ugly at your house, man," I told him. "Your mom has been drinking every night. And not just a few glasses of wine, dude. She's been getting shitfaced. She gets pissed and starts screaming at Jacob.

I can hear her from my house." Thankfully my grandparents were getting hard of hearing and hadn't heard Wendy Cassidy-Malcolm screaming at her husband like the hag she was. "Then when she's done screaming and throwing shit, she goes to bed and Jacob takes his frustration out on Annabelle. The first night you know about, but Anna didn't tell you everything."

I knew when Annabelle found out I'd told her brother everything, she was going to get pissed at me, but I couldn't let that shit keep going on without him knowing. So I told Noah about how Annabelle had been woken up one night over the summer to Jacob pulling her out of bed and slamming her against the wall. How he'd slapped her over and over again, splitting her lip and putting bruises all over her arms.

I felt my rage starting to boil up all over again just thinking of how she had looked when she'd knocked on my window afterward. Her lip had been bleeding and she'd had black and blue fingerprints on her soft peaches-and-cream arms. She begged me not to do anything, pleaded for me to just stay and hold her that night and the rest of the weekend. By the time I'd had to go to work that Monday, I'd been a little more sane, but not by much. I'd kept my hands off Jacob Malcolm, but I'd made sure that he knew I was watching him.

Of course he hadn't heeded my threats for more than a week or so before he'd woken Annabelle with a slap to her beautiful face. She'd climbed through my window that night with a red handprint on her cheek. I'd paid a visit to the fucker at work the next day and given him a few handprints of my own. He'd told everyone he'd gotten his black eye from walking into a door, and Annabelle had been able to sleep in her own bed for several more weeks without having to worry about her stepfather hurting her.

"A few weeks ago he did it again," I bit out as I glared off into space, flashes of Annabelle holding her bleeding nose making my hands fist on my thighs. "She begged me not to say anything to you, and I didn't out of loyalty to her. But I made sure Jacob knew I wasn't playing around. He still walks a little stiff from where I punched him in the ribs."

"So she's been scared all summer?" Noah's voice was hoarse, his blue eyes nearly cobalt with emotion. "He's been beating on her and she's been so scared that she doesn't even sleep in her own bed. Why didn't she tell me?"

I shrugged. "Probably because she knows that you'll do something crazy. Like kill the fucker." It was what I wanted to do to the bastard. But it was the image of her begging me with tear-filled baby-blue eyes not to do anything that would take me away from her that had kept my instinct to destroy that little prick in check.

"Has he touched her since?"

"She says he hasn't but she's terrified that he will. She doesn't get enough sleep because of it and I think she's starting to struggle in school. I saw one of her test papers sticking out of her backpack the other day and the grade on it wasn't one I would expect Annabelle to get." She was so damn smart. What the fuck was she doing making D's?

Noah jerked to his feet and started pacing. "What the hell am I going to do?" he muttered, but I knew he wasn't asking any of us. He was talking to himself, like he always did, raking his fingers through his blond hair.

If you looked at him and Annabelle you would have no doubt that they were brother and sister. They had the same platinum-blond hair, the same light blue eyes, even the same nose. On Noah it gave him a pretty-boy kind of face, one that girls went crazy for every Friday night when he took the stage. On Annabelle it gave her an almost delicate elfin quality and it only increased my instinct to protect her.

"We could kill the motherfucker," Wroth spoke up for the first time letting us all know that he hadn't been so lost in his nightmarish memories that he hadn't been paying attention. "I'm not against slicing that fucking loser up."

"I'm with you there, dude." Devlin pushed his long dark hair back from his face, grinning evilly. "You're a beast. You could hold him down while we took turns slicing him open."

"We'll call that plan B," I muttered. The whole idea would have made me happy, but I knew that Annabelle would be upset. Probably not that we actually did it, but that we would get in trouble. She was always trying to protect us, when that was exactly what we wanted to do for her. "Noah, what are you gonna do, man?"

"I don't fucking know, bro. I don't fucking know."

Annabelle

My stomach was growling and I still had over an hour to go before I could lock up the garage. I was exhausted after spending all day at school dealing with the drama that went with high school: bitchy girls, boys who thought they were men trying to either get me to notice them or wanted to push my buttons because of old vendettas against my brother and his friends, pop quizzes as well as tests that I should have studied for but hadn't remembered to, teachers complaining and lecturing… The list went on and on.

On top of all that, I'd come into the garage with plans to study for the exam I was supposed to retake on Monday after turning on the water works with my history teacher. Mr. Wake was in his mid-forties, but he was still a sucker for a pretty face and tears. I'd been desperate enough to pull one of the tricks I hated other girls for pulling. I'd gotten a D on my last history test and the grade I'd gotten today hadn't been any better. If I didn't get my grade up, the vice principal would be sending a letter home to my mother and I just couldn't deal with that crap at the moment.

For the most part, my mother ignored me. She liked to pretend I didn't exist and I was more than happy to let her. It was how things had always been between us, even before my father had died and she'd married Jacob Malcolm.

My plans to study had been thrown in the trashcan when I'd gotten off the bus in front of the garage and seen the way everything was backed up in the office. We only had one full-time mechanic. Wade Cutter was a freaking genius when it came to anything that involved an engine. His social skills, however, needed some serious work. Noah and Liam had worked part time, apprenticing with Wade up until last year. Liam's cousin, Wroth, had come back from his deployment overseas and Liam had quit soon after.

Noah had still been apprenticing up until he had graduated this past May. Now he lived in the apartment above the garage and helped out more in the office than in the garage. When I'd stepped into the office it was to find Noah with grease smeared across his face and hands as he tried to sort through the paperwork on the desk. Six different customers had been standing around, shooting daggers at my brother.

"What's going on?" I'd smiled politely at a few of our regular customers, but two of them were strangers to me.

Noah nodded his head at the strangers without taking his eyes off the computer. "Idiot number one has been driving around on bald tires for a while now. Thought he could make the long drive from New Jersey to Mississippi on them. Didn't work so good for him when one blew out and he took off the bumper of idiot number two. Idiot number two needs a new bumper and for some reason a new carburetor, but thinks that idiot number one should pay for said carburetor."

I looked at the two strangers and forced a smile for them while my brother continued to call them both idiots. Noah had become one hell of a mechanic, but his social skills were nearly as bad as Wade's when it came to dealing with customers. He had no patience for stupid people and no filter to make him keep his mouth shut. Not that it mattered all that much. My dad's garage was the only one in the county so it wasn't like we were going to lose business because of my brother's rudeness. Still, it helped make things a hell of a lot easier when you were nicer to the customers.

At least it made it easier on me. Since I had to run the office Wednesday through Saturday, I was the one who had to field angry phone calls. Usually because of the way Noah had treated someone, but there was the occasional irate old farmer who needed a new part but had been told to 'fuck off' because Noah had been too busy to deal with them.

When Noah continued to glare at the computer, I'd nudged him out of the way and took the invoice slips from his hands. "Go help Wade. I got this."

Noah grunted something under his breath and slammed the door that led into the garage bay behind him. I gritted my teeth, sucked in a deep breath for patience, and smiled up at the two men my brother had called idiots. "Gentlemen, can I get you to take a seat for a few minutes? I'll be right with you, I promise." For extra measure I turned up the brightness of my smile and fluttered my long lashes at them.

The displeased expressions on their faces cleared marginally and they both took seats in front of the window that acted as our waiting room for such occasions. Once they were out of my way, I dealt with the other four customers who had been waiting to pick up their vehicles that had either needed a new part or an oil change. It took less than ten minutes to get them to pay and out the door with their keys in hand.

Once the majority of the chaos was out of the office, I turned my full attention on the remaining two men and started to put their information in the computer. Our system was outdated and needed to be handled with kid gloves. Something that Noah still didn't understand.

It took over an hour to get everything sorted because I had to call both customers' insurance agents to make sure we were going to get paid. There was only one problem. There was no way insurance was going to cover a carburetor for a simple fender bender. Explaining that proved to be futile and I took to calling the stupid man Idiot Number Two, if only in my head. It was after five before I had the payment from the would-be conman.

Around six, Noah appeared in the office, freshly showered and changed into his usual old T-shirt and faded jeans he wore to his weekly gigs at Floyd's Bar. "Wade is almost finished with the Buick. They'll be picking it up in the morning, so go ahead and start on the invoice for that. If they get here early I'll just take care of them so you don't have to."

I raised a brow at him. "Whose Buick is it?"

"Mrs. Farris."

"Then I really, really, really hope you have to deal with her." I'd grinned up at him. "She still hates me." Mrs. Farris had been both Noah's fifth-grade teacher and mine. She had adored Noah, but when I'd become her student it had been like night and day in how she'd treated me. I tried not to let it bug me, but it still did. I'd never had a teacher dislike me until that old hag.

"Let's hope, kid." Noah had leaned over the desk, brushed a kiss over my cheek and left the office with a grin on his face.

Wade had finished up the Buick and left over half an hour ago, and I still had a mountain of paperwork to deal with before I could lock up.

My tummy flipped at the thought of what was going to happen after I closed the garage for the night. Zander was supposed to pick me up. We were going to get a hamburger and then I would be spending the night in his room again. My heart kept teasing me that this was like a date, while my brain kept scolding me that it was just Zander being Zander. He was looking out for me, making sure I ate and that I was safe.

The inner battle between my heart and brain was distracting and I still wasn't finished with all the paperwork by the time an old truck pulled up in the parking lot. Groaning, I stacked all the papers together and left them on the desk so I would remember to do it in the morning. It took a few minutes to shut down the computer, but at least I'd put the money in the safe earlier and didn't have to worry about that. Grabbing my backpack, I locked the garage door and then the front door on my way out.

Zander was already out of the truck. He stood leaning against the passenger door, a tired smile on his sinfully sexy face. It was dark out, but the streetlights made it possible for me to notice that his eyes were green and shooting gold flames. The smile told me he wasn't raging, though.

Reaching out, he took my backpack off my shoulder and tossed it in the back of the truck. "Long day?"

I shrugged. "I've had longer."

Zander grimaced. "Yeah, I bet you have, babe." He opened the passenger door and stepped back. "I'm starving. How about you?" Before I could even nod my head, my stomach growled loudly, causing him to grin. "I'll take that as a yes."

"It's been a while since lunch," I muttered as I climbed up into the truck with his help. His hand touched my back and I couldn't help how I reacted. Goose bumps popped up on my arms and legs, and I shivered. I knew it was just Zander helping me in, not him touching me because he actually wanted to touch me. His grandmother had taught him to be a gentleman where members of the opposite sex were concerned. Well, for the most part. My heart didn't seem to care because it melted a little more for him as he closed the door and jogged around to the driver's side of the truck.

He started the engine and shot me a frown as he turned to back out of the parking lot. "You haven't eaten anything since lunch? That was what, eleven thirty?" I nodded and his jaw clenched. "I don't like that, Anna."

Stupidly, my heart gave a little delighted shiver at his calling me 'Anna'. He was the only one who ever shortened my name, and it made me feel as if I were special to him because of it. Liam Bryant had his own nickname for me, but Anna was so much better than Anna Banana.

"We were busy most of the evening," I explained. "And then Noah left for the bar so I couldn't go get a snack or anything. Besides, I knew you were going to pick me up. I didn't want to ruin my dinner."

Zander pulled out onto the road, but his hands were clenched around the steering wheel. "I'll bring you something next time. I don't like you being hungry and not eating."

Ah, Z.

I smiled to myself as he continued to drive toward the only burger place in West Bridge. We didn't have a McDonalds or anything; just a locally owned place called The Burger Shack, which was ten times better than any fast-food chain. It was only eight thirty on a Friday night, and the place was crowded when Zander pulled into the parking lot.

He opened his door and waited for me to scoot across the bench seat to climb out on his side. His hand shot out to take mine as he helped me down, but he didn't release it once he'd shut the door. Pulling me close, he linked his fingers through mine and we went in.

Inside, it was so full that Zander released my hand and wrapped his arm around my waist, keeping me close as we made our way to the long line of people waiting to order. A few people saw that it was Zander and immediately stepped out of the way. West Bridge was a small town, which meant there were very few places to hang out on Friday nights. Most everyone came to The Burger Shack to hang out more than to actually eat.

"Annabelle!"

I turned at the sound of my name and smiled when I saw my friend waving at me from a back booth. Chelsea made a face and waved her arms again. Beside me, Zander groaned. "Of course they would be here," I thought he muttered under his breath, but the noise level was so loud that I wasn't sure if I'd heard him right.

Chelsea turned her head away and I watched her stare dreamily up at the guy sitting next to her. I shook my head at the sight of my brother stuffing a burger in his mouth, seemingly unaware of the adoring way his girlfriend was watching him. Chelsea was probably my closest friend, but she had been Noah's girlfriend first. I didn't know how those two had stayed together as long as they had because they tended to argue more than anything else. Still, I figured they would be together forever and my friend would one day be my sister-in-law.

We ordered our burgers with extra chili fries to share and waited for the order before turning to find a place to sit. I figured Zander would want to sit with Noah and so I started walking toward the back table, but he caught hold of my elbow and pulled me down into a booth with him closer to the front. I was surprised but definitely happy that we were sitting alone.

Zander handed over my wrapped burger, his brows raised. "Is this okay?"

"Yeah, Z. This is great." I took a sip of my sweet tea before smiling up at him. "Thanks."

"Is it enough?" He sounded concerned. "If you want something else, I'll order it for you. How about some fried mac and cheese?"

I couldn't help but laugh. "This is plenty, Z. I swear. I probably won't even eat all of this."

He didn't look convinced. "Okay, but we're getting dessert afterward. Okay?"

Damn it. My heart was going to be a puddle of goo if he didn't stop. "Yeah, okay."

I took my time eating my burger, mostly eating the chili fries, which were my favorite. Thankfully it was the extra-large order, because Zander was like a wild animal when he ate. His burger was gone in no time as well as half of the fries. When I was full I offered him the rest of my burger and it was gone within a few seconds. He licked his lips before wiping them with a napkin. "You want a slice of pie here or should we wait and get ice cream?"

I blinked, coming out of the daze I'd been in after watching his tongue swipe across his full bottom lip. "Um… ice cream sounds good," I murmured before taking a gulp of my sweet tea in hopes of cooling myself off.

Zander grinned. "Good. That means we can get out of here before your brother comes over to ruin our night."

My heart jumped. He didn't want Noah interrupting us? I couldn't help wondering why. Was it because he was having a good time with me and didn't want my brother getting all big-brother on him? Was this really a date? My heart and head were both confused and hoping, but I didn't want to act stupid so I bit down on the inside of my cheek to keep from blurting out something I'd regret.

He stood and picked up the tray that had our trash on it. He was back from throwing it away before I could get to my feet. Zander took my hand and linked our fingers as he headed for the door. I glanced over my shoulder as we waited for a few other people to enter The Burger Shack to glance at Noah and Chelsea. My friend waved and I lifted my free hand to wave back, but Noah was watching me with narrowed eyes. That look made me glad that we were going for ice cream and not sticking around. I didn't need Noah going all brother-bear on Zander.

Outside, the night air was turning cooler and the scent of rain was on the wind. Zander stopped by the passenger door to his truck and while he opened the door for me I closed my eyes and enjoyed the clean fragrance. I'd always loved the rain, even the thunder and lightning. For me it was calming. The rain could wash away the past, while the thunder and lightning seemed to energize me.

Zander tugged on my fingers and I opened my eyes to find him staring down at me with an odd expression on his sinfully sexy face. The lighting was too dim for me to see his eyes, but at a guess I would have said they were green with those damn gold flecks flaming down at me. My heart jumped in my chest, excitement making my blood practically sing.

I didn't dare blink for fear of making him step away from me. *Kiss me. Please, kiss me.*

An old farm truck backfired as it left the parking lot, causing me to jump. Zander shook his head, as if he was trying to clear it, and then smiled down at me a little sadly. I wanted to cry, feeling like I'd lost out on something special. "What flavor do you want?" he asked as he helped me into the truck.

"I don't know," I told him honestly. Ice cream had been the furthest thing from my mind just then.

He closed the door and came around the truck to get in behind the wheel. "Let's get several and share, then," he suggested as he started backing up.

"Okay."

It was barely a two-minute drive down the street to the little ice cream shop that had been open back when my dad was a little boy. The owners were an older married couple and they both greeted us when we walked into their shop. They had only ever sold seven flavors, but every now and then they would get a new flavor in by accident. Butter pecan was my favorite and the old couple always made sure they had some on hand.

Mrs. Welsh smiled fondly at Zander as he glanced from one flavor to the next. She and her husband were one of the few people in West Bridge who didn't look down their noses at him because of his OCD. "How are your grandparents, Zander dear?"

Zander met the old lady's gaze and smiled. "They're good, ma'am. Thanks for asking."

"What would you like, Annabelle?" Mr. Welsh asked as he grabbed an ice cream scoop. "The butter pecan is calling your name, I bet."

I grinned over the counter at him. "I think we'll take two scoops of everything, Mr. Welsh. Two spoons, please."

Zander turned to face me as Mr. Welsh scooped up the ice cream into one large, disposable dish for us. "You are the only chick that gets me, Anna."

I felt my cheeks fill with pink from the sheer pleasure that little statement gave me, but I shrugged off his compliment in hopes he wouldn't see my blush. "That's why we're such good friends, Z."

"You're my best friend, Anna."

I lifted a brow at that. "Not Dev or Noah?"

He shook his head. "No, babe. Neither one of them get me like you do. I never talk to them like I talk to you. Without you, I'd probably lose what is left of my mind."

My heart turned over. "Zander…"

"Here you go, kids." Mr. Welsh set the dish loaded with ice cream on the counter, pulling Zander's attention away.

He paid for the dessert and we went over to the toppings station. I grabbed the can of whipped cream while Zander drowned most of our ice cream in hot fudge sauce, nuts, marshmallow cream, and gummy bears. As

I started to cover the dish in the whipped cream, I noticed that he had made sure to leave the butter pecan alone when he'd been putting on the toppings.

It wasn't that I got Zander so much; he got me, too. He knew what I liked and didn't. He was so considerate, so gentle and caring. It hadn't been hard to fall for him. Unfortunately, I kept falling a little more every day.

Zander

Tell her.

That damned voice in the back of my head kept whispering those two words over and over again. Wanting me to confess, needing to prepare her for what would happen when she went in to work the next morning.

I couldn't force the words out, however. I knew that if I told her what I'd done—that I'd gone over her head and told Noah exactly what was going on in her house—she would think I had betrayed her. I'd promised her repeatedly that I wouldn't go to Noah, but I couldn't let things continue the way they were at home. If something happened to her and I hadn't done everything in my power to make sure she was safe…

I punched the side of the bed and glared up at the ceiling. Just the thought of her getting hurt made me insane. My fucked-up mind couldn't deal with it and I wanted to destroy something.

From my connecting bathroom I heard the water turn off and tried to relax, not wanting her to worry. I'd convinced her to shower here rather than sneaking into her house to do it. Since it was Friday night I knew my grandparents wouldn't think twice about me taking a shower so late. I was usually out until early morning because of OtherWorld's gig and they were used to me showering when I got home.

That is if they actually happened to hear anything at all. They both wore hearing aids and took them out when they went to bed. That was one of the reasons I hadn't moved out when I'd graduated high school. Devlin and I had even talked about renting a house or something together, but I hadn't wanted to leave Gram and Gramps vulnerable like that. What if someone broke in and they didn't hear anything? They could get hurt and I would seriously lose my shit then.

The other reason I'd decided to stay was because I knew Gram needed some help paying for her medication. It was so expensive that she'd been known to go without just so she could instead buy groceries when I was younger. Now that I was working full time and getting a decent paycheck every week, I was able to help her with that. I paid most of the bills so she didn't have to worry about whether or not she had her blood pressure medication or electricity that month.

The bathroom door opened and Annabelle stepped out dressed in one of my T-shirts and a pair of boxers. All other thoughts evaporated from my mind at the sight of her like that. Her long, platinum-blond hair was hanging around her face in wet tangles. The shirt I'd loaned her fell to mid-thigh, practically swallowing her small frame up. The old, black boxers I'd given her to sleep in peeked out from under the shirt as she walked toward the bed.

I quickly sat up and pulled one of the pillows over my crotch to hide the evidence of my raging hard-on. She flopped down on the bed beside me, turned on her stomach and scrunched the pillow under her head. She looked tired, but no less beautiful.

Tell her.

My mouth remained closed. If I told her, and she got upset, I wasn't sure how I would handle it. Would she stop trusting me? Stop sneaking through my window when she needed me? Would I lose her?

Clenching my jaw, I reached out and turned off the lamp beside my bed before lying down next to her. She was quiet, way too quiet for Annabelle. Concerned, I reached over and pushed her long, damp hair back from her face. A streetlight and the moon were both shining through my window, giving her skin an ethereal glow. "What's wrong?" I whispered.

"Just tired," she murmured, but I could tell she was lying. She might have been tried, but there was something on her mind. I could practically see the wheels in her mind turning.

"Talk to me, babe. You know you can tell me anything." *And I won't tell Noah unless I have to.* I gritted my teeth as that damn voice taunted me. Guilt was eating me alive, but I knew I'd done the right thing. I just hoped she would see it that way.

Her lips lifted in a small smile that didn't reach those baby-blue eyes that fucking owned me. "I'm just being silly, Z. Honest, I'm fine."

Without thinking, I cupped her cheek in one hand. "I'd walk through hell for you, you know that, right?" *Please remember that tomorrow*, I mentally willed her.

She turned her face into my palm. Her eyes closed and she smiled a little bigger. "Me too, Z. Me too."

"Come here," I muttered and pulled her closer. She turned on her side and pillowed her head on my shoulder. Fuck, that felt good. It felt so fucking perfect. Like she belonged there. One of her slender arms draped over my stomach and I brushed a kiss across the top of her head. "Goodnight, Anna."

"Night, Z." She yawned and her eyes closed sleepily.

I laid there for hours just listening to the sound of her breathing. Even with the guilt churning in my gut, my fucked-up mind was calm. Over the last few months I'd realized that she brought me peace. I wasn't up twisting the doorknob fourteen times, or closing my dresser drawer fourteen times, or turning off the bathroom light—yeah, fourteen times. With her, like this, I didn't feel like my mind was broken. I was able to see past the obsessions and think clearly.

I couldn't tell you when my OCD first started messing with my life. I couldn't remember a time when it hadn't affected it. Even in kindergarten kids would whisper about me. Parents hadn't wanted me to play with their kids; either they were too much of a bigot or scared I would rub my OCD off on their special little brats. It hadn't really mattered that much to me.

I'd had Noah and Devlin from the time I could walk, and then Annabelle, followed almost just as quickly by Noah's girlfriend, Chelsea. I hadn't needed anyone else. A few years back, Liam had moved to West Bridge because his old man had died. With Liam I'd gotten two more friends to add to my short list since he'd brought Wroth into our little group. Well, I guess three if you counted Marissa, but she was still too young to understand that I was broken. One day she would and who knew what would happen then. She might be just like those other fuckers who looked down their noses at me, or she might be just as amazing as Annabelle and would look past my fucked-up mind.

I considered myself lucky to have all of them as friends, but I knew if I had to give them all up it would be Annabelle I would miss the most. Just thinking about being without her was enough to make me feel like there was a boulder sitting on my chest, making it almost impossible to breathe.

By morning I might have to face life without her. That was the scariest thing I'd ever have to face. Ten times more terrifying than Wroth Niall in a rage and being the one he was ready to tear apart.

I sucked in a deep breath, trying to calm my heartrate. She wouldn't hate me for long. She couldn't stay mad forever. I'd find a way for her to see it from my point of view. I had to keep telling myself those things over and over until I was finally able to relax once more. Tightening my arms around her, I brushed a kiss across her forehead and breathed in the fragrance of my shampoo in her hair.

Before I was ready, my eyes began to grow heavy and I was drifting off to sleep…

The Rocker Who Betrays Me

She was gone when I opened my eyes the next morning. I pushed down the disappointment and got out of bed, knowing that Gram would come looking for me if I wasn't out of bed in time for breakfast.

I sat down at the table with my grandparents and ate the food that Gram placed in front of me, but I didn't taste any of it. Gram asked me twice if I was feeling okay, and I forced a smile and assured her I was fine. The concern in her hazel eyes told me she didn't believe me, but I wasn't about to blurt out what was bothering me.

Gram loved Annabelle and she would skin my hide if she knew I'd done something to hurt her. I couldn't tell her the reasons why I'd broken a promise to the girl who was more my best friend than anyone else on the planet. There would be an all-out war between my grandparents and Mrs. Cassidy-Malcolm. Annabelle would get put in the middle, and she would end up hating me even more than I suspected she already did.

Or would, once she talked to Noah.

Gramps was always grumbling about the grass and having to mow it. I didn't know why he was so fussy about it because I'd been mowing it since I was twelve. After breakfast I went out to get the yard work done before he could open his mouth about it. By the time I came back in, just a little over an hour later, Gram had a glass of her sweet tea waiting for me.

I gulped it down, enjoying the sugar shock to my system that always came with a glass of Gram's special sweat tea, before heading back to my room and grabbing a quick shower. I was just pulling a clean shirt over my head when my bedroom door opened and Devlin walked in. He barely glanced at me before flopping down on my bed.

I caught the pillow he threw at my head easily. "Thought you and Liam were going fishing this morning?" At least, that's where he and Liam usually spent their Saturday mornings.

Devlin clenched his jaw. "That was the plan until Tawny called him and asked him to drive her to Nashville."

I swallowed back a curse and dropped down on the edge of the bed to put on my boots. "That bitch is trouble." Liam and Devlin were normally inseparable on the weekends. Well, before Tawny came into Liam's life. Now Liam was ditching Devlin and anyone else for that stupid coke whore.

"Yup."

I combed my fingers through my damp hair and stood. "So what do you want to do?"

"Wroth said he was putting hay in the barn today. Want to go out there and give him a hand? See if Mary Beth made one of those cherry pies?" He grinned as he sat up on my bed. "I could really go for a slice of one of her pies."

I was up for anything that didn't involve us going near the garage. Maybe I was acting like a pussy, but I wasn't ready to face Annabelle if she was going to hate me. It would be best to let her temper cool off a little before I saw her again. I'd even go out to the Niall's farm and carry heavy-ass bales of hay to avoid a confrontation with her.

I grabbed the keys to my truck and called a goodbye to Gram as we headed out the back door. "I probably won't be back for dinner," I told her. "We're going out to the Niall's farm to help out."

Gram smiled fondly up at me, and my heart twisted with love for the little wrinkled-face lady who had raised me. "You two are good boys. Tell Mary Beth I said hello."

It was a twenty-minute drive out to the farm. Devlin spent the time trying to find something decent to listen to on the radio, but our only radio station only played old country music. We were close enough to Nashville to get some of their stations, but the closer we got to the farm the less of a signal we got until we were mostly just listening to static. Frustrated, I turned the damn thing off and we were silent for the last five minutes of the ride.

Wroth's farm was one of the largest in the county, but a few years before, his father had nearly lost it to the bank. Wroth had enlisted in the marines and used his sign-on bonus to get his old man caught up on their mortgage. While he was away, he'd sent money home as often as possible to help keep it running, but it had been Liam who had helped out the most. He'd worked at the garage part time, helping Devlin's dad work on engines. After Wroth had come home from his deployment, however, he'd quit the garage.

Of course that was the same time he'd started dating Tawny. Fuck, if there was ever a chick I hated it would have been that bitch. She was sucking all the good out of my friend and turning him into a person I didn't recognize anymore.

I drove past the old farmhouse about half a mile before I reached the barn. Wroth was standing on the back of his truck surrounded by huge bales of hay that he'd cut and baled himself over the last few days. Stopping a few feet away from the other truck, I got out and walked toward the barn with Devlin.

"Zander! Devlin!"

I couldn't help but grin at the excitement in Marissa's sweet little voice. She was standing in the barn entrance with an orange kitten in her arms. Liam's little sister was nine and was always following Wroth around. You would think that someone as scary looking as Wroth would terrify any kid who went near him. That wasn't the case with Marissa. She might have been the only person alive who didn't cringe at the sound of his beast-like voice or cower when he went all rage-monster. I was pretty sure that Marissa was the only person Wroth actually cared about.

"Whatcha got there, Rissa?" Devlin asked as he scratched the kitten behind the ears. It was tiny, nothing more than a ball of fur.

"This is Peaches," she informed him. "Wroth found her last night. He nearly ran over her with his truck. She doesn't have a mommy, so he brought her home to me to take care of."

I tried not to snicker at the thought of the beast known as Wroth Niall picking up a stray cat and bringing it home. I bet the poor kitten had been terrified at the sight of the ex-marine. I knew better than to speak those thoughts aloud, though. I wasn't about to push the rage-monster's buttons. I didn't have a fucking death wish.

"Want some help?" I asked the beast, who was tossing bales of hay onto the ground two at a time like they were nothing.

"I'm not gonna say no, dude."

Smirking, I started carrying the bales already on the ground inside the barn. There was already a small stack against a back wall so that was where I put the rest. After a few minutes of talking to Marissa, Devlin started helping and before long we were finished—with the first load at least. It took three more loads before the job was done.

Covered in sweat, we went down to the farmhouse for lunch with Mary Beth. As soon as we walked through the door, I knew Devlin was going to get what he came for. The smell of Mary Beth's famous cherry pie filled the entire house, making me want to sit down and never leave.

"Marissa, put Peaches in your room, baby." Mary Beth was running around the kitchen putting together freshly cooked roast beef sandwiches. "And wash your hands."

"Dad not coming?" Wroth asked as he took his place at the table.

"He's still in town. Wade is putting new brakes on the pickup." Mary Beth set the sandwiches on the kitchen table before turning back to the fridge to take out the potato salad. I didn't know how she did it, but she always had a batch of potato salad on hand whenever I came over. Devlin might be a sucker for her pies, but for me I'd steal Mary Beth away and marry her just for that damn potato salad.

Mr. Niall was at the garage. I couldn't help but tense up at the thought of what was going on down there this morning. I grimaced, wondering if Annabelle hated me yet.

Fuck. I hoped not.

Chapter Five

Annabelle

The garage was empty when I walked into work that morning. The old Buick was gone, letting me know that Mrs. Farris had already picked up her car. I grinned to myself as I opened the door to the office.

"Thanks for handling the Buick for me," I told Noah as I walked past the desk and into the break room to grab one of the donuts Wade always brought in on Saturday mornings.

After pouring myself a cup of the strong black coffee Noah favored, I went back into the office and sat down on the edge of the desk. I was stuffing my face with the blueberry-filled powdered donut when I glanced at my brother. He hadn't spoken so much as a word since I'd walked through the door and that just wasn't like my brother.

"What's up?" I asked, causing powdered sugar to come out of my mouth in a cloud.

Noah wasn't normally a brooding kind of person. Even when he was sick he always had a smile for me. That wasn't the case right then. His face was so grim it looked like he'd never smiled a day in his life. His blue eyes were darker than I'd ever seen them and his jaw was clenched so hard that I worried he was going to break the crown on his back tooth he'd gotten in the fifth grade.

He just sat there, his eyes full of a mixture of emotions that confused me as he watched me. I knew instinctively that whatever was bothering him, it wasn't good. My brother was the kind of guy who could find the good in any situation. Mostly. The look on his face right then told me that he'd come across a situation that held very little good, however.

I licked the powdered sugar and blueberry filling from the corner of my lips before wiping my mouth with the napkin I'd snatched in the break room. "You're starting to worry me here, Noah." I laughed, trying to break the tension that was filling up the office.

He moved so fast I nearly yelped in surprise when he grabbed hold of both my hands and held them tightly in his much bigger ones. "Why didn't you tell me, Annabelle?" he asked in a voice rough with the same emotions that were swirling in his eyes.

Everything inside of me went still with dread. I forced a smile for him and shook my head. "Tell you what? I'm not following here, Noah."

His hands tightened around my fingers, but what shocked me was the desperate look on his face all of a sudden. "I know, honey. I know what's been going on at home. About Mom and Jacob. About the beatings. I know that you've been sleeping in Z's bed the last few weeks. Why didn't you tell me? Why, Annabelle?"

I closed my eyes as I was consumed with a mixture of emotions that rivaled those I'd seen in Noah's eyes. I hadn't wanted to tell Noah about what was going on at home because I knew he would worry and stir up trouble, not just for me but also for himself. I didn't want to drag him into the middle of it when his relationship with our mother was tedious at best. As for his relationship with Jacob, well, let's just say there were plenty of reasons why Noah had moved out the day after graduation. Our stepfather had been at the very top of that list.

After Mom had married Jacob, he'd thought he could jump in and take over the running of the garage. There had been dollar signs in Jacob's eyes, but Noah had made it clear real fast that the douchebag wouldn't touch our father's legacy. The garage had been left to Noah and me, period. There had been no stipulation on age or even a small share of it for our mother. Two days after our father's funeral, a lawyer had shown up with a will our dad had made.

The terms had been simple. We would inherit as long as we continued to run the garage and kept Wade on as a full-time mechanic for as long as the older man wanted the job. Having been raised to take care of the office practically from birth, both Noah and I hadn't been concerned about keeping the garage open. Even at fourteen and sixteen, we'd been able to run the place smoothly with Wade as our mechanic. Mom had tried to contest the will, but she hadn't made it far before a lawyer had ordered her to back off.

When Jacob had realized that he wasn't going to be cashing in on our profits, or sell the garage—which was what I really think he'd wanted to do—he'd gone ballistic. I was sure that Jacob and Noah would have started throwing punches if Wade hadn't stepped in. Their relationship had been tense ever since, and Noah had been counting down the days until he could get out of the house we'd both grown up in.

Noah was looking for a reason to beat the hell out of our stepdad. So, yeah, I hadn't wanted him to know what was going on at home.

My heart clenched as I fought back tears. *Don't you dare cry, Annabelle. Not now. Not yet.* If Noah knew about what was going on, and from the look on my brother's face he probably knew it all, then there was only one person who could have told him. Pain sliced through me and I jerked my hands out of Noah's grip and crossed to the windows.

Zander must have told him. After promising me over and over he wouldn't, he'd gone to Noah with it. I thought I could trust him with anything, but obviously that wasn't true. He'd shattered my trust in him, but of course he must have known that he would.

Don't cry. Don't cry. Don't. Fucking. Cry.

My mind couldn't comprehend why he'd done it. Was he tired of me sleeping in his bed? Was my coming to him for help so often messing with his life? My heart suddenly felt like it was broken and I fell into one of the chairs by the window as I put my head in my hands, fighting the tears with a desperation that nearly stole my breath. That must have been it. Zander was tired of having to play the white knight for me. Especially when he could have been out fucking any other girl.

"Annabelle." Noah pulled my hands from my face and I looked at him through tear-blinded eyes, but still I refused to let them fall. I was not going to cry in front of my brother over a guy I'd been stupid enough to put all my trust in. "Honey, you should have told me things were bad at home. It isn't safe. We have to get you out of there."

The fear of sleeping at home was nothing compared to the pain I was feeling right then. It drove home just how differently Zander felt for me than how I felt for him. To him, I was just his friend's bothersome little sister that he had to take care of—and he no longer wanted to do that. While I...

I loved him.

"It's fine," I muttered. My voice was choked with the tears that I was holding back. "I'm fine. There's nothing to worry about."

Noah released my hands only to grasp my elbows. He made an angry sound in the back of his throat as he shook me, just enough to make me lift my eyes to meet his. "Stop it, Annabelle. Just stop it. Everything is not fine. Jacob could hurt you bad and then I'd kill the sonofabitch. For your safety and my sanity, you aren't going home ever again. I'll figure out something, but until I do you have to stay with me upstairs."

"No. There's no room." I couldn't let him move me in with him. I couldn't burden him with me and my problems. I still had two weeks before

I turned seventeen. Noah was nineteen and needed his own space, to live his own life. I wasn't going to rob him of that.

"I'll take the couch and you can have the bedroom," he told me, determination overshadowing his blue eyes instead of the emotional cocktail I'd seen just a few minutes before. "The bus drives right by here on the way to the house, so getting to school won't be an issue." As he spoke, I saw his shoulders actually become less tense, as if he'd finally found the good in the situation after all.

"Noah, no." I tried to reason with him. I couldn't let him do this. "Mom won't like it. She'll be pissed and she isn't going to let me live with you."

"What the fuck is she gonna do, Annabelle?" he demanded. "She has no job, no income except for what we give her. Jacob's measly little paycheck every week won't keep her in the wine and vodka she's so accustomed to getting every night. If she so much as opens her mouth about this, I'll cut all that off."

I shook off his hold on my arms. "Noah, you aren't listening to me. Please, don't do this. It's only going to start trouble. You have your life to live. I can't move in with you."

His eyes suddenly went darker than I'd ever seen them. Big hands cupped my face tenderly, showing me loud and clear the difference between him and Jacob. My brother would never touch me with violence. Never. "You listen to me, Annabelle Marie, and you listen good. I don't want to have to repeat myself." I started to speak, but he quickly shushed me. "No, honey. Just listen. You are the most important person in the world to me. I would do anything for you. Anything. Keeping you safe is the only thing I care about. Don't you ever fucking argue with me about that."

The battle to keep my tears at bay was suddenly lost, but my tears had nothing to do with Zander right then, and everything to do with how much love I felt for my brother in that moment. I realized in that moment that our father had done an amazing job raising his son. Noah reminded me so much of Dad, not just because he and I both looked so much like him, but with his amazing heart and determination to take care of me. My brother was a man that any father would have been proud to call his own.

Seeing my tears, Noah groaned like he was in physical pain and pulled me against his chest. "Don't cry, Annabelle. Please, honey. I swear it's going to be okay. I'll make sure you're safe. I'll take care of you."

I wrapped my arms around his lean waist and buried my face in his chest as his arms contracted around me. "I-I love you," I whispered brokenly.

I felt his lips on my forehead. "Love you, too, Annabelle."

I felt drained the rest of the day.

Noah went out into the garage bay to help Wade when a few customers came in, and I sat down behind the desk to finish up the paperwork I hadn't finished the night before. People came in to set up appointments for tire rotations, oil changes, and sticker inspections or to order parts for vehicles so they could do it themselves. I handled it all on autopilot.

I had a smile planted firmly on my lips all morning and well into the afternoon. It was only after my jaw began to ache that I realized what I was doing and wondered if I looked as much like a puppet as I felt. Rubbing at the ache in my cheeks and temples, I handed Mr. Niall the keys to his older-model pickup truck once he'd signed the invoice slip for his brake replacement.

"Thank you for your business, Mr. Niall. It's always a pleasure to see you." My smile was a little less forced for the still handsome man who looked so much like his only son. The two Niall men were drop-dead gorgeous in a masculine kind of way, but Mr. Niall was so much less intimidating than his son. Maybe it was the eyes. The things his son had seen while on deployment to war-torn countries didn't haunt James Niall's eyes like they did Wroth's.

Mr. Niall winked down at me from his magnificent height, something else he had in common with his son. "Thanks, Annabelle. Appreciate the quality service, sweetheart. You and that brother of yours should come out to the farm and have dinner with us one night. You look as if you could use one of Mary Beth's home-cooked meals."

A small laugh escaped me, relieving the tightness in my chest ever so slightly. "Thanks, Mr. Niall. I would love to have some of Mrs. Niall's homemade yeast rolls."

His face brightened. "Good. Good. I'll let her know. Be expecting Wroth to tell you what night."

"Sounds like a plan." I stood and walked around the desk so I could walk with him to the front door. "Drive carefully, Mr. Niall. Tell Mrs. Niall I said hi."

"You're a good girl, Annabelle. Don't you ever change, honey." He waved as he walked through the door and I watched long enough for the older man to pull out of the parking lot before turning back to my desk.

The pickup truck was the last scheduled appointment we'd had for the day. It was already two in the afternoon and we only stayed open until three on most Saturdays unless someone had scheduled a later appointment. Since

I doubted we would have anything that would need my attention—especially since Noah was more than capable of dealing with any last-minute arrivals, I grabbed my backpack and went up to the apartment above the garage.

My dad, George Cassidy, had built the garage with his own hands when he was twenty-one years old. His grandparents had left him a nice little nest egg when they had passed away and he'd taken that money and invested it in the two-story garage, using the upper floor as his residence.

Even back then the county hadn't had its own garage, forcing people to drive into Nashville to get any repairs done. Dad had known what he was doing when he'd provided a service that everyone had needed so desperately. He'd started out on his own, and then when Wade Cutter had moved to West Bridge, he'd taken him on, paying him with commissions instead of hourly. The two had made a great team.

When Dad had married my mother, she'd rushed to spit out a child for her husband so that he would buy her a house. She'd hated living in the apartment above the garage.

Even back then I was sure my mom had only married him because he'd been on the rise to making a good living. Not many people in West Bridge could afford my mother's expensive tastes in alcohol, at least not in our part of town. And I was sure that the ones who had memberships at the local country club just outside of town didn't think Mom was worthy of their time, let alone good enough to marry.

It might sound harsh, but I wasn't blind. I knew that my mother liked to think she was a queen, but the truth was she was just white trash. She hadn't helped dispute that label by marrying Jacob, either. The creep was racist and was the kind of guy who gave good ol' country boys a bad name. I was pretty sure that Jacob was a member of a local hate group. Most of the folks in West Bridge hated him, and I was high at the top of the list of people who wanted to see the bastard swimming with an anchor tied to his feet.

The apartment was actually a nice place to live, in my opinion. It had a small kitchen with a small laundry room off to the side, a living room big enough to hold a large couch and loveseat plus the big-screen television that Noah had bought for it. The bedroom was a decent size, with a queen bed and dresser. The only bathroom was in the hall between the living room and bedroom, but it had a large tub/shower combo, not to mention the toilet was separated by a door that offered privacy to those needing to use the bathroom while someone else showered.

I tossed my backpack on the couch and dropped down on the edge of one of the cushions. I glanced around carefully, trying to imagine Noah and I sharing the apartment like he wanted us to do. The couch was long, but it doubled as a bed since it had a pull-out mattress folded inside. It should be long enough so that his long legs didn't hang over the ends. Maybe we could make it work after all.

If our mother didn't cause trouble, that is. Noah didn't think she would because he gave her a monthly allowance from the profits we made from the garage. He'd threatened to make that disappear if Mom wanted to stick her nose in it. However, I wasn't so sure she wouldn't. She was a drama queen and was liable to stir shit up just for the hell of it. I was still sixteen for two more weeks, and even when I turned seventeen I wasn't sure if she couldn't get the cops involved because I would still technically be a minor.

Anxiety clenched in my gut at the thought of Noah being hauled away in cuffs because he'd wanted to take care of me. Jacob and Mom would probably have a good laugh watching Noah go to jail.

Oh, Christ. I couldn't let my brother get in trouble. No way. He had a bright future ahead of him with not only the garage but with his music. Noah had an amazing voice. He could go far in the music world if he was able to stick with it.

Damn it.

I couldn't let him risk going to jail over this. I couldn't let him throw away his chances of doing something amazing with his life and his career. I couldn't....

"You going to study?"

My head snapped up at the sound of Noah's voice. He was standing in the doorway with grease smeared over his cheek and forehead. He looked tired, but I didn't see so much as a sign of worry on his handsome face. Did he not understand what he could be losing if I stayed there?

"Noah, I have to go home."

His lips tightened and he moved away from the door, slamming it shut behind him as he crossed to the couch and glared down at me. "Don't start this again, Annabelle. Everything is going to be okay. You have absolutely nothing to worry about. I've already taken care of it, actually. Devlin, Wroth, and Z are going to pick up Chelsea and stop by Mom's house. They are going to pack up everything you need and bring it over. I've told Mom what's going to happen and what won't happen if she doesn't let you stay here with me."

He dropped down on the edge of the couch beside me, a smug-ass grin on his face. "She tried to run her fucking mouth, but I shut her bitching up real quick when I told her she wasn't going to get two dimes out of me if she tried to make a scene over this. I told her plain and simple that she had two options. One, you get to live with me and I still pay her the money she lives off of. Or, two, I call CPS, tell them what she's been doing and allowing Jacob to do, and the money stops and she goes to jail for child neglect and endangerment. Either way I would still get to keep you since I have a stable job, my own place to live, and a bunch of other crap that would qualify me as a capable family member to look after you."

"So she's really going to let me stay here?" I asked, biting the inside of my cheek to contain my hope.

Noah's lips lifted in a sad kind of smile. "Yes, Annabelle. She doesn't have a leg to stand on. She can't do shit to make you go back." He leaned his head back and closed his eyes, what sounded like a tortured breath leaving his chest. "I still can't believe you were going through hell and I didn't know." He opened his eyes and met my gaze. "Don't you know that you are all I have left, Annabelle? I'd be lost without you, sweetheart."

I threw myself into my brother's arms, not caring that he was covered in grease and grime and going to get me filthy. A broken sound somewhere between a sob and a laugh choked me as it bubbled out of my throat.

I was going to be safe, and Noah's future wasn't going to get thrown in the trash because of me.

Everything was going to be okay. We were going to be just fine.

Chapter Six

Zander

The ride back to my house was a quiet one. Devlin and I both had our jaws clenched, our faces tight with determination. Noah had called Wroth's house and we'd all decided we would be there with Chelsea when she went in to pick up Annabelle's things. Honestly, with just Wroth there we knew Chelsea would have no problems getting the things that Annabelle needed, but I wanted to be there.

I fucking needed to be there.

Since Wroth was the one who had spoken to Noah, I had no idea how Annabelle was handling all of this. Wroth had simply told us that Noah wanted him to pick up Chelsea and grab Annabelle's things. I was lucky to have gotten that much of an explanation out of the dude. Wroth wasn't much of a talker; he said as little as possible most of the time.

I pulled into my driveway but didn't move to get out of the truck. Devlin and I remind quiet, both of us lost in our own thoughts as we waited for Wroth's mother's old Jeep Cherokee to pull into the driveway that separated mine from Dev's. When it did, a normally perky Chelsea jumped out of the front passenger seat with a look on her face that seriously made me glad I wasn't the one on the receiving end of her temper.

Devlin opened his door and I followed behind quickly. Glancing at my house, I saw my grandmother standing in the front window watching, and I shook my head at her. The look on her face told me she knew that whatever was going on in my fucked-up head wasn't good. She put her fingers to her lips, concern on her wrinkled but still beautiful face. I waved once and jogged to catch up to Devlin and Wroth who were standing on the front steps of Annabelle's front porch.

Chelsea stood by the door, her finger holding down the doorbell without letting up on it. From inside the house I heard Wendy Cassidy-Malcolm cursing as she stomped to the front door. "I'm coming. I'm coming," she yelled.

Chelsea didn't release the doorbell until the door opened to a fuming Mrs. Cassidy-Malcolm. "What the fuck do you four want?" she snarled before lifting a Dixie cup of what smelled like fruit punch to her lips.

We all knew that it wasn't just fruit punch in that cup. She was notorious for loving her vodka and wine, and from the way her eyes were bloodshot, and with the way she seemed unsteady on her feet, we all knew she was more than three sheets to the wind. My guess was vodka was her drink of choice that night. Annabelle had told me that her mother loved to mix her alcohol with fruity juices, normally adding a third of the bottle to her concoctions.

Chelsea crossed her arms over her busty chest. She and Noah's mother had never gotten along and neither had made a secret of that. Noah had started dating Chelsea our freshmen year and they had been connected at the hip ever since. The two might have fought like cats and dogs at least once a day, but they made up before either fell asleep every night.

Mrs. Cassidy-Malcolm hadn't liked Chelsea from day one because Chelsea wasn't shy about her feelings for the other woman. That's one of the things I liked so much about my friend's girlfriend. You always knew where you stood with her because she told you straight to your face. She was a little spitfire. There had been more than a few occasions where she'd missed school over the years because of suspensions from getting into fights. Not all of them had been with girls, either.

"Noah told me he already talked to your drunk ass, so don't act stupid, bitch. I'm here to get Annabelle's things. These guys are here to make sure you and your fucking loser of a husband don't get in my way."

Mrs. Cassidy-Malcolm took a long swallow from her Dixie cup. "Jacob isn't here."

"Good." Chelsea went to walk into the house, but the older woman didn't move aside.

I tensed, ready to step in if they started fighting. I would have paid good money to see Chelsea kick her ass, but I didn't want to have to bail her out of the county jail when she got arrested for assault. Beside me, Devlin started to step forward just as I did, but Wroth was closer and much more effective. He stepped up behind Chelsea and crossed his arms over his chest.

Something on his face must have gotten through to Mrs. Cassidy-Malcolm's drunken mind because she gulped and stepped back in the next second.

The three of us followed Chelsea through the living room and down the hall to Annabelle's room. I went to the closet and pulled out a duffel bag and the only suitcase on the top shelf. Chelsea crossed to the dresser and started opening drawers, tossing in bras and panties while I took clothes out of the closet without taking them from the hangers.

As I put the first load of jeans in, my fingers brushed over a pair of soft panties and everything inside of me went white-hot and my body hardened. Muttering a curse under my breath, I tried to ignore the hard-on that was making it uncomfortable to walk—just from touching Annabelle's fucking underwear, and helped to finish packing up her clothes.

Devlin produced a few boxes and he started tossing in the few things on top of her dresser and nightstand before taking the pictures off the walls. It took less than twenty minutes to pack up the room with the three of us working together while Wroth stood guard at the door. I grabbed the suitcase and the duffel bag while Wroth and Devlin each took a box and Chelsea had the small overnight bag she'd used to pack up the things Annabelle needed from the bathroom.

As we walked through the house, we found Mrs. Cassidy-Malcolm sitting on the couch with a full cup of her fruit punch and vodka mixture, watching a rerun of a sitcom. She didn't lift her eyes from the television as we left. We loaded everything into the back of my truck and headed to Noah's apartment.

It took less than five minutes to get to the garage. Wroth pulled up behind me and he helped Chelsea and Devlin unload my truck. I just sat behind the wheel for several long minutes. I needed to man up and go up to the apartment and face Annabelle, let her have her pound of flesh for going behind her back the way I had.

Knuckles knocking on my window forced me to lift my head to find Devlin standing beside my door. He had Annabelle's suitcase in one hand and her duffel bag slung over his shoulder. He didn't say a word, but the look in his eyes said he had my back. Scrubbing a hand over my face, I stepped out of the truck and took the suitcase from him as he led the way up the back steps to the apartment that took up the top floor of the garage.

Wroth had left the door open for us and I swallowed hard before entering the apartment behind Devlin. The sound of the television greeted us and I quickly glanced around, searching for Annabelle. Noah was in the kitchen, pulling out slices of pizza from one of several boxes and loading it onto a plastic plate. Wroth was already sitting on the couch, but there was no sign of Chelsea or Annabelle.

Devlin dropped the duffel bag on the floor beside the old recliner. "Got any beer?"

"Yeah, there're a few left over from Wroth's last visit." Noah grabbed a paper towel and folded it in half before picking up the paper plate. "Thanks for getting Annabelle's things, guys. There's plenty of pizza, so make yourselves at home. I'm gonna take this in to Annabelle. She's not up for company right now. We can watch a movie or something."

I dropped the suitcase beside the duffel bag and held out my hand for the paper plate. No way was I just going to sit out there when the only person I wanted to be around right then was in another room. "I'll do that."

Noah lifted a brow at me but didn't say a word as he relinquished Annabelle's plate of pizza. Clenching my jaw, I moved across the living room to the bedroom door and knocked twice before opening it. Annabelle was lying on the bed with her back to the door. The TV that sat on top of an old dresser was tuned to some old sitcom that I knew she liked, but from the way her head was pressed into the pillow I knew she wasn't watching it. Chelsea was in the connecting bathroom, putting away Annabelle's things but stuck her head out when I entered the bedroom. Like Noah, she lifted her brows when she saw me standing there but didn't say a word as she pressed her lips together and left the room.

I waited until the door was closed behind her before stepping farther into the bedroom. As I stepped closer, I could hear her sniffling, and my stomach twisted.

She was crying. Fuck. Her tears were like daggers slicing through my chest.

Her back was still turned to me when I sat down on the edge of the bed and placed the paper plate on the nightstand. Her shoulders tensed and I knew she knew it was me and not her brother, but she didn't lift her head to look at me as I kicked off my shoes and lay down behind her. A small sob left her when I wrapped my arms around her waist and pulled her back against my chest.

"I'm sorry, Anna." Another small sob that left me feeling like I was being shot with a fucking machine gun escaped her and I tucked her closer. "Don't hate me, baby. Please don't hate me. I had to tell him. If anything happened to you I would lose what little was left of my fucked-up mind." I pressed a kiss into the hair at her temple.

She moved so quickly I didn't have time to react. One minute I was facing her back, the next I was assaulted by the bluest eyes in the world. Tears were pouring down her beautiful face, but she wasn't glaring at me. Her arms wrapped around my shoulders and she buried her face in my chest.

"I c-couldn't hate you, Z. Not ever," she whispered brokenly.

Some of the tightness around my heart eased at her confession that she didn't hate me and I stroked my hands down her back. "Don't cry, Anna. Please, don't cry."

"I want to be m-mad at you, but I c-can't." She rubbed her face against my shirt. "I was so hurt that you broke your promise, but I understand. Really, I do. You're tired of having to take care of me so much, and I'm sorry you've had to. If I'd known it would be so simple to just tell Noah and let him take care of everything, I would have told him months ago and you wouldn't have had to deal with my crap." She lifted her head, pushed away from me and finally sat up. A small, sad smile lifted the corners of her lips. "You can go back to doing whatever it is you do, Z. I promise not to bother you again."

If her tears had been like knives and bullets, her words were like fucking grenades, eviscerating my heart with each syllable that left her perfect mouth. So that was what she thought? That I'd broken my promise to her by telling Noah because I was tired of taking care of her? Was she out of her fucking mind?

"Anna, that isn't why I told him," I began, but she shook her head, offering me yet another sad smile as another tear spilled from those baby blues.

"It's okay, Z. Really." She scooted to the edge of the bed and stood, leaving me lying there, unable to find the words to tell her she was wrong. "I need a shower. Thanks for helping the others bring my things. I swear it's the last time you'll ever have to do anything for me."

"Anna…"

She opened the bathroom door and glanced back at me over her shoulder. "I owe you so much, Z. I'll never forget that. Maybe one day I can repay you for all the help you gave me." She gave me another sad smile that made my stomach roll with nausea, and then she was stepping into the bathroom, leaving me alone.

All day I'd been stressing over how to deal with Annabelle's anger, her possible hate of me for breaking my promise. Never once had I thought she would think I'd done it to get away from her. This… I didn't know how to deal with this. She was beyond hurt. It was almost as if I had broken her heart.

And that just wasn't acceptable to my fucked-up mind.

Annabelle

I waited for several long minutes until I heard the bedroom door close behind him. Then and only then did I let go of the tears I'd been desperate to hide from him. I'd been helpless to keep some of them at bay, but I'd be damned if I'd let him see me completely break down. That would be the ultimate humiliation.

I heard the soft click of the bedroom door finally closing and rushed to turn on the shower to drown out my broken sobs. I dropped down beside the tub and pressed my forehead against the cool tiles as the scalding tears flooded out of me.

I only had myself to blame. I'd pretended that Zander had let me climb through his bedroom window because he secretly loved me as much as I loved him. The night before had only driven that hope home for me. The way he'd treated me all evening and then held on to me so tightly as I'd fallen asleep... All of that hope had crumbled into a pile of ashes that morning when I'd realized that he was probably only trying to let me down easy.

Zander Brockman didn't want to be my white knight. He wanted his life back and I couldn't blame him. He was a great guy and he deserved to have the life he wanted.

It wasn't his fault that my heart was shattered, that I couldn't fucking breathe for the pain. I'd lost him...

No, I'd never really had him.

If I was lucky, I wouldn't have to face him again. I'd no longer be living next door to him so I wouldn't risk running into him every day. He had to work and I still had school, so avoiding him wouldn't be hard. That was the only way I'd ever be able to move on.

There was a tap on the bathroom door and I lifted my head as the door opened a few inches. My heart stopped, thinking it was Zander and my humiliation would be complete. When Chelsea's dark blond head appeared around the edge of the door, I was able to breathe again, barely.

Her eyes landed on me where I was huddled up against the bathtub. Sympathy filled her dark blue gaze. She closed and locked the door before dropping down onto the bathroom floor beside me. Holding open her arms, I let her pull me against her and I bawled like a baby until my throat was raw.

The weekend dragged by.

I tried to study for my make-up test, but couldn't take in anything I read. My head ached from crying myself to sleep Saturday night and most of Sunday morning. Thankfully, Noah left me alone. I guess he realized I wasn't in a good place because he brought me a Pop-Tart and a glass of orange juice—his equivalent to breakfast in bed—before heading out to spend the day with Chelsea.

Monday, I took the bus to school and went through the day on autopilot. Somehow I managed to get a B on my make-up test, but I honestly didn't know how. Maybe my teacher took pity on me since I had dark circles under my red-rimmed and bloodshot eyes. Who knows, I was just glad to have the whole thing behind me.

After school I returned to the garage and worked a few hours in the office before climbing the steps to the apartment and doing my homework in bed. Noah had tried to talk to me, but I hadn't had the energy to do more than answer him with as few words as possible. Even Wade had tried to get me to smile, a rare thing for the old mechanic, but I wasn't able to make my face muscles work to satisfy him.

That became my routine for the rest of the week. School, work, then straight to bed to do homework. I didn't sleep much during the night. I no longer needed to worry about a possible surprise attack so it wasn't because I was scared to close my eyes. It was the lack of a certain warm body lying in bed next to me that kept me awake most of the night. I missed Zander.

Missed his hogging the bed, missed his warm body curled behind me, holding me all night. Missed the damn scent of his harsh soap and mint shampoo he used. Missed the sound of his heart beating under my ear and the sound of his slight snore when he was tired after a long day of working.

I missed talking to him every day, damn it.

I should have been happy to be out of my mother's house. I was safe with Noah, and I knew that it was where I needed to be. My heart, however, didn't care that I was supposed to be happy. It missed Zander the most.

Finally, Friday arrived and I was able to pass a calculus quiz and a history exam without much trouble. Neither were the A's that I was used to, but at least they were high enough scores that my teachers didn't give me disappointed looks and a frigging lecture as they handed back the papers.

The last bell of the day rang and I tossed all my books into my backpack before following the rest of my classmates out. Pushing my hair back from my face, I headed to my bus, wanting nothing more than to get to work and have the week end.

"Annabelle!"

Great. Now I was hearing things. My mind told me that it was just a figment of my imagination, but it was my heart that had my head snapping up at the sound of Zander's voice calling my name.

From across the parking lot, I spotted Zander climbing out of his truck and my heart actually stopped for a second. He was still dressed in his work clothes, but he wasn't as disheveled as he normally was at the end of a workday. Briefly I wondered what he was doing there, since his workday didn't end until five and it was only two thirty. That thought was quickly brushed aside as my gaze ate up the sight of the beautiful boy/man walking toward me with a determined gait to his step.

The uniform jeans and work shirt that stated he worked for the county DOT fit him well—the jeans hanging low on his narrow waist and the shirt pulled tight over his lean, muscular chest that I'd been aching to lay my head on. His hair was unkempt, as if he'd been running his fingers through the slightly curly locks all day. Even from the distance that still separated us, I could tell he had dark shadows under his hazel eyes, but there was no hazel remaining today; just pure green jade and a few golden flecks.

My heart twisted painfully, wondering how close to the edge he was feeling. The fewer gold flecks in those amazing eyes of his, the more his OCD seemed to rear its head.

I stood on the sidewalk, frozen with a mixture of excitement at seeing him for the first time in nearly a week and anxiety after the humiliating way I'd cried all over him. Other students had to move around me as they rushed to catch their buses or whatever ride they had home.

As Zander came closer he thrust his hands into the front pockets of his jeans. His jaw was clenched but his gaze was locked on me. I swallowed hard, wanting nothing more than to throw myself into his arms and beg him to hold me one more time. *One more damn time.* The only thing that kept me from doing just that was the knowledge that he wouldn't want that. He was done holding me.

"Um…hi?" I greeted with a forced smile when he was only a few feet away.

"Hi." His voice came out rough, as if he hadn't spoken much that day.

I adjusted my heavy backpack on my shoulders and glanced at his truck, expecting to see Devlin sitting in the passenger seat. Of course he wasn't since I hadn't seen him the first time I'd looked that way. It wasn't like Devlin Cutter would have been hard to miss, after all.

"What are you doing here?" I asked. "Is everything okay?"

He shrugged. "I took half the day off."

I frowned. "You did? But you never do that." Not even when he was sick. He'd had the stomach flu at the beginning of the summer but he'd still gone to work. No one had wanted to be on the road crew with Zander that day.

He pulled his hands free from his jeans and offered one to me. "I couldn't wait until after work to see you. Thought maybe I'd give you a ride home. Come on."

I barely hesitated before putting my hand in his. My heart was doing backflips in my chest and my head was so curious, wondering what was going on, that it didn't yell at me as I placed my hand in his much larger one. He linked his fingers through mine and everything inside of me seemed to relax for the first time all week. Suddenly it was easier to take a deep breath. My heart seemed to trip over itself as it started beating normally again. Stupidly, tears burned my eyes and I kept my face averted so he wouldn't see them as he led me to his truck and helped me into the passenger seat.

I busied myself putting on my seatbelt as he climbed behind the steering wheel and started the truck. I kept my eyes on the buses that were slowly leaving the parking lot while he put the truck in reverse and backed out of the space he'd been lucky to find so close to the front of the school.

Somehow I was able to get my tears under control before he pulled into traffic and I let myself look at him again. His jaw was still clenched, but his shoulders didn't look nearly as tense. For a brief second I wondered if he had missed me as much as I'd missed him over the past week, but quickly called myself an idiot for even thinking that it might be a possibility. He'd probably been jumping on his damn bed Saturday night he was so happy to be done with having to take care of me.

"How was school this week?"

"Not bad. I passed my make-up test and the ones we had today." I leaned forward to fix my backpack where Zander had placed it at my feet, just to have something to do.

"I knew you would get your grades up if you weren't so stressed at home." He shot me a tight smile as he braked long enough for the bus in front of us to drop off a few students in front of several houses. "Everything else going okay?"

No, I wanted to scream at him. *No, everything else is not going okay. I can't sleep. I haven't eaten. I miss you so damn much. But you don't want me, Z. You don't want me, and I'm dying.*

Instead I forced another smile to my lips and shrugged. "Everything is good."

I expected him to smile back, relieved that I was okay now that he had fixed everything for me and no longer had to worry about how I was coping. He didn't smile. If anything, his jaw tensed even more and he turned his attention to the road as we followed behind the bus.

I bit down on the inside of my cheek and turned my head to watch the passing scenery through the passenger window as he drove on. Fall was my favorite time of year, and not just because it was my birthday. I loved the changing colors of the leaves and the cooler temperatures that teased at the coming winter. I was the type of girl who would rather be in a hoodie and sweats than a bikini top and shorts.

The trees passed in a blur and it took me several minutes before I realized we were no longer behind the bus, the same bus that would have driven past the garage. Blinking, I realized we were on one of the back roads that led to the Niall's farm, one that not even they used all that often.

"What...?" I broke off when Zander hit the brakes and turned off the truck in the middle of the rarely-used dirt road. He unsnapped his seatbelt before turning on the bench seat and unsnapped mine.

He moved so fast I didn't have time to think about my own reaction as he moved across the seat and wrapped his arms around me. Zander pulled me against his chest and buried his face in my hair and I melted against him, because it was exactly what I wanted.

"Fuck, I've missed you." His voice came out rough, bordering almost on a growl. "I know it's only been a week, but it feels like longer."

I pressed my face into his chest, inhaling the mixture of sweat and soap. I loved the scent because it was completely Zander. "Missed you, too," I whispered.

His hands stroked up and down my back and I thought I felt his lips in my hair, but figured it was wishful thinking. "I wanted to come see you on Sunday, but Chelsea thought you needed time to calm down. So I've waited

56

all week, feeling like my damn heart would explode if I didn't see you, but I gave you your fucking space Anna."

Confusion flooded my head. Why would he want to see me if he was so damn glad to be done with me? Not understanding anything, I pulled back, even as my heart was screaming at me that we needed more of Zander's hug than answers. "Why?"

He frowned. "Why what?"

I pushed at his chest, needing more space so that I could think clearly. "Why did you want to see me so bad if you were so glad to be rid of me? I figured you would have been celebrating with Devlin or something this week?"

The frown turned into something dangerous. His face hardened and his eyes took on that glow that told me his head was not in a good place. "For someone so smart, you can be a fucking idiot sometimes, Annabelle." My mouth fell open, not sure how to react to that slap in the face. "I didn't tell Noah what was going on because I was tired of taking care of you. I would fucking take care of you for the rest of my life and never complain about it. I didn't care if you climbed through my window. Hell, it was something I looked forward to because when you were sleeping in my bed, I found the kind of peace I've been searching for all my life."

My heart clenched painfully at the look on his face. His eyes started to turn back to hazel, his face unclenched and the way his lips tilted upward I knew he was telling me the truth. The look passed quickly and his eyes went back to the green and gold glow.

"You were hiding from the problem and I knew I couldn't let you keep doing it no matter how much I loved being your hero. I was scared to death you were going to get hurt, and your grades were slipping. You deserved a better life than the one you were leading, babe."

Tears burned my eyes, but this time I didn't try to hide them from him. "Z—"

He cupped my face in his big, rough hands. "It's okay if you hate me, Anna. I'll take whatever shit you want to throw at me for breaking my promise. What I can't handle, what my fucked-up mind can't deal with, is you thinking I wanted to get rid of you. You're my best friend, the only person who has ever gotten me and has never judged me. I've felt like I couldn't fucking breathe without you this week. All I want is for you to be safe." Using his thumbs under my jaw, he tilted my head back so that I had no choice but to meet his eyes head on. "Do you understand that?"

An errant tear spilled free. "Yes, Z." It came out as a whisper, but it cut my throat on its way out, fighting for freedom past the huge lump choking me.

More gold flecks filled his eyes, but they didn't turn back to hazel. The gold flamed down at me and I watched in fascination as he lowered his gaze from my eyes to my lips. Everything inside of me screamed in an intoxicated kind of excitement as I watched him lick his full bottom lip, as if he were thinking about tasting my mouth. Before my eyes, I watched his inner struggle, to kiss me or not.

Seeing that need in his eyes, that hunger that matched my own, made me suddenly feel powerful. Mix in his explanation of why he'd broken his promise and I realized that I'd been seriously blind when it came to Zander Brockman. Maybe he did care about me—want me—just as much as I did about him.

His inner struggle was making those gold flecks disappear again and I knew instinctively he wasn't going to follow through with the kiss that I would have begged him for. Not wanting to lose this chance to have something I'd only been dreaming about, I lifted my hands to cover his on my face. Pulling his big, beautifully rough hands from my face, I moved closer.

Zander inhaled through his nose, making his nostrils flare in a way that was unspeakably sexy. Still holding onto his hands, I placed them at my waist and pressed my chest against his. The rapid beating of his pulse at the base of his neck caught my attention and I lifted one hand to touch it. His heartrate matched my own and gave me courage to do the one thing I knew he wouldn't.

"You're such a good man, Zander." I brushed my lips over his jaw.

"I don't feel like a good man right now, Anna."

My lips lifted slightly in a smile. "That's okay. I like it when you're bad, too." I let my lips skim along his jaw until I came to his chin. Abandoning the pulse at the base of his throat, I combed my fingers through the hair at the back of his neck and pressed another kiss to his slightly rough chin. "No one has ever kissed me before, you know," I murmured. "I've never really wanted to kiss anyone until this summer. Then I kind of fell hard for this guy."

His jaw clenched again, harder this time than it had been earlier. "Who?" His tone was low and rough, sounding a little gravelly and making the fine hairs on my body lift with excitement.

My small smiled turned into a grin. "Just a guy I know. He's a little rough around the edges, but I like him that way. He's got a bad reputation around this small-ass town, but no one realizes he's got the biggest heart." My other hand covered the middle of his chest, right over his racing heart. "He's the kind of guy every scared little girl should have as a hero."

A few more flecks of gold returned to his incredible green eyes and he leaned his forehead against mine. "Christ, Anna. I thought you were talking about some fucking tool from school."

An unladylike snort left me. "That's the stupidest thing I've ever heard you say, Z."

"Maybe." He shook his head as he pulled back. "I'm no good for you, Annabelle. You shouldn't want me. I'll only bring you down, baby."

My fingers tightened in his hair. "Don't ever say that to me again, Zander Brockman. I'll accept anything else that leaves your lips, but don't you ever put yourself down to me." It was my turn to force him to meet my gaze. I kept a strong hold on his hair, knowing that I was probably hurting him as I did it, but what he'd just said had not only pissed me off but hurt me. "You are the best man I know, second to no one. Not even my brother. You are a strong, kind man and I care about you. Very much." *With my whole heart.*

"Anna—"

"If you're going to say something to try to talk me out of it, you might as well hold your breath, because I don't want to hear it." I glared at him. "Hearing you say you aren't good enough for me only pisses me off, Z. I know what I want and that's you. You are the best thing in the world for me. No one else will do."

His lips twisted in a disbelieving smile. "Stop it. You know…"

I couldn't stand to hear another word coming from that sexy-as-sin mouth a second longer. I tugged his head down the few inches that separated us and sealed my lips to his, stopping whatever he might have said. His entire body stiffened.

All my anger at him over the way he'd put himself down evaporated in the force of the heat that consumed my entire body as I kissed Zander. His hands at my waist contracted but, after only a brief uncertain moment, he pulled me against his hard body, taking control and deepening the kiss. Surprised and thrilled from the way he was taking over, I opened my mouth.

His tongue brushed over mine and my senses stopped everything they were doing in that moment to take stock of his taste. Holy God. He tasted of the cinnamon candy he liked so much but also something else. It was just as spicy as the cinnamon but something much more potent, yet it was sweet too. Like the honey his grandmother put in her oatmeal cookies.

With a curse Zander pushed away from me and raked his hands through his hair. "Fuck. Fuck. Ah fuck, fuck, fuck."

Still lost in his taste, it took me a few seconds before I was able to make a coherent thought. I felt a sudden sense of loss. I'd only had it for a moment, but I already missed the feel of his hands on me, his lips on mine, his body heat soaking into my own. The next was disappointment. I wanted more, so much more.

"Zander."

"I didn't bring you out here to do this, Anna." He leaned his head back against the seat and closed his eyes as he breathed in deep breath after deep breath through his nose. "I just wanted to talk. To make you understand..." He broke off and shook his head without opening his eyes. "I told you I'm not a good man."

"Was kissing me so wrong?" I whispered, hating that look of self-hate I saw on his face. Was that because of me? Had I forced this and made him hate himself because of it?

His eyes snapped open and he turned on the bench seat to face me. "Baby, kissing you feels like the most right thing in the world. But you're sixteen and I'm almost nineteen. In this state, that makes you underage and me a bad man in the eyes of the law."

I lifted a brow at him. "You're only two years older than me, Z."

It was his turn to glare. "That doesn't mean anything, Annabelle."

I smirked at him. "Actually it does. I'm going to be seventeen in a little over a week, and you're still eighteen for several more. Even if you were up to four years older than me, you wouldn't be breaking any laws. It's called the Romeo and Juliet Law."

"How do you even know that?"

I shrugged, still smirking at him. "I might have gone to the library and looked it up." His brows lifted and I couldn't help but blush. "I spent all summer daydreaming about you wanting me as much as I want you. I knew you would think your age would be a problem and I wanted to make sure that you wouldn't get in trouble if by some miracle you decided you did want me."

Zander growled something under his breath and started the truck. "Swear to me you aren't joking, Anna."

My smirk vanished. "I have a copy of the law in my backpack. Do you want to see it?"

"Fuck, yeah I do."

My stomach did a little flip. Did that mean he wanted it to be true? I dampened my suddenly dry lips with the tip of my tongue. "Okay." I reached for my backpack and pulled out the folded and creased sheet of paper that I'd photocopied from the library.

He pulled it from my fingertips and his green and gold gaze scanned over each word as he read it. Twice. I watched as he swallowed once, twice, a third time. Then, without looking at me, he put the truck in gear and drove me back to the garage.

Stepping out on his side, he offered me his hand and helped me out. I was about to turn to go into the office when his hand tightened around my fingers and I watched in fascination as he lifted my hand to kiss my knuckles. "I'll see you soon, baby."

My heart did a summersault in my chest and I grinned as I left him standing there and went into the office to get to work.

Chapter Rock Eight

Zander

"You sure this is what you want, man?"

Noah leaned his head back on the couch in the back room at Floyd's Bar. He wasn't drinking his usual beer, and he'd had a faraway look in his eyes ever since he'd gotten to the bar half an hour ago. I'd known this was coming tonight, just as Devlin and Wroth had, but Liam had been busy elsewhere all week—meaning he'd been getting high with Tawny—so Noah's decision was news to him.

"Yeah, man. This is what I want," Noah assured Liam, but I could see the pain in his eyes. He might have decided that this was what he needed to do, but he wasn't a hundred percent sure that it was what he *wanted*.

I was a million percent sure that it wasn't what I wanted. Noah was leaving the band right when we'd been starting to get noticed. We'd had two managers stop in to Floyd's over the last few months, all saying we had potential, but none of them had made us an offer to sign with them. Still, we were sure that it was only a matter of time now until we found the right manager.

Noah was worried that even if we did get a manager and then a record deal afterward, he wouldn't be making the money he needed to support himself plus Annabelle. I knew he was only thinking about his and his sister's future, but that didn't make his leaving any easier for my fucked-up mind to understand.

Or maybe it was the thought of what would happen once OtherWorld did actually get a record deal and we had to leave Tennessee. Would I be able to just follow my band-brothers and leave Annabelle behind? Especially after she'd confessed that she cared about me just as much as I did about her.

"But country music? Really?" Liam lifted his beer to his lips and took a long pull from the bottle. I didn't think he needed the added buzz of a few beers. From the way his eyes were dilated I could tell he'd already been into the coke.

Noah's lips lifted in a forced smile. "Yeah, man, really. Chelsea and I actually went up to Nashville last week and I played for some radio executive. He was impressed with me and said he'd be in touch."

That wasn't news to me and the other's either. We knew he was going to go the country route and that he was even talking to Chelsea's dad about asking her to marry him. Her old man liked Noah and was pretty cool about their relationship. He'd even offered to help them out with money if they decided to move up to Nashville, promising to pay their rent if it came to that.

Noah and Chelsea moving, however, meant that Annabelle would be moving with them.

Motherfucking hell.

I lifted my beer to my lips and swallowed the rest of its contents in one gulp before reaching for another on the small table between the couch and the old musky love seat that I was sitting on with Devlin.

Liam's brows lifted but after a few seconds he shrugged. "Huh. Well, good luck, dude. I'm gonna miss you."

"Thanks," Noah muttered and turned his gaze toward the ceiling. He was quiet for several minutes before he let out a forced laugh and sat up a little straighter. "I want to be there when you guys audition my replacement."

"Don't do that to yourself, man." Devlin sat forward on the loveseat and grabbed another beer. "No one wants to see who's replacing them on any level."

"Nah, it'll be okay. It will make me feel better about leaving you fuckers. I want to make sure that whoever takes over for me will get you where you deserve to be." His smile this time wasn't nearly as forced as it had been. "Don't want some idiot wannabe bringing down my boys."

We waited until the last song that night before Noah made the announcement that it was going to be his last show at Floyd's. We had a pretty big following from the surrounding area and no one was happy about Noah's news. Several chicks in the front row started crying, until he told them that he was going country solo. That had a few of them drying their tears, but not many.

I gritted my teeth as we left the stage after the last song. I wanted to get as far away from Floyd's Bar and my band-brothers as fast as possible. My fucking mind felt like it was bouncing around in my skull and all I wanted was the sweet peace that only one person could bring me.

I didn't even wait to see if Devlin was going to get a ride home with one of the others before I was jogging out to my truck and burning rubber as I backed out of the parking lot. I drove over the speed limit and kept twisting the knob on the radio even as I tried to fight my OCD not to do it fourteen times while the fingers of my other hand tapped over and over again on the steering wheel. Fourteen. Fourteen. Four-fucking-teen.

I didn't know why I was stuck on the number fourteen. I couldn't remember why it was so important, but my brain was obsessed with it. I was starting to hate that damn number and how it was destroying my life.

By the time I pulled into the parking lot of the garage, I hadn't calmed down any. Jerking open the door of my truck, I jumped out and slammed it behind me. Taking the steps up to the apartment two at a time, I tried to think of something—fucking anything—other than the taste of Annabelle's lips earlier that afternoon.

Fuck.

Fuck.

Motherfucking sonofabitch.

Fuck.

I reached the top of the steps and lifted my fist to knock, but the door opened before I could. Annabelle stood on the other side of the doorway, her long pale blond hair tousled, her sleep clothes rumpled and her eyes a mixture of sleepy and worried. "What's wrong?" she demanded as soon as she saw my face. "What is it?"

Stepping through the door, she grasped my arms, pulling me easily across the threshold into the apartment. "Z, you're scaring me. You're shaking."

I pulled my arms free and wrapped them around her. I opened my mouth, but nothing came out. My voice was locked in my throat from the boulder of emotion blocking its exit. Instead I pulled her against me as tight as I could get her and buried my face in her sweet-smelling hair.

Having her that close, being able to touch the only thing that mattered to me, made it easier to breathe and I sucked in one deep gulp of air after another for the first time all night. Tears of relief stung my eyes and I kept my face in her hair until I could control myself, not wanting her to see my weakness.

Soft fingers trailed up my back under my old T-shirt and stroked up and down my spine. I let out a shuddery breath and kissed the shell of her ear.

"Sorry," I got out in a voice still rough with the emotions still churning through me. "I didn't mean to scare you."

"Are you okay?" she murmured softly.

"Better now," I assured her and, with my arms still wrapped tightly around her, lifted her a few inches off the floor so I could carry her to the couch.

I dropped down onto the old piece of furniture and pulled her across my lap, wishing to God and anyone else who was willing to listen to my silent prayer just then, that I could keep her like that for the rest of my life. Things were changing way too fast and I wasn't able to keep up. I was losing Annabelle with every passing second, but there wasn't a damn thing I could do to stop it. Soon she would be in Nashville and I would be who knew where. I just wanted to hit pause on everything, holding her and soaking up every moment of having her in my arms.

Her fingers stroked through my hair as she held my head against her chest. The feel of her soft hands, the soothing strokes as she combed my hair back from my face, and simply having her in my arms, were slowly calming all the noise in my head to a soft murmur and I was able to think clearly once again. Finally I lifted my head and met her concerned blue gaze.

"Hi," she whispered softly with a small smile.

"Hi, baby."

"Want to talk about it?"

I shook my head. I didn't even know where to begin to start and even if I did I couldn't have voiced the craziness that was eating up what was left of my sanity. As if she understood all of that and was okay with it she lowered her head to my chest, but continued to stroke her fingers through my hair. "Okay."

We sat there like that for at least an hour. Neither of us spoke, neither one so much as moved except for her fingers through my hair. It was only when she fought back a yawn that I realized I'd woken her up, acting like the crazy man that I was.

"You should go back to bed," I muttered, thinking about her and pushing down my need to hold onto her and the last thread of sanity I still had.

"I won't sleep if I do. I'd just lie there thinking about you." She lifted her head and met my gaze. "Don't send me away, Z. I'm happy where I am."

Fuck, she knew how to gut me. "I'm not going to send you anywhere you don't want to go." I glanced down at the old couch we were sitting on. Figuring it was long enough and wide enough for us both, I kicked off my boots and positioned us so that she was lying in front of me. I kept her back to my front and reached for the remote that was in its usual spot on the arm of the couch.

I promised myself I'd only stay for a little while. I just wanted to hold her for a few more minutes.

Turning the television on, I found a channel that wasn't stupid infomercials before lying back. There was an older afghan that Chelsea had brought over and left a few months before and I pulled it off the back of the couch and over the both of us. Annabelle snuggled back against me, making my body throb from wanting her, but I just gritted my teeth and kissed the back of her head.

Just a few more minutes, but I knew I was lying to myself. I couldn't bring myself to leave her. Would I ever get enough of this?

No. Never.

Within minutes her breathing evened out and I knew she was asleep. Soon my own eyes began to drift closed, but I didn't fight it. I kissed the top of her head again and I let sleep claim me...

The high-pitched cackle of a cartoon witch jerked me awake the next morning. My eyes snapped open and for a few seconds I didn't recognize where I was. Then the warm body wrapped around my own shifted and I breathed a little easier when I realized I'd fallen asleep holding Annabelle. My body instantly woke up and I had to bite back a groan as her thigh brushed over my throbbing hard-on.

Needing a distraction —and fast —I glanced at my watch and saw that it was still pretty early, but that Gram would be up and making breakfast. She wasn't used to me not coming home on Friday nights, not like she had been before Annabelle had needed me to be home. She would worry and I didn't want that.

I leaned up on my elbow and brushed a kiss over Annabelle's temple. "Hey, are you hungry?"

She yawned and blinked her eyes open. "I could eat," she murmured sleepily and snuggled against my chest a little deeper.

I stroked my fingers down her cheek, soaking up the feel of her in my arms like that a little longer, storing the memory away for a rainy day. Fuck, it felt good. It felt right. Like she was meant to be right there in my arms forever. Muttering a curse, I lowered my head and brushed my lips over her closed eyes. "Come on, baby. We'll eat and I'll bring you back in time for the garage to open."

She didn't move for a long moment, keeping her face buried in my chest as she sucked in a few deep breaths. Was she crying? I grasped her chin carefully between my fingers and tilted her head so I could see her face. Her eyes were damp, but no tears had fallen yet.

"Anna—"

She shook her head and gave me a trembling smile. "I'm good, just really happy right now. Does that make sense?"

My gut clenched. "Yeah, babe. It makes perfect sense." Because even though I was stressing over the future and knowing I'd be without her, in that moment I was happy. Having her in my arms, knowing her feelings ran as deep as my own, I was the happiest I'd ever been in my life.

By the time we pulled into my grandparents' driveway, I could smell her breakfast in the air. I climbed out of my truck and turned to help Annabelle out before shutting the door. As we walked to the back door, her gaze went to her mother's house next door.

Things had been quiet over there the last few days, but I'd seen Mrs. Cassidy-Malcolm getting her mail the day before. She'd been holding her usual cup of punch and vodka, stumbling as she walked back to her house. As for Jacob, I hadn't seen him at all, although I knew he was there since his car was there in the evenings when I got home each night.

I stopped before opening the back door. "I'm glad you're out of there, Annabelle."

Her jaw clenched and she nodded, giving me a small smile. "Yeah, me too."

I pulled her close, stealing a hug before I finally opened the back door and stepped into the kitchen. Gram was standing at the stove, stirring the gravy. She was humming to herself as she cooked and I pulled Annabelle with me as I went to hug the old woman.

Gram grinned up at me when I tapped her on the shoulder. "Zander, I was starting to wonder if you were coming home."

"I slept at Noah's last night," I informed her and nodded toward Annabelle. "I brought company."

Gram's eyes fell on the girl beside me and her entire body seemed to light up. She practically pushed me out of the way to get to Annabelle. "Oh, honey. I'm so glad to see you." She pulled Annabelle into a squeezing hug that proved just how strong she still was, but Annabelle was hugging her back. When she stepped back, her eyes had darkened with concern. "How are you?"

"I'm good, Mrs. Brockman. I hope it's okay that I came over."

Gram narrowed her eyes. "Girl, you know you will always be welcome at my table. Always. You're one of the family, honey."

Annabelle started blinking rapidly and I knew she was fighting tears. Not wanting her to feel embarrassed, I distracted Gram. "I'd really like some scrambled eggs, if you don't mind making them, Gram."

"Of course I don't mind." She turned back to the stove. "You two kids sit down. Annabelle, how do you want your eggs?"

She cleared her throat before speaking. "Scrambled is fine, Mrs. Brockman."

Gram turned to glare at her as I pulled out a chair for her at the kitchen table. "I wish you'd call me Gram, honey."

Annabelle opened her mouth, but no words came out. It wasn't the first time Gram had asked her to call her that but, when she was little, her hag of a mother hadn't wanted her to. Now there wasn't any reason for her not to start calling my grandmother Gram, and I'd have been lying if I said I didn't like the idea.

Once she was seated, Annabelle smiled. "Okay. Thank you, Gram."

Gram was just putting the bowl of gravy on the table when Gramps took his usual place. He greeted Annabelle with one of his rare smiles. "Good to see you, girl."

"You too, sir."

My grandparents caught up with Annabelle over breakfast and she was laughing by the time she helped Gram clear away the table. I glanced at my watch and realized that the garage would be opening in fifteen minutes. Grimacing, I stood and grabbed my keys. "I'd better get you back to the garage, Anna."

She glanced at the clock above the stove and gasped. "Noah is going to be worried if I don't get back in time." She quickly hugged Gram and then brushed a kiss over Gramps' cheek as she followed me to the back door. "Thanks for having me, Gram."

"You come back anytime, Annabelle." Gram stood at the back door as I helped Annabelle into the truck and waved as I backed out of the driveway.

Annabelle was quiet for several minutes as I drove her back to the garage. When she finally spoke, her voice sounded sad. "Thanks for that, Z. I didn't realize how much I missed your grandparents until this morning. You're so lucky to have them."

I knew exactly how lucky I was. My grandparents had supported my mother when she'd come home from college pregnant. They hadn't judged her as most of the people in West Bridge had when she'd had me. Then when she'd died of breast cancer, they'd made sure I stayed with them instead of letting my father's family adopt me. My father's family had had little to do with me until my mother's death, but as soon as she'd died they'd suddenly wanted custody of me. My grandfather had fought them tooth and nail until my other grandparents had given up. It was then that I knew exactly how lucky I was to have them love me so much.

Pulling into the garage, I saw Devlin's dad's truck already in its normal spot along with Noah's. Noah's truck hadn't been there when we'd left that morning, so I figured he'd just slept at Chelsea's the night before. Getting out, I helped Annabelle down, but didn't move toward the garage's office. I didn't want to see Noah or Wade and I didn't want them to see me saying goodbye to Annabelle.

Holding onto her hand, I pulled her close and brushed my lips over her cheek. I felt her shiver and it took everything in me not to pull her against me and kiss her the way I really wanted to. Lifting my head, I met her bright blue eyes. "Tonight I'll bring pizza and a movie from Blockbusters. Okay?"

"Sounds good," she breathed.

Unable to resist, I brushed another kiss over her cheek and reluctantly let go of her hand. "Seven?" She nodded and I climbed back into my truck. "Call my house if you need me."

Annabelle

Noah and Wade were already working on someone's car when I entered the office. Sitting down behind the desk, I was glad to be alone for the moment, needing to soak up the incredible morning I'd had with Zander.

It felt like bubbles were in my blood. I was walking on clouds as I went back and forth from the office to the back room. I wanted to hold on to the feeling and never let it slip away.

Waking up with Z's arms around me had been something I'd missed all week and, for the first time, I'd gotten a full night's sleep. My heart had felt like lead when I realized he'd have to leave me soon, but then he'd asked me to have breakfast at his grandparents' house and I couldn't help the tears that had nearly spilled free. How could something as small as going for breakfast have brought me to tears so easily? For the first time in forever I'd felt truly happy, and it was all because of Zander Brockman.

Without realizing it, a stupid grin lifted my lips and I was still sporting it several hours later when Noah came into the office to wash his hands and grab a quick snack. My brother opened his bag of chips as he sat down on the edge of my desk where I was sorting through invoices for our latest parts shipment.

"Zander put that stupid look on your face?"

My head snapped up and my grin faded as I glared up at Noah. "Shut up," I snapped at him, not wanting him to make fun of the bubbly feeling I was still having.

He popped a Dorito into his mouth. "Don't get all defensive, Annabelle. I'm just curious what or, more to the point, who put that silly grin on your face. I like it. Looks good on you, baby sis." He shrugged and popped two more Doritos into his mouth. "If it was because of Z then I'm cool with that. He's good for you."

I bit the inside of my cheek. "Really? You'd be okay if we…?" Noah shrugged again and my heart melted with love for my brother. "Thanks, Noah."

He grimaced. "Don't thank me yet, honey. We still have to talk about Nashville. The way things are looking we might be moving up there by the end of next month."

"Nashville isn't that far away. I could see Z on the weekends…" Noah was shaking his head. "Why not?"

He tossed his now empty bag of chips in the trashcan by my feet and wiped his cheesy fingers on his grease-stained jeans. "Don't tell Z, but when I went to Nashville this week, I told the radio exec about OtherWorld. He gave me the number of a guy and I've been talking to a manager who wants to hear the band. As soon as I find my replacement, I'm setting up a meeting for them. If this guy likes what he hears, then the band will be moving to California to start looking for a record deal."

I gasped, seeing the pain in my brother's eyes. "I'm sorry, Noah." Tears burned my eyes and I tried to keep them at bay, but a few fell free. Noah was giving up so much to take care of me. Anyone who knew my brother knew that OtherWorld was his life. His giving them up and even helping them in the process must have been killing him. I didn't know if he was going to be happy going solo, but I knew it wouldn't fill the void OtherWorld did.

I was costing him OtherWorld. He was leaving the band because of me, so that he would be able to take care of me. I was choking with the regret I felt over ruining his life. Things would have been so much simpler if I'd just kept my mouth shut. I could have dealt with Jacob if I'd known just how much I would fuck up Noah's life.

He lifted a hand and wiped away my tears. "This isn't your fault, Annabelle. I don't ever want you to think it is. I'm the one who is making this decision. You didn't force me. I'll still have music, so it's not like I'm giving it up completely. I have you and Chelsea. That's all I need. Nashville will be a good fit for the three of us."

"But—"

Noah clenched his jaw and stood, walking around the desk. "No buts. I've got work to do."

"Noah…" He stopped at the door and turned his head to look at me. "I love you."

His face relaxed. "Love you, too."

My grin didn't return for the rest of the workday. I spent the hours trying to go through the invoices and other paperwork that needed my attention, but I couldn't remember what I'd read or actually done with it all. My mind was caught on the fact that Zander could be leaving me in just a matter of weeks. Part of me was ecstatic about the opportunity for him and OtherWorld, but a bigger part was heartbroken.

Zander would move to California and become a rock god. There would be girls, so many fucking girls. He'd hook up with them all, live the life of the badass rocker I knew he would be. He'd forget all about me...

Muttering every vicious curse word I knew, I tossed the paperwork into a filing cabinet and locked up the office before stomping up the stairs to the apartment. My chest was so tight I felt like I was going to pass out from the pain. I practically ran into the bedroom and locked the door behind me before falling onto the bed and crying like the baby I was.

Z was going to leave. OtherWorld was too good for that manager Noah had mentioned not to want to help them move up in the rock world. As long as they found someone with the right vocals to take over for Noah, there would be nothing to stop them from getting signed.

Sob after sob shook my body, each of them leaving my throat tortured and raw. My heart was breaking and Zander wasn't even gone yet. I knew it was only a matter of time, though. The countdown had already begun and it was just a matter of weeks before he would be gone. I wanted to beg and plead for him to stay in Tennessee, for me. *For us.* I'd love him for the rest of my life if he would just stay and hold me.

The tears came faster, the sobs so intense I felt like I was destroying all of my organs. It wouldn't have mattered if I had. The second Zander was gone, I wouldn't need any of them. And he was going to leave.

I wasn't going to beg him to stay. I wouldn't plead. Not because I thought Zander wouldn't, but because I knew he would. Z was just too good of a man. If I begged him to stay, I knew he would and I couldn't do that to him. I couldn't ask him to stay when I knew he deserved to be out there sharing his music with the world.

Turning over onto my back, I wiped away the last of my tears and glared up at the ceiling. My head was killing me from all the crying I'd done, my entire body aching like I'd just been hit by a bus, but I'd come to a decision that I was going to stand by. I'd take what little time I had left with Zander and cherish every damn second of it. I'd live off the memories forever if I had to, but I wasn't going to ask him to stay. I wouldn't be selfish.

I'd already ruined my brother's life.

I wasn't about to ruin Z's.

The Rocker Who Betrays Me

By the time I heard Zander's truck pulling into the garage's parking lot, I'd gotten myself under control. I'd showered, changed into a pair of running shorts and a tank top, and then put chilled spoons on my swollen eyes. There were no signs that I'd had a complete breakdown just a few hours before. I couldn't let him see that I was so close to shattering into a million pieces at his feet.

Zander knocked on the door and I forced myself to take a few extra seconds to compose myself before I opened it. As soon as my eyes fell on him, I had to fight back the urge to cry again. *No, Annabelle. Just stop it.* Ruining two men's lives in one week wasn't going to happen. I forced back the tears and let my eyes trail down over the delicious boy/man standing on my doorstep, needing to commit everything about him to memory for those days I knew I'd need it the most.

Dressed in old jeans and one of his favorite Nirvana T-shirts, Z looked good enough to eat. His hair was rumpled, as if he'd been running his fingers through it, and his eyes were green with those damn gold flecks I loved so much burning down at me. I wanted to throw myself into his arms and never let go, but that wasn't possible with his hands full.

He held a box of pizza in one hand with two VHS Blockbuster rentals on top. In his other hand he had a bag that was full of chips, drinks, and my favorite chocolate bars— Reese's. Smiling at the sight of the familiar orange candy wrapper, I reached out to take the box of pizza from him.

"Where's Noah?" he asked as he followed me into the kitchen.

"Probably at Chelsea's." I hadn't seen my brother since our talk earlier that day, but Chelsea's was the most likely place he'd be. He couldn't go more than a few hours away from her. I thought it was adorable the way they were together. Even when they were arguing—which was at least once a day—you could see how much they loved each other shining out of their eyes.

Setting the pizza on the counter, I grabbed a stack of paper plates before opening the box. When I saw what toppings were on the pizza, my heart clenched so hard I had to suck in a deep breath. Half the pizza was covered in enough meat to feed an army—or at least one hungry Zander Brockman. The other half of the pizza had sliced tomatoes, green olives, and just a little bit of bacon. Exactly how I loved my pizza.

He hadn't called to see if that was what I'd want, he'd just known.

Gulping in a shuddering breath to fight back the urge to break down and sob like a baby again, I busied myself with piling our plates with slices of pizza while Zander fixed us each a glass of the sweet tea he'd brought. I carried our plates into the living room before going back for the videotapes. It was only then that I actually looked at the titles on the Blockbuster boxes.

Z was normally all about action movies, so I was surprised at the first movie. *Fear* starred one of my favorite actors, Mark Wahlberg, as the obsessed villain who falls in love with the teenaged Reece Witherspoon. Glancing at the second movie, I nearly laughed. I wasn't a big fan of scary movies, but I'd still watch them if I had someone to watch them with. I had avoided watching *Scream*, though. Movies that could actually happen were so much worse for me than ones that had monsters and ghosts.

Deciding to get it over with first, I put *Scream* in the VCR and dropped down on the couch beside Zander.

"You just had to, huh?"

Z grinned at me before taking a huge bite of his pizza. "I got you Wahlberg, baby. That's about as far as I can go."

I grinned back. "You'd better not make fun of me if I scream."

"Wouldn't dream of it." He grasped my hand and tugged me toward him. "If you get scared you can hold on to me. I won't ever let anything happen to you, Anna."

I melted against his side and rested my head on his shoulder. Watching a scary movie didn't seem nearly as bad all of a sudden.

Zander

I stretched and had to bite back a groan when my aching body brushed against the warm female snuggled so tightly against me. Blinking open my eyes, I realized that for the second night in a row I'd fallen asleep on the couch with Annabelle in my arms.

Grinning at my good luck, I brushed my lips over her ear and pulled her even tighter against me. Shit, this felt good. Right, so damn right. It didn't matter that my dick was as hard as a sledgehammer. I wasn't about to let that fucker ruin the peacefulness of the moment for me. This was my paradise and I wasn't in any hurry to leave it.

The night before had been perfect. We'd watched movies and eaten pizza. I'd gotten to hold Annabelle during the scary parts of both movies I'd rented and then we'd stretched out together on the couch to watch old episodes of *Happy Days* before falling asleep. As far as dates went, it had been a great one for me. Considering I'd slept over and hadn't fucked the brains out of my date, it was definitely a first for me.

My throbbing body didn't consider it nearly as great as I did, however. I was rock hard and the tip was already damp with need for the beauty sleeping so peacefully in my arms. Biting back a curse, I shifted to try and adjust my aching flesh. Sleeping in my jeans was not something my dick thought was amusing. The way it was pressed into the zipper at that moment was the punishment I obviously deserved.

Annabelle sighed softy and I glanced down at her in time to watch her lashes flutter upward, revealing those incredible blue eyes. As soon as she met my gaze, her pink little tongue slipped out of her mouth to dampen her ripe lips. Groaning, I leaned down to brush my own tongue over her bottom lip.

Just a taste. One. Little. Taste…

I knew it was a mistake as soon as I made contact. Her taste exploded on my tongue and it was like my entire body was set on fire. No one had ever affected me the way that Annabelle did. No one. My dick was now trying to drill its way out of my jeans. I didn't care. All I wanted was more of her taste on my tongue, her hands on my body, her soft sighs in my ears.

Before I could make the move to take more, she was already demanding it. Soft fingers combed through my hair and pulled my head down until our lips met. I thrust my tongue deep, wanting to taste every square inch of her hot little mouth. My hands developed a mind of their own and started exploring. I touched every inch I could reach, but tried to avoid her amazing tits because I knew once I touched them I'd need to focus all my attention on them to give them justice.

I was lost in the moment. Her taste was making my brain fog over, her fingers tangled in my hair as if she were scared to release me in case I stopped kissing her. I wanted more, yet I didn't ever want to stop what we were doing to explore what exactly 'more' would feel like. Nothing could ever feel better—feel this right—like when I was kissing the girl who owned my motherfucking soul.

Sharp teeth nipped at my bottom lip, surprising me enough to lift my head so that I could see her face. Annabelle was straining against me, trying to get as close to me as humanly possible. The need that was shining back at me from those sky-blue eyes matched my own. "Please," she moaned. "Z, please."

I lifted a hand that noticeably trembled with my own need to rub across her kiss-swollen bottom lip. "Please what, baby? What do you want?"

"You," she whimpered. "I want you. I want…" She trailed off and grasped my hand, bringing it down to her left breast. "Touch me here."

I cupped her through her shirt and realized she wasn't wearing a bra. How the hell had I missed that? I'd been avoiding looking at her chest all night, but I should have at least noticed that little detail. She fit perfectly in my hand, driving home the fact that this girl was made just for me.

Rubbing my thumb over the hardened nipple, I watched as her eyes half closed and she arched her back, moaning my name. My dick nearly ripped through the zipper and I had to release her long enough to unsnap and unzip my jeans before I hurt myself. I was back to holding her amazing breast in my hand within a second, but her gaze had followed my hand as I'd rearranged myself. The need that had been shining in her eyes just moments ago became an inferno as she gazed down at my throbbing dick tenting out of my jeans through my boxers.

Under her watchful gaze, my dick flexed, enjoying her attention and wanting more. Curious, she lifted her eyes back to mine and I saw the silent plea in those blue depths. "Can I?" she asked almost shyly.

Ah, fuck. There was no way I could turn this girl down, but I knew as soon as she touched me that I'd lose what was left of my restraint and take things further than I was sure she was ready for.

As if she knew my inner battle, she smiled that smile I loved so fucking much and stroked her fingers over my stubble-roughened jaw. That smile said so many things. That she got me. That she understood. *That she was mine.* "It's okay," she murmured and brushed her lips over my chin. "You can just kiss me again if you don't want me to touch you."

I caught her hand in mine and brought it to my lips, kissing each knuckle as I begged God for willpower. "I want you to touch me, Anna. So fucking bad it's making me shake. But once you do I'm not going to be able to hold back, and you deserve better than me turning into a damn caveman and taking you on a fucking couch where you brother can come in at any second and catch us."

"We could take this into the bedroom," she offered, the shyness returning.

I cupped her chin in my hand and kissed her lips tenderly before pulling back. Now that I was able to control myself somewhat, I wasn't about to get in over my head again. "I'm not going to fuck you, Anna."

The shyness and need faded from her eyes so fast it was like I'd dropped a bucket of ice water over her. She tried to pull away, but I wouldn't let her go. I wrapped my arms around her and pulled her roughly against my chest. "You're not the kind of girl a guy fucks, Anna. You're the type of girl a guy should take his time with. Cherish and love her like she deserves. That's what I want, baby. That's how it will be if I'm ever lucky enough to get that chance."

She melted against me, no longer trying to push away. Her arms wrapped around my neck and she lifted her head, showing me the tears that were already spilling over. "Z—"

"You're so beautiful, Annabelle. So fucking beautiful." I lowered my head and kissed away the tears that streaked down her face. "How'd I get so lucky? Huh? How did a sweet girl like you fall for a fuckup like me?"

"Don't say that," she whispered. "You aren't a fuckup. You're a good man, Z. That's why I love you."

My heart stopped at those last three words. I closed my eyes, trying to savor everything about them. The way her lips had formed each word, the sound of her sweet voice, how her eyes had shone with love despite the continued tears. "I don't deserve you, Anna."

She blew out a huff and snuggled against my chest. "You deserve everything you want, Z. Maybe one day you'll understand that."

Yeah. I doubted it, but…

Maybe.

Annabelle

School on Monday was a hell of a lot better than it had been the week before. I was able to focus more on what the teachers were saying instead of staring off into space… Okay, mostly I didn't stare off into space. I got the majority of what the teachers were trying to make me learn. The rest of the time I would daydream about Zander.

He'd surprised me when he'd spent Sunday night with me. With Noah home and Zander having to work the next morning, I was sure he'd go home and sleep in his own bed. Which had kept me depressed most of Sunday afternoon while he was at home with his grandmother. He'd shown up at eight with a large Tupperware container full of Gram's spaghetti and an entire loaf of fresh baked French bread smothered in garlic butter.

I'd eaten with him and Noah in the living room while they watched a football game on television. I'd gotten bored less than halfway through the game and pulled out my history book to study for the test that we were supposed to have on Friday. The guys had kept quiet for me and I was able to sit beside Zander instead of having to go into the bedroom.

I don't remember when I fell asleep, but around eleven I'd felt Zander lift me and carry me to bed. As he'd laid me down in the middle of the queen-sized mattress, I'd pulled him down with me. "Don't go," I murmured. "Stay with me."

In my half-asleep state I wasn't sure if I was asking for him not to go that night…or ever. When he'd chuckled deeply and started taking off his boots, I was thankful he'd assumed it was for the night. Smiling through the pain, I'd scooted across the bed and waited for him to take his jeans off before crawling into bed with me and pulling me close.

The lights were off, something I was glad for because I hadn't wanted him to see my tears. I needed to savor every second I could get with him, I reminded myself, and buried my face in his chest to soak up the scent of his body wash and aftershave. I needed to memorize everything about him, including his scent.

I was starting to relax again when the door cracked open and I heard Noah's voice. "Gram knows you're not coming home?"

"Yeah, man." Zander's voice had caused his chest to vibrate and I'd been unable to contain my shiver of desire. He'd felt it, his arms tightening around me as he tucked me closer.

The feel of his hardness was unmistakable, but he didn't try to kiss me or even touch me beyond just holding me close. If he was aching just a fraction as much as I was, then I knew he had to be in pain, but neither of us dared to start anything. I didn't want the first time Z made love to me to be when my brother was in the next room and could hear us. Gross.

"Night, then. Night, Annabelle." Before I could respond, the door had closed behind my brother.

Zander was gone when I got up for school that morning. Vaguely I remembered him kissing me goodbye before he'd left. He had to go home and get ready for work so I knew he wouldn't be there when I got up. Didn't mean I wasn't disappointed to wake up without him beside me, his lips brushing softly over my ear or cheek. Still, I was ten times happier this Monday than I'd been the Monday before, so I was able to get through the day with little difficulty.

With the last bell still echoing in my ears, I walked out to my bus and was about to get on when I saw a familiar truck across the parking lot. Frowning, I stepped back and waved at the man sitting in the driver's seat and the little girl who was practically bouncing with excitement on the passenger side.

Wroth Niall said something to his favorite person in the world and I watched as Marissa giggled and he got out of his older-model truck. As his scary big body got out of the truck, he waved me over and I didn't hesitate to go. Scary, Wroth might be, but I trusted him just as much as I did Noah and Zander.

"Hey," I greeted when he stepped back from the driver's side door, holding the door open for me. "What's up?"

"Zander called me this morning and asked if I'd pick you up since I was going to be in town anyway." He helped me into his truck. "We're doing auditions this evening."

My heart clenched and my gut rolled, but I tried to make my smile not look forced as I greeted Marissa. The girl threw her arms around me and started talking a mile a minute about her day at school. I was thankful for the distraction so I didn't torture myself with the realization that this audition was one step closer for OtherWorld getting their big break and taking Z away from me.

As soon as Wroth pulled up in front of the garage I hurried up to the apartment with Marissa to change and drop my backpack on the bed. When I returned to the living room, Wroth was stretched out on the couch with the remote in his hand, completely comfortable enough in my brother's apartment to make himself at home.

Marissa had unpacked her backpack and had her homework spread across the coffee table. I went into the kitchen to grab all three of us a snack. Placing the milk and cookies down beside Marissa, I sat down on the floor with her and helped her with her math homework.

Even at nine years old, Marissa was the prettiest girl I'd ever seen in my life. I could picture her older, those amazing blue eyes and that long dark hair making the boys beg for her attention. I pitied them all, because I knew that, with Wroth and Liam around, those guys would never get beyond a friendly hello before they were knocked on their asses. Marissa would have to learn to put her foot down with those two overprotective beasts if she ever wanted a boyfriend.

It was six before I heard the rest of OtherWorld's members arrive. I heard the engine of a powerful old car and looked out the window to see Liam getting out of the driver's seat of his girlfriend's old Corvette. When the passenger door opened and Tawny stepped out dressed like the streetwalker I knew she was, I had to bite back the curses that would have had Wroth tearing into me for cussing in front of Marissa.

Liam and Tawny headed for the apartment steps just as Zander's truck pulled up. Devlin's truck was right behind him and I couldn't stop the stupid grin that lifted my lips. Did that mean he was going to spend the night with me again? My heart leaped at the possibility and I no longer cared that my brother's apartment was about to be infested with Tawny's skank ass.

Liam didn't bother to knock when he got up to the apartment. Letting himself in, he instantly released Tawny's hand the second his eyes fell on his sister. "Hey, Anna Banana." Ugh, I hated it when he called me that. He seemed to have a thing about giving everyone a nickname and that was what I'd been stuck with from the first day we'd met.

"Rissa," he greeted with a laugh and bent to lift the little girl into his arms. He dropped down on the couch beside his cousin and started asking questions about Marissa's day.

Ignoring her brother's girlfriend who parked herself on the edge of the couch beside of Liam, Marissa gave him a minute-by-minute account of her day. I had to admit that Liam had once been one of my favorite people in the world until he met Tawny. He'd been a great guy up until he'd gotten involved with Satan's sister and fallen into the depths of hell with the first taste of drugs she'd offered him. But even now, when he wasn't on my list of favorite people, I couldn't help but miss my friend as he gave Marissa his full attention. Tawny or no Tawny, Marissa was and always would be Liam's main priority.

And the bitch knew that and tried to keep him away from her as much as possible.

Rolling my eyes at the jealousy I saw shining in the devil's sister's eyes, I turned my full attention on the two men now walking through the apartment door. Devlin entered first with a bag of groceries under each arm. I took one from him and glanced inside, seeing the fixings for some killer sandwiches. Sighing, I gave him a mock glare.

"I guess I'll be crafting these beasts, huh?"

Devlin's eyes were full of amusement, but he pouted those lips of his at me. "Pwease, Annabelle. Pwetty pwease?"

"Funny." I started to turn for the kitchen when Zander walked in holding two more bags. "Really? What else is in there?"

"Stuff for those barbeque sausage things you make in the crockpot. Some chips and dip, a few frozen pizzas." Devlin shrugged. "We want to make a good impression on the dude that takes over for Noah."

Another pain clenched at my heart and I stumbled a moment before putting a smile on my face and dropping my grocery bag on the kitchen counter. Devlin disposed of his own and Zander placed his beside mine before wrapping his arms around my waist and brushing a kiss over my cheek from behind. "I'll help," he murmured against my ear.

I shook my head. "No. You've worked all day. Sit down and relax." I turned in his arms and stood on tiptoe to brush a quick kiss over his lips. I heard several shocked grumbles coming from the living room but ignored them. Their opinion on what was going on between Z and me wasn't important.

Zander's hold on my waist tightened, pulling me closer for a deeper kiss that left me breathless before stepping back with a sexy smirk and going into the living room to sit beside Devlin. I just stood there, trying to recover from his amazing kiss. A silly grin spread across my face and I finally started on all the food that Devlin wanted to use to impress Noah's replacement.

By eight thirty, Noah had come up from the garage and was showered. Chelsea had arrived and was helping me finish up the last of the sandwiches and the rest of the food Devlin had requested I fix—even though I kept having to fix extras when he and the other beastly men in the apartment kept stealing the food as I made it.

The guys wanted the atmosphere to be casual for these rehearsals. Except for Wroth, who had his acoustic guitar, and Zander, who had his bass, no one else was going to be playing. They wanted the guy who took over for Noah to be able to work with minimal music, needing to know the full range of his voice before they offered anyone the position.

Three guys showed up at just after eight thirty and the guys made small talk with each of them, offering them a seat on the couch and to make themselves at home with all the food I'd made. While they snacked on the sandwiches and barbeque sausages, I took my time inspecting each of them.

They were all young and seemed cocky enough to think they would be good for the open vocal position. Two of the three even seemed decent enough and might have even made the band a good fit just on their attitude alone. One definitely fit the part of rocker material, with his long dark hair and tattoos that seemed to take up the majority of the space on what skin I could see.

He wasn't bad to look at, but something about him made me a little uneasy. Maybe it was the way his eyes kept going to Marissa who was sitting on the floor by Wroth coloring her little heart out. Every few minutes I would shoot a glance at the big beast and realized I wasn't the only one who was aware of the attention the little girl kept getting. Even Liam was sober enough to realize the tension vibrating off his cousin and wasn't blind to the reason.

After a few more minutes of Wroth sitting there with murder in his eyes, I took Marissa into the bedroom and turned on the smaller TV set and let her get comfortable with a G-rated movie before returning to the others. As I entered the room, I realized a fourth guy had arrived to audition and I stopped dead in my tracks when I spotted him.

His hair was just slightly on the long side and looked recently dyed, but the jet-black color suited him. I also noticed fresh ink on his arm, still glossy from the ointment that needed to be constantly applied to a new tattoo. Even with the new hairstyle and fresh ink, I recognized the guy. It would have taken a blind person not to realize that this guy was Anthony Huntington. He lived on the uppity side of West Bridge with his snotty-as-hell mother.

He hadn't gone to school with us because his mother had sent him to some big-bucks, high-class private academy well over an hour away. Still, the few times I'd seen him in town, I hadn't gotten the 'I'm better than you' vibe from him. Unlike his mother who looked down her nose at everyone she saw.

This new version of Anthony shocked me speechless, however. He'd been a very handsome boy with his slightly shaggy, sandy-blond hair and hazel eyes. Now, with that jet-black hair and that badass ink on his arm, I had to admit that the guy was seriously sexy.

I greeted him with a shy wave as I took the spot on the floor between Zander's feet and everyone else in the room got comfortable. Noah was going over the requirements of the audition. Telling them to relax and sing whatever cover song they were most comfortable with, but one that would show off their vocal ranges best.

They went in order of who had arrived first and I leaned my head against Zander's knee as I watched intently as they each took their turns. The first two didn't have the voice that OtherWorld was looking for, and some of the tension in my stomach actually started to ease. Of course my instant guilt over being glad that those two guys had basically bombed filled me with self-hate.

The third guy, the one who had set most of us on edge because of his bizarre attention to Marissa, actually had a decent voice. I might have hid an evil smile, because I knew that there was no way in hell Wroth would let that prick become a part of OtherWorld. No one said anything, though, just letting him sing the cover of a Skynyrd song.

By the end of the song Noah was nodding his head, but when his eyes landed on me, asking my opinion, I shook my head. He stood and offered his hand to the three other men. "Thanks, guys. I appreciate you all coming by tonight. Give us a couple of days and we'll let you know. We're going to let this guy get something to eat before we let him sing for us."

They all shook Noah's hand and filed out of the apartment. While they did that, I offered to make Anthony a plate. The new version of the guy I'd always known to be so preppy smiled up at me. "You don't have to do that, Annabelle. And the name isn't Anthony any longer. I changed it two days ago. I'm Axton Cage now."

My eyes widened. "Really?"

"Call it a late rebellion against the dictator that is my bitch of a mother." He winked up at me and for some reason I couldn't help but grin at him. "I would take a glass of tea, if you have it, though."

"Sure. I'll get it for you now."

It took less than a minute to get his drink and when I retook my place at Zander's feet, he stroked his fingers through my long hair and dropped a kiss on top of my head. I leaned into him, loving the feel of his lips on me even if it was just on my head.

Everyone else around us seemed to settle down to get comfortable once more. Wroth even went into the bedroom to ask Marissa to join us again, but she had crashed while watching the movie I'd put in for her. As he took his place on the now empty couch, he nodded for Axton to sit down beside him and asked him what song he wanted to do.

Axton scratched his chin, thinking about his selection, and then shrugged his lean shoulders. "Let's mix it up, man. If you want to hear my full range I'd need to do several songs for you guys. Let's start with Aerosmith, then go into some Skynyrd, and end it with some Metallica. That okay with you?"

Wroth shrugged. "Which songs?"

Axton grinned. "Surprise me."

I nearly snorted at the arrogance of the guy, but held it back as Wroth's talented fingers started the first few chords of Aerosmith's "Angel." All urges to snort or laugh at the new guy evaporated as soon as he opened his mouth and everyone in the room became entranced with the man we knew was going to take over for Noah.

As I listened, I couldn't fight back the tears that suddenly threatened to choke me. From the first note that left Axton Cage's mouth, I knew that there was no way OtherWorld wouldn't go far with this guy front and center for them. He wasn't just good; the man had a fucking gift. And it broke my heart into a million pieces. One look at OtherWorld performing with Axton singing their songs and any manager with a working brain would sign them on the spot.

Swallowing hard, I glanced at Noah. The look on his face was a mixture of amazement and gut-wrenching pain. He knew as well as I did—as well as everyone in the room—that not only was Axton going to fit with the band, but that this guy was better than even he had ever hoped to be. The pain in my heart at the knowledge that I was even closer to losing Zander than I had been just thirty minutes ago, doubled at the pain my beloved brother was going through right then.

The Aerosmith song faded easily into the Skynyrd song, "Free Bird," and even though Axton's vocal range changed, it only showed just how talented he really was. I lowered my gaze to the floor, hiding the tears that were so close to spilling over. I wanted so hard to hate Axton, wanted it with every fiber of my being, but I couldn't. None of the pain I was feeling was his fault. He'd just shown up to a freaking audition, unknowingly ripping my heart from my chest with that amazing voice of his, and shattered it into a million little pieces.

I couldn't hate him. Not when he was going to help the man I loved succeed in his goals.

The Rocker Who Betrays Me

Skynyrd drifted seamlessly into Metallica's "Nothing Else Matters" with Wroth's talented fingers. Glancing at Zander, watching him keep beat with the bass, seeing how much he loved being a part of this music world, I lost the battle. One tear escaped from my eyes and was quickly followed by a hundred more. I stood, keeping my face averted from everyone as I went into the bedroom and shut the door quietly behind me.

I quickly tore off my clothes as I entered the bathroom. Turning on the shower, I climbed in before the water even had time to warm. My knees gave out and I slid down in the corner of the tub, letting the cold water beat down on me as the first sob tore my heart loose from my chest. Pulling my knees up to my chest, I hid my face in my raised thighs and cried for the loss of the man who wasn't even gone yet.

Zander

It was late when Axton left, but I had a grin on my face as I pulled off my shirt and jeans before climbing into bed beside Annabelle.

I thought she was asleep but, the second I wrapped my arms around her waist, she turned in my arms and brushed her lips over mine. My body was still humming from the high of the amazing jam session I just had with the guys. That plus my constant ache for her and the taste of her lips was like a detonator on my self-control. With a growl I didn't even realize had left me, I turned onto my back and pulled her across my chest.

My hands tangled in her long pale hair, holding her head at the angle that I wanted it. Thrusting my tongue deep into her hot little mouth, I couldn't help thinking of thrusting into her heat elsewhere. My left hand tightened on her amazing ass, pulling her down harder against my aching dick as I ground into her sweet spot through whatever pajamas she was wearing.

Her soft gasp of pleasure only revved me up that much more. Ah, hell she felt so good. I could have gotten off just rubbing against her like that and, as lost in the feel and taste of her as I was, I might have done just that if there hadn't been a knock on the door two seconds before it opened.

I kept Annabelle right where she was, but stopped kissing her as her brother stuck his head around the corner of the door. He couldn't see anything since the room was almost completely dark other than the small ray of light that was shining from behind Noah.

"She has school in the morning, dude. Don't keep her up too late," Noah spoke quietly and I could hear Chelsea laughing at something on the television in the living room. "Night, man. Night, Annabelle."

I had to clear my throat before I could answer him. "Night."

"Night, Noah." Annabelle's voice was soft, full of all the desire that I was still making her tremble against me with. My hand tightened on her ass, letting her know that I was just as far gone as she was.

After another few seconds, Noah shut the door and Annabelle tried to search for my lips again. With a groan I turned us so we were both on our sides facing each other in the dark. It took a little while before my eyes adjusted to the darkness, but finally I could make out the shape of her face. Lifting a hand that trembled, I stroked a finger down her cheek.

"We shouldn't," I told her even as my body was screaming that I was a fucking idiot.

"Wh-why not?" Her breath hitched as her soft hands traced over my bare chest. Her fingertips trailed over my stomach and straight for the top of my boxers, and I reluctantly caught her hands, lifting them to my mouth to press kisses to each palm. "Please, Z."

I squeezed my eyes shut, knowing I shouldn't let it go further, but I wanted her so fucking bad. Muttering a curse, I pushed her to her back and promised myself I'd just get her off, nothing more. I wouldn't dare take something that I didn't deserve, and I sure as hell didn't deserve to be the one to take her virginity. I was too much of a fuck-up, too fucked-up in the head, to ever be worthy of something that precious.

Jaw clenched, I kissed my way from her lips, down her neck and straight for her amazing tits. Motherfucking hell. The thin straps of her pajama top came down way too easily and then I was wrapping my lips around one of her sweet nipples. Her breath hitched as I sucked harder, but she just barely kept from moaning. I quickly turned my attention to her other tit. Fuck —how did this one taste better than the other?

Selfishly, I wanted to take my time with her —Make her first orgasm be something she would remember for the rest of her life —but it was already late and she needed to get up early for school. Reluctantly, I left her tits and kissed down her flat stomach to the waistband of her pajama shorts. Eagerly she lifted her hips as I tugged them down.

The heat and scent of her desire nearly crippled me with need. Touching her smooth, soft thighs, I had to bite back a groan when I felt her need damp on the inside of her slender legs. Lowering my head, I kissed each thigh and realized for the first time why it was so easy for Liam to get so addicted to the drugs he poisoned himself with every day. If they tasted this good, if they made him feel this alive and hard, then no wonder he couldn't stop. No wonder he wanted more and more and more.

My dick flexed against the mattress and I drowned my groan by burying my face between Annabelle's sweet-smelling legs. I wasn't the kind of guy who enjoyed eating pussy often. I'd only done it a handful of times and had hated every second of it. Yet from the second I tasted Annabelle, I realized maybe it wasn't that I didn't like eating pussy, just that I didn't like tasting anyone but the girl now withering under my tongue.

I couldn't get enough of her taste, the feel of her tiny clit under my tongue and the heat scalding me from her opening. Unable to resist, I teased my middle finger around her opening and pushed in ever so slightly. "Z, oh, God." Her walls clenched around my fingertip, trying to suck me deeper. My dick thickened even more, my balls tightening. Holy shit, I was going to get off just from licking her pussy.

Annabelle was getting close. I could feel it in the way her body was tensing, the way her walls kept contracting harder around my finger, and especially in the way her sweet cream flowed faster and faster. I lapped up every drop, desperate for more. Her little gasps and pants were driving me crazy and my balls were so tight I knew it was going to be over in less than a few seconds.

I moved quickly, knowing I was going to hell anyway so what was once more crime against me? I pulled my throbbing cock out of my boxers and rubbed the pre-cum-covered head over her drenched pussy lips, teasing it over her clit. Once. Twice. The third time I thrust my middle finger into her a little farther, not quite deep enough to touch her virginity, and she came apart for me.

Fuck, I wished the lights were on so I could see her as she soared with her orgasm. I wanted to know what her face looked like when she fell over the edge of release, wanted to see how her body glowed with the pleasure.

Biting back a curse, I gave one last stroke over her wetness before I had to cover the head of my dick as I came harder than I had ever come before. My back arched so hard it was a wonder I didn't break my spine. Gritting my teeth, I held back the yell of release that was shredding my throat for freedom.

When I could breathe again I climbed out of bed and went into the bathroom to clean myself up. Returning to the bed, I used a warm, damp cloth to wipe away the rest of her sweet-smelling cream. She was lying there, her breathing finally evened out, and from the glow of the bathroom light I could see her sleepy expression. Pink filled her cheeks as I cleaned her up and then brushed a kiss over her lips.

I took the washcloth and towel back into the bathroom and returned to her. Pillowing her head on my chest, she snuggled as close as she could get and let out a long breath that sounded almost sad. I wanted to ask why she was sad but couldn't find the words—and honestly, I was scared shitless of what her reason really was. Neither of us spoke as we drifted off to sleep in each other's arms, holding on as if we would never let go.

I spent every night that week at Noah's apartment. Sometimes Annabelle and I slept on the couch, but more often than not we took the bed and she begged me to touch her. I barely had any self-control, and each night I came closer and closer to taking something I knew I didn't deserve.

On Friday I left work early to pick her up from school. I took her home with me because Gram had been asking me to bring her back. My two favorite girls in the world spent the afternoon talking away and making dinner for Gramps and me. Annabelle didn't know much about cooking, but Gram took her time with her, showing her how to do everything.

Sitting down to dinner that night, I savored every bite on my plate because I knew the girl I loved had helped make it. She blushed every time I would make an approving groan and Gram would giggle to herself while Gramps ate his own dinner with a half grin on his normally taciturn face. The gruff old man had a soft spot for Annabelle but, then again, who wouldn't? She was special.

Noah was closing up the garage early that night so Annabelle didn't have to go into work. I was taking her with me to Floyd's Bar for our gig, but I didn't understand why Noah wanted to torment himself by going too. I hated to admit it, but Axton Cage sounded so much better with us than Noah did. It wasn't that Noah didn't have the voice to make it in the business, but after jamming with Axton, I had realized—hell, we'd all realized—that Noah wasn't the right voice for OtherWorld.

I'd felt guilty for feeling that way all week. It felt like I was being disloyal to Noah, but I couldn't feel guilty for being glad that we'd found Axton. Noah would do better doing country music; his voice just suited that style better. Didn't mean I wasn't torn up at having to say goodbye to a band member who I thought of as a brother. I knew that with Noah officially out of OtherWorld, I was one step closer to losing him…and Annabelle.

Refusing to think about that—because my fucked-up mind would probably shatter if I did—I left Annabelle with Chelsea in the back room at Floyd's Bar while I helped the guys set up for that night's gig. We were all somber as we set up our gear, all of us hurting a little because it was going to be the first time we played a show without Noah. Even Axton was quiet, as if he knew how hard this was going to be for us, and felt our pain just as deeply.

Once everything was set up we joined the girls in the back room and had our usual beers. I sat beside Devlin on the old loveseat, Annabelle on my lap. She kept shooting her brother questioning looks and after a few minutes Noah nodded his head. I felt her tense for a second or two and then she was turning her head and smiling brightly down at me. She stroked her thumb over my bottom lip and I pressed a kiss to her soft skin.

"You boys ready?" Floyd's gruff voice, nearly as scary as Wroth's, asked as he stuck his head into the room. "The place is packed as usual. Even got a few new faces out there."

"Give us five," Devlin told the old man, and with a nod Floyd left us alone again.

Wroth and Liam stood along with Devlin. I sat Annabelle on the loveseat before joining them, hating having to leave her. Noah seemed hesitant as he stood with us. Axton remained on the chair, watching us, letting us have this goodbye with our friend. I watched as Noah swallowed hard before giving Wroth a one-armed hug. Out of everything else that was going on right then, watching that big man swallow with difficulty while he hugged Noah nearly ripped my heart out of my chest.

Clenching my jaw, I took my turn hugging my friend, my brother. Turning away, I grabbed another beer and swallowed the entire thing in two gulps. Annabelle caught my hand as I headed for the door, following my band-brothers. Her touch and the reassuring squeeze she gave me had the power to ease some of the tightness in my chest. Bending, I brushed a quick kiss over her slightly parted lips.

I waited on stage for Devlin to get us started and found Annabelle in the crowd. She was standing between Noah and Chelsea. There was a bright smile on her lips, but even from where I was standing with the lights shining down on me, I could see the tears in her beautiful blue eyes.

Putting it down to her being emotional for her brother, I winked at her, hoping to make her laugh. Her lips opened in a small laugh, but I couldn't hear it over the noise of the crowd. I wanted to tell her right then and there that I loved her —that no matter what happened in the future, I would always love her.

Devlin counting us down for our first song of the night kept me from doing just that, and I turned off everything in my mind except for the music. I didn't see the crowds while I played with my band. All I could hear, see, fucking feel, was the music that seemed to radiate out of me with the force of a tropical storm that was quickly turning into a hurricane.

The Rocker Who Betrays Me

Nothing in the world had ever felt as good as being on stage, sharing my love and need for my music. Nothing had ever gotten me as revved up, as high. Nothing could make me feel like a god more than my music…

No, that was wrong. Annabelle could do all of that with just her smile. All she had to do was look at me with those baby-blue eyes and I felt like I could conquer the world. She was my high. She was the goddess to my god. I might want the music, but I needed her more. If she asked me, I would throw down my bass right then and there and walk away from it for the rest of my life. I would give up anything and everything if she wanted me to.

Being a rock star didn't seem as important when faced with the possibility of losing her forever, something I knew would happen if I stayed with OtherWorld. I would happily quit and follow her and Noah to Nashville, find a job working for the DOT there. And then, when she was old enough, I'd put my ring on her finger, put my baby in her belly.

Everything inside of me went simultaneously hot and cold. I wanted all of that, damn it. I wanted it and more, but I wasn't good enough for Annabelle Cassidy. I didn't want to destroy her life like that. She deserved so much more, someone better than the monster that was in my head. I couldn't ruin her life by being selfish. I wouldn't. She was too good, so special, to have to live the rest of her life with my fucked-up mess.

But I wanted to be selfish…

If you asked me how well the show went that night, I couldn't have told you. My mind had shut down and I'd played on autopilot. I didn't hear the screams for one more song, or see the reactions on my band-brothers' faces as we left the stage and returned to the back room where more beers were already waiting on us.

Grabbing two, I swallowed one before my ass had even hit the loveseat and quickly tipped the other to my lips. Vaguely, I heard the others laughing and someone patting Axton on the back. From the groan I heard I was pretty sure it had been Wroth doing the patting. Someone sat beside me and I was surprised to see it was Liam. Usually he went off with Tawny right after our gigs, either to get some pussy or more drugs, I didn't know. Didn't care.

"You alright, man?"

I nearly laughed at my junky friend asking if *I* was alright. I bit back the laugh, though. I wasn't sure how I could hold back the other emotions churning deep inside of my gut if I did.

Noah walking into the room with Chelsea and Annabelle, distracting me long enough to calm down. I held out my hand for her, wanting just a little more time with her. *God, please. I won't ask you for more, I swear. Just a few more days with her is all I want. When she moves to Nashville, I'll let her go. Just give me a few more days.*

Annabelle placed her hand in mine, but when I gave it a little tug, wanting her to sit down on my lap as she had before the show, she gave me a tight smile and shook her head. My brows lifted and my hand tightened around hers, ready to pull her down forcefully if I had to. She pulled her hand away and turned her head, looking at the door she'd just come through.

Curious, I followed her gaze only to find a man in his late thirties, dressed in an expensive suit, standing in the doorway. Noah stepped forward, shaking the man's hand as if he knew him already.

"Glad you could make it, Rich." Noah encouraged the other man to come in, grinning. "I told you that you wouldn't be sorry if you came out. After that show I'm sure you will agree with me."

"You got that right, boy." Rich glanced from one of my band members to the next, only stopping for a few seconds on each of us, but I could see the excitement in his eyes when I met his gaze. "I like your sound. I think I can take your band far, if you're willing to let me try."

I shot a look at Noah, who was still grinning. He wrapped his arm around Chelsea's shoulders and she kissed his cheek quickly before pulling away and went to hug Annabelle. I watched the girl I loved continue to wear her bright smile, but I was more than sure that she was blinking back tears as she let the smaller blonde hold her.

"Mind telling us what's going on?" Wroth's scary-ass voice brought my head around, turning my attention back to what was going on around us.

"When I was in Nashville last week, I told the radio exec about OtherWorld. He gave me Rich Branson's number and told me to mention his name so Branson would take me seriously." Noah shrugged his shoulders. "Once we found Axton to take over for me, I knew that you guys were ready, so I asked Rich to come out and listen tonight."

"Rich Branson?" Axton repeated the name, a frown tightening his brow. "Aren't you one of the top managers in California?"

The Branson guy was grinning even bigger now and even I could see the narcissism in this asshole. "That would be me. If you guys are willing to sign on with me, I can guarantee you a record label contract within the next year. Hell, within the next month if you boys aren't scared of coming out to Cali with me."

My heart stopped at his words. Holy shit. Here it was, my chance to go after the dreams I'd had almost my entire life. I had known it would happen one day, but now that the chance was staring me right in the face, I couldn't breathe.

Branson continued, laying all the details out for us, and my heart still didn't beat. We had a week to get our life in West Bridge in order before going to California. He'd send a bus for us, give us a taste of what life on the road touring would be like. Around me, the others were going crazy, laughing and slapping each other on the back. We'd made it. OtherWorld was going to be something special.

All I had to do was leave Annabelle behind.

The noises around me, added to those in my head, were making it hard to think straight. I jumped to my feet, grabbed hold of Annabelle's arm and pulled her out of the room with me. The exit was just a few feet to the left and I dragged her outside with me.

The air was cool and I sucked in one lungful after another. My entire body was shaking and when I looked at Annabelle I realized that I must have been scaring her. She cupped my face in her soft hands. "What's wrong?" she murmured soothingly.

"I…" I broke off, not sure what I was going to say. Shaking my head, I covered her hands and closed my eyes. "Things are just going too fast. I can't slow it down. It's too fast for me to wrap my head around and I need to make sense of it."

I heard her breath hitch as she inhaled sharply and forced my eyes open. "I know," she whispered. "It's kind of scary. I'm kind of scared too. But I know this is what you've always wanted. Here's your chance. Don't let your fear of change take that away from you. You're too good at what you do to let this slip through your fingers. OtherWorld is going to go places; you're going to become the rock gods I've always known you would be." Her arms wrapped around my neck and she buried her face in my neck. "I'm so proud of you, Z."

Hearing her say those words, letting her put it all into perspective for me, was exactly what I needed. For the first time since Branson had opened his mouth, I felt like my heart was beating again. This was happening and I was going with OtherWorld on this crazy rollercoaster that I knew it would be.

She was right. This was everything I'd ever wanted. All I had to do was say goodbye to her.

Motherfucking hell.

Annabelle

The guys wanted to go out and celebrate, but since I couldn't go to any of the places they wanted due to my age, they settled on going back to the apartment. Wroth, who was the only one old enough to actually buy booze, brought enough beer and liquor to qualify us as a small bar. The stereo was on full blast and the apartment was crawling with fans who had followed us back from Floyd's Bar—most of them girls.

I sat on a pillow in a corner with Chelsea for most of the night, not wanting to get in Zander's way as one person after another congratulated him and his band members for their success. I didn't move when I saw one chick after another kiss his cheek and smile at him, offering him their bodies on a fucking platter as they looked up at him through their fake lashes. Even if what I really wanted to do was scratch up every prettily made-up face that went near him, I didn't.

No, I sat there and every time he glanced at me, I smiled brightly for him, not wanting him to see how I was slowly dying inside. I refused to let him, or anyone else, see how close to breaking I really was. I just had to keep this up for another week, and then I could fall apart. Then I'd be able to mourn the loss of the boy/man I loved more than anything or anyone. Once he was gone, I knew he wouldn't come back. I'd be just a vague little memory that entered his head from time to time while he rocked out on stage every night and fucked a different girl after every show.

Chelsea pulled the beer bottle out of my hand, forcing me back from the self-torture I was putting myself through as I imagined the guy I loved touching someone else the way he'd been touching me for the last week. The look on Chelsea's face was full of sympathy and compassion as she replaced the empty bottle with a fresh one.

Lifting her own full bottle of beer, she tapped hers to mine. "Here's to being the unselfish chicks who let the men we love have the futures they deserve."

Hearing her say that, I felt guilt tighten my already churning stomach. "It should be Noah out there with them, getting ready to start the rock-star lifestyle with OtherWorld."

Chelsea's blue eyes darkened and she lifted her beer to her lips, swallowing deeply before speaking. "No, Annabelle, it shouldn't. Noah has some serious talent, and yes he deserves to go far in the music world, but he and I both know that it wasn't going to be the rock world he'd succeed in. The radio exec told him what we've always known. Country is where his voice belongs, not rock. And you know what?" I shook my head, not sure if she really wanted me to answer or not. "I'm glad."

Her chin trembled ever so slightly before she clenched her jaw and forced a smile to her beautiful face. "I'm so glad, Annabelle. His going solo saved us. I could barely handle the groupies that hung around the bar on Friday nights. How was I going to deal with the ones that follow bands from city to city? The ones who just want to say they fucked a rock star? Yeah, I know he loves me, but that doesn't mean shit when they're drunk and they have available ass just begging them. How was I supposed to not break apart when he was out on tour without me? Huh?"

"Chels…" I honestly didn't know what to say, because she was voicing every fear I had running through my own head. That was going to be Zander. He would be the drunken rocker with all the girls throwing themselves at him, and he wouldn't resist. He wouldn't have to.

She took a smaller sip of beer this time. "No, girl. This is the life I can live with. I can handle this one. He's promised me that we can tour with him when his career takes off. I'll be able to handle it because I know the only piece of ass he will be getting every night will be mine." She winked and I had to laugh at the pleased look on her face.

Hearing her voice her opinion on my brother's need for a new career path actually made me feel a little better. The guilt of ruining Noah's life had been festering to the point that I was in fear of an ulcer. With Chelsea's confession that all the new changes were probably going to save their relationship, I could feel some of the knot in my stomach ease.

Sipping at my own beer, I glanced back at where I'd last seen Zander. He and Devlin had been talking to a small group of two girls and three other guys in the kitchen, but they were gone now. One of the girls had kept touching his arm, flirting with him and tossing back her fried bleach-blond hair. I didn't think he would do anything with that little ho-bag, but I didn't put it past the chick to actually throw herself at him.

Turning my head, I searched the room for him and found him sitting on the arm of the couch talking to Noah, who was standing with Wroth and some chick who looked like the type I pictured the big ex-marine would go for: long hair, longer legs, and big boobs. Yeah, that was exactly how I figured Wroth Niall liked them.

As if he felt my eyes on him, Zander turned his head and caught my gaze. I offered him the same bright smile I'd had affixed on my face all night and gave a small wave. He stood and brushed past Wroth like he didn't even see him as he crossed the living room and crouched down in front of Chelsea and me.

Taking my beer from me, he lifted the bottle to his lips and swallowed the rest of its contents before handing the now empty bottle to Chelsea and taking my hand. He pulled me to my feet. "Let's get some air, baby."

I let him lead me outside where several other people were standing around smoking, drinking, and laughing. It was a good thing we didn't have any neighbors because obviously everyone was having a great time, some of them a little too much fun from the looks of it. I just wished I could have been as happy for OtherWorld as I was pretending to be. Zander linked his fingers through mine and we walked down the stairs and around the back of the garage where no one else had dared to venture, at least not yet.

I inhaled the cool fall air as we stopped and leaned back against the garage. I didn't want to look at him—too afraid I'd fall into a sobbing mess at his feet—so I looked up at the stars instead. Despite the coolness of the night, the sky was crystal clear, not a cloud in sight. The stars twinkled down at me, mocking me for wanting to wish on each and every one of them. Wish for Zander to stay, for things to be different. For him to have a different dream, one that included settling down somewhere and starting a family. Or whatever. Anything, damn it, anything that wouldn't take him away from me.

But that wasn't his dream and I loved him enough to want to make this dream of his a reality.

His fingers tightened around mine and he stepped in front of me, blocking out my view of the stars. I swallowed hard, forcing back my pleas for him to stay, and smiled. "What?" I demanded with a laugh when he just stood there looking down at me with such intensity. I couldn't see the color of his eyes, but I would have bet they were green with flecks of gold fire right then.

"I'm going to buy you and Gram a cell phone. That way if you need me, I'll only be a phone call away. We can talk every day, and I'll come back to visit as often as I can."

My heart skipped a beat. "R-really?"

"Yes, Anna, really. I need to be connected to you. I need to know that you're safe and back here in Tennessee waiting on me. That you care enough to wait until I'm in a position to come back and get you." He took a step back and raked his hands through his hair. "Look, I know this probably sounds stupid to you, and I would totally understand if you don't want to take this chance with me. I'm a bad risk, Anna. My head is all kinds of fucked-up and I'm probably going to make your life a living hell because of that."

I stood there, completely stunned by what was coming out of his mouth. I didn't want to hope. Hope was such a dangerous emotion and it could rip me apart if I let myself feel it. Watching him made that impossible, though. Being this close to him, hearing words leave his mouth that broke my heart because of all the self-hate I could hear in them, I couldn't *not* hope.

Muttering a curse, he caught my chin between his thumb and forefinger, so gently it finally broke me. A few tears spilled out of my eyes and down my cheeks. I could only make out the shape of his face but even in the darkness I could see the intensity in it. "I love you, Annabelle. I love you so damn much. Say you'll wait for me. I'll come back for you, baby. I swear it."

Fuck you, hope. You'd better not break my heart.

More tears fell and I didn't try to hold them back like I'd done all night. With a broken sob I threw my arms around his neck. "I love you t-too, Z-Z." His arms wrapped around my waist hard enough to lock the air in my chest, but I didn't care. "I love you. Of course I'll wait. I'll wait as long as I have to. I only want to be with you. I love you so much it hurts."

His body was shaking, but he kept a tight hold around my waist. "Thank God," he breathed. "I was going crazy, baby. This is what I want, the music and all that shit, but I want you too. You deserve so much better than me, Anna. It was killing me because I didn't think I had the right to ask you to take a chance on me—on a future with me. I know it's selfish, but right now I don't give a damn."

A choked laugh bubbled up in my chest. "You really are crazy." I felt him tense even more and laughed again. "Crazy for thinking I wouldn't want to be with you. I want it all, Z," I admitted with another sob that hurt my chest from the force of it. "I want you to have your dreams and I w-want to be a part of them. I love you and it was killing me to have to smile all night and pretend I was over the moon when all I wanted to do was beg you to stay or take me with you. I wasn't about to ask you to stay, and I knew I couldn't go with you. Not yet." Tears were pouring down my face and now soaking his shirt, but neither of us seemed to really notice or care. "I love you."

"Fuck," he muttered with a groan that turned into a tortured whimper. "Ah, fuck." He kissed my neck but didn't lift his head. His shoulders shook harder than the rest of his big body. When I felt his tears soaking into my shirt, my heart clenched painfully and my own tears fell faster.

"I love you," he breathed. "I love you."

It was nearly dawn before the last person left. Wroth was crashed out on the couch, taking up all the available space on it and still his big feet hung over the end of one of the couch arms. Devlin was asleep on the loveseat and, given that he was the second tallest guy I knew, the sight was something I couldn't help laughing at. Or taking a picture of. I took several with the Polaroid we'd had for forever. Sticking one to the fridge, I took the other with me into the bedroom to hide in case he decided to tear the other one into a thousand pieces.

In the bedroom, I found Axton asleep by the closet. I didn't want to know what he'd been doing to fall into a drunken sleep there, and I didn't have the heart to wake him. Thankful that he had all his clothes on, I tossed a throw over him and I went into the bathroom to get ready for bed.

Noah had left half an hour before with Chelsea, deciding to sleep at her house rather than finding a place to crash on the floor. Liam and Tawny had been the first two to leave earlier, and I wouldn't say I was sorry. Even high, I could deal with Liam, but Tawny was another story. High or stone-cold sober I couldn't stand her for longer than five minutes and even then that pushed the boundaries of my tolerance for the bitch.

After brushing my teeth I washed my face and turned off the light as I went back into the bedroom to climb into bed. I wasn't sure how long I lay there just staring at the dark ceiling before Zander came to bed. It wasn't long at all, but it felt like hours. I knew that I needed to get used to not having him to hold me at night, but for now I was going to savor every second I had with him.

I still couldn't believe what had happened earlier. I was still smiling because that damn emotion, hope, was making me plan our future already. Z would go to California and OtherWorld would get their record deal. They would record their first album and he'd come home before he went off on his first tour. Then, when he got back from that, I'd be eighteen and we could start our life together in California.

After hearing how Tawny was going to be moving out to California with Liam and even bragging how she would be touring with her rock-star boyfriend, I knew that Z and me actually had a chance. This could happen for us.

With a happy sigh I snuggled against him, moaning softly when he brushed a butterfly-soft kiss over my eyes and whispered he loved me before his breathing evened out and he fell sound asleep. Fighting back a yawn, I let my own eyes close and fell asleep within minutes.

The next few days flew by. Zander turned in his notice at the county DOT and started getting things set for his trip to California. He bought me a cellphone and matching ones for Gram and himself. We spent as much time at his grandparents' house as possible because I wasn't going to make him choose between spending time with me and his gram when I knew he loved us both. When I saw him slip his grandmother a wad of bills, knowing he was just trying to make sure that she had enough money for her monthly medication, it took everything inside of me not to start sobbing like a baby.

Zander was really a good man and I fell a little deeper every day that week.

I tried to look forward to the fact that Friday was my seventeenth birthday, instead of how sad it was going to be to tell Zander goodbye on Saturday morning. OtherWorld was going to do one last gig at Floyd's Bar and then Zander was taking me to dinner. It would be just the two of us, and I was going to take advantage of every second we had that night.

Our last night together.

At least for a while, anyway. He'd already promised to come back for Christmas and stay until New Years. I believed him. He'd only ever broken one promise, and that had been for my own good—something I had started to quickly understand that week. Without the guilt of ruining Noah's life, I knew that Z telling him what was going on at home had been the right decision to make. For all of us.

"How do I look?" I asked Chelsea with a frown at my reflection in the bathroom mirror.

She'd done my makeup at my request and had even helped me pick out my outfit. I'd left my long, platinum-blond hair down, and curled the ends just enough to give them a little wave. My eyes seemed to pop at me in the mirror's reflection, my lips looking bee-stung and glossy. The dress she'd helped me pick out was one of her own and ended several inches higher on my thigh than it had hers the few times I'd seen her wear the little red dress.

It felt like it had taken forever for me to get ready and Chelsea had sent Noah off to the bar with Zander and Devlin, not wanting them to get impatient with how long it was taking me. I'd been reluctant to have her ask them to go on ahead, wanting to spend every spare second with Zander that night, but Noah had kept on coming to the bedroom door asking if I was ready or not.

The girl who now had my brother's ring on her finger stood in the bathroom doorway with a small grin teasing at her lips. "That depends. How hot were you trying to look, girl?"

I couldn't help the blush that flooded my cheeks, making my eyes stand out that much more in my well made-up face. "Supernova," I mumbled. I wanted to stand out tonight. I wanted Zander's eyes on me and nowhere else. I wanted...

"Well, you pulled that off, sweetie." My future sister-in-law gave me a sly wink and turned back into the bedroom. "Now let's get your hot little ass to that bar and make Zander Brockman sweat until he can get you alone later."

My blush only intensified at the thought of being alone with Z later, but I had a silly grin on my face as I followed Chelsea out of the apartment and down to Noah's truck. She climbed up into the jacked-up monster without any problems whereas I had to struggle to hold on to my dignity as I attempted to get up into it in the heels I was wearing. Finally, with a muttered curse, I tore off the high heels—also borrowed from Chelsea—and tossed them onto the floorboard of the truck before climbing in.

Chelsea was still laughing her head off at me when she pulled my brother's truck into the over-crowded parking lot of Floyd's Bar. I put the damn heels on again as I got out of the truck and reached back in for my purse. We were running late, and it was all my fault. By the time we entered the bar through the back door, OtherWorld was already out on the small stage Floyd set up for them every Friday night.

Noah was waiting for us in the back room. He kissed Chelsea hello before turning his gaze to me. When he did, his eyes almost popped out of his head, his jaw dropped and it took him several attempts before he could speak. "Um..." He cleared his throat. "You...? Wow, Annabelle."

My brother's reaction made my silly grin return and I took his offered free hand as he led us out to the bar. As the parking lot had suggested, the place was packed to capacity and then some. Between the two hundred or so people talking and singing along with the band, plus the loudness of the music, I could barely hear myself think.

There was barely any room to move between people, but Noah guided us through the thick crowd to the front where OtherWorld was playing. I took a quick glance around, noticing how many chicks were in the front row. All of them were chicks except for Noah, who stood like a bodyguard between Chelsea and me. I saw girls crying as they shouted out at the band, some of them already without their bras on because they had tossed them onto the stage. I couldn't help but roll my eyes at that. Really? Did these chicks think that by giving some guy their bra they would pick them out of the throng of other females around them?

I was the stupid one for even thinking that, of course. That was exactly how Wroth and Devlin had actually picked some of the chicks they had hooked up with over the past year. They picked whichever bras they liked the most and left with their owners. I was pretty sure Z had done that same thing a few times before I'd started slipping into his window most nights.

I knew the instant that Zander saw me. His playing turned to pure shit and I glanced up at him to see why. His eyes were glued to me and he was barely playing his bass. The way his gaze was raking over me, I knew he liked what he was seeing and that made me start to tremble. Ah, Christ. I wanted him so badly.

Liam drifted across the stage, still playing his own bass, and bumped his shoulder against Zander's. Zander didn't even move, just continued to stand there staring hungrily at me. My panties grew damp, my nipples aching in the pushup bra I'd bought earlier that week at the mall in Nashville. Would it hurt anyone if we left right then? I mean really?

As the song came to an end, Zander finally seemed to come out of his daze. He shook his head a few times and muttered something to Wroth, who was giving him a questioning look. I couldn't hear anything he said over the noise of the crowd around me, but whatever he said had Wroth grinning. Moving toward the edge of the stage, Zander cocked a finger, waving me over, and I went without the slightest hesitation.

Bending, he brushed his lips over mine in a quick, soft kiss that made my heart shudder in my chest. I wanted to linger but, behind him, the guys were already starting up the first chords of the next song. I started to back away, but Z stopped me. His hand caught mine and he tugged me closer as he pressed his lips to my ear. "Was that the reaction you wanted?"

Blushing even hotter, I nodded. "Definitely."

I felt more than heard his chuckle. "As soon as this show is over, you're mine, Anna." He pressed a kiss to the sensitive spot just under my ear, causing me to shiver deliciously. With a grin he straightened and easily started playing along with the others.

For the rest of the show his eyes never strayed from me, but his playing didn't turn to shit again. I couldn't keep my gaze off of him any more than he could me. Tomorrow didn't matter right then. All I could see was that night.

Our night.

Annabelle

I wanted to leave as soon as Zander stepped off stage, but my brother grabbed my hand and held on to it tightly before I could follow after them. I pouted up at Noah, but he just grinned and pulled Chelsea and me through the sea of fans to the back room.

Several other girls had already followed the band back, but Floyd's one and only bouncer was keeping them at bay. Noah gave him a small nod as he pulled us past the whining chicks. The door to the back room was closed, which confused me. That door was rarely closed.

Using his foot to push the door open, Noah stepped in, only then releasing my hand as he and Chelsea turned to face me. Behind them, OtherWorld was already waiting, grins on everyone's faces. "Happy birthday to you, happy birthday to you."

I didn't know why, but tears instantly burned my eyes. I tried to blink them back, but it was no use. One tear spilled down my cheek followed by ten more. My heart was full in that moment. With all of my old friends, plus one new one, singing "Happy Birthday" to me, I realized that I was going to miss more than just Zander. I'd miss Liam calling me Anna Banana and Devlin's smiling aquamarine eyes as we teased each other. I'd miss Wroth's scary scowl that lightened every time he saw little Marissa. Hell, I'd even miss Axton, whom I'd only known a week but had somehow become someone I counted as a friend.

Stepping around everyone else, Zander produced a cake with a candle shaped into the number 17 while he and the others continued to sing. Lighting the candle, he stopped in front of me just as the last 'happy birthday to you' was being sung. "Make a wish, Anna."

Ignoring my tears, I closed my eyes and sucked in a deep breath. *I wish for more of this. More of my family and friends and times like this.* Opening my eyes, I blew out the candle to the cheers of everyone around me. Zander shoved the cake into the hands of the closest person behind him, which happened to be Chelsea. "Okay, we did the cake and song. Now I'm taking the birthday girl out for dinner and her present."

Before anyone could even open their mouths he grasped my hand and pulled me out of the room and then through the back door. Biting the inside of my cheek to hold back the excitement that was starting to bubble over inside of me, I remained silent as he practically dragged me toward his truck. With his big, quick steps I couldn't keep up in my heels.

Noticing that I was having trouble keeping up, Zander stopped and swung me up into his arms. A giggle spilled out of me and I wrapped my arms around his neck as he jogged the rest of the way to his truck and opened the driver's side door. Placing me on the seat, I scooted over toward the passenger side but didn't get more than a few inches before Zander was beside me.

"No," he growled when I started to move over again. "Stay close." He caught my hand and brought it to his lips. From the glow of the parking lot lights, I could see that his eyes were green with only a few flecks of gold shooting fire down at me. This wasn't my OCD messed-up Z staring down at me; it was my hungry Z, and from the looks of it he was starving. "I don't think I can breathe if you don't."

My heart shuddered in my chest. "Z—"

He released my hand and turned on the truck. Backing out of his usual space, he quickly got us out on the road before draping his arm over my shoulders and pulling me closer. Closing my eyes, I laid my head on his chest and hugged my right arm around his waist. Tears burned my eyes again, but this time I was able to hold them back.

Don't think about tomorrow. There's only tonight.

Zander drove on, but I didn't bother to open my eyes. I only wanted to savor this. Christmas felt so far away so I'd have to live off of memories like this until then. He pulled up in front of the pizza place and ran inside to get the food he must have ordered earlier. He was back within a few minutes with a small pizza box and a huge bag full of two orders of the baked spaghetti I liked so much as well as salads and two slices of my favorite chocolate mousse cake.

Setting our food in the empty space by the passenger window, Zander climbed back in and drove us to the garage. I already knew that Noah and Chelsea weren't coming back that night. Chelsea had promised me complete privacy with Z, her birthday gift to me. Honestly, it was the best gift she could have given me simply because it was all I wanted.

Somehow he carried the food and held my hand all the way up the stairs to the apartment. I couldn't seem to find the words to protest even though I knew I should have. His hands were full, but I ached for every touch I could get from him that night. Releasing me long enough to let me unlock the door, he quickly grasped my hand again and led me inside.

Placing the food on the counter in the kitchen, Zander made a small growling sound deep in his throat as he pulled me against his chest. His arms were tight around my waist as he buried his face in my hair and breathed in deeply, almost as if he were trying to memorize my scent.

Don't think about tomorrow.

There is only tonight.

"I love you," he murmured in a quiet voice. "Don't you ever fucking forget that, Annabelle."

There is only tonight.

Only. Tonight.

Forcing back the tears, I put a bright smile on my face and lifted my head, meeting his green eyes. "I won't, Z. I love you too. Remember that, okay? When everything else is going crazy around you, remember that I love you. Promise?"

"I promise," he breathed as he lowered his head and brushed his lips over mine.

It was almost like he was scared to kiss me too hard, too deep. Each brush of his lips over mine was butterfly-soft. When his tongue brushed over mine, it was such a tender caress that I had to tighten the hold I had on my tears. My hands wrapped around his neck, but I didn't deepen the kiss. If he was scared to deepen our kiss, then I wasn't going to push him.

Lifting his head, he brushed his nose against mine and smiled down at me. "Hungry? I ordered your favorites."

Don't think about tomorrow.

Swallowing hard, I nodded. "Yeah, I'm starving."

"Good. Go sit in the living room. We can have a picnic on the floor." I started to protest, wanting to help him, but he pushed me toward the living room. "Go on. I'll make our plates and get drinks. It's your birthday, baby. Let me take care of you."

Giving in, I went into the living room. Instead of turning on the TV, I picked out a few CDs and put them in Noah's stereo. Bon Jovi's "Always" flowed from the speakers and I sat down on the floor in front of the coffee table as Z brought in the box of pizza before going back for drinks and then our plates of food. Sitting beside me, he brushed another soft kiss over my lips before picking up his fork.

Don't think about tomorrow.

I wasn't hungry all of a sudden, but I picked up my fork and took a small bite of my baked spaghetti. Zander watched me for several minutes and I put on that damned bright smile for him as I took another bite. He shifted and pulled something out of his jeans pocket. Placing whatever he'd taken from his pocket on the table, he dropped his hand but kept his eyes on my face.

I blinked down at what he'd put on the table. It was a simple thin-band gold ring. Hands trembling, I picked the ring up, staring at it like it was the most precious thing in the world. "Wh-what's this?" I choked out through my tight throat.

"It's a promise."

My eyes snapped up to his, noticing that nearly all the gold was gone from his eyes now. "A-a promise?"

He nodded and took the ring from my shaking hands. Taking hold of my right hand, he placed the ring on my ring finger. "Yes, Anna. A promise. A promise that one day I'll put this ring on the finger it belongs on. A promise that tomorrow isn't goodbye. It's a 'see you soon.' But mostly it's a promise that I won't ever stop loving you. Ever." He rubbed his thumb over the gold ring that fit so perfectly on my finger. "This ring was Gram's. She stopped wearing it years ago because it kept slipping off her hand, but when I told her I didn't know what to give you for your birthday, she gave me this. Do you like it?"

Without me even realizing it, I'd lost the rein I'd been trying to hold on my tears. I could barely see the ring on my hand through the flood of them. "I l-love it, Z. Thank you."

Groaning, Zander lifted his hand to wipe away my tears. "I didn't mean to make you cry, baby. That's the last thing I want to do tonight."

"These are happy tears." *Mostly.*

"Doesn't matter. I hate seeing any tears in your eyes." He lowered his head and kissed away more of my tears. "It tears me apart, Anna. You have no idea how special you are to me and seeing these tears destroys me."

The pain I heard in his voice was doing the same thing to me.

There is only tonight.

As that thought echoed in my head yet again, I turned my head and met his lips. My kiss wasn't soft like his had been all night, it wasn't tender. My kiss was hungry—starving. My fingers thrust through his hair, holding him right where I wanted him the most. He didn't hesitate, didn't try to stop me, but kissed me back just as hungrily and pulled me onto his lap.

I forgot about the food—who needed to eat? Tomorrow didn't matter. Neither did tonight. All I wanted was now. Right now, with his taste exploding on my tongue and his hands on my body. Our kiss deepened, his tongue skimming over mine, tasting me as much as I was him.

His fingers felt hot against the backs of my thighs as he skimmed his fingers under my dress. He cupped my ass in both of his hands, squeezing hard. I loved how he was touching me. Loved this uncontrollable passion I'd unleashed in him with my kiss.

Zander's hands dipped into my panties, his fingers caressing over the seam of my ass. The small tease made my already soaked panties flood with liquid heat. Finding me drenched, Zander jerked as if I'd actually burned him. I could feel the growl building in his chest long before he released it. Pulling back, he lowered his eyes, watching like a tiger ready to pounce as he lifted the dress, slowly exposing inch after inch of my body.

When he saw the color of my panties, the ones that matched my black and red pushup bra, I saw the last of his control shatter in his eyes. Z practically ripped the dress over my head before getting jerkily to his feet. He wasted no time in lifting me into his arms and carrying me into the bedroom.

The sheets felt cool against my overheated skin as he laid me down on the mattress. He paused long enough to pull his shirt over his head and kicked off his boots. Unsnapping his jeans, he left them on as he followed me down onto the bed. My legs were already spread for him, letting him fall right between them as he found my lips and kissed me so roughly I wondered if my lips would be bruised the next morning.

I didn't care if they were. This kiss was wild and I loved it, but it was over far too soon. His damp lips left mine to graze down my neck and over my collarbone. His fingers were pushing my bra straps down my shoulders even as his lips were kissing each swollen globe. With a vicious curse he pushed one hand under my back and unsnapped my bra with ease. My breasts spilled free and he tossed my bra across the room without looking where it landed.

Those green eyes were eating me up. Taking in my flushed body, my diamond-hard nipples that were throbbing for his mouth, my damp thighs and drenched panties. I could feel the pounding of my raging heart between my legs, the ache growing so intense that I was sure all he had to do was breathe on me there and I would fall off the edge and into the abyss of mind-shattering release.

His mouth captured my left nipple, sucking hard. I didn't try to contain my whimpers as he made a meal of my breasts. He went from one to the other and back again until I wasn't even sure what my own name was anymore. I couldn't think through the torturous pleasure, had no clue what was going on around us except for how good it felt.

Talented fingers caressed over my stomach and found the elastic of my panties. He tugged on them and I lifted my hips so he could pull them off. His mouth followed his fingers, making me cry out in protest as his lips left my nipples. Z grinned wickedly against my stomach before dipping his tongue into my belly button. Lower he kissed, until his breath was almost washing over my dripping pussy lips.

Only then did he lift his eyes to mine. "Tell me you love me," he commanded.

"I love you," I breathed without hesitation.

He kissed my mound, making a high-pitched little moan leave me, but his eyes never wavered from mine. "Tell me you want me."

"Yes. Oh, God, I want you." His lips pressed against my clit, but he didn't open his mouth to suck or lick. "I want you so bad, Z. I love you so much. Please. Please, make love to me."

His body tensed. "Is that what you want?"

"So much," I moaned. "I need you inside of me, Z. Please. Give us both this memory. Something we can live off of for the next few months."

Z didn't speak; his only answer was to bury his face in my aching pussy. My fingers tangled in the sheets beneath me, fearing I would rip his hair out if I tried to touch his head. My hips lifted off the bed of their own volition, pressing hard against his amazing mouth. I was close, so frigging close. My vision started to narrow, my thighs trembling, my heart nearing the point of explosion it was pounding so hard.

I was gasping, moaning, pleading for him to come inside of me. I wanted it all tonight. I needed him inside of me. I was hanging by a thread that could drop me at any second. It felt so good. I didn't want it to end, yet I wanted to come so badly.

With a groan that seemed to be torn from his chest, Zander pushed his jeans down his hips, taking his boxers with them. He kicked them off and grabbed something from one of the pockets as he turned back to me. On his knees he tore the wrapper in his hands open and rolled the condom over the gleaming head of his amazing cock. I wanted to touch him, but I knew from the look on his face right then that it wasn't a good idea. He was just as close as I was, if not more so, and I wanted this to end with him inside of me.

With the condom in place he lowered his head, kissing me softly again. I moaned as he rubbed the tip of his cock over my wet folds. It wasn't the first time he'd done that to me, and he knew how much I loved it when he teased me like that. But tonight I wanted more. I spread my thighs wider for him, offering him everything I had to give.

His breath seemed to be trapped in his lungs as he positioned himself at my opening. He caught my gaze and watched me closely as he started to push into me. I wanted to watch, wanted to see his cock being swallowed by my pussy, but he didn't move back so I could. He was pressing me into the mattress, his body feeling so deliciously heavy on top of mine. The walls of my pussy felt stretched as he entered me, filling me up in a way that made me see stars from the sheer pleasure of it.

Zander rocked his hips back and forth, going a little deeper with each careful thrust into me. I arched toward him, wanting him deeper, wanting more of all this pleasure his body was offering. I could feel the effort he was exerting to hold back, could see in the tension on his face that it was costing him to not just dive deep and take what he wanted.

I lifted my hand, stroking my fingers over his cheek. He stilled above me, his eyes closing as he leaned his face into my caressing hand. "I'm sorry, baby." With a groan he thrust deep, breaking through the last barrier that separated us.

He'd moved so fast and hard that the sharp stab of pain was over before it had even begun to affect me. My need never faded. With the feel of him so deep, it only revved it up, and I pulled his head down to mine, kissing him hungrily as he started to move inside of me once more.

With his chest rubbing against my own, I couldn't help but feel how hard his heart was beating. The tempo only matched my own. He felt amazing deep inside of me. My inner walls contracted around him with each thrust, my breathing coming in quicker pants and gasps as I begged him for more.

His pace increased, driving me closer and closer to the edge of release. It felt so good that I tried to twist away from it, not wanting it to be over yet.

There is only tonight.

Tears burned my eyes and throat as I remembered that there really was only tonight. I tried to hold them back, but I was too vulnerable right then. My emotions were an open book to him like this and I couldn't hold on to the tears. As I fell over the edge into the abyss of an earth-shattering orgasm, I couldn't contain the sob that felt like it left my insides torn to shreds.

Above me I watched through my tears as Zander's eyes grew damp. His body tensed with his own release and he threw his head back, moaning my name even as the first tear spilled from his green eyes. He fell forward, seemingly unable to support his own weight. His head buried in my neck, my hair hiding his face.

I wrapped my arms around his shaking shoulders as we both let go of our pain, our feelings of loss that would come with the morning. "I-I love you," I whispered brokenly.

"Fuck, Anna, I love you too."

Zander

I woke up at dawn. Annabelle's warm, soft body was tangled around mine and I would have given anything to get to stay like that for just a few more hours. I couldn't, though. The tour bus that Rich Branson had sent for us had arrived yesterday and we were supposed to leave at seven.

The bus was parked at Wroth's farm and I'd taken my things out there the day before. I'd talked to Devlin and he was supposed to pick me up from the garage. Glancing at the clock on the nightstand, I realized he would be there soon. I clenched my jaw, trying to hold on to my emotions as I glared up at the ceiling.

I knew this would be hard, but it was turning out to be unbearable. Maybe it was because I'd made her mine so thoroughly, or maybe it was just because I'd never had to leave her before. Fuck, I didn't know, but it felt like my heart was cracking with each ticking of the clock. My throat was tight, choking me with the lump of emotion that was trying its damnedest to get free.

Lifting onto my elbow I gazed down at Annabelle as the sun rose, giving her skin a soft glow as it lightened the room through the open curtains. Last night had been perfect. We'd made love three times before falling asleep in a tangle of arms, legs, and sheets. She was so beautiful, so fucking special. And all mine.

I kept trying to convince myself that Christmas wasn't all that far away, but it felt like fifty years instead of a matter of weeks. I didn't want to leave her, not now. Not ever.

But I was going to. This chance might not ever come around again, and it would mean I could give Annabelle everything she deserved. I would be able to afford a nice house anywhere she wanted to live. I could shower her in all kinds of beautiful things that would make her eyes sparkle. Our kids wouldn't ever have to want for anything.

It was also my dream. I would get to play my music for the world and, soon, I could share that with Annabelle.

That didn't make it any easier. As I forced myself to get out of that bed, I felt like I was ripping my heart out of my chest and leaving it on the pillow beside her. She was so exhausted from our amazing night together that she didn't even shift as I pulled on my clothes. Zipping up my jeans, I heard Devlin's truck pulling up downstairs.

Fighting back tears, I leaned over and brushed my lips over her forehead. "I love you, Anna. Don't you ever fucking forget that, baby." She let out a small sigh and snuggled deeper under the covers, a smile lifting the corners of her kiss-swollen lips.

Two tears forced their way out of my eyes and with a pain-filled moan I turned away from the sight of the girl who owned every part of my soul, leaving her behind when all I wanted to do was hold her close. Picking up my shoes, I didn't bother to put them on as I left the apartment.

Devlin was waiting behind the wheel of his truck, looking like he hadn't slept at all the night before, but he was grinning like a damn Cheshire cat so I knew he'd had a good time. I walked barefooted to my truck and pulled out the registration and title to the vehicle from the glove compartment before putting the keys on top of the two pieces of paper in the driver's seat. I was leaving it for Annabelle. She could drive it or sell it, I didn't care which, but I couldn't leave without her having that last part of me.

Not wanting Devlin to see how close to the surface my emotions were, I opened the passenger door of his truck and threw in my boots. Climbing in, I didn't bother to speak to him as he backed out of the parking lot. Unable to stop myself, I took one last look up at the apartment and saw her standing in the doorway. Even from where I was, I could tell she was crying, but there still was a smile on her beautiful face.

Annabelle lifted her hand, waving goodbye. I had to swallow several times before I could breathe again. *Fuck. Ah, motherfucking hell.* My eyes stung, my heart hurt, and my head was already a tangled mess without her. Lifting my hand, I waved once before forcing my eyes away from the sight of the only chick who would always own my heart.

Annabelle

"That's the last of the heavy stuff," Noah said and groaned as he and Chelsea's dad, Ben, put the old couch we'd had in the apartment back in West Bridge down in our new living room in Nashville.

I didn't bother to glance up from where I was sorting through the boxes that were still stacked in the middle of the living room, trying to get all my stuff together so I could start unpacking in my new room. Noah and Chelsea had found this apartment on their last trip to Nashville the week before and we'd wasted no time in moving into it this weekend. I started my new school on Monday, but I couldn't find any kind of enthusiasm for it.

I couldn't find much enthusiasm for anything, really. It had been three weeks since Zander and the others had left, and I hadn't heard a word from him. Every time I'd tried to call him, there had been no answer and I'd had to leave a message. There had been no return calls, no texts, no anything. I didn't know whether to worry, be mad, or cry.

A million things had been filling my head. That he had lost his phone had been my first thought. Quickly followed by him regretting spending that last night with me, and wanting nothing to do with me now. And the worst… That he'd gone from my bed straight into someone else's and wasn't about to look back. That last one made me hurt to the point that I couldn't breathe. I didn't know what to do because I had no clue why I hadn't heard from him. If he'd lost his phone, then he probably didn't even realize that I had called. But if he'd been ignoring my calls, I didn't want to keep knocking on a door that he wanted to keep closed.

A firm hand touched my shoulder and I jerked, not expecting the touch. Noah's hold on my shoulder tightened. "Easy, honey. It's just me." He smiled down at me, but I could see the concern deep in his blue eyes. "Ben asked three times if you wanted something to eat and you didn't hear him."

I forced a smile to my lips as I looked over at Chelsea's dad. "Thanks, Ben, but I'm not hungry."

Ben smiled back. "Well, I'm going to order a few pizzas, sweetheart. So you can eat later if you feel like it."

I nodded, but knew I wouldn't be eating. Food held no appeal for me, it hadn't practically from the moment I'd waved goodbye to Zander from the front door of the apartment in West Bridge. I only ate when Noah made me, and only then forcing it down through a throat that had been tight with tears for the past three weeks.

It took over three hours before I had my room unpacked. When I was done I took a shower to wash away the dust of the move and grabbed the keys I'd left on my dresser. I didn't know why Zander had left me his truck and then acted like I didn't exist, but I was glad to have the trusty old piece of metal.

Noah, Chelsea and Ben were in the kitchen eating the pizza Ben had ordered earlier, so I called a quick bye to them before rushing out the door. Our apartment was on the second floor so I ran down the stairs before anyone could ask where I was going. Starting the truck, I put it in gear and headed out of the city.

I'd been arguing with myself for the past two weeks about whether or not I should go see Gram, but I suddenly felt like I couldn't breathe if I didn't. I didn't know if it was because I wanted to know if she'd heard from her grandson or if I just needed one of her hugs, but I had to see her. All the way to West Bridge I had to fight my tears, sometimes losing the battle.

With my hands on the wheel, I couldn't help but glance at the little gold ring Zander had put on my finger. A promise, he'd said. That ring was a promise that it looked like he'd already broken. Yet as upset as I was, I couldn't find the strength to take it off. It hadn't left my finger since he'd put it on there.

I had to drive past the garage to get to Gram's house. It was closed today, but it would reopen on Monday. Chelsea and Noah were going to drive down every day to keep it running, but we'd been talking about just selling it and banking the money in case of an emergency. After talking to Wade, and finding out he was ready to retire anyway, we hadn't felt as guilty about selling it and possibly leaving him without a job. Still, it was the last connection we had to our father, and I was just as reluctant as Noah to let it go.

The Rocker Who Betrays Me

Pulling into the driveway of Gram's house, I could smell whatever she'd made for dinner still lingering in the air. For the first time in weeks my stomach growled and I jumped out of the truck. As I walked toward the back door, I couldn't help but glance over at my mother's house. The yard needed mowing and Jacob's car wasn't in the driveway, making me wonder if she'd kicked him out.

I had no way of knowing because neither Noah nor I had heard so much as a word from our mother. It seemed like she was completely happy to have us both out of her life. Oddly enough, the thought of my mother practically abandoning me didn't hurt anywhere near as bad as Zander possibly having done the same.

Chin trembling from that thought, I knocked on the back door and waited for Gram to answer it. The door opened less than a minute later and Gram stood on the other side, wiping her hands on her apron and smiling welcomingly at me.

"Annabelle," she greeted, with so much warmth in her voice that some of the ice around my heart thawed slightly. "Honey, it's so good to see your pretty face. Come in, come in." Taking my hands she pulled me into her kitchen, her eyes skimming over me with a maternal eye. "You've lost weight, honey."

I bit my lip, nodding. "Yes, ma'am. Just a little."

She released my hand and went to the fridge, pulling out containers of leftovers. "Well, you sit down. I'm going to feed you and I best not hear any complaining. She took the containers to the stove and started heating up whatever she'd cooked for dinner. From the living room I could hear the television and Gramps coughing every now and then. "I still haven't learned how to cook for just me and Zander's grandfather. I keep thinking Zander will walk through the door and I need to fix enough for his bottomless stomach."

Her voice was so full of sadness that my chin trembled even more. "Ha-have you heard from him?" I asked as I sat at the table.

Without turning to face me, Gram nodded. "He calls every few nights on that cellphone of his. Makes sure I have enough blood pressure medicine and everything else. He's a good boy, my Zander. Always taking care of his grandma."

I had to swallow my sob. So he hadn't lost his cellphone. Blinking back tears, I sat there, trying to smile for Gram when she glanced at me over her shoulder every few minutes. When the food was heated up she put it all on a plate and set it in front of me with a glass of juice. "Now, you eat all of that and I'll get you a slice of pie I managed to save earlier."

My fingers shook as I lifted my fork, but I clenched them around the utensil so Gram wouldn't see. Somehow I ate half the food she'd put in front of me, but I didn't taste any of it. My stomach roiled, protesting the food, but I didn't let Gram know that I was so close to being sick. While I'd eaten she'd gone on and on about how Zander was doing.

From what she told me, the band had an apartment in West Hollywood that they were sharing. They'd already made a recording of some of their songs and three record labels wanted to sign them. Rich Branson was holding off for a little longer before accepting any of them because he wanted to squeeze as much money out of the label as possible. Branson had advanced them some money and Zander had already mailed her a check so that she could get her next month's worth of medication.

I'd been happy to shovel food into my mouth as Gram had talked. It meant I didn't have to keep up with the conversation. I could see how proud of her grandson she was, could hear it in her voice as she spoke so lovingly of him. I knew what a good guy Zander was, she didn't have to tell me that. What I couldn't understand was why he hadn't wanted to talk to me.

I didn't eat everything on the plate, but Gram still offered me a slice of pie. Unable to eat another bite without throwing up what I'd already eaten, I declined her offer and quickly made my goodbyes. The little old lady hugged me close and kissed my cheek as I stepped back. "You come back and see me anytime, Annabelle. You promise me."

I smiled through my tears. "Yes, Gram. I promise." I kissed her wrinkled cheek. "I'll see you soon."

All the way back to Nashville, I let myself cry, not caring when the sobs felt like they were tearing my heart loose from my chest cavity. I wanted to get it out of my system before I saw my brother again. I didn't understand what had happened, why he didn't want me anymore, and maybe that was why it hurt so much. The not knowing why was killing me.

Pulling into the apartment complex's parking lot, I slid into the space that was reserved for our apartment and grabbed the cellphone I'd left on the seat while I'd been at Gram's. Wiping away the last of the tears I'd let myself cry on the drive up, I punched in the number I knew by heart now. Lifting the phone to my ear, I waited for him to answer.

"You have reached—"

Hearing the automatic voicemail, I turned the phone off and threw it on the floor. "Why, Z? Why?" I whispered to the empty truck cab. "Why did you break your promise already?"

Zander

"Yo, Z. Your phone is ringing again, man."

I lifted my gaze from where I'd been watching my fingers strum the strings on my bass to frown at Axton. He had my phone in his hand and he tossed it to me. Catching it with ease, I glanced down at the little screen, my stomach clenching as I prayed it wasn't Annabelle again. I didn't think I had the strength to ignore yet another call from her.

Seeing that it was my grandmother, I opened the little flip phone and put it to my ear. "Hey, Gram."

"Merry Christmas, Zander, honey," Gram greeted me happily.

I'd hated disappointing her when I'd told her the month before that I wouldn't be able to make it home for Christmas. She'd understood, though. I had work to do in California, after all. We were still recording our first album and the process was taking a lot longer than anyone had first thought.

"Merry Christmas, Gram. How are you and Gramps feeling?" The last time I'd talked to her she'd had a dizzy spell and Gramps was fighting a bad case of flu.

"We're good, honey. How are you and the boys? Are you eating enough?" Her concern for not only me but my band members as well made my chest tighten.

"Everyone is doing good, Gram." My fingers started strumming over the strings on the bass again, unconsciously playing a Christmas song.

Everyone except me. I didn't say that aloud, though. No use in making Gram worry. I hadn't been okay since the day I'd left Tennessee, and from the way my head had yet to calm down, I knew I wasn't likely to be ever okay again.

"That's good, honey…" She paused and I knew there was a reason she'd called other than wanting to tell me Merry Christmas. It didn't surprise me because Gram rarely called me using the cellphone I'd given her. She didn't understand the damn thing, couldn't see the numbers very well because she refused to wear her glasses, more often than not. "Annabelle came to see me this morning."

Everything inside of me jerked as if I'd been electrocuted from the mention of her name. My fingers fumbled over the strings of the bass until I forced myself to stop and I leaned back in the chair I'd been parked in all morning, closing my eyes as pain exploded inside of me.

I thought I was handling being without her. As long as no one mentioned her name, I was able to keep my head on straight—straight enough to make it through the day at least. Her calls had been few and far between lately, something I was both thankful for and hated. She'd called at least three times a day in the beginning, but in the last few weeks she hadn't called at all. Until the night before. I'd been lying in bed when the phone had rung and it had taken everything inside of me not to pick it up. To just hear her voice one more time.

I hadn't let myself listen to the voicemails she'd left. Had made Devlin delete them for me because the temptation to hear her beautiful voice would have been too hard to resist if I'd been the one to do it. I didn't want to know if she was crying or cussing, if she still loved me or hated my guts. It was safer not knowing. I could pretend when I didn't know for sure. Gram hadn't said anything about her to me and I hadn't asked her if she'd heard anything from Annabelle or Noah.

It was better not to know what was going on with them. *With her.* She was better off…

"Oh yeah?" I tried to keep my tone even and I was proud of myself when my voice didn't crack with all the emotion choking my throat.

"Yes. She's been coming to visit every few weeks, but I hadn't seen her in a while. I guess now that the garage has been sold she can't make it down as often. She drove your truck down from Nashville. Brought me a box of those chocolate-cover cherries she knows I like so much and gave Gramps a tin can of that popcorn he loves." Gram went on and on for a few minutes, telling me what a good girl Annabelle was and how she had missed her since she'd moved to Nashville.

"Anyway, she mentioned that she was trying to reach you, honey. She's lost some weight, says she's been fighting the flu like Gramps was. Poor thing didn't look well at all."

Concern for Annabelle made the ache in my chest throb. When I didn't say anything, however, Gram let out a small sigh. "I didn't know that you hadn't spoken to her since you'd left, Zander. I thought you two were talking as much as we were?"

I clenched my jaw. "No."

"Oh… Well, anyway, she wanted me to tell you that it was important that she talked to you. I even gave her your address so she could send you a letter, because she says she knows you probably don't want to talk to her." Gram's voice became the one I remembered so well as a kid. The one she used when she was done playing games and wanted real answers. "Did you do something you shouldn't, Zander Brockman?"

Another shot of pain sliced through my body. I wasn't going to go down that road with my grandmother. It would probably break her heart to hear that I'd been doing a lot of things I shouldn't lately. "She's better off without me, Gram. I knew that before I left, I just tried to convince myself otherwise."

"Ah, honey. You know that isn't true. You and Annabelle have something special. Don't throw that away because you're doubting yourself." Gram's soft scolding made tears prick at my eyes.

"Gram…" I broke off, not knowing what to say to that. She didn't know what I'd been doing since I'd left Tennessee, and I hoped to God she never did. She had no idea just how far I'd fallen.

"Okay, honey, okay. I'm not going to put my nose in your business. I know that you're a grown man now. I just promised Annabelle that I'd pass along her message. Even if you don't get your head out of your ass, she's still going to send you a letter. Do yourself a favor and at least read it."

"Yeah, Gram." There was no way in hell I was going to read it.

"I love you, honey. Merry Christmas."

"I love you, too."

She hung up and I glared down at the silent phone in my hand.

"Gram okay?"

I didn't bother to lift my head as Devlin dropped down onto the long couch in our living room. We all lived in the five-bedroom apartment owned by Rich Branson. Apparently he put all his new talent up for the first year as part of their contract. The place was huge and must have been costing the dude out the ass to rent for us, but I wasn't going to complain. It kept a roof over my head while I sat around doing nothing on the days we weren't in the studio recording.

"Yeah."

"How about Gramps?" Devlin drummed his fingers on the leather couch's arm.

"He's fine." *Go the fuck away. Leave me alone.*

"Uh-huh," Devlin muttered. He was quiet for a while, but I could feel his eyes on me, watching me carefully. He'd been doing a lot of that lately. I didn't blame him. If I were him I'd be watching the crazy dude a little closer too.

I'd had a lot of plans when I stepped on that damn tour bus all those weeks ago. I would go off to California and chase my dreams. When I got to a place where I could take care of Annabelle, I'd bring her out to be with me. We could have a happily-ever-after like she deserved.

The first two days I'd avoided my phone when she had called because it had hurt too much to be without her. It had taken us a week to get from Tennessee to California since Rich had offered us a real rock-star experience. We were playing at Hard Rock and other huge bars across the country and staying in the penthouses of stupidly expensive hotels.

I'd been diving into any bottle of liquor I could get my hands on, and—trust me—there had been plenty for me to drink. I wasn't sure I was sober at all that entire week. My pain was easier to deal with when I was drinking. My heart didn't ache nearly as bad for the girl I'd left behind when I was halfway through a bottle of expensive bourbon. I was numb and I liked that sensation.

Being in a constant numb state had its consequences, though. I'd found that out by the end of that week. I'd done things I couldn't take back. Things that still haunted me. Things that had proven to me just how undeserving I truly was of Annabelle.

I hadn't had anything harder than a beer since and I sure as hell hadn't messed up like that again. My head, however, was still a mess. It was like a fucking hurricane in there, tossing shit at me at a hundred miles an hour and sometimes it became too much.

Which was why Devlin—and everyone else—walked on eggshells around me. It didn't take much to set me off. The simplest things would send me over the edge into the abyss of craziness that left only destruction in my wake. I'd trashed hotel rooms that week and since then destroyed our apartment more than once. I'd started fights I knew I couldn't win—yet somehow had. My fucked-up head was pushing me toward the edge of insanity and I wasn't sure if I wanted to fight it anymore.

Hell, I'd even been so desperate for my end to come that I'd punched Wroth. He hadn't obliged me. Wroth kept an eye on me, though—they all did. No one understood, though. They didn't know what I was going through. Not even Devlin, whom I'd been friends with since we were little kids, could get what I was going through. He'd never gotten me. No one had except for Annabelle.

How long I sat there staring down at the damn phone, I wasn't sure, but the sky was getting darker outside when it started to ring again. I jerked when I saw the number on the screen. Annabelle.

The air in my lungs turned to ice, making it hard to breathe. I closed my eyes, hurting like I'd never hurt before, and hurled the damn cellphone across the room. It exploded into a hundred pieces against the opposite wall.

Chapter Fifteen

Annabelle

Present Day

I just wanted to go home.

It had been over a month since I'd seen my brother and sister-in-law. Even longer since I'd seen Audrey, Ben, and Mieke. I was homesick, but not for my house or my own bed. I was homesick for my family. From the looks of it, I wasn't going to get to go home anytime soon for even a brief visit.

Things were still ugly in California. I had an obligation to Gabriella and I wasn't going to back away from what was required of me. That didn't stop me from missing Noah, Chelsea and the kids so much, though. Our nightly talks on Skype or on FaceTime just weren't enough. I wanted to hug them and be hugged.

At least I was in Southern California now. Gabriella was home, tucked into bed with Liam in the house that Emmie and I had been able to buy for them near Gabriella's cousin Alexis. At Emmie's invitation I was now sleeping in one of her guest bedrooms rather than living out of a suitcase in a hotel. Being around her and her adorable family helped with my homesickness, but at the same time made it that much worse. Especially when I saw her with her kids.

Sighing, I tried to toss my growing depression aside as I got out of bed and stepped into the shower in my en suite. By the time I returned to the bedroom it was to find I'd missed a call from home. *Mieke.* My heart clenched when I glanced at the time and realized she was probably too busy by now to call her back. That girl was crazy busy with taking prep tests for college and I was so freaking proud of her.

Swallowing my disappointment, I dressed and went downstairs for breakfast. Emmie was already sitting at the kitchen table with her baby son when I walked in. Jagger gave me an adorable grin and a small wave as I went to the coffee pot for a giant mug of strong black coffee.

"Morning," Emmie greeted. "Sleep well?"

It was the third night I'd slept at Emmie's house and I'd slept better there than I had in the hotel. "Pretty good. What about you?" I turned to glance at her, taking in the dark circles under her big green eyes that she couldn't hide with makeup.

"I got a few hours."

I nodded, knowing for a fact that a few hours of sleep for Emmie was a hell of a lot more than she had been getting. I doubt she'd gotten a full night's sleep since the attempted kidnapping of her daughter, Mia.

The housekeeper, Gail, came into the kitchen with an empty coffee cup. "Good morning, Miss Cassidy. Would you like something to eat?"

"I'll just make myself some toast, but thanks." I took a sip of my rich coffee. Somehow I'd gotten addicted to Jesse Thornton's special recipe over the last few weeks. It had been the one thing that I'd basically been living off of after the hell Emmie and I'd had to deal with concerning the hospital, feds, press and any number of other shitty problems we'd been faced with. Now I basically lived off that damn recipe and my stomach was definitely not my friend for it.

"Okay. If you need anything let me know." She placed the empty cup in the sink and went down the hall to what I assumed was the laundry room.

Emmie stood and walked over to the sink, rinsing out her cereal bowl before turning to face me. "Well, have you thought about my offer?"

I frowned down into my coffee. The day before, Emmie had made me an offer that I didn't know if I was willing to accept or not. We'd made a great team working through the shit storm with Gabriella and the press and all the extra crap. Things could have been a hell of a lot worse if we hadn't worked together like we had.

She wanted me to go into business with her. Meaning, turn her small client list and my slightly larger list—larger, yet not as well known—and merge. It was an amazing idea, offering me resources for the clients I already had that I hadn't been able to before. Sure I had connections, but I doubted the president had the kind of connections that Emmie Armstrong did. With her as my partner I could open so many doors for my people.

It also meant moving across the country. Not seeing my family as often as I was used to. It was that thought alone that was holding me back. "I'm still thinking about it, Em." I lifted my eyes and met her understanding gaze. "Can I have a few more days? I promise to have an answer for you by the weekend."

She shrugged. "Take as much time as you need. I'm not going to take back the offer so consider it an open invitation." She crossed back to the table and lifted her son into her arms. Jagger wrapped his arms around her neck happily, pressing a wet kiss to his momma's cheek. "And just so you know, us being partners doesn't mean you can't still live in Tennessee. I know what's waiting on you back there and realize how hard it will be to just uproot yourself like that. That's the joys of technology, Annabelle." With a wink she left me alone in the kitchen.

After eating my toast I grabbed the keys to my rental and headed out. It was only a few blocks from Emmie's house in Malibu to the one Gabriella now lived in with her rocker fiancé. If I didn't have to go into the city later I would have walked the short distance, but my lunch meeting was important and I didn't want to be late. I parked behind Liam's SUV and stepped out of the cute little sports car I'd rented.

There was another vehicle already in the driveway that I didn't recognize. Figuring it was one of Gabriella's relatives, I climbed the steps to the front porch and pressed the doorbell. Liam opened the door with a welcoming smile on his face. His clear blue eyes were so much more welcoming than the drug-clouded ones I remembered so well.

"Anna Banana," he greeted with a grin. He lifted his coffee cup to his lips, taking a large swallow before stepping back. "Come in. She's in the living room."

I stepped into the house, dropping my keys on the table by the door. "How is she feeling?"

"Cranky," he said with another grin. "Come on, I'll protect you."

Laughing, I followed him into the living room. My gaze went straight to the couch where Gabriella Moreitti was sitting with a fleece throw over her legs. She was sipping at a mug and pouting. As soon as she saw me, her eyes brightened. "Please tell me I get to go somewhere today?"

"I don't care what Anna Banana says. You're staying right there." Liam bent and kissed his fiancée's lips before sitting down on the couch's arm beside her. "I mean it. You're lucky I let your sexy ass out of bed."

Brown eyes brightened, but she glared up at him. "No, you're lucky I let *your* sexy ass out of bed."

Liam shrugged. "Same difference," he said with a sexy wink for her.

I snorted and pulled a few files out of my bag. "Sorry, babe. I haven't come to spring you from your imprisonment yet. I just needed you to sign these before I send them to the record execs. Since your doctor says you can't sing for a few more weeks, we have to postpone the scheduled time already set up with the producers."

Her pout only got worse. "I'm completely fine. I don't know why everyone wants to baby me. I could sing if I wanted to."

"But you're not going to," Liam told her, not giving in when she turned those big pleading eyes on him. "Your new material will still be there when your doctors give the okay. Until then you aren't going to do anything but sit here and keep me company."

"Baby, I know you love me, but even I need a break from myself every now and then. I know you're probably climbing your mental walls right now wondering how soon you can get out of the house for an hour to yourself." Liam opened his mouth to protest but quickly shut it again when she grinned at him. "It's okay. I still love you."

"Okay." I set the files on the stone coffee table in front of her and sat down on the matching chair across from her. "You can go over those and let me know what changes you want. I'll drop them off on my way into the city."

"Hey, Brie. Do you want more tea while we're in here?" I glanced up as Natalie Cutter stuck her head into the living room. "Oh, hi, Annabelle."

I smiled up at her before letting my gaze drop to the small baby bump under her white T-shirt. "Hi. How are you?" The few times I'd gotten to talk to Emmie's assistant, she'd told me she was having some blood pressure issues.

Natalie smiled. "No headaches today, but I'm sure that will change by the time I get over to Emmie's. Can I get you a cup of coffee or something while we're still in there destroying the kitchen?"

"No, thanks. I just swallowed half a pot over at Em's."

"Brie?"

"No, thanks, Nat. And you don't have to clean up in there, you know. We have a housekeeper who is supposed to be by later." Gabriella lifted her eyes from the documents I'd given her. "Devlin couldn't have made that big of a mess."

"If it had just been Dev, probably not. But you know if you get those two together that they do more playing than anything else." Natalie rolled her eyes and turned back toward the kitchen. "Let me know if you need anything. You should rest as much as you can."

Gabriella grimaced. "Why does everyone treat me like a baby? I'm fine now."

"And that's the way we want to keep you," Liam muttered as he lifted his mug to his lips. Draining the rest of his coffee, he stood. "I'm going to get another cup and see what kind of mess those two jackasses made."

I sat back in my chair after he left the room. "I didn't expect you to have company. If I had, I would have called before I came over."

Gabriella waved her hand dismissively. "You're always welcome here, babe. I love seeing you. Natalie, Devlin and Zander just brought us some breakfast this morning. Natalie offered to do the dishes but Dev wouldn't let her so he designated himself and Z to clean up. Apparently she's in there cleaning up their mess plus our earlier one."

Without my realizing it, my hands started to shake at the mention of Zander. Clenching them into fists, I sat up a little straighter in my chair. "Like I said, I wouldn't have come if I'd known you had company."

I wanted to jump up and run from the room. I didn't want to be in the same *state* with Zander Brockman let alone the same house. For weeks I'd had to deal with seeing him in passing at the hospital. Each time I'd seen him it had felt like I was being stabbed in the chest with a knife.

I'd avoided so much as looking at him, but the few times I'd found myself giving in, it was to find his tortured green eyes staring at me. Green without the gold flecks. I'd felt destroyed seeing his eyes like that. Other than that first time he'd spoken to me, he'd kept his distance and I had been both glad and hurt to my very soul that he hadn't tried to talk to me. Was it really so easy to forget all about me? To ignore me for so many years and pretend like I didn't exist when I was in the same fucking room as him?

With all the hell I'd had to deal with over the last month, having to see him so often had been the worst part of all. I'd barely slept at night torturing myself over Zander Fucking Brockman.

Gabriella smirked at me. "So, it's true?"

I blinked, not understanding her. "What?"

"That you and Z once…?"

Pain sliced through me at her question. I tried not to think about that time in my life, but that wasn't possible. Ever. Something always reminded me of my time with Zander. Gabriella had no way of knowing what I'd gone through after Zander had left me. She didn't know the lows I'd fallen to just to try to get him to talk to me on so many occasions. No one but Noah, Chelsea and Rich Branson knew how desperate I'd been to have Zander open a letter or pick up a fucking phone and have a five-minute conversation with me. Gabriella had no clue of the shame I still felt for trying so many times over the years to reach out to a man who had made it perfectly clear I didn't matter to him. I couldn't yell at her for asking a question that felt like it was tearing my heart out of my chest. Sure it was a small, innocent-enough question, but it hurt nonetheless.

"Yeah," I muttered and had to clear my throat. "Another lifetime ago, but yeah."

The amusement left her face. "I'm sorry, Annabelle. I wasn't trying to be a bitch. It's just that when Liam told me that you and Z..." She shrugged. "Well, I couldn't really believe it. You two are so different. I mean, you're so put together and he's...well, not."

"Have you found any changes you'd like to make yet?" I changed the subject without even caring that I was being obvious about it. "I have a lunch appointment so, if you don't mind, we need to hurry this along."

Her eyes filled with sympathy. "Just that I want a few extra days to do those new songs I've been working on. And talk to Emmie for me about getting OtherWorld into the studio with me so we can record the newest song I wrote."

I pulled a legal pad out of my bag and scribbled that down before I forgot. She used my pen to sign where she needed to before handing everything over. With them in hand, I didn't bother to waste time putting them back in my bag. Standing, I gave her a small smile. "I'll be in touch. Take care of yourself until then."

Gabriella snorted. "No worries there."

From the kitchen, I heard Liam laugh followed by two other male chuckles. How was it that I could still pick out his deep laugh? Why the hell did it still make my heart race to hear it? Tightening the hold I had on my bag, I headed for the door. "I'll call you," I called as I picked up my keys from the table where I'd left them and opened the door.

"Bye, babe."

Closing the door behind me, I paused long enough to suck in a deep, steadying breath. I hadn't even seen Zander and I still felt like my chest was being sliced to shreds. Sucking in another shaky breath, I started toward my rental, on legs that felt unsteady.

Halfway to the car, two things happened at the same time that did conflicting things to my heart. My phone rang and when I looked down at my screen, my heart melted. Also, behind me, the front door opened and someone called my name, making me turn to ice. No, not someone... Him.

Pretending like I didn't hear him, I swiped my thumb over my phone and lifted it to my ear. I'd already missed one call that morning. I wasn't about to do it again. "I miss you so, so, so, so much."

The delighted sound of Mieke's husky laugh caused my eyes to sting with tears. Fuck, I missed that kid so much. "I miss you more."

"That's just not possible, baby." I pressed the button on my key to unlock my car and tossed my bag into the passenger seat before walking around to the driver's side. Behind me, I heard heavy footsteps. My heart started racing, but I kept my full attention on the beautiful girl on the other side of my phone. "How is the test prep going? Think those tests this fall will kick your butt?"

"I got this," Mieke said with confidence in her voice. I had no doubt that she did. She was so damn smart, so talented. She could be or do whatever she wanted, something I'd told her from the first time I held that little angel in my arms. "When are you coming home?"

"Annabelle," Zander called my name again and my fingers reflexively tightened around my phone.

I didn't look up as I leaned against the driver's door and closed my eyes. "I'm not sure, baby. Listen, I need to talk to you about something. Emmie Armstrong has made me an offer. A really good offer."

"That's exciting, but you don't sound like you are." Concern colored the teenager's voice. She always could pick up on people's emotions so easily. It was part of what made her so special.

"Anna."

He was getting closer and it was almost as if I could feel him as he drew nearer. The small hairs on my entire body stood at attention, as if they yearned for his touch. Hearing the way he'd always shortened my name—something I hadn't heard in so, so long—made it feel like there were razorblades in my throat when I swallowed. "I don't know if I'm excited or not. I don't even know if I'm going to take the offer. I want to talk to you and the others about it first."

"Anna." Zander's voice was so close now and I turned my head away, keeping my eyes on a house in the distance so I wouldn't look at him. I couldn't look at that man when I was talking to my favorite person in the entire world. I just couldn't.

"Who's that?" Mieke demanded. "Where are you?"

"I'm leaving Gabriella and Liam's house. I have a lunch meeting with the exec from Tasha Vowel's record label." Tasha was one of my clients who was a complete diva. She'd been pissed the last few weeks because I'd been so busy with Gabriella that I'd had to put her issues on hold. Noah had helped me out as much as he could with the little bitchy singer, but it hadn't been enough to satisfy her. Now I was on cleanup duty.

"But that isn't Liam Bryant. I've heard his voice a lot over the last few weeks." Mieke sounded suspicious and I couldn't help but smile at how protective her husky voice sounded. "Who is it?"

"No one that matters," I assured her, not daring to tell her who it was. Mieke wasn't stupid, though. She'd figure it out, but I'd worry about that later. "I have to go, Mieke. I love you."

"I love you more."

A strangled laugh escaped me. It was full of all the love I had for that girl. "Love you most." I disconnected before she could argue and just stood there, still staring at the house in the distance.

He was behind me, less than two feet away. I could feel his body heat, could smell his cologne. A huge part of me wanted to continue to pretend he wasn't there and just get into my rental. Drive away … maybe even run over his fucking foot in the process. A smaller part of me wanted to know what the hell he wanted.

Glancing down at my phone to make sure the call had really disconnected, I turned to face the man who had destroyed me so utterly and completely. I refused to look anywhere but in his eyes, not wanting to take in the details of how he'd changed over the years. I'd already done that weeks ago and hated myself for how much more attracted I was to this version of Zander Brockman than I'd been to the boy/man version.

"Do you need something?" I kept my voice neutral and mentally gave myself a pat on the back.

Flecks of gold flamed down at me out of green eyes. Was he having an off day, or were his green eyes because of me? Clenching my jaw, I told myself I couldn't care less either way. Of course I was a big fat liar. My heart was crying out for me to touch him, to comfort him. Where were the hazel eyes that had owned me all those years ago? I wanted them. I wanted him to be stable enough to have them.

Idiot.

Zander stood there, his eyes never leaving mine, as he seemed to have an inner struggle. I knew the instant he gave up. He thrust his hands into his jeans pockets and smiled down at me. Not just any smile. It was a smile I remembered well, the one he'd always reserved for me all those years ago. My heart clenched at seeing it now. "Are you busy tonight? I'd like to take you to dinner, maybe catch up."

I couldn't stop my eyes from widening in surprise. What the hell? "Are you fucking serious?"

Another shrug. "I've stayed out of your way while you and Emmie were so busy with Brie's stuff, but now that things have calmed down I was hoping we could… I don't know, talk?"

"You want to talk? Now?" My voice was rising with my anger, but I couldn't help it. Seventeen years of pain, of gut-wrenching hurt, and anger— *so much anger*—was beginning to boil in my veins. "Where were you when I wanted to talk to you seventeen years ago? I called Rich Branson, begging him to make you talk to me. Just for a minute. One little minute. I mean after everything, I thought I at least deserved that. How about twelve years ago when I called again, sobbing with my desperation to just have you answer the damn phone? Where the fuck were you when I wanted to talk, Z? When I fucking *needed* you?"

His entire body tensed, his face going pale. I watched through angry eyes as he swallowed hard and lifted a hand toward me. I slapped it away—no way could I handle his touch right then—and reached for the handle of my car. "I don't want to talk to you, Z. It's too late for talking."

"Anna…"

"No!" I screamed, so close to breaking I hated myself a little right then. "No." I whispered it that time, fighting back tears. "Goodbye, Z."

Annabelle

Somehow I made it through the lunch meeting with the record-label dick. It hadn't been easy, that was for sure. I still had anger simmering in my gut along with all the other emotional pain that Zander always stirred up in me. Add to that a record label exec who thought he was entitled to stroke my thigh under the table while we shared a meal and discussed Tasha Vowel's future with his label, and it had really made for the afternoon from hell.

The exec, I'd been able to handle, although I knew that if I'd had Emmie's name backing my own I wouldn't have had to deal with his shit in the first place. Still, I'd had a professional smile on my face as I'd stabbed my fork into the back of his hand. He'd muttered a curse, grinned at me, and then proceeded to give me what I'd come for. Tasha Vowel had been pleased with the results when I'd called her.

It had been Zander who had rotted my brain, making it impossible to concentrate on anything else. I hadn't even called my family back in Tennessee to talk to them about Emmie's offer like I'd planned. Noah would have known immediately that something was wrong with me, and my overprotective big brother would have been on the first flight out to California. Right then, that wasn't something I wanted even though I ached to see him.

I ate dinner with Emmie and her family that night and then went to bed early. As I climbed into bed, my phone buzzed, alerting me to a FaceTime call from my brother. I didn't have the energy to rehash my day with him, though. Turning my phone off, I pulled the covers up over my head and closed my eyes, hoping for sleep.

A firm, urgent knock on my bedroom door startled me awake half a second before the door opened and Emmie walked into the room with a cordless phone in her hand. "Annabelle, it's your brother. He says it's an emergency."

My heart stopped and everything inside of me went cold. I jumped out of bed, not caring that I was only in a T-shirt and panties, and took the phone from her. "Noah?" So many bad memories were flooding my mind that I knew my brother clearly heard my terror.

"She left, Annabelle. She just up and left." His voice held no less terror than my own. And anger. Lots and lots of anger. I could hear my nephew's voice in the background, but couldn't make out what he was saying. The blood was rushing through my ears, making it nearly impossible to hear anything. "Shut up, kid. I'll deal with you in a minute... Annabelle, she sent Ben a text about thirty minutes ago telling him where she was. He says she's fine. I'm going to beat you, boy. You just wait. I'm going to beat the hell out of you for keeping this from us." We all knew that wasn't going to happen, but I knew Noah was struggling with the same bad memories as I was. My brother sounded wild, his fear making my own rise. "She's out there, Annabelle. She's in L.A."

"I'll just go pick her up at the airport. She's fine, I'm sure of it." *Oh, God, please let her be okay.* I couldn't fucking go through this again. She had to be fine.

"No, Annabelle. You don't understand, honey. Mieke is already there. Ben said she wasn't coming to see you." At those words, some of my fear faded and was replaced by ten tons of dread.

Ah, fuck.

The hand holding the phone dropped to my side and I fell onto the edge of the bed, my legs no longer willing to hold me up. That stubborn girl. My beautiful, stubborn girl.

"Annabelle?"

I slowly lifted my head to look at Emmie. "Um... I need to go out." Good, I was able to get out a full sentence. At least I hadn't fallen off the edge. Yet.

Her brow furrowed. "Of course. Is everything okay?"

My chin trembled. "I don't know," I whispered.

"Can I do anything?"

Clenching my jaw, I forced myself to my feet and straightened my spine, resolved as to what was to come. "I need Zander Brockman's address."

Zander

Ding. Dong.

I ignored the doorbell. I hated the sound of the damn thing. I'd been debating on just disconnecting it altogether. No one ever rang it the way I needed them to and my OCD always went haywire because of it. Tonight, however, it was easy to ignore the damn thing.

Seeing Annabelle today had been equal parts heaven and hell. I hadn't been able to get my fill of simply looking at her. For weeks, ever since I'd seen her again that first day, I'd been struggling to stay away. The only thing that had kept me from demanding her attention was that she was so busy all the time. At times it had looked like she was going to drop from exhaustion from all the chaos that she and Emmie had to deal with each day.

Now that things were calmer, I'd been trying to find a way to see her. I wanted another chance with her, a do-over—something. Anything. I was tired of feeling so numb, hadn't even realized just how numb I actually was until I'd seen her again that day in the hospital waiting room. Seeing her again had untwisted something inside of me, and for the first time in seventeen years I was able to breathe again. This morning I'd been handed the chance to try and start the ball rolling for us again.

Only to blow it.

What was I expecting after seventeen years of avoiding her and anything that might be connected to her? I'd skipped award shows where I'd known her brother was up for a country music award. I'd left parties when I'd realized that Noah and Chelsea Cassidy were on the guest list. Fuck, I'd even stopped going back to Tennessee except for when I absolutely had to. When Liam had his accident and we all stayed on Wroth's farm, it had been the first time I'd even been in the state in over ten years.

Ding. Dong.

Gram and Gramps had both died not long after I'd gotten to California. First Gram that January and Gramps only a few weeks later. It had been like he couldn't live without her and had gone in his sleep one night. I understood how he felt. Fuck, it was the same for me even seventeen years later with Annabelle. Sure I hadn't died, but I wouldn't call what my life had been like without her *living*.

I'd flown out for my grandparents' funerals, but that was all. I hadn't even stayed overnight, leaving the sorting of the house and other things to a lawyer. Some might think that I was being disrespectful, not sticking around to properly mourn the people who had raised me.

I considered it self-defense. The temptation to see Annabelle had been too strong. If I'd stayed even a second longer, I would have been up in Nashville knocking on her door. Knowing she was better off without me, I'd jumped back on the plane Rich had chartered for me and returned to L.A.

Ding. Dong. Ding. Dong. Ding. Dong. Ding-dong-ding-dong.

Shaking my head at the continued ringing of that damn doorbell, I lifted my glass of bourbon to my lips and swallowed half the contents. The hundred-inch flat-screen that took up one wall of my penthouse apartment was on, but the volume was muted. *SportsCenter* was on, but I didn't care who had won whatever baseball game that day, or who was playing whom in a pre-season football game.

It was only on because Devlin and Harris had spent the evening at my place. We'd ordered pizza and wings, having a guys' night while Natalie had gone home to rest after working most of the day at Emmie's house.

I swallowed the rest of my bourbon, grimacing at myself as I thought about my best friend's wife. I wasn't sure why I'd gotten so hung up on Natalie… No, that was a lie. I did know. She was the first person to try to understand me since Annabelle. She'd reminded me so much of the girl I had loved—still loved—that I'd confused affection for something else and nearly ruined not only my friendship with her and Devlin, but also their chances together in the process.

Ding-dong-ding-dong-ding-dong.

Muttering a curse because obviously whoever was at the door wasn't planning on going away, I jerked to my feet and started toward it.

Ding-dong-ding-dong-ding-dong-ding-dong.

My hand was lifted, about to open the door and snarl at whomever was on the other side when my fucked-up head realized that the bell had rung fourteen times. Frowning, I opened the door, figuring it was Devlin or Natalie, hoping for the impossible and that it was Annabelle.

It was neither.

I found a beautiful girl on the other side of the door. No, she wasn't just beautiful. There was something almost surreal about her. I put her age at somewhere in her late teens, but I wasn't sure. She could have been in her twenties for all I knew. She was tall, at least five-foot-eight, with long, curly dark hair and green eyes that had patches of gold in them. Her complexion was a soft tan color, making me wonder if it was natural or if she just spent a lot of time in the sun. Her body was slender, with just a few curves in the right areas, but my gaze kept going back to her eyes. There was something about them—not just their color but also the shape—that reminded me of someone.

There was a mixture of emotions churning in those green and gold eyes: wonder, amusement, anger. That particular mixture confused me, because I didn't understand any of it. Sure, I'd seen young girls like her with wonder in her eyes because she was meeting a member of OtherWorld. I experienced that daily. The amusement confused me, but not nearly as much as the anger.

"Yeah?" I asked, realizing that we'd been standing there staring at each other for several minutes with neither of us speaking.

"She was right. It *is* like looking into a mirror." Her voice was husky and full of the wonder I'd seen in her eyes.

My brows lifted. "Excuse me?"

The amusement only increased. "You don't see it?"

"See what, kid?"

She rolled her eyes, the amusement being replaced with more of the anger. "Never mind. Can I come in? I expect she will be over here soon. After I texted Ben with where I was, he was supposed to wait thirty minutes before he told his dad. I figured that was enough time to at least get in the door." When I didn't move, she pushed past me and walked toward the living room, her green and gold gaze taking in my apartment. "Nice place you have here. I like your view."

I stood at the open door, unsure what I was supposed to do. Who the hell was this girl and what was she doing here? I had no idea, but my gut was churning as I watched her, and I couldn't help but feel like she belonged there. She sure as hell acted like she belonged there. Shaking my head to clear it, I closed the door and followed her into the living room.

My guest sat on the couch, where Harris had been only an hour before, and picked up the huge universal remote that controlled almost everything in the room. She studied it for less than two seconds before figuring the thing out and turning to the weather channel. It had taken me two weeks to figure out how to even turn on the flat-screen with the damn thing.

"Oh, look. It's raining in Nashville." She sighed and sat back before flipping the channel again. "I love the rain."

"Me too," I found myself admitting as I sat in my favorite chair. My eyes were still on this kid's face. Why couldn't I stop staring? It wasn't like I was interested. Just the thought of that turned my stomach. No, it was something else. She had a glow about her, and I was so intrigued.

She grinned and dropped the remote, leaving the volume on mute. The wonder was clearer in her beautiful eyes now, eclipsing the amusement and anger. "Mom told me. She told me everything about you, actually."

"Oh, yeah?" I had no clue who this girl's mother was, and couldn't understand why she would be telling her daughter all about me. Very few people knew the real me anyway, so I doubted that this kid knew very.

She laughed, the sound husky and beautiful. My heart skipped a beat at the sound and I rubbed at my chest as if I were in pain. What the fuck? "You don't believe me, but you will."

"Whatever, kid."

"I'm hungry. Got anything to eat?" She stood gracefully, as if she'd spent years dancing or something. Without waiting for me to answer, she walked into my kitchen and I heard the door to my fridge open. "Gross, don't you ever clean this thing out? This carton of eggs went bad in May. It's freaking September."

I didn't cook often—more like ever. The eggs had been put in there by the housekeeper from the service I used long before I'd gone on the summer tour with OtherWorld and Demon's Wings. I hadn't called the housekeeping service since I'd gotten home this week, so it was hard to tell what she would find in my fridge.

"I just got back from tour. I've been meaning to get the housekeeper in here for a good cleaning," I found myself explaining, and then frowned at myself. I didn't explain myself to anyone, why should I start with this kid?

"Ah, that would explain the loaf of bread that has mutated into some kind of yeast monster. Scary stuff, right there. I'd be careful if I were you. It might attack you in your sleep." She laughed again—making my chest ache yet again—and reappeared in the living room. "But seriously, I'm hungry."

I grabbed my cellphone from the coffee table where I'd tossed it hours ago. "Pizza?" Devlin and Harris had polished off the last of the pizza and wings we'd ordered earlier.

"No, thanks. I don't like pizza. Can I have something else?"

"Who doesn't like pizza?" I muttered to myself as I pulled up a few of the local restaurants I liked that I knew would deliver.

"I have a lactose problem," she said and shrugged as she sat down on the couch once more. "I like Chinese."

I pulled up the number for my favorite Chinese place and handed her the phone. "Order what you want."

She clapped her hands excitedly before taking the phone from me and putting it to her ear. "You want something too?" I shook my head and she shrugged as she waited for someone to answer on the other end.

While she ordered, my doorbell rang again. I gritted my teeth, not wanting my OCD to go into overdrive when I had a mystery guest sitting in my living room. Then I realized that whoever was at the door was ringing it enough times.

"That's Mom," my guest lowered the phone from her mouth and muttered before returning to ordering enough food to feed a small nation. How the hell was she going to eat all that?

Shaking my head at her, I stood and slowly made my way to the door. I had no clue who was going to be on the other side, but at least they hadn't put my OCD into overdrive. Glancing back at the kid who was still ordering food—six egg rolls, and I had no idea where the fuck was she going to put them—I opened the door.

I knew it was her as soon as the door started to open. I felt it in my bones and not just because she pushed hard on the door, knocking the damn thing into my shin. My entire body was like an Annabelle detector and as soon as we were sharing the same air, I could feel her. She blew into my apartment like a hurricane, pushing past me as if I weren't even there, and stormed into the living room.

Rubbing at the sore spot on my leg, I followed after her. The kid had finished ordering her food and was staring patiently up at Annabelle. Even from where I was standing, I could see the amusement dancing in her eyes. "Mieke, what the fuck are you doing? Do you realize how scared I was when Noah called me? Do you?"

"Hi, Mom. It's so good to see you too." She grinned and Annabelle stumbled over whatever she had been about to say. I stood in the doorway, confused as hell. Annabelle grabbed hold of the girl who had just called her 'Mom' and pulled her to her feet and then into a hug that should have squeezed the breath out of the kid.

"You are in so much trouble, do you hear me?" Annabelle was still raging even as she hugged the kid, but I thought I heard a small sob in her voice. "I'm grounding you until the end of time. I was so scared when Noah called. You can't do shit like this to me." Finally she pulled back, staring down at the girl who was her freaking daughter. "I love you so much."

"I love you too, Mom." The girl glanced my way and smiled. "I told you she would be here soon."

Annabelle stiffened as if just then realizing I was in the room. What was she expecting? I fucking lived there, after all. She crossed her arms over her chest and glared at me. What the fuck? I hadn't done a damn thing to her to earn that icy glare. "What did she tell you?" she snarled.

"Nothing," the girl assured her mother. "Honest, Mom. I was waiting on you."

The two females shared a long look I didn't understand. I didn't understand any of this. Motherfucking hell, I was still trying to wrap my head around the fact that Annabelle had a daughter. She had a kid. *A. Kid.* Someone other than me had touched her. I'd always known she would find someone else. It was something I'd told myself I wanted for her—and yeah, I'd had nightmares about the faceless sonofabitch who would one day take my place in her heart. Still, I'd known she deserved so much better than my fucked-up ass. But having the proof of what I'd wanted for her thrown down my throat like this was like having my chest sliced open with a katana.

Knowing the girl was Annabelle's daughter had me taking a closer look at her. Now I understood why her eyes had held me so entranced. They weren't Annabelle's clear blue that I loved so much, but the shape was exactly like hers. So were her nose and those lips. Those were the only similarities that mother and daughter shared, meaning the girl favored her father...

Motherfucking hell. Shit. Oh shit. This kid—this teenaged girl... How old was she?

Suddenly, I couldn't breathe. All the oxygen left my lungs and I couldn't suck in another breath. My gaze met the green and gold eyes that I knew were reflected back at her. She was so beautiful.

And mine.

Annabelle and I had made love three times the night before I'd left and we'd used a condom every time, I reminded myself. But... Fuck, the *but* was killing me. There had been that one time during the night when I'd gone twice without changing condoms. *Fuck.*

How had I not known she existed? She had to be sixteen years old and I was just now setting eyes on her. How...?

Motherfucker.

Memories of Annabelle being so desperate to contact me flooded my mind. The letter she had sent and I'd returned unopened because I'd been terrified of reading about how much she hated me for abandoning her. She hadn't tried to contact me for months after that. I hadn't heard another word from her until a few weeks after Gramps had died. She'd somehow gotten Rich's number and started calling him daily. Rich had gotten frustrated with her and finally told me to call her, but I hadn't. Too much of a pussy. There was no way I could call her and still stay sane. I'd wanted to hear her voice so damn bad, but I couldn't call her. She deserved better than me. After that, there hadn't been so much as a murmur from her until five years later. Rich had said Annabelle had been hysterical, and now I couldn't help but wonder what had happened.

Ah, God, I'd fucked up. Fucked up so badly.

Nausea rolled in my stomach. I'd not only fucked up with Annabelle, but I'd evidently fucked up with my kid, too. I'd lost out on so much of her life and I had no one to blame but myself.

"I think he knows," my daughter-motherfucker, my daughter—whispered to her mother.

Annabelle's blue eyes glared without sympathy at me from across the room. "Yeah, looks like it. Took him long enough."

Annabelle

I knew the second he connected all the dots and found the truth. I didn't have to see his eyes to know they were completely green now. He'd gone past his normal boundaries and he wasn't coping well with what my daughter—*our* daughter—had thrown into his lap. His face twisted in agony and I was pretty sure he'd stopped breathing.

I took a sick sense of pleasure knowing how destroyed he was in that moment. That was the same feeling I'd had when I'd discovered I was pregnant two months after he'd left me without a backward glance and with a broken promise. That was how I'd felt when I'd fallen when I was six months pregnant and had been so scared I was going to lose my precious baby. And it was how I felt times ten million when five years later I'd nearly lost my reason for living.

Every time, I had tried to tell him what was going on, but he couldn't be bothered to return my calls or even open a damn letter. Memories of pulling that letter out of the mailbox, the red stamp on the front saying 'return to sender' without it having been opened, still had the ability to slice at something deep inside of my heart. I'd needed him so much during those terrifying times and he wouldn't give me so much as five minutes of his time.

My pleasure at his destruction lasted only five seconds. I couldn't stand there, watching the man who still owned part of my soul falling into the abyss I knew he was so frightened of. His body started to shake and he took a stumbling step toward us. My instinct was to protect my child and I stepped in front of Mieke. He shook his head as if to clear it as he moved past us.

"Don't leave," he muttered. "Please…just don't leave."

Zander stumbled down the hall and struggled to open a door. Seconds later I heard him retching and my heart ached. Swallowing hard, I turned to face my kid. Concern darkened her green and gold eyes. "Is he going to be okay?" she whispered.

I cupped her cheek with one hand, rubbing my thumb under one beautiful eye. "Maybe not tonight, but he will be soon." Zander was stronger than he knew and I wanted to help him deal with what must be a nightmare for him. "What were you thinking, honey? Why did you do this?" I was still trembling on the inside from how scared I'd been when I'd gotten that call from Noah.

Mieke's chin trembled for a brief moment, her eyes continuing to travel down the hall to where her father was still throwing up. "I heard his voice when I talked to you this morning. I knew it was him, Mom. I just knew. Something inside of me needed to see him, to put a real person to the voice I'd heard. To the man you've told me so much about over the years. Don't be mad. Please? I…I just needed to *see* him."

I dropped my hand and closed my eyes. I'd never lied to her about who her father was. If she asked about him, I told her. She deserved the truth about the man who had helped me create her. I'd told her everything I remembered about him. Everything…except that he had destroyed me when he'd broken his promise to come back for me. But I knew she knew that. My girl was so special, she could practically feel the emotions in the air, and I knew she had known just how utterly broken I'd been when Zander had decided I wasn't important enough. But I liked to lie to myself and pretended she didn't know.

I stroked my fingers over her hair and asked the one question I was dying to know—although I was pretty sure I already knew the answer. "How did you know where he lived, Mieke?"

"It wasn't hard to hack his email and bank accounts. I got his address off his bank statements. But I didn't mean for this to happen," she whispered. I blew out a frustrated breath through my nose. Damn it, she was too smart for her own good. It wasn't the first time she'd 'hacked' someone to get the information she wanted. "I didn't mean to upset him this much."

"I know, honey. I know." From down the hall I heard Zander groan, curse viciously, and then vomit again. "Sit down. I'm going to go check on your…dad." It felt so strange saying that word, but once it was out it seemed so right that it made my heart ache all over again.

"Tell him I'm sorry," she murmured as she sat. I didn't answer her as I walked down the hall. She had nothing to be sorry for, but if she wanted him to know she was, then she could tell him herself.

Zander was on his knees in front of the guest bathroom toilet, his head in the bowl as he retched yet again. There wasn't anything left in his stomach now and he was just dry-heaving. Seeing him like this gave me no pleasure and I was ashamed of myself for feeling it earlier. I wouldn't wish this pain on anyone, especially not him. This was just the beginning, too. How was he going to handle knowing everything?

Finding a washcloth, I dampened it with cool water in the bathroom sink and knelt down beside him, wiping it over his brow. He jerked when I touched him, his tortured eyes lifting to mine as tears spilled down his face. "I didn't know," he muttered.

I just nodded as I continued to wipe his face. I didn't know what to say to him right then, so I remained quiet. He didn't need words at the moment. Hell, I didn't know what he needed. I knew nothing about this Zander.

"Knew I wasn't good enough for you, Anna." He let out a moan and closed his eyes as I wiped the cloth over his jaw. "I'm a fuck-up."

I sighed and stood long enough to rewet the washcloth. Seventeen years ago, I would have argued with him, but I didn't know how to defend him now. Maybe he had been a fuck-up back then and I'd just refused to believe him. Love was blind, and I'd loved him so much. When he'd left, I'd lost a part of myself that I doubted I'd ever get back.

I lifted the washcloth to his face again, but he grabbed my wrist, stopping me. "How much do you hate me, Anna?"

That question had me biting the inside of my cheek. Honestly, there had been times I'd thought I'd hated this man all the way to my core. And then I'd look at my daughter and realize that I couldn't hate the man who had given her to me. Pulling my wrist free, I returned to wiping his brow. "Starting to feel better?" I kept my voice quiet, not wanting Mieke to overhear us.

"Don't," he muttered.

I frowned. "Don't what?"

He scrubbed a hand over his face, pressing his thumb and index finger hard into his eyes. "Don't be nice to me. Don't take care of me. I don't deserve it. I never did."

"I can't," I whispered. Maybe he didn't deserve it, but I couldn't stop myself from helping him. I never had been able to. My heart would probably always be weak where this man was concerned.

"Mom?" Mieke called. "Is Dad okay?"

Zander flinched at the word 'Dad', jerking in pain like he'd been shot. "Fuck," he muttered, rubbing his hand across his chest. "She's killing me."

I stared at him for the longest time, trying to decide how to explain Mieke to him. "We'll be out in a minute, Mieke."

"I like her name," he said as he pushed up from his knees and sat on the edge of the tub. "How did you come up with it?"

I lowered my eyes to the cloth in my hand, concentrating on folding it perfectly so I didn't have to meet his eyes. "It's a Dutch variation of my middle name. Her full name is Mieke Zandria Cassidy." I could feel his gaze drilling into the top of my head as I whispered her name. "She is part of me and you. I wanted her name to represent us both."

"It's a beautiful name, Anna."

"I thought so too." I looked up long enough to give him a brief, sad smile before turning my gaze back to the cloth. "She's everything I've ever wanted, Z. I should tell you about her..."

"Does she have my OCD?" he asked, his face looking haunted.

I quickly shook my head, knowing that he'd always worried about passing his mental illness on to any child he might happen to have. I remembered him always telling Noah that he wasn't sure he wanted kids when he was older, that he didn't want to subject a poor kid with what he'd always had to live with. "She doesn't have it."

His body noticeably relaxed. "Thank fuck for that. Look, I want to hear everything about her. From both of you." He scrubbed a hand down his face. "Give me a minute to clean myself up, babe. I can't face her like this."

Zander left me there and I watched him walk in the direction I could only assume was his bedroom. I set the damp cloth on the sink and went back to the living room. Mieke was sitting where I'd left her, but her face was full of anxiety. I sat down beside her and pulled her into my arms.

"I'm sorry," she whispered. "I didn't realize... I'm sorry."

I tucked her head under my chin and tightened my hold around her. "It's okay, baby. You wanted to see him and I understand your need to. Everything will be okay. I swear."

She let out a shuddery breath and we sat there in silence while we waited for Zander to come out of his bedroom. He was gone five minutes and when he sat down on the coffee table in front of us, he'd changed his clothes and his hair was damp from the shower. His face was still pale, but there was a new determination in his eyes. Eyes that weren't all green anymore. There was more gold now and I was proud of him for grabbing hold of his control for his daughter.

Slowly, Mieke lifted her head and met her father's gaze. She swallowed hard and gave him a tight smile. "I'm sorry I upset you. When I decided to come here I didn't realize how hard it would be for you. I mean, I knew it was hard for me, but I didn't know it would make you..." She broke off and sucked in another shaky breath. "I'm sorry."

"You have nothing to be sorry about, Mieke. Ever. I was upset—am upset—but not at you, sweetheart." He gave her a smile I remembered from our childhood; one I'd grown to rely on as we'd gotten older. It was full of so many different things that I knew our girl needed right then: reassurance, understanding…love.

Zander held out his hand and she didn't hesitate to take it. His smile didn't waver as he looked at her. "Tell me about yourself. I want to know everything about my daughter."

Mieke's eyes quickly locked onto mine, as if she were almost frightened to talk about herself. I tried to mirror Zander's smile. "How about I start from the beginning?" She nodded and I cleared my throat. "Mieke was born three months early. She and…her twin sister."

My eyes were on Mieke's but I could practically feel Zander's reaction. The air went completely still around him and I gave my daughter a watery smile. Thinking about her sister always ripped open old emotions and memories that were painful.

"We have another daughter?" His voice was raspy, but I didn't so much as blink, not daring to break eye contact with Mieke when she needed me.

I swallowed around the lump in my throat. "No, we had another daughter. Mieke and her identical twin were born three months too early because I'd fallen and it put me into labor. They couldn't stop it so they had to take both babies by C-section." A tear spilled from Mieke's green and gold eyes, and I lifted a trembling hand to wipe it away. "There were complications. They were too early and I nearly lost them both."

"Go on," he whispered roughly, encouraging me when I would have stopped. The memories were overwhelming me.

"The doctors knew there was going to be no helping Michelle… That's what I named her, Michelle Anna Cassidy. I used a variation of your middle name and my first for her," I explained.

"It's beautiful, Anna."

"She was. Even as small as she was, she was so beautiful. Just like Mieke."

"Wh-what happened?"

"Mieke's lungs were better developed than Michelle's, but there was a hole in her heart…and other complications with it. The doctor said that even if I'd carried to full term, that Mieke's heart would still have had issues. Michelle's was perfect, but there were so many other complications with her that there was no way to help her. The doctors came into my room and told me that I could lose one daughter…" The first tear fell, but I didn't bother to wipe it away. Every time I cried for Michelle, I never wiped away the tears. It felt like I was wiping away her memory if I did. "…Or both. I didn't understand what he was telling me at first, and I was barely out from under the anesthesia, but I remember the doctor looking at Noah and explaining that they wanted to give Michelle's heart to Mieke."

Without releasing her father's hand, Mieke tugged her shirt down until the top of her scar was visible on her chest. It was just a faded white scar now, not the angry red it had been for the first years of her life. As she'd grown, the scar had gotten smaller, but it was still a big scar. "Mom didn't lose her, Dad. Michelle is still alive as long as my heart beats."

I glanced at Zander then. Saw the way his whole body seemed to shudder in agony. I knew how he was feeling. It was like your heart was bleeding. Every time I looked at Mieke, I felt that way. I expected him to jump up, to turn away from us, as his eyes filled with tears. When he didn't, but just tightened his hold on Mieke's hand, I was surprised but proud of him.

We were all quiet for a long moment, each of us lost in our own thoughts. Finally I cleared my throat and went on. "Noah and Chelsea gave Michelle a funeral. Mieke and I both had to stay in the hospital for a long time afterward—Mieke much longer than me, of course. They buried Michelle beside my dad, which was pretty close to Gram and Gramps too, if you ever want to go see her."

I hadn't known until after my brother had buried Michelle that Zander's grandparents had died. He must have kept it out of the papers, probably to make sure I didn't go to the funeral. At that time, it had just been one more blow to my heart. I had hoped to take Mieke down to West Bridge and share her with her great-grandmother, if not her father. I knew Gram and Gramps would have loved her… And yeah, I knew the old lady would have beat her grandson with a spoon the second she found out he hadn't been in contact with me since he'd left, not letting me tell him he was going to be a father.

"I do," he choked out. "Soon."

I nodded. "Okay." I went to visit her every Sunday when I was home. Yet another reason I didn't know if I was going to be able to take Emmie Armstrong up on her offer. Maybe if I could work from Tennessee, like I'd been doing, but not if I had to be in California so often. I knew she'd said that becoming partners didn't mean I had to leave Nashville, but I had a feeling that California would be where I was most needed.

"I got to go home when I was six months old, Dad." Mieke continued when she realized I was reluctant to go on. I didn't want to get to the other part. I didn't want to remember…

"I looked like a little drowned rat with no hair, but by the time I was two I was where everyone said I was supposed to be. The doctors always said I'd be tiny, but by the time I was four I was taller than average. Mom says I'm still a shrimp because I get my height from you and I should probably be taller." She smiled for him, the one to reassure him this time.

"And because I have Michelle's heart, I like to think that I can live enough for both of us. I try to, anyway."

"You do, sweetheart," I assured her. "You do."

Zander nodded, agreeing readily with me. "Yeah, honey. You do." His gaze turned to me all of a sudden. "That was why you called Rich. Because of the babies… But what happened later? Why did you wait until then to try and call me again?"

I closed my eyes. Remembering what had happened when I'd lost Michelle was hard to face every day, but at the same time I'd always been thankful for what time I'd had with her. I'd gotten to hold her for a few minutes before they had taken away both my babies and only returned with one. What had happened five years later…? That's the one memory I hated to remember. It was the one that I woke up in a cold sweat to some nights.

"It's okay, Mom." Mieke squeezed my hand and I opened my eyes, smiling for her. It would always ever be just for her when I smiled with those memories running through my head.

"You're scaring the hell out of me here, Anna." Zander's voice growled at me. "What happened? What put that look on your face and how the fuck do I erase it?"

I opened my mouth but the sound of the doorbell stopped me. I frowned, glancing at the clock on his wall beside the television. It was nearly midnight, so who the hell could be at his door? Jealousy shot painfully through my chest. Was I about to come face to face with one of Zander's many lovers? I didn't know if I could handle that after just ripping my heart open by telling him about our daughters and then having to face the near tragedy of losing Mieke five years later.

"That's my food," Mieke surprised me by saying as she got to her feet. "They had your card on file so I charged it to that. Is that okay, Dad?"

"Yeah, that's fine, sweetheart."

She rushed to answer the door. Zander and I stayed where we were, our gazes lovingly watching our daughter. She said something to the delivery boy and then set the two bags of food on the table by the door. After the boy left, she stepped halfway out the door and pressed the doorbell thirteen more times.

Zander chuckled. "I guess you really did tell her all about me."

"I never lied to her when she asked about you, Z. She deserved to know."

His jaw clenched and he nodded, but didn't say anything more.

Returning to us, she grinned at her father. Setting the two bags on the coffee table beside Zander, she started taking out cartons of delicious-smelling Chinese food. Finding the egg rolls, she stuffed half of one in her mouth before continuing her task.

"Are you going to eat all of this by yourself?" Zander didn't look like he believed it could happen, and I threw my head back, laughing for what felt like the first time in forever. He frowned at me. "You mean she can?"

"And more," I assured him.

My kid could put away some food.

My kid.

I never thought I would say those words, but watching Mieke stuff the last egg roll into her mouth, I realized it felt right. She was so beautiful, so full of life, and completely perfect. When she'd told me about Michelle always living as long as her heart still beat, I'd lost my shit. It had taken everything in me to stay where I was and not run back to the bathroom. But I knew I couldn't do that. She needed me. Annabelle needed me.

While she ate her noodles, fried rice, and honey chicken, she told me a little more about herself. Annabelle remained mostly quiet while Mieke spoke of her childhood. I now knew she had to wear braces when she was twelve, but only for a year. I now knew she liked raspberry sherbet, and hated pickles. I even now knew that she was a year ahead in school and would be graduating this year from high school. My kid was some kind of freaking math genius and she had her pick of colleges.

I liked hearing Mieke talk, but what I really needed right then was to know what had happened when she was five. What had put that haunted look on Annabelle's face? What was worse than losing one of our babies?

I waited until Mieke was leaning back against the couch beside her mother. Her stomach was finally full and she had a content smile on her face. The second I asked about it, the small smile that was on Annabelle's lips disappeared and Mieke sat up a little straighter, but she looked more concerned for Annabelle than anything.

"I'd just turned five," Mieke said, her tone soft as if she were afraid to speak too loudly. "Mom was out of town with Uncle Noah for a charity concert and I had a field trip to the Parthenon in downtown Nashville. Aunt Chelsea was supposed to go with my class, but Ben was sick and she had to take him to the doctor."

"Ben?"

Mieke smiled a little easier this time. "My cousin. He's a year younger than me, and my best friend. He has a sister, Audrey. She's three years younger than me."

"Do they look like Noah?" I asked Annabelle, curious about my old friend's kids. Did they look like him, like Mieke looked like me? Or did they look like Chelsea?

She nodded. "Ben is his double, but Audrey looks more like Chelsea."

I turned back to Mieke. "Okay, so you were on a field trip?"

"After we walked through the Parthenon we had lunch out on the lawn. I ate my lunch and then some of the other kids started playing. I didn't want to, so I stayed on my blanket and fell asleep. The teachers were more concerned with watching the ones running around than me." She shrugged. "So they didn't notice when someone grabbed me."

Annabelle let out a whimper and I instinctively grasped her hand as my heart started racing. "What?" I didn't mean to shout, but I didn't have control over the volume of my voice right then.

Mieke nodded as I felt Annabelle tremble with the memories. "There had been a lot of visitors at the Parthenon that day. One of them was a woman who'd just lost her daughter to cancer. When she saw me just lying on the blanket, she took me."

Annabelle stood up so quickly I didn't know how to react. She combed her fingers through her long, pale-blond hair, scattering the streaks of hot pink. "I can't," she whispered. "I just can't do this."

"Anna?" I'd never seen her like this. It gutted me to see it now. The look on her face told me she was reliving a nightmare. She was shaking and looked so pale it was as if what Mieke was telling me had happened only the day before and not nearly twelve years before.

She turned to face me with eyes that were wild. "Some psycho took our baby, Z. She just took her in the middle of a crowded place and no one even saw her. She had her for two days. Two. Days. Do you know how that feels? Do you? To have the reason you get up in the morning missing and not knowing if she's okay? If she were cold or scared? If someone was *hurting* her?"

My throat tightened and I couldn't breathe, let alone speak, so I shook my head. I had no clue what she had felt then, but if it was half as bad as what I was feeling right then, just hearing about what had happened, then I could imagine.

"This girl?" She pointed at Mieke with a finger that shook. "She is my reason for breathing and I couldn't wrap my arms around her. I couldn't hold her and tell her everything was going to be okay. She was scared and alone with a woman who could have done anything to her. At the time we didn't know if it was a man or a woman, a pedophile or what. The local cops brought in the Feds, but they had no leads and after the first day they told me that statistically I wasn't ever going to get her back."

"Mom, I'm okay. It's over. That was years ago. She didn't hurt me." Mieke tried to soothe her mother, but Annabelle shook her head and let out a sob that cut me to the quick.

She turned accusing eyes on me. "I didn't want to believe them. I refused. I tried calling you. I tried so many times to just get you to speak to me for a minute. Two seconds. *Anything.* Our baby was missing and I n-needed you."

I reached for her, unable to not touch her a second longer. I grabbed her trembling hand and pulled her down onto my lap. A broken sob seemed to tear from her chest as she clung to me. "I needed you," she whispered.

I buried my face in her hair, letting my tears fall. "I know. I know."

"You b-broke your promise." If she had hit me, I couldn't have hurt more. I almost wished she would hit me. Beat the shit out of me. I needed it, fucking deserved it. Maybe the physical pain would relieve some of the emotions choking the air out of me right then. "I needed you—*we* needed you and you just left us. You didn't want us."

"I did want you," I groaned into her hair. "I wanted you so bad I hurt."

Annabelle shook her head, still sobbing. "No. If you had, you would have come back. You wouldn't have broken your promise."

I didn't argue with her. There was no use right then when she was so distraught, and I didn't have the emotional strength to go down the road of what I'd been feeling back then—what I still felt now. All my energy was focused on Annabelle and how she was falling apart in my arms.

A soft hand touched my arm and I lifted my head just enough to see Mieke standing beside us. She had one hand on my arm, but the other was rubbing her sobbing mother's back. "Please don't cry, Mom." Annabelle's sobs abruptly stopped but turned into little hiccups that tortured me just as bad as her sobs had. "And don't take your pain out on Dad. If he'd known, he would have been there with you."

Hearing her defend me like that to her mother shamed me. I didn't deserve her taking up for me like that. I'd left her mother and, in my refusal to face my pain and self-hate, I'd essentially left Mieke as well. I'd failed them both. I deserved everything Annabelle threw at me and so much more.

Eventually Annabelle cried herself to sleep, her arms still wrapped around my neck. I lifted my eyes from the beautiful girl, who had turned into an even more exquisite woman, to meet my daughter's tired gaze.

Mieke gave me a sad smile. "She always does this when she remembers…" She broke off and shrugged. "I guess it exhausts her."

I brushed my lips over Annabelle's forehead and stood with her in my arms. "Come on," I told the girl. "You and your mom should get some sleep."

I carried Annabelle down the hall to my bedroom and laid her in the middle of the king-sized bed. Pulling the covers over her, I glanced at Mieke who was standing on the other side of the bed. "You two take the bed. I'll take the couch."

I had another bedroom, but I'd turned it into my music room. It had my keyboard and guitars in it. I'd fix that in the morning, I promised myself. I wanted Annabelle and Mieke to stay with me for as long as they were going to be in California. I didn't want to waste another second away from them.

Mieke lifted her green and gold gaze from her mother, startling me yet again with their unique blend of the two colors. Her eyes couldn't be labeled as hazel; there was too much green. The gold was just enough to catch your attention and hold it. "Would you… Will you lie with us for a little while? I'm tired, but I don't think I could fall asleep right away." I blinked, surprised by her softly spoken question, and she bit her bottom lip. "Please? Just for a little while?"

Giving her a nod, I climbed in on the right side of the bed beside Annabelle. Instinctively, I wrapped an arm around her and pulled her against my chest. She let out a soft, shuddery breath and burrowed against me as if she was desperate to get closer in her sleep.

Mieke kicked off her shoes and turned off the light as she climbed into bed on the other side of her mother. With the door still open, I could see her worried face as she watched me holding her mother so close. "She acts so strong that sometimes I forget how vulnerable she really is." Mieke stroked a hand down Annabelle's arm, seeming so much older than she really was.

We lay like that for several long minutes, both of us quiet as we watched Annabelle sleep. My gut was churning, my mind racing from what Mieke had told me earlier. Maybe I hadn't been there to feel the fear when my daughter had been taken, but I felt it right then. Annabelle must have lost her mind...

"How did they find you?" I couldn't help but ask, my mind stumbling over all the things that could have happened to my little girl when she'd been snatched.

The hand that had been stroking up and down Annabelle's arm lifted to her mother's hair, combing her fingers over the hot-pink strands. "Mrs. Viars didn't hurt me, Dad. So don't torture yourself about that, okay?" She continued to stroke Annabelle's hair, as if she needed to soothe her mother even though she was sleeping. "She took me to her home and fed me mac and cheese, played Barbies with me. I was scared, but only for a little while. She was nice but distraught from the loss of her daughter. Later they told me that it was because I reminded her of her little girl that she took me. Her mind was protecting her from the pain of the recent loss, and seeing me confused her."

I swallowed around the lump in my throat, relief washing through me as she told me about her time with this Mrs. Viars woman. "But how did they find you, sweetheart?" I needed to know or I knew I'd never get another second of sleep for the rest of my life.

Mieke smiled, as if knowing how badly I needed her answer. "Mrs. Viars' sister came to check on her two days after she took me. When she saw me and realized I was the little girl the entire state was looking for, she called nine-one-one. She didn't want the cops to scare me, or her sister to get hurt, so she told them to be gentle. A woman, a Fed I guess, knocked on the door a few minutes later and took custody of Mrs. Viars." She shrugged. "I don't remember a lot after that. It became kind of crazy. I remember a cop picking me up and wrapping a blanket around me because I was still in Mrs. Viars' daughter's nightgown and it was chilly outside. I remember being a little scared about all the strangers and the flashing lights of all the cop cars. One woman might have come into the house, but there were at least twenty cop cars outside."

"Was...your mom there?"

"No. They wouldn't let her come to the scene. The cop put me in the back of an ambulance and let me play with his badge on the ride to the hospital. He stayed with me while a doctor checked me over to make sure I wasn't hurt. Someone brought her and Uncle Noah to the hospital." I saw her chin tremble and lifted my arm from around Annabelle to pull her closer.

"Mom was a little hysterical at first, but when she saw me she tried to keep her calm. I remember her smiling even though she was crying pretty hard. She grabbed me and wouldn't let me go. She had never squeezed me that hard until that day. She had always been so careful when she hugged me up until then. Uncle Noah was crying too, and I thought that was crazy because I'd never seen him cry before. Seeing his tears scared me more than anything else had during that entire time." She swallowed with difficulty and continued with a whisper. "It was only then that I realized something bad had happened. That what had happened to me had been something some little girls didn't come back from."

"Mieke…" I rasped out, tears burning my eyes. I didn't try to hold them back. Letting them fall freely, I pulled her even closer, practically squishing Annabelle against my chest in my need to hold Mieke just as close.

Motherfucking hell. I should have been there. I should have been there to hold her and her mother. Maybe if I had, none of that would have happened. Mieke wouldn't have been taken… And maybe Michelle would have been there too. A choked sob escaped me.

Annabelle sighed my name in her sleep and wrapped her arms around me. She pressed a kiss into my chest, and I felt it even through the cotton of my shirt. Mieke draped an arm over her mother, her hand on my back as she held me just as close as I held her. Together we sandwiched Annabelle between us, protecting her from the bad memories.

Mieke fell asleep a little while later. The sound of her even breaths mixed with her mother's calmed me enough that I was able to relax, but it was hours later before I even began to feel like sleeping. I didn't dare move, but watched with a new determination as my two girls slept.

I hadn't been there for them when they had needed me the most, but that stopped now. I was done hiding from my past fuck-ups. That shit was over and it was time I moved on instead of hiding from them and Annabelle. None of it mattered now.

I had a daughter to get to know and try to make up for not being in her life until now. My gaze dropped to the sleeping beauty curled against me, holding on to me as desperately in sleep as I wanted to hold on to her forever. "I love you, Anna. I'm not going anywhere ever again," I promised her. "Tomorrow our new lives start. I swear to you, baby. We'll start the life we should have had all along."

Annabelle

The ringing of the doorbell startled me awake. I jerked my head up, my eyes instantly opening. When I found myself in a room I didn't recognize, I tensed. With the blinds open I could see that the room was painted in warm browns and the bed was a huge California king with chocolate-colored sheets and comforter.

And Zander Brockman was sound asleep beside me, his arm still around my waist, anchoring me to him.

The events of the night before flooded back into my mind and I dropped my head back onto the pillows as I tried to breathe through the memories I'd had to relive. I knew all about Layla and Jesse Thornton's torment when their twin boys had been born so prematurely, but at least they hadn't had to say goodbye to one of their precious babies. I understood exactly how Emmie had felt when Mia had almost been taken. She'd only had to live with the thought of her daughter being taken for less than an hour. I'd had days to imagine what was happening to my little girl in the hands of a stranger. The only thing that ever got me through it was imagining Michelle as Mieke's guardian angel, watching over her twin during the time her sister was gone.

Thinking of my little baby in Heaven, watching over her sister, brought me peace and I was able to smile as a tear spilled from my eyes. I didn't wipe it away. I'd never wipe away the memory of Michelle like that.

The sound of a voice I vaguely remembered followed by Mieke's quiet reply had me lifting my head again. Frowning, I glanced at the bedroom door, slightly ajar. Seconds later the door was pushed open and the light was switched on, a frowning Natalie Cutter standing in the doorway.

Zander groaned and lifted his head to glare at the woman. "Go away, Nat. I'm trying to sleep here."

She crossed her arms over her chest, making her baby bump stand out. "I can see that. My question is, why do you have guests? You never have guests. Especially not overnight ones."

My eyes widened at what she'd said. Was her question seeking an actual answer, or was she telling me that Zander never had women in his apartment? I kind of hoped it was the latter, but quickly scolded myself at feeling such a stupid emotion where this man was concerned. Zander and hope just didn't fit well with me. They never had.

His arm still around my waist, Zander pushed up onto his elbow. Yawning, he took his time answering the woman. "You know Annabelle," he grumbled as he looked at her once more. "And that beautiful creature beside you is our daughter, Mieke."

Natalie stood there for a full minute as if she hadn't heard him. She didn't so much as bat an eyelash. Then it was like someone had slapped her because she jerked and turned her head to give Mieke a thorough going-over with her blue-gray gaze. "Oh, my god," she whispered and lifted her hand to her lips. "You look just like him."

Mieke shrugged. "That tends to happen. It's called genetics."

I shot my daughter a frown, not appreciating her sarcasm. Why was she being rude? Having worked with the other woman, I'd discovered that she was not only nice and a good person to have in your corner when you felt like you were being pulled through a war zone, but she had a good heart. Natalie adored her stepson and the love she felt for her husband was unmistakable.

Natalie's gaze narrowed before turning back to Zander. "No one ever mentioned you having a daughter, Z. This is all a little bizarre for me."

"It's a long story, Nat. One that will have to wait until I've had a few cups of coffee. Do you mind making a pot while Anna and I get up?"

The other woman shrugged. "Sure. I'll get on that. I'm calling Dev, too. I can't believe he didn't tell me."

"Probably because he didn't know," Mieke grumbled as she turned to go back toward the living room.

Natalie blinked after the girl. "For real?"

"Coffee, Nat. Please." She shook her head as if to clear it, then nodded. "Shut the door."

The door had barely shut behind her when Zander dropped back down onto the pillows, pulling me across his chest as he did. "It felt good to sleep with you in my arms again," he murmured before brushing a kiss over my forehead.

Yes, it had, but I didn't tell him that. There was no way in hell I was going to fall back into old habits where this sexier-than-sin man was concerned. "I need to get up." I tried to pull away but he only tightened his arms around me. "Seriously, Zander. I have things to do."

"Whatever it is you think you need to do, it can wait five minutes." His tone was coaxing. His hands remained locked around me, but his fingers started rubbing soothing—and arousing—little circles just above my hips.

I squeezed my eyes shut, trying to ignore the little thrills of arousal that were waking up my entire body in a way it hadn't been in far too many years to count. Feeling his damp, hot lips against my cheek and then lower to my jaw had me biting back a whimper. *No, Annabelle. Stop this now before you can't stop yourself.*

I jerked away from him and jumped to my feet, straightening my wrinkled clothes to avoid looking at him. When some of the trembles had left my hands, I turned to face him. He was sitting up in bed with the covers pulled up to his waist. Ah, thank God. I wasn't strong enough to keep myself from climbing back into bed with him if I'd seen the proof of his arousal that I'd felt only seconds ago flexing against my stomach. He was still wearing the sweatpants and old T-shirt from the night before, but that didn't mean I wouldn't see his cock standing at attention through those layers of clothes. If there was anything I remembered about Zander, it was that he had nothing to be ashamed of in the cock department.

"Last night changes nothing between us, Zander. The only difference between this morning and yesterday is that you now know about your daughter."

"Our daughter," he corrected with a smug grin.

I rolled my eyes, ignoring his interruption. "It's actually a relief that you know about her now. It's obvious that she loves you and you should take advantage of the fact that she wants to spend some time with you. She's going to college next year and then she's going to be so busy with all of that, she will forget about everything and everyone else."

It was still hard to believe that Mieke had skipped from fifth grade to seventh and now she was in her final year of high school. Because she'd been born so prematurely, the doctors had feared that she would have development delays that would affect her not only physically but also mentally. Considering the fact that she took after her father and he was so tall, even with Mieke's above average height some could say that she was on the small side. As for mentally, her IQ was beyond average and bordering on genius.

Hence how she had been able to hack into her father's bank statements and find his address.

She was growing up way too fast and all I wanted was to hit the pause button so I could hold onto her a little longer.

Zander's brow furrowed as he glared at me. "I plan on spending every spare second I have with our daughter, Anna. But I want to get to know you again too. I have so much to make up for, not just to Mieke, but to you as well. The only thing that has changed about how I feel about you is time, and time has only made me love you more."

I flinched at the word love. It felt like a physical blow to my chest it hurt so much. The sad part was that, even when I'd tried to hate Zander Brockman, I had still loved him with what little bit of my heart was left after he'd shattered it. Letting him back into my life and even more so into my heart was not an option, however. I knew I wouldn't survive this time around if I let myself believe in him again.

Clenching my jaw, I finished tugging the majority of the wrinkles out of my shirt and turned for the door. "You should hurry, Zander. Maybe you could show Mieke around the city. She would enjoy that. I have meetings today. More loose ends to tie up so I can get back to Nashville." *And as far away from you as humanly possible.*

"Damn it, Anna. Come back and talk to me," he called after me.

I ignored him, something I'd learned from him how to do like a pro. Natalie and Mieke were in the kitchen. Natalie was by the coffee maker while Mieke sat at the island in the middle of the huge room. Seeing the look on my daughter's face startled me. Why was she glaring at Natalie Cutter like she was the enemy? What the hell was her problem?

I touched her arm and her angry eyes lifted from where she was shooting daggers into Natalie's turned back. "What's wrong with you?" I whispered so as not to embarrass my child. I would never do that to Mieke.

The anger and pain in her eyes gutted me, but I didn't understand why she was feeling like that. "She rang the doorbell forever, so I got up to answer it. But by the time I got there she was using a key to get in. A *key*, Mom. This chick has a key to Dad's apartment, and it's more than obvious that she is pregnant. Did he start a new family without us? Did he?"

I let out a deep, frustrated breath. The pain in her eyes and voice was excruciating to see and there was nothing I could do about it. Mieke had built up some kind of fairy tale in her mind —that one day her father would ride in and swoop the two of us up and we'd be a family again. I'd turned a blind eye to it, and only now did I realize how big of a mistake that had been. I knew Zander hadn't started a family, but if he had, Mieke would have been destroyed right then.

"Honey, I know this is hard for you, and I understand why it would hurt you to think that your dad had a new family here while… But don't stress yourself over this. Natalie is married to Devlin Cutter. That's his baby in her belly. Trust me when I say that Dev would cut off your dad's nuts and shove them down his throat before he let your dad touch his wife. Okay?"

Mieke shook her head. "That wasn't the case over a year ago when the band was having issues and Dad and this Devlin guy were fighting over *her*."

I couldn't help but blink at the venom in Mieke's voice any more than I could help the stab of pain straight to the center of my chest. Over the years I'd bent over backward to avoid any news about OtherWorld, but I knew that Mieke had kept up with the band through social media groups as well as the tabloids and entertainment shows. Even though Noah and I had tried to beat into her head that most of the tabloid stuff was just rumors at best, she had still continued to read anything she could get her hands on.

But even I had heard people talking about the possibility of OtherWorld breaking up due to an inner conflict between the band's drummer and bassist. Apparently there had been a bet between the two best friends, and that bet had led to the breakup between Natalie and Devlin for over a year.

Mentally shaking away my pain, I grasped Mieke's elbow a little firmer. "Nothing is going on between Nat and your dad, sweetheart. And even if there were, that is his business. Don't get pissed because he has a life here."

"But I am pissed," she cried, her voice rising.

Natalie turned her head and raised a brow at the two of us. I gave her a small, grim smile and tugged on Mieke's elbow. "Excuse us, Natalie. I need to—"

Mieke jerked away from my hold. "You don't need to do anything." She turned the full force of her glare on Natalie. "Are you knocked up with my little brother or sister, or what?"

Natalie's lips twitched for a moment and then she was tossing her head back and laughing out loud. "Are you serious?" Mieke's glare only turned icier and Natalie's laugh stopped, but she was still grinning. "No, kid. This is one hundred percent Devlin Cutter's baby girl. That thing between your dad and me was never more than friendship. Cool your jets, princess. I'm not the competition around here. Actually, you don't have *any* competition. Z has always kept his demons to himself, but now I can see why he's never hooked up with anyone while we were on the road."

Mieke's shoulders actually dropped in relief. "So Dad hasn't ever had a girlfriend?"

154

"No girlfriend that I've ever seen, honey. And hookups were few and far between." Natalie turned her blue-gray eyes on me, as if she was speaking solely to me now. "I'm not going to tell you the dude was a monk, but honestly it's a pretty close call on that end. I always wondered why," — she shrugged —"but now I don't have to wonder anymore."

I wasn't lying when I told Zander I had meetings all day. There were things that needed my immediate attention so I could get my ass back to Nashville where it belonged. So I left Mieke—reluctantly—with Zander, who promised to show her all his favorite places in the city. Natalie had still been there and had promised she would plan them out a day and then send me an itinerary so I would at least know where my daughter was.

Pulling my rental car into Emmie's driveway, I rushed inside and started up to the second floor when I nearly ran straight into the solid chest of Nik Armstrong. Letting out a squeak, I thought for sure I was going to fall backward down the stairs when strong hands caught me around the waist and steadied me.

Nik's hands didn't linger, just steadied me and let me go as soon as he was sure I wasn't going to fall. "Whoa there, Annabelle. You okay?"

I grimaced and nodded up at him. "I'm good."

Clear, ice-blue eyes narrowed on me as he lifted a brow. "Emmie said you went over to Z's last night. Everything okay?"

Mentally I groaned but gave him a tight smile. He was bound to find out anyway so there was no use in lying about it. "My daughter decided to come into town. She's going to be staying with her dad until I'm ready to go back to Nashville. Since she should be in school right now, it looks like I'm going to have to rush through what still needs my attention so I can get her stubborn ass home."

Ice-blue eyes darkened for a moment and then he threw his head back and laughed out loud. "Are you telling me that Zander Brockman is the father of your daughter?" I didn't return his laugh, merely nodding, causing Nik to abruptly stop laughing. "What the fuck? I had no idea he had a kid."

I shrugged. "Neither did he until last night."

The amusement faded completely and he glared down at me. "You kept his kid from him, Annabelle? Really? I thought better of you than that. That's a low thing to do to anyone."

Anger boiled in my veins at his instant judgment. I liked Nik —really, I did. He was a nice guy—mostly. He loved his family and his band-brothers, and when it came to his friends he was always ready to fight in their corner. However, anyone outside his small group of family and friends wasn't honored enough to see the good guy he was. To everyone else, and especially to the paps, Nik could be a total dick. He had no idea what had happened between Zander and me, and honestly he had no room to judge. "This really isn't any of your business, Nik. But even if it were, get your facts straight before you start condemning people. I tried to tell Zander I was pregnant so many times, I lost count. He didn't want anything to do with me and completely ignored every attempt I made to get in contact with him. He didn't want to know."

I pushed past him as I finished climbing the stairs. At the top, I turned to glare down at him. "The Zander you know isn't the same guy I was once in love with. I have no idea who this new version of him is, and I'm not even sure I want to know. If you think you should take sides, by all means take the side of your friend. But I'll be damned if I'm going to sit around and let anyone make me out to be the bad guy in all of this. So fuck you, Nik Armstrong. Fuck you and anyone else who wants to believe that I kept Zander's daughter from him on purpose."

Without waiting on a reply, I hurried to the room that Emmie had lent me and rushed through a shower before dressing and throwing all my things into my suitcase. I'd find a hotel later, but there was no way in hell I was going to sleep under the same roof as Nik Armstrong.

Suitcase in hand, I rolled it downstairs and put it in my trunk before going to the small guesthouse that Emmie had turned into her office. I'd heard her telling Layla Thornton just a few days ago that she was going to find some office space downtown because she didn't want to chance putting her family in even more danger by having clients coming in and out with her kids so close.

I didn't bother to knock on the front door. Stepping into the little guesthouse/office, I saw Emmie's secretary sitting behind her desk typing away. Rachel glanced up long enough to offer me a smile and nodded her head toward the closed door of Emmie's office, which had once been a bedroom. "She's free. Go on in."

I gave her a nod in appreciation and stepped into Emmie's domain. The little redhead was standing by the window looking out at the ocean as the waves hit the beach, a cellphone pressed to her ear. "I'm glad Dallas is feeling better and that Cannon didn't catch it," she was saying into the receiver. "No, don't worry about it. I'll take care of it for you. You just take care of your family, Ax. Yes…Okay. Love you, too. Bye."

She turned to face me as she placed her cell on the big desk behind her. "Hey. Everything go okay at Zander's last night?"

I glared down at her, still seething over my run-in with this woman's husband. "It went better than expected, seeing as my daughter forced my hand and ended up meeting her father for the first time last night."

I was watching Emmie's face, so I wasn't surprised to find her unaffected by my statement. I should have known that Emmie knew about Mieke and who her father was. Emmie knew everything about everyone she dealt with. It was one of the reasons she'd gone so far in her career so quickly. It was how she'd gotten the connections in the music world that she had. She had everyone she so much as spoke to investigated before she even shook their hand.

That didn't mean I didn't feel as if I'd been emotionally violated. She'd sent her henchman, Seller, to find out all the dirt he could on me before offering me the partnership deal. "How did he take it?"

I shrugged. "After he stopped throwing his guts up, he took it pretty well. How long have you known? About Mieke and Z, I mean?"

Emmie gave me half a smile. "About five minutes after I saw your reaction to Z at the hospital a few weeks ago. Seller gave me a full report the next day, but I'm not stupid. I can do basic math and I'm really good at reading people."

"And obviously you didn't share this intel with your husband."

Green eyes narrowed. "Nik knows that I can't always tell him things. If it's important to him, our family, or the band, then fine, but I can't tell him everything that I know about my clients and he understands that."

"Well, he knows now. He was all kinds of ready to defend Zander. Since you offered me this partnership knowing all the dirty little details, I'm assuming you don't care one way or another."

"Annabelle, that is your business. I wasn't going to use it to convince you to go into business with me. I wasn't even looking for shit like that when I had Seller do the background check. All I wanted to know was if it would be risky doing business together. That's it. You're great at your job and you have awesome PR skills that I sometimes lack. During all those press conferences, I wanted to tell the paps to go fuck themselves, but you kept your cool. I need someone like that with me when things go to hell. And since you've been thinking about my offer, I have to at least assume I have something to offer you as well."

She sat on the edge of her desk and crossed her arms over her chest. The look on her beautiful face was completely serious. "If Nik said something to upset you, I'm sorry. He's a guy and guys tend to support each other even without knowing all the details. The OtherWorld guys are good friends with the Demons and that isn't going to change. But Nik's opinion doesn't mirror my own. I still want you to be a part of this with me. Please, keep considering it."

I knew Emmie's reputation so I knew good and well how much that 'please' had cost her pride. That she had admitted to needing me soothed my own pride. A little. Pushing my hair away from my face, I crossed my arms over my chest, mimicking her. "Would I really get to work from Nashville?"

I hadn't realized I was going to even ask that question when I opened my mouth, but once it was out, I knew that I was going to take her offer seriously. Maybe it was a good idea after all. Maybe it would make my life easier and I'd have more time with Mieke and the important things I'd missed out on in the last few years.

Green eyes brightened, as if she knew I was weakening toward her. "Yes. You would probably be home more often than you are now if we were partners. I'm not saying I won't need you here or in New York or wherever the hell a shit-storm might be, but you will be in Nashville most of the time. We will share the workload together, and I plan on hiring a whole team to help us out. With the way technology is right now, we could do a lot of our important meetings via Skype or whatever else there is out there to help with that crap."

The excitement in her voice was contagious and I found myself weakening that much more. Damn it.

"Between the two of us and Natalie, we can train a competent team that will make our lives so much easier. We can delegate, something Nik has been begging me to do for years now. All I need is you, Annabelle. You're the missing piece to the puzzle to make all of that possible."

Cursing under my breath, I dropped down into one of the chairs in front of Emmie's desk and buried my face in my hands. "I'll probably regret this tomorrow, but what the hell." Dropping my hands from my face, I extended my right hand toward her. "Okay, fine. Let's do this thing."

Zander

It seemed easy enough to please Mieke as we spent the day out exploring L.A. I showed her all the sights that had entranced me from the first day I'd stepped off that tour bus seventeen years before. She listened intently as I talked about why certain places meant so much to me. Mostly they were places that spoke to me the most when I was writing a song.

For Demon's Wings, they relied on Nik to do most of the song writing for them. He had a real talent for writing music and had sold his songs to other artists over the years. Hell, we'd even bought a few of them. More often than not, however, my band and I took turns writing our own songs. The majority came from me, but each of us had written at least a few over the years.

Mieke ate up everything I told her and found a few places she loved along the way. By dinnertime I could tell she was getting tired, though. The emotional events of the night before added to the excitement of that day were catching up with us both, but I was reluctant to end our time together. I knew what was coming, knew that when I got back to my apartment, Annabelle wouldn't be there. That thought alone made me not want to go home.

We still had dinner to get through, though. I had mixed feelings about that. I'd asked Natalie to get the guys together for a meal somewhere low key so I could break the news to them all myself. Since Wroth and Marissa were getting ready to go back to Tennessee, I knew I had to do it now or I'd have to wait. I was excited to get to introduce my daughter to them, but anxious about their reactions to the news. Honestly, I wanted them to jump on me and kick my ass. I wanted them to be pissed at me and give me the beating that I deserved for missing out on so much of my kid's life. Not to mention how much I'd put Annabelle through over the years.

Traffic was hell and Mieke and I arrived at the restaurant in West Hollywood fifteen minutes late. I turned my car over to the valet and put my hand at the small of Mieke's tiny waist as I guided her into the little Italian restaurant. The hostess was busy, but I didn't need her assistance to get us to the table Natalie had reserved for our group. I could see Wroth's wide shoulders and Devlin's dark head from the entrance and steered my daughter in their direction.

We had a back table well away from most of the other diners. Axton, Liam, and Devlin spotted me at the same time and grinned at me like the idiots they were until they saw the girl at my side. Natalie must have already told Dev about Mieke because he shot me a supportive grin. Wroth, Axton and Liam shot me killer glares and I quickly lifted my hands.

"She's not jailbait," I rushed to assure them. For fuck's sake, why would they think that right off the bat? I was the least likely out of all five of us to go after the younger chicks. I rarely whored around like these fuckers had in the past. Now that they were all in stable relationships, they were ready to start judging me? Fuck that shit.

"Bullshit," Wroth growled in his scary-ass voice. "How old are you, girl?"

Mieke didn't back away from the giant who looked like he could swallow her whole in one bite. "Sixteen, sir." She was polite, but her voice was cool, as if she were sizing the beast up and wasn't sure if she liked what she saw. Yet.

"Motherfucker," Liam grunted. "What the hell are you doing, Z?"

Didn't they see the resemblance? It had taken me two seconds after seeing Annabelle to realize that Mieke was mine. I opened my mouth, ready to explain everything, but suddenly my throat was too tight to get out so much as a squeak. It was time to admit to them just how much I'd fucked up, but no words could squeeze through my tight throat. Glancing down at Mieke, I grimaced and hugged her to my side, loving her so damn much that my heart squeezed just getting to hold her like that. I held on to her for a long moment before turning back to my bandmates.

"This is Mieke," I rasped out. "Mieke is my daughter. Mine…and Annabelle's."

Three out of four mouths dropped open at the same time as three pairs of eyes widened and looked at my daughter with a new appreciation. I looked down at Mieke, trying to determine her reaction to all these rockers looking at her like she was an alien with three heads. She was smiling a little shyly and there was a little pink in her cheeks, but her green and gold eyes were bright with excitement. I hugged her closer and brushed a kiss over the top of her head.

"Annabelle didn't tell you about your own kid for sixteen years?" Axton was the first to speak and there was pure contempt in his voice. My spine went straight as I glared down at the man, but before I could even open my mouth to defend Annabelle, he continued. "How could she do that to you, man? That's so fucked up."

"Yeah, why would she keep something that important from you?" Wroth demanded. "Fuck, man. I've been in Tennessee more often than not over the years. All she had to do was tell me and I would have told you."

I was so pissed I couldn't find my voice for a second. How could these fuckers talk about Annabelle like that? Didn't they remember her at all? That they were talking about her like that—*and in front of my kid*—had rage bubbling in my veins.

"I can't believe this," Liam muttered. "How could she do this? That bitch."

I felt Mieke stiffen against me, her anger as strong as my own. Out of all the reactions I'd imagined getting from these four men, this was not one of them. I never in my wildest dreams would have figured they would put the blame on Annabelle's shoulders. This wasn't her fault. She'd tried to contact me repeatedly and I'd turned my back on her every damn time.

"Don't call my mom that," Mieke snapped at Liam, turning the full force of her glare on the bassist. "You know nothing about her or what she's been through over the years. How dare you point the finger at her and make her out to be some wicked witch." She pulled away from me, her gaze full of all the contempt that had been filling three out of the four men's eyes. "And even if she were, you of all people don't have any room to judge. How many rehabs have you been in, Mr. High and Mighty Rock Star? How close have you come to killing yourself over the years, chasing after the next big high? Oh yeah, I know all about you. All of you. So tell me, Liam Bryant, which is the bigger evil of the two of you? Huh?"

Liam's blue eyes darkened, but his mouth snapped shut and he lowered his gaze to the table, a muscle in his jaw twitching as he clenched his teeth together.

"Yeah, that's what I thought." Mieke turned her gaze to Axton next. "You don't know my mother, you never did. So don't pretend that you do." She looked at Wroth next, now completely ignoring Axton, letting the rock god know that he wasn't worth her time.

If you want the God's honest truth, I'd tell you that Wroth scared the ever-loving hell out of me. My daughter, however, had bigger balls than any man I knew because she turned her venomous glare on that huge hulk of a beast without so much as flinching. "And you. You think it would have been so easy for her to go down to West Bridge? Show up at your farm with a kid on her hip and ask you to pretty please tell Zander Brockman he was a daddy? She wanted *him* to know, not you or any other jerk-off. Him. My dad. So shut your mouth about my mom, you dick."

Wroth's mouth slowly closed and he blinked at Mieke several times without speaking. She rolled her eyes at him, obviously fed up with him and the rest of my bandmates. "What, nothing to say, big man? No big and bad comeback?" Her glare turned even icier. "Yeah, I thought so. You know what? Fuck you all. My mother is one hell of a woman and I'm not going to breathe the same air as anyone who is going to talk shit about her." She lifted her head, pride rolling off her just as strongly as her anger. She flipped them off with both hands and turned to walk away, not even gracing them with a backward glance.

I waited until she was several feet away before turning my own glare on the three men who had just put down Annabelle. Over the years we'd had our ups and downs. We were closer now than we'd ever been, but we'd never be like the brothers Demon's Wings had always been to each other. For me, this just pushed us back to before we'd cleared the air and tried to become a family instead of just bandmates. I couldn't put up with these fuckers talking about Annabelle like that. If they said so much as another word about her, I'd gut them. Even Wroth.

"Do you guys not remember anything from all those years ago? I was so fucked-up all the time I couldn't have taken care of Annabelle and a kid. Annabelle tried to tell me, but I was too stupid and hurting too much to listen to her. We all know that if I'd so much as heard her voice I'd have been back in Tennessee and said to hell with OtherWorld. So I stayed as far away from anything that even resembled a connection to her or Noah." I raked my hands through my hair, trying to grab hold of my control but quickly losing hold. "I'll admit it. I was a fucking pussy. I wanted this world *and* her, but didn't think I could have them both. Didn't think that I deserved them both. I'm the one at fault here. I'm the one to blame for missing out on watching my baby girl grow up. You know nothing about what Annabelle went through, or how much she needed me to be there with her, and I wouldn't even pick up a fucking phone. So don't go sprouting your shit to anyone else. I won't have Annabelle's name dragged through the mud while you and the press make me out to be the victim. I'm not. I was a goddamn pussy."

"Z—" Axton started, but I lifted a hand, cutting him off. The look on my face must have told him that now was definitely not the time to try and reason with me, because he sat back down and shrank in his chair.

"No, I don't want to hear your shit right now. I'm going after my daughter. I don't want to see any of you fuckers for a while. Go home and play happy families while I go and try to put mine back together." Following Mieke's example, I flipped them a double bird and rushed after my little girl.

I caught up with Mieke out on the street. She was standing by the valet who was eyeing her in a way that made me want to put a fist through the kid's face. I didn't like the desire in the boy's eyes as he looked at my little girl. Stepping in front of her, I blocked the guy's view before handing over my valet ticket. Once he was out of sight, on his way to get my car, I turned my full attention on Mieke.

Her eyes were damp, but she hadn't let a tear fall. My pride in her only grew. The way she'd just stood up to my bandmates—and especially to Wroth, something grown men would piss themselves doing—told me that Annabelle had raised our daughter right. To not take shit from anyone. I pulled her against my chest and kissed the top of her head.

"That didn't go as I was expecting."

She snorted. "Oh, yeah? What did you think would happen, Dad?"

"That they would take turns beating my face in while we ate a three-course meal." That made her laugh and I was rewarded when she wrapped her arms around my waist and hugged me tight. I couldn't resist kissing the top of her head again. "Everything you said in there was justified, sweetheart. I know I'm the one to blame for missing out on so much of your life. But that stops now. I want to be a part of your life as much as you will let me."

Mieke lifted her head and I saw one tear finally spill down her cheek. "You think I blame you?" I shrugged, not sure how to answer her, not without crying like a fucking baby. She sighed and shook her head. "Dad, I don't blame you. I don't blame Mom, either. Okay, so I'm not exactly a hundred percent happy with either of you about it, but I don't really blame anyone. You two were young and you both made some bad decisions..." An odd expression crossed her face and she laughed at herself. "I sound like my guidance counselor right now."

"No, you sound like an adult. I don't think I like that." I lifted my hand and wiped away her tear with my thumb. "I don't want to miss out on anything else, Mieke. Will you give me a chance to be a part of your life? Let me make up for some of the past?"

Another tear spilled over her bottom lashes and she gave me a wobbly smile. "Yeah, Dad. I'd like that."

"Z..." Both our heads turned at the sound of Devlin's voice. I lifted a brow at my best friend, not sure what to expect from him after what had just gone down in the restaurant. He'd remained completely quiet throughout the entire thing and I had no idea what he'd been thinking.

"Hey," I greeted, tightening my hold on my daughter. I knew he wasn't a danger to her physically, but after what had just happened inside, I wanted to shield her from the possible emotional pain that anyone else could load onto her small shoulders.

Devlin grinned and turned his gaze to the girl in my arms. "Natalie told me all about you this morning. Mieke, right?" He held out his hand and after a slight hesitation she shook it. "I'm Devlin Cutter. It's a pleasure to meet you, Mieke."

"Yeah, you too."

He lifted his phone in his other hand and shook it back and forth at her. "I have this great pizza place on speed dial that makes the best pizza in the world. Want to order a couple and go back to your dad's place? I can call my kid and you two can get to know each other too."

"She doesn't eat pizza," I hurried to tell the taller rocker.

"Who doesn't eat pizza?" he grumbled.

"It's a lactose thing," I explained and Mieke grinned up at me, obviously happy that I had remembered.

"Okay, new plan. I'll order pizzas for us and pasta for the lovely lady. Then call my wife to let her know I'll be late getting home followed by a call to the Thorntons to tell my kid to get his ass over to your place." Dev rolled his aquamarine eyes at Mieke, still grinning. "If he asks nice enough, he might get to bring Lucy."

My apartment was crowded with people, pizza boxes and the biggest takeout container of spaghetti I'd ever seen. Thankfully Natalie had gotten someone from the housekeeping service in to clean up my apartment while I was out with Mieke all afternoon. She'd even had the fridge stocked with drinks and groceries.

We were all in the living room now, the huge flat-screen on mute as we all talked and got to know my daughter better. Natalie had decided she felt up to having dinner with us, something that rarely happened since she was having blood pressure issues with her pregnancy. She'd brought her sister, Jenna, with her. I was happy to see Jenna and Mieke getting along so well. It was nice to see that the other teenager had accepted my kid so quickly.

The two girls sat on the long couch with Jenna to Mieke's left and Lucy Thornton and Harris to her right. Apparently Harris hadn't had to ask nicely to bring his best friend. Lucy had batted her big dark eyes at her father and he'd caved within seconds. Typical. Jesse Thornton loved his adopted daughter just as much as his biological sons—maybe even more, because she was his baby girl.

It made me hope to have that kind of relationship with Mieke one day —to share the bond and love that Jesse and Lucy did so seamlessly with my little girl.

Fuck, I had to quit calling her a little girl. She was sixteen, looked even older. My Mieke was nearly a grown woman. Motherfucker, I'd missed out on so much I'd never get back and that didn't sit well with my already fucked-up head.

The other kids were letting Mieke do most of the talking, and I was happy to hear her stories about growing up with a country music star like her uncle Noah. The country music scene wasn't nearly as hardcore as our rocker world. Mostly it was more family orientated and every summer she would go on tour along with her cousins, Ben and Audrey.

The way she talked about her cousins, aunt and uncle, I could tell that she loved them. They had been there for her when she and her mother had needed their support the most, and I couldn't even imagine how I was going to ever repay Noah for helping Annabelle take care of Mieke over the years. I doubted Hallmark made a card that said, "Thanks for playing daddy to my kid while I was off playing rock star."

It was nearing nine thirty when my doorbell rang. No one moved until it had hit the fourteenth ring, every one of them knowing it would put me off for the rest of the night if I didn't hear it fourteen times. Leaving my guests to finish their meal and conversation, I stood and answered the door.

Opening it up, my heart skipped a beat at the sight of Annabelle standing on the other side. Not only was my heart happy to see her, but my body instantly reacted at just the sight of her, and I shifted from one foot to the other to relieve some of the tightness in my jeans. "Hi," she greeted quietly.

I shot a glance over my shoulder, saw that Mieke was lost in whatever she was telling the entranced people around her, and then stepped out of the apartment, leaving the door only slightly ajar so I could get back in. "Hi." I lifted a hand, needing to touch some part of her to remind myself that she was real, that she was actually standing there in front of me.

I caught hold of her fingers and she stiffened for a second before seeming to force herself to relax. Her hand was so soft, so delicate. I wanted it stroking over my chest, over my thighs and wrapping around my aching cock.

"How did it go today? Did you and Mieke get along well?"

"We had a great time. I think she likes it here." I grimaced, knowing I had to tell her the rest. "I had Natalie set up a dinner with just the guys. Everyone but Devlin tried to put the blame on you." I watched as her jaw clenched and she lowered her eyes, not allowing me to see what she was feeling.

"Before I could set them straight, Mieke tore them a new one." That had Annabelle's head snapping up and I grinned. "Even Wroth. She's got guts, I'll give her that. But then again, look at her mother." I tightened my hold on her hand. "You did a great job raising her, Anna. She's an amazing kid."

Annabelle swallowed hard once, twice, and then cleared her throat. "I saw that you had guests, so I don't want to interrupt. Natalie messaged me earlier and said that she'd gotten your spare room sorted for Mieke. I don't mind her staying with you while we're in town, but we'll be leaving the day after tomorrow."

The thought of her leaving didn't bother me as much as it might have before, because I wasn't going to sit around in California while they went back to Tennessee without me. I'd be on the same flight with them, camped out in their front yard if I had to. I needed to be with them, but there were also things that I needed to do in Tennessee. First was to visit my baby daughter's grave and tell her how sorry I was for not being there to hold her. And second, win back what I'd thrown away all those years ago when I'd left without Annabelle Cassidy.

"Thanks for letting her stay with me." I rubbed my thumb across the back of her hand and had to suppress my smirk when I saw gooseflesh pop up along her arm. So she wasn't any more immune to me than I was to her. That definitely worked in my favor. "Will you be at Emmie's?"

She shook her head. "No. Nik and I had words this morning and I'd rather stay as far away from him as possible for the moment. Like the OtherWorld guys, he blames me for not telling you about Mieke."

I dropped her hand, afraid that I'd crush it if I didn't. "I'll talk to him." I hadn't been expecting Nik to take sides in this shit-storm. I appreciated him sticking up for me, but not at the cost of Annabelle's feelings.

Annabelle snorted. "Don't bother. I'm not going to lose any sleep over what Nik Armstrong might think of me. I'm just going to get a hotel for the next few nights."

"No." There was no way in hell I was going to let her stay at a hotel. I was greedy for every second I could get from her, not to mention I would worry about her being alone like that. Whoever had shot Gabriella was still out there; who knew what else that crazy bitch would do next.

Sky-blue eyes narrowed on me, blond brows lifting. "No?"

"Don't stay at a hotel, Anna. There's no use wasting your money when I have a perfectly good bed right here." I thought it was a good enough argument to make.

Her brows only lifted higher. "You have two bedrooms, Zander. One of them is Mieke's and, while I love that girl with every breath in my body,

I'd rather not have to see a chiropractor in the morning. She's all over the place when she sleeps, all legs and arms that kick and flail."

"So take my bed…" Blue eyes turned glacier and I rushed to continue, "…and I'll take the couch. I swear I'll keep my hands to myself. For now."

Those eyes I'd always loved—would always love—lost some of their frost, but she was still narrowing them at me. "You're awfully cocky, Zander Brockman. How did I forget that about you?"

I ignored her question, knowing without a doubt she hadn't forgotten so much as the smallest detail about me over the years. Fuck, it was the same for me. "Stay here, Anna. Let's give Mieke a taste of what having both her parents under the same roof would feel like."

Annabelle lowered her eyes to the carpeted hallway and I knew I'd hit a nerve for her. By the way she sucked in a shuddering breath, it must have been a painful nerve. Damn it, I hadn't meant to hurt her. My goal in life from that day forward was to never hurt her again.

"Hell, Anna. I'm sorry. I didn't mean—"

She shook her pale-blond and hot-pink hair back from her face, lifting her gaze back to mine. The look in her eyes was so sad it broke my heart a little more. "You're right, Z. It would be nice for Mieke to have us both for once. Even if it is only for a few more days."

I thrust my hands into the front pockets of my jeans so I wouldn't reach out and tuck a stray strand of hot-pink hair behind her ear. "I'm going back to Tennessee with you and our daughter when it's time for you to go, babe. I want to see Michelle's…grave." Just saying that one word felt like I was being stabbed directly in the heart with a thousand daggers. "Plus, I want the chance to get to know Mieke better…and you."

She flinched at the last part and took what seemed to me to be an involuntary step back. "It would be good for you to see where Michelle is buried, and I love the idea of you spending more time with Mieke. She's going to enjoy that. But I am featured nowhere in your future. I'm nothing but your daughter's mother. It begins and ends there, Zander. Our chance was over a long time ago."

"Maybe it was, but then again, maybe it wasn't. We'll never know unless we try, Anna." I was going to try my damnedest to prove to her our time wasn't over.

It was just the beginning.

Chapter Rock Twenty One

Annabelle

From the second I stepped off the plane in Nashville, I felt like I could actually breathe again. I didn't know if it was because I was finally home again after so many weeks away, or because everything and everyone I loved was there, or maybe even if it was because I was so close to Michelle when I was in Tennessee. None of the reasons mattered. I was simply happy to be home. Where I belonged.

I stood with Mieke and Zander as we waited at baggage claim for our luggage. Either Emmie or Natalie had been able to get Zander a ticket on the same flight as Mieke's and mine, and had snuck and upgraded our two seats to first class with Zander. I rarely flew first class, not because of the money—no, my brother still made enough off his royalties, and my own income was enough to keep my daughter and me comfortable for a very, very long time. I just didn't see the point in wasting money for first class when all I needed was a seat on a plane that was taking me in the direction I wanted to go.

Mieke didn't have any luggage to pick up since she'd only brought her backpack and a carry-on with her. I had two carry-on cases as well as a larger, heavy case I'd had to check. Zander had only brought one large bag that he'd checked. Seeing our bags coming our way now, he reached for both before I could even try.

Turning to me, he took both my carry-on cases, stacked one on top of each of the larger bags, and smiled that smile that had always melted me. "I think I see your brother." He lifted his chin in the direction of where people were waiting for the disembarking passengers. "Bet he'll be happy to see me, huh?"

I bit down on the inside of my cheek. Noah had been unusually quiet when I'd told him Zander was coming back with me. A quiet Noah was an unpredictable Noah. I had worried about his reaction to the sight of his old friend the entire flight home. Would he punch Zander on sight? Wait until we had gotten to my house—that just happened to be right next door to my brother and sister-in-law—before taking a swing at Z? Or would he put the past behind him, as I was trying so hard to do, and welcome his old friend home?

Just as I wasn't sure how Noah would react, I wasn't at all sure how *I* wanted my brother to react. For Mieke's sake, I hoped Noah would keep his cool and would welcome her father back with a manly one-armed hug and a pat on the back. For me? I had no idea how I wanted things to play out. Sure I wanted my brother to vindicate me, to at least punch the man who had broken my heart. In the face. Twice. Yet, at the same time, I didn't want Zander hurt.

Yeah, I was conflicted. Having spent some time with the delicious rocker again, my emotions were all over the place and I didn't know if I wanted to punch him in the face or kiss him. The way my feelings continued to flip back and forth was giving me whiplash. And a headache.

Over the last few days, I'd gotten to know Zander again without even realizing I was doing it. I spent most of my days out, taking care of business so I could get back to Tennessee as quickly as possible. Emmie had moved lightning fast and had gotten our partnership contract drawn up. I had it in my carry-on so I could go over it a little more in-depth as well as let my attorney look it over before signing it.

My nights, however, had been spent at Zander's apartment. It had just been the three of us each night. We would spend the evenings eating dinner together, mostly takeout. After dinner we would all sit in the living room, watching a movie—or at least pretending to. The movie was usually forgotten halfway through, at which point the huge flat-screen was put on mute and Mieke would tell her father some silly story from her childhood. She would talk until she grew tired and then she would go to bed.

Leaving me all alone with Zander Brockman. The father of my child. The man who had broken my heart...but was trying to put it back together. Not once in the few nights I'd spent at his apartment had he tried anything. He'd kept to one end of the long couch while I'd stayed on the other end. All he wanted to do was talk, so talk we did. Without even realizing it, each night I wouldn't stop talking until hours later. He would ask question after question if for some reason I happened to stop talking.

He wanted to know about me, about what I'd been doing the last seventeen years. Was it hard for me to finish high school being a single mother? *I hadn't finished. I'd had to quit because it had gotten too hard to get out of bed some mornings, so I'd gotten my GED.* When had I stepped in as Noah's manager? *I'd always acted in some way as his manager, but it wasn't until Mieke was in school that I really took over that responsibility.* Why had I kept it up when Noah had retired? *I was good at it and I'd had clients lining up, begging me to be their manager.* Did I enjoy my job? *Most of the time, yes. But there were times when I wanted to punch one of my clients in the balls—or the tit—and tell them to go fuck themselves.*

Even odder, Zander never once asked a question that was overly personal. Such as, if I'd dated anyone over the years, or even if I currently had a boyfriend.

I was glad for that small reprieve. I'd never been all that good at lying to Zander; at least I hadn't been in the past. Now, I didn't want to test those waters and embarrass myself by telling him there had been an endless line of guys who had wanted me and I'd let them have me. If he saw through that lie, I didn't think I could ever face him again.

Pathetically, while Zander had broken his promise right from the start to come back for me, I'd kept my own to him. I'd promised him I'd wait as long as he needed me to, and stupidly I had. There hadn't been another man in my life since the morning Zander had driven away. I could lie to myself and say that I hadn't gotten involved with anyone else over the years simply because I didn't want to risk getting hurt again. That was partly true, but not all of it.

Mostly, I guess I'd been secretly hoping that Z would eventually come back for me. That was why I'd given our baby girls variations of our names. It was why I'd done so many other stupid things throughout the years as I'd prayed for him to come back. For me.

Oh, yeah. I was definitely pathetic.

"Uncle Noah," Mieke called out excitedly and rushed ahead of us to wrap her arms around the man who had stepped up to the plate and been the father figure that my daughter had needed for the last sixteen-plus years.

I watched as my brother wrapped Mieke up in a tight hug, swinging her around twice just to make her squeal in delight. Even though he had two kids of his own, Noah had never treated Mieke any differently than he did Ben and Audrey. To him, Mieke was just as special as his own kids.

Setting Mieke back on her feet, Noah took a step back so that he could look his niece over. "Have you grown another inch?" He lifted a brow at the teenager. "Yeah, I think you have."

"I wouldn't doubt it," she assured him.

The Rocker Who Betrays Me

Noah's smile started to dim. "I'm mad at you, Mieke. You scared the life out of me when Ben told me you were gone. All I could think about was…" He broke off and I knew he was remembering what we'd all gone through when Mieke had been kidnapped. He shook his blond head at her. "Don't you ever do that to me again. You hear me?"

Mieke kissed Noah's cheek, a soft smile on her beautiful face. "Yes, sir. I promise."

"Good." Keeping one arm around her shoulders, he turned to finally look at me—and the man standing next to me. Noah kept his gaze on me, as if trying to figure out what I was thinking.

For a long moment he accessed me before finally lifting his blue eyes to meet hazel. Yes, hazel. Zander's eyes had been more often hazel than green the last two days and, while I was glad he was being so calm about all that was going on in his life at that moment, I couldn't help but wonder why. The Zander I remembered would have had all green eyes, with little to no gold in sight.

The two men locked gazes and stood there staring each other down for nearly a full minute. I glanced at Mieke, who was watching her uncle and father, biting her bottom lip as she felt the tension radiating off of them both.

It was Zander who made the first move. Letting go of the luggage, he took a step forward and offered his hand to the man who had once been one of his closest friends. Noah hesitated for a brief moment before lifting his hand and shaking Zander's. "Good to see you, Z."

"You too, Noah. Looks like life has been treating you well. Congrats on your two kids." Zander stepped back but didn't immediately take hold of the luggage again. "I'd like to talk to you later, if that's possible."

"Yeah, sure, man." Noah glanced back down at Mieke. "Let's get you home. Your Aunt Chelsea wants to hug you…before she takes a wooden spoon to your behind."

Mieke snorted, knowing that Chelsea would never do anything of the kind. Chelsea was the least likely person to raise her hand to a child in the world. It had surprised me just how patient she had been with our kids, even from the start. Even when I'd been ready to rip my hair out, Chelsea had been the calm one. She was the best mother, too. Making sure that not only did her kids have someone to support them, but Mieke did as well when I couldn't be at special events. When Mieke had been taken, she'd blamed herself since she'd had to back out of chaperoning the fieldtrip. I'd been losing my mind at the time, but I'd still stopped long enough to hug her and tell her that out of everyone who could have been blamed, Chelsea wasn't even on the list. Her son had been sick and she'd had to take him to the doctor. No one was going to ever blame her for what had happened to Mieke. I'd gut them if they even tried.

"Okay, well, we'd better get this over with, huh?" Mieke smirked up at her uncle.

Noah helped Zander with the luggage as we headed out of the airport and to the SUV that belonged to my brother. While the men put the cases in the back, I started to jump into the front passenger seat, but Mieke beat me to it. "I've missed Uncle Noah. Do you mind if I sit up front with him?"

I blew out an exasperated sigh at my daughter, knowing from the amused gleam in her green and gold eyes that it was more about me sitting with her father in the back seat than how much she had actually missed her uncle. For some reason I didn't call her out on it, though. I tapped her on the ass with my hand as she climbed into the front passenger seat before climbing into the back seat directly behind her.

Several minutes later, once all of our luggage was sorted so that Noah could see out the rear mirror, my brother got behind the wheel and Zander climbed in beside me. Seeing that I was sitting beside him, Zander grinned and scooted a few inches closer than were actually necessary considering how big the back seat of the SUV was. Draping his arm across the back of the bench seat, he turned ever so slightly toward me, his long fingers playing with the ends of my ponytail while Mieke pointed out some of her favorite places on the ride home.

My house was just outside of the city, in Green Hills, Tennessee. It was a more affluent area and several celebrities lived there. I lived on a corner lot in a smaller two-story house that had three bedrooms. Noah and Chelsea lived in the house to my right, while across the street was an ex-linebacker for the Tennessee Titans. His house was considerably larger than either Noah's or mine, but then again, he needed the extra room with all the kids he and his wife kept popping out on a regular basis. Seriously, in the five years they had lived across the street, I couldn't remember a time when that chick hadn't been pregnant. They had a total of six kids with one on the way. Noah teased them, saying that they were starting their own football team. The dude never really corrected him, so I assumed that was his goal.

Pulling into his own driveway, Noah honked the horn three times before opening his door. No sooner had we stepped out of the SUV were we surrounded by my sister-in-law, niece, and nephew. I got hugs from the kids before Ben was wrapping his arms around Mieke and hugging her tight. They talked in hushed voices, but I didn't try to listen in to the conversation. Those two were best friends, but I knew neither would do something that would actually get the other hurt. Although their plan for Mieke to fly to California on her own without saying a word to anyone had skated the line, I knew that Ben wouldn't have done it if he'd thought his cousin would be in any real danger.

"He's grounded for the next month," Chelsea informed me as she followed my gaze to our children, who had their heads close together, whispering back and forth animatedly.

I snorted. "I told Mieke she was grounded until the end of time. It will last the rest of the week...if I'm lucky." I was a pushover when it came to my kid and we both knew that she could break me and my resolve with something as little as a trembling lip and crocodile tears in her beautiful eyes.

"So..." Chelsea's blue eyes went to the back of the SUV where Noah and Zander were unloading our cases. "How are you dealing with all of this? Are you really going to let him stay in your house?"

I gritted my teeth. Mieke had made the offer to her father, wanting him to stay with the two of us while he spent some time in Tennessee. She'd been so excited that I hadn't tried to talk either of them out of it. After all, we'd done well enough staying in Zander's apartment for the last few days. He'd been the perfect host, giving me his bedroom while he slept on the couch. He'd turned his spare room into a beautiful room for Mieke and she'd been thrilled with it.

We'd actually gotten along pretty well over those few days. We'd talked about Mieke and her many stages up until present. His favorite had been her superhero stage where she would take up for anyone she thought was being bullied. Yeah, that stage had kept everyone on their toes. I'd been called for meetings with her principal so many times that I'd lost count. Each time the grumpy old man had wanted to suspend Mieke, and I'd just laughed in his wrinkled old face, daring him to punish my child for defending not just herself but others who couldn't.

Zander had been so proud when I'd told him about that time in our daughter's life, and so our pattern had started. I'd work all day, while father and daughter got to know each other better, and then the three of us would have dinner together. After Mieke would go to bed, I'd stay up talking to Z about her. Telling him all the special things about our not-so-little girl.

I could lie and tell you that I'd only done it for my daughter; that Zander deserved to know all the little things I was sure Mieke wasn't telling him about herself. But it was more than that. I found myself enjoying our quiet times together. It reminded me so much of how things had been before life had stepped in and sent us both in completely different directions.

"Where are these going, Annabelle?" Noah called as he headed across the large yard that separated our houses.

"Show Zander to the guest room, Noah. Just leave the rest in the laundry room. I need to wash everything in both my cases and Mieke's." I glanced back at Chelsea and gave her a quick hug before following after Noah and Zander. "Please tell me you cooked?" I demanded, glancing at her over my shoulder. The other woman nodded and my stomach growled just thinking of one of my sister-in-law's home-cooked meals. I'd been living off of way too much takeout over the last six weeks or so.

"Come on over around seven," Chelsea called after me and I waved as I entered my house.

The house was basically spotless. Normally when I was out of town on business, Mieke would stay next door with Noah, but I had a cleaning service come in once a week to dust and vacuum so that I didn't have to come home to a musky-smelling house. Stopping by the front door, I took off my thin jacket since it was getting chilly out now that fall was sneaking up on us. Toeing off my sneakers, I left my socks on before climbing the stairs to make sure Noah was showing Zander to the guest room.

All three bedrooms were on the second floor. Mine was at one end of the house, closest to the street, and Mieke's was at the other end. The way Noah's house was laid out, Ben's room was right across from Mieke's, and they usually kept their windows opened so they could talk to each other when they were in their rooms.

The guest room was right in the middle of the upstairs and only slightly smaller than the other two rooms. It had its own bathroom, just as the others did. I hoped Zander would be comfortable in there.

As I stepped onto the second-floor landing, I could hear my brother talking to Zander. The door to the guest room was slightly ajar and it wasn't like Noah was trying to keep his tone quiet. "You'd better not hurt her again, Z. If I see so much as a single tear in my sister's eyes—or Mieke's for that matter—I'll put a bullet in your head this time."

I rolled my eyes at the threat in my brother's voice. He was completely serious and I was sure that Zander knew that. Noah hadn't changed much in the last seventeen years. Sure he'd grown up, become a good man, but he was still so much like the boy—my big, bad, over-protective brother—I remembered from our youth.

"You don't have to worry about that, Noah. I've got my priorities straight now, man. For me, making Mieke and Annabelle happy is all I want in life. I'm hoping that their happiness will include me being a part of their lives, but I'm willing to take what they are willing to give me." Zander sounded so serious that my heart actually stopped for a second. "Nothing's changed, at least not for me. I love your sister, Noah. I will always love her. And my daughter... There is nothing and no one in this world I love more than that girl."

I didn't realize that Noah was quiet for so long until he spoke again. I'd been too lost in what Zander had said about still loving me to produce a thought that wasn't a jumbled mess because I was suddenly a melted puddle of goo. So when my brother did speak again I jumped at the sound of his voice. "Good. That's real good to hear, bro. But that doesn't mean I won't kill you if you hurt either of them."

"Not gonna happen, dude." Zander chuckled deeply and after a slight pause so did Noah. When I heard the sound of what must have been the men slapping each other on the back, I moved quickly down the hall to my own room, closing the door quickly.

My heart was racing after hearing Zander confess that he still loved me, my emotions all over the place. I didn't know how to react to those words—to the knowledge that the man I was pretty sure I still loved—loved me back. I was scared—no, I was fucking terrified—of getting hurt again. I was skeptical, because how the hell could he still love me after all those years apart? But mostly, I was angry. If what he'd said was true, that he loved me—always had and always would—why the hell had he stayed away for so long?

Chapter Twenty Two

Zander

I couldn't sleep.

It wasn't because I was in a bed I'd never slept in before, in a house I'd only stepped foot in that afternoon. After too many years of touring with OtherWorld, I could sleep anywhere, any time of day. It was something that you learned to do to survive out on the road. Otherwise you ended up a zombie while on stage trying to perform for tens of thousands of fans.

I couldn't sleep because my head was pulling me in so many fucking directions that I was getting lost inside it. Being back in Tennessee, being in Annabelle's house, felt…right. This was where I should have been all along. That I hadn't been, that I'd missed so much time away from the woman I loved—away from our beautiful daughter—made me hate myself in ways my fucked-up head couldn't understand.

Glancing at the clock on the nightstand, I saw that it was barely after midnight. Annabelle had gone to bed just after ten and Mieke hadn't been far behind her. Tomorrow was Thursday and my daughter needed to go to school, especially since she'd missed so much of it by going out to California. I'd kissed Mieke goodnight and then gone into the room Annabelle had so graciously given me. I knew how lucky I was that she had let me stay with her. She could have told me to fuck off and get a hotel room, but thankfully she hadn't. I didn't know if it was because of Mieke…or if maybe she wanted me around, too.

A man could hope.

A quick shower and then I'd flopped down on the comfortable mattress. I hadn't moved since. Just lain there staring at the ceiling as so many thoughts ran through my head.

Wanting to see Michelle's grave was the one that stuck out the most. Maybe put some flowers on my grandparents', too, while I was there. I wanted to tell them and my baby girl how sorry I was that I hadn't been strong enough to face my mistakes and beg Annabelle for forgiveness—beg for another chance after fucking up so badly seventeen years ago. I wanted Michelle to know that even though I hadn't gotten to hold her—*fuck, I wished I'd gotten the chance to hold her just once*—that I loved her just as much as I did her sister.

I wanted to tell my gram that I was sorry I hadn't been the man she and Gramps had raised me to be. I wanted to beg her for forgiveness for all the things I'd done to mess up so many innocent lives. But what I really wanted was for her to hug me one last time and tell me that even though I'd screwed up, that she still loved me.

My chest started to tighten to the point that I could barely draw in a breath. Tears stung my nose and eyes, but I blinked them away. My OCD was suddenly going off-the-charts crazy, and without realizing it, I started tapping my fingers on my chest. Fourteen. Fourteen. Four-fucking-teen. Why did it have to be fourteen? Why couldn't it have been three? Why couldn't it have been nothing? Fuck, I just wanted it to stop. Nothing had ever helped. Not the meds that I'd been given as a kid, not the therapist I'd tried when everything felt like it was so fucking out of control.

The only thing that had ever helped was Annabelle. For seventeen years I'd been without her and suffered through one out -of -control -OCD episode after another. The world probably thought I was insane. I'd have to agree with them.

Gasping for breath, I jerked out of bed and stumbled across the room. With shaking fingers I managed to open the door and went straight to the closed door of Annabelle's bedroom. I didn't knock. There was no time. I needed her. Now.

As soon as I was inside her room, the scent that was so uniquely her own filled my nose and some of the tightness eased in my chest. *Not nearly enough to calm me.* Moving forward, I headed straight for her bed in the middle of the room.

Before I could reach it, Annabelle gasped and pushed herself up on the bed. Reaching for the lamp on her nightstand, she quickly snapped it on, her eyes searching the room frantically until they landed on mine. "Z?" Her voice was overflowing with concern and I fell to my knees beside her bed. I buried my face in the comforter, hiding the tears that I could no longer keep at bay. My hands clenched her covers and I swallowed back one sob after another.

Soft, soothing hands stroked through my hair. "Z, what's wrong?" she whispered. "You're scaring me."

That was the last thing I wanted to do. Lifting my head, I let her see my tears as I tried to find my voice to tell her what I needed. "I want… No, I need to see Michelle's grave."

Her eyes widened. "Now?"

My throat was closing up again so I nodded. Annabelle's hand moved from my hair to cup my jaw, scruffy with a day's worth of beard. "Are you sure?" I nodded again and her eyes filled with understanding. "Okay. Let's go. Get dressed and meet me downstairs."

Scrubbing the back of one hand over my face, I stood on shaky legs and hurried back to my room. I grabbed the first thing I saw, jeans and a white tank. It was probably chilly out, but I didn't waste time by looking for a jacket in my luggage. I pulled my boots on without bothering with socks and then quietly descended the stairs.

Annabelle was already waiting there. She was in sweats and a hoodie with a large throw folded and draped over her arm. She had her keys in her other hand and her purse tossed over her shoulder. She lifted a finger to her lips as soon as I reached her. "Mieke will be okay while we're gone, but if she wakes up before we leave she's going to want to go with us. It's always harder on me to visit Michelle when Mieke is with me," she murmured quietly.

I nodded and followed her into the garage. A new red Tahoe was parked beside a cute, girly Jeep that I knew was Mieke's. She'd told me Noah had bought it for her for her sixteenth birthday. Guilt and something else—pure, agonizing jealousy—churned in my stomach. It should have been me who had given Mieke her first vehicle. It should have been me buying her everything she needed, wanted, and spoiling her rotten.

Annabelle climbed behind the wheel of the Tahoe and opened the garage door, and then started the large SUV. I climbed in on the passenger side and she shot me a grim smile before backing out. Once she was on the street, she hit the button to close the garage and turned in the direction of West Bridge.

Neither of us spoke for the longest time, but with each minute I didn't say anything, I saw her tense a little more. Blowing out a sigh, she glanced at me once before turning her eyes back to the nearly empty road. "I sold your old truck. It broke down on the highway one day when I was on my way to one of my doctor's appointments. So I had Noah sell it to some junk yard that used it for parts."

I didn't know how to respond to that, and I didn't think she really wanted me to. She just needed to talk, so I let her. All the way down to West Bridge she talked about random things. Like how Mieke had dared her to put the hot-pink streaks in her hair, but the joke had been on Mieke when Annabelle realized she liked the streaks and continued to get them touched up every month.

I was so enthralled with what she was saying that I was surprised when Annabelle pulled to a stop in a church parking lot. Reluctantly I turned my eyes away from Annabelle's profile and looked out the windshield at the graveyard just beyond the church. I knew this place well. I remembered standing here, holding Annabelle's hand when she buried her father, and her doing the same when my mother had died of breast cancer. I remembered coming here and watching as my grandmother had been lowered into the ground beside her daughter and doing the same just a few weeks later with my gramps.

Somewhere out there in that graveyard was my baby girl.

I closed my eyes and sucked in several deep breaths. When the passenger-side door opened, I snapped my eyes open and found Annabelle standing there, holding out her hand to me. Her eyes were so sad, glazed with tears that mirrored my own. "They say the first time is always the hardest," she assured me. "And I wish I could tell you that each time gets a little easier, but honestly for me, it never has." She lowered her eyes to the blanket draped over her arm, but still held out her hand, waiting for me to take it. "I usually bring a blanket and spread it on the ground beside her headstone. I lie there and put my hand over where I think she is resting and pretend I'm rubbing her back."

A tear spilled from her right eye and the sight unglued me. I jumped down from the SUV and wrapped my arms around her. I hugged her against me, wanting to take away all the pain that I'd seen in her blue eyes. Quietly I closed the door and lifted her into my arms, tucking her head against my chest. I remembered where her father was buried, and since she'd told me she'd put Michelle next to him, that was the direction I started walking.

It didn't take long to find what I was looking for. There was plenty of light coming from the church's parking lot and the moon was shining brightly, as if offering both of us comfort that night. Carefully, I placed Annabelle on her feet and took the large throw from her. I spread it over the ground right beside the little headstone that read:

Michelle Anna Cassidy
Beloved Angel Who Will Forever Be In Our Hearts

The date of her birth was the same date of her death. If I'd thought seeing my daughter's grave would help me in any way, I was wrong.

179

Devastatingly wrong. My knees buckled and I fell onto them beside the headstone. Bowing my head, I let my tears fall freely.

Annabelle left me to my grief for several minutes, as if she knew that I needed the time to myself. But then she knelt beside me, her head resting against my arm and her soft fingers entwining with mine. Having her there, offering me the comfort I hadn't given her when she had needed it the most, shamed me, but I didn't pull away from her. I needed her. Needed this.

Still holding onto my hand, she leaned forward and touched her free hand to the ground where I was sure Michelle rested in her casket. "Hey, sweet girl. Sorry I haven't been to see you in a few weeks. Work got a little crazy, but Mommy's home now. I won't be going away again for a while."

It didn't surprise me to hear Annabelle talking to the little girl buried there. Neither did the pure love I heard in her soft voice. What surprised me was the peace that washed over me from watching and listening to her. A small smile tilted at her lips as she continued to speak to our daughter.

"Mieke has been sneaky, but I guess you already know that. She talks to you more often than I do. Did you watch over her while she flew out to California?" She laughed a little shakily, but it was oddly filled with joy. "You're such an amazing angel, watching over your sister like you do. I can never repay you for taking care of her for me."

A few more tears fell from Annabelle's eyes, but she didn't pause as she continued to speak to Michelle. "I brought someone to meet you tonight. I think you've been on his mind a lot lately because he couldn't even wait until morning to come here to see you." Her fingers tightened around mine, offering me comfort in that little squeeze. "He's your daddy, baby. And I know he loves you just as much as I do."

Annabelle lifted her head then and I met her gaze. I lifted my hand, wanting to wipe away her tears, but she stopped me. "No. Don't ever wipe away a tear that is for Michelle." She swallowed hard once, twice, and then tried to smile. "I'm going to walk back to the SUV and give you two some time to catch up. You can talk to her if you want. It's what brings me comfort. But you can just lie here and be close to her. Whatever helps, do it."

She wrapped her arms around my neck, burying her face in my neck for nearly a full minute before releasing me and getting to her feet. I watched as she walked back to her vehicle and was safely inside before turning my attention back to my daughter's grave.

Now that I was here, I didn't know what to do, what to say. For several long minutes I just sat there, staring down at the headstone, my eyes tracing over each letter. Eventually I lay down and put my hand in the same spot that Annabelle had touched. Closing my eyes, I pictured what Michelle would look like. Mieke was her identical twin so they would look exactly alike, but I wondered what her personality would have been like.

Without realizing it, I found myself asking her that question. Once the first words were out it became easier to talk to her and before I knew it my chest wasn't hurting nearly as badly as it had when I'd been in bed. It felt like I talked to her forever, finding it just as easy to talk to Michelle as I did Mieke.

It was getting late and as much as I wanted to spend the rest of the night right there, I knew we needed to get home to Mieke, who might wake up and be worried that we weren't there. I sat up, still rubbing little circles on the ground where Michelle rested. "I'm so sorry, honey. I love you so damn much. Please, if nothing else, believe that. I'll spend the rest of my life trying to make up to your mom and sister for not being there when they needed me—when you needed me. Out of all my regrets, my biggest is that I didn't get to hold you." Tears streamed down my face, but I didn't wipe them away. Like Annabelle, I would never wipe away a tear that was for Michelle. "I'd give up my last breath to get that time back, to hold you and tell you how much I love you."

A soft hand touched my shoulder, but it didn't startle me. I'd sensed Annabelle long before she'd reached me. I covered her hand, squeezing it and silently thanking her for being there with me. "How do you leave?" I asked her. "How do you get up and leave her every time?" I needed to know how she did it, because even though I knew we needed to get home to Mieke, I couldn't bring myself to stand up and walk away from this little grave.

"You take a deep breath, tell her you love her, and take one step at a time," Annabelle whispered. "Don't worry, Z. She knows we love her, and she will be waiting right here for us to come back."

The sun was just coming up when we walked into the kitchen. My heart was still feeling heavy, like it always did after a visit to West Bridge to see Michelle, but I was also feeling more at peace than I had in a long time. Maybe for the first time since I'd been told Michelle wasn't going to make it.

Seeing Zander at our daughter's grave—watching how completely torn apart he was over the loss of our little girl—it had healed something inside of me. Not because he'd been in so much pain; no, I didn't take pleasure in his pain now. It was because I had him to share the pain with. Sure my brother and sister-in-law had hurt at the loss of Michelle, but they would never truly feel how heartbroken I'd been—still was—at the loss of my baby. Zander did, though.

Pulling out a chair at the kitchen island, Zander sat down heavily. I moved to the coffee pot, hitting the button to start a pot of the strong brew Jesse Thornton had taught me to make. With the sound of the liquid hitting the bottom of the coffee pot filling the kitchen, I moved to stand beside Zander. He'd been so quiet on the drive back, his eyes looking lost with very few flecks of gold in sight.

I ached for him, knowing exactly how hard it had been for him to stand up and walk away from Michelle. Unable to see him like that and not offer him some kind of comfort, I wrapped my arms around his neck and buried my face in his chest. Damn, he smelled good. My body instantly took notice of the delicious scent and reveled in the heat of his body so close.

He didn't even hesitate as his arms wrapped around my waist, his hold almost crushing me against him. He held on until long after the last drop of coffee had dripped into the pot, but I didn't try to move away. I needed this more than coffee.

Fuck, I needed this more than anything.

Zander sucked in a deep breath and let it out slowly. "I stayed drunk for two weeks after I left you that morning."

I went completely still against him. *Here it comes, the reason he didn't come back for me.* I knew that whatever left his mouth shouldn't matter now. Seventeen years had gone by since it had happened. That didn't mean I wanted to stand there and let him break my heart all over again by hearing what had been so terrible that he hadn't wanted to come back for me. That he couldn't even pick up a phone or a pen and tell me goodbye like he should have so that we could have at least had some kind of closure.

I didn't move away, though. I stood there, waiting for him to continue because I knew he needed to get it out, to purge it so he could move on. I just hoped I could move on, too.

"For the first two days, I avoided the cell I'd gotten so we could talk like I'd promised. Just thinking about hearing your voice would make my chest hurt, and I knew that if I heard you cry, I'd have been back in Tennessee in a flash." He tightened his hold even more, cutting off my air, but I didn't care. I wasn't sure I would have been able to breathe even if I could. "I pussied out and avoided the pain, then drowned it in any bottle that Rich Branson handed me."

He said his old manager's name more like a curse than anything else. I remembered the paps going to town when the story had broken about Demon's Wings dropping Rich Branson, the restraining order that Emmie had to take out against the old man, and even the assault charges that Rich had tried to file against Nik Armstrong for knocking him out. Within a month, OtherWorld had cut ties with their manager and signed on with Emmie. With two of his biggest clients gone, and the reasons for it spreading like wildfire, Branson had been bankrupt within a year.

"The booze made the pain of missing you…not better, but I guess easier to deal with." He blew out a harsh breath, as if frustrated with himself. "It numbed me up and I stayed that way for a full week."

"You said you were drunk for two weeks," I murmured and felt him nod his head but didn't dare look up at him. I didn't know what I would see in his eyes right then and had no idea if I could deal with what I would see.

"Yeah. At the end of the first week, on the last stop of our pseudo-tour that Rich arranged to give us his version of a real rocker experience, I woke up in a hotel room with three girls lying on top of me."

I shut my eyes tight, trying to block out the mental picture he'd just put in my head. I couldn't, ah fuck, I couldn't. Before he'd left, I'd known that there was a huge chance that something like that would happen, that he'd cheat. But after that last night, after he'd made love to me all night long, I'd thought my fears weren't anything to worry about.

Sucking in a deep, pain-filled breath, I tried to pull away from him. Zander didn't let me move back more than an inch before tightening his hold. I still didn't lift my eyes to meet his and he didn't try to force me to, but I could feel his gaze drilling into the top of my down-bent head.

Tears stung my eyes and clogged my throat, my heart breaking for the second time in my life over this man. I didn't expect it to hurt this much, didn't think I could still feel this kind of pain over something that had happened another lifetime ago.

"I went a little crazy when I opened my eyes and saw what I'd done. Tore the fucking room apart. It took Wroth and Devlin to calm my ass down. When I was able to think a little clearer, Dev told me that nothing had happened. I'd passed out and the girls had just stuck around. Later, I found out Branson had paid the girls to make it look like I'd fucked them." His voice was full of a menace I'd never heard before from Zander.

Slowly, I lifted my eyes and met his dark green and gold eyes. "Y-you didn't...? But..."

Zander lifted a hand that noticeably shook and wiped away a tear that I hadn't realized had fallen from my eyes. "The second week I stayed drunk because I realized I'd been right all along. I wasn't good enough for you. I didn't fuck those girls, but what about the next time? I was a fucked-up mess and you deserved so much better than that. I wanted my rock-star dream and I wanted you, but I couldn't have both. I picked one over the other. You deserved a man who would pick you over anything and everything else, Anna. That guy wasn't me."

I swallowed back the lump in my throat. "So why couldn't you just tell me that?"

He flinched at the chill in my tone. "Because I knew if I heard your voice, I'd throw away my dream and be home with you. I'd have given it all up in the blink of an eye if I'd talked to you, baby. But I was too much of a pussy, and too much of a selfish bastard to do that. Part of me liked the lifestyle I'd found with OtherWorld. I was living the dream I'd envisioned for myself for most of my life. Playing my music for thousands of fans every night, hearing them chant our name, seeing them rock out with us. It was a high all its own. I wasn't ready to walk away from that yet."

184

Oddly enough, I understood where he was coming from. Even at sixteen I'd known that Zander would always pick his music over anything, me included. I'd even accepted it—or so I'd told myself. Hearing him admit it now was like being punched in the chest. I didn't know what hurt more, the thought of him cheating on me just days after making me a promise to come back for me … or having him say out loud that I'd come in second place.

No one wanted to be second best, damn it.

I pushed against Zander's chest until he dropped his hands and took three steps back. "From the time you started playing with my brother in the garage, I knew you were destined for great things, Z." My voice was raspy from the tears I refused to let fall. I'd cried enough that day. I wasn't going to shed another one. Not when I'd known better, but still hoped for something more…

Fucking hope destroyed lives.

"I knew it and yet I let myself fall in love with you anyway. I knew it even though I let myself believe you when you gave me your grandmother's ring and promised me that you would be back. I can't blame you for something when I knew better than to hope I would ever mean more to you than what everyone could see you ached for." I pushed my hair back from my face and finally met his gaze. My eyes ached, but not with tears. They were dry now. So dry I doubted I'd ever cry again. "So if anyone is at fault here, it's me. I'm the one who hoped for something I knew I couldn't have—even if it was just a small piece."

His face tightened, but I turned away from him, hurting too much to worry about his own pain right then. I loved him so much—I probably always would—that seeing his pain would only increase my own and I'd want to comfort him. To tell him it was going to be okay.

This time I couldn't do that.

Going to the coffee pot, I poured two cups of the strong coffee and placed his on the island in front of him before moving into the living room and quickly made my way upstairs. I went to Mieke's room, pausing at the door to suck in several steadying breaths before I knocked twice and opened it.

My daughter sat up, pushing her tangled curls out of her face as she yawned. "What time is it?" she grumbled.

I had no idea. Glancing at the digital clock on her nightstand, I saw that it was just after six thirty. "How about pancakes for breakfast?" I offered, needing something to do to distract myself from the pain that was cracking me from the inside out.

Gold-tinted green eyes brightened. "Can I call Ben and Audrey to come over?"

Somehow I kept my smile in place. "Let's just keep it to us and your dad this morning." I was exhausted—emotionally and physically—after only an hour of sleep the night before. If my niece and nephew came over for breakfast, I'd probably lose what was left of my sanity trying to keep up with all their excited chatter.

Mieke's eyes widened as if her sleepy mind had just remembered that her father was in our house. "Okay. I'll be down in a few minutes." I nodded and turned to leave. "Mom?"

I stopped at her hesitant tone, my back to her, and glanced at her over my shoulder. Praying my smile didn't crack my face, I lifted a brow at her. "Yeah, baby?"

"I love you. You know that, right?"

If I thought I couldn't hurt any more than I already did that morning, I was wrong. I could and did hurt more, but at least this hurt was the good kind. "I love you too, honey."

Chapter Twenty Four

Zander

"I wanted to fly out to Cali and punch you in the face."

I didn't blink at the words that left Noah Cassidy's mouth. Fuck, if I had been him, I would have done just that. "Why didn't you?" I couldn't help but ask, wondering why he hadn't gone out there and beaten the hell out of me.

Noah shrugged before lifting a bottle of beer to his lips and taking a large swallow. "Annabelle asked me not to. She said she wanted to tell you. I guess she figured since it had been just the two of you to make those babies, it should be just between the two of you. Then she fell…" He shook his head and placed the half empty bottle of beer on the table between us before raking his hands through his pale-blond hair.

The look on my old friend's face gutted me. "How did it happen?" I'd known that Annabelle had fallen, that it was why she'd had the twins so early, but she hadn't gone into details. I hadn't pushed her to talk about it, not wanting to hurt her more than I knew she already was.

The other man grimaced and glanced around the room we sat in. We were in what Chelsea had called Noah's man cave. It was what I would have expected of my friend to have in his little hideaway from the outside world: classic car posters on the walls, huge flat-screen taking up one wall, and a mini fridge stocked with beer beside a card table that didn't look like it had been used for much card playing. A Grammy sat on a shelf in a corner—I assumed it was the one he loved the most because the rest of his awards were in the family room, decorating the walls. Noah had done well for himself in the country music world, with platinum records and country music awards of every type. I was proud of him.

Blue eyes that were nearly identical to his little sister's finally found mine again and the agony in their depths was like a punch to the stomach. All the air rushed out of my lungs as I waited for him to tell me.

"I was in Memphis that day. Chelsea and Annabelle were out doing some shopping and girly shit. They had just left the mall when some kid who was skipping school nearly ran them over in the parking lot as they were walking to my truck." He shook his head. "Chelsea told me she didn't see Annabelle fall, she was too busy cussing at the kid who didn't even bother to stop to see if he'd hurt them. When she turned around, Annabelle was on the ground. She'd fallen on her ass, but that didn't matter. She was already so big with the twins... Chels said that there was a puddle of blood just pouring out of Annabelle. A mall security guard called an ambulance, but by the time they got to the hospital they knew they would have to take the babies."

Noah pressed his thumbs into his eyes, as if trying to block out the images that were ingrained there. "I got to the hospital as they were bringing her into her room, and the doctor tried to tell her about Michelle. She was in shock and still half under the anesthesia they'd given her for the emergency C-section. I had to sign the papers for the heart transplant since she wasn't coherent enough and I was technically her legal guardian."

I grabbed my beer off the table and downed the nearly full bottle in two swallows. Even after hearing most of the story from Annabelle, it was hard as fuck to hear it again from Noah's point of view. I could have lost them all that day. Not just little Michelle, but Mieke and Annabelle, too. Just the thought left a gaping hole in my chest.

"Let's not talk about the heavy shit, man." Noah drained his bottle before tossing it in the trash and reached into the mini fridge for two more. Uncapping them both, he offered me one before once again leaning back in his chair. "How have you been? You fuckers have done well for yourselves. Even heard that y'all were gonna take a break from touring for a while. That true?"

After the disaster the summer tour had turned into, I doubted any of us wanted to tour again anytime soon. "Yeah. It's true. We all need a break from everything, not just touring."

Noah nodded. "Yeah, that shit gets old fast. Learned that quick enough once the kids were born. It's hard to keep everyone happy when you're touring, making new music, and have a family to take care of. After ten years, I was done. I'd made enough money to keep us happy for the rest of my kids' lives, but I still work. Couldn't completely give up the music. I help produce for my label and still write a song every now and then."

I opened my mouth, ready to tell him that he was done considering Mieke as one of his own. Now that I was in her life, I would make sure she was taken care of. Before I could even get the first word out, one of the cellphones on the table buzzed and I grunted when I realized it was mine.

Grabbing it, I saw that it was Natalie and quickly answered, shooting Noah a quick look. "Hey."

"Hi," she greeted with a small laugh. "What's going on?"

"You know what's going on. I sent you an email." I'd sent it hours ago, but knowing how crazy her schedule was at times, I figured she'd just gotten it if she was calling now. After what I'd told her in that email, I'd expected her to call as soon as she read it.

"Yeah, I got that. I'm looking at it right now, actually. I'm just not sure I believe my eyes. Maybe these damn headaches from my blood pressure are playing tricks on my eyes. No way you sent this. Not you."

I took a long pull from my fresh beer and leaned back, frowning up at the ceiling. "Well, I did. Figured you should be the first to know. And be the one to tell Emmie."

"What about the others?" she demanded, sounding exasperated and more than a little concerned. I knew the concern was for me and she was wondering what the fuck was going on, but I didn't owe her an explanation. I didn't owe anyone that except Annabelle and maybe Mieke.

"Fuck the others," I growled, still pissed at the way they'd rushed to put the blame on Annabelle about Mieke. They had all tried to call and text me, but I wasn't up for hearing their voices let alone a cheap-ass apology. Noah raised a brow at me but didn't say anything as he silently continued to drink his beer.

"Is that why?" she murmured, as if trying not to be overheard. "Because of what happened the other night?"

"No, Nat. This has nothing to do with them." And it didn't. The decisions I'd made earlier that day had nothing to do with my bandmates. "This is just something I need to do. For myself and only myself. Fuck everything else."

There was a long pause on Natalie's end and I could almost see the wheels turning in her beautiful head. Blowing out a tired-sounding sigh, she started grumbling to herself. "Fine. I'll take care of this. I don't want to have to be the one to tell Em, though."

"So don't. I'll tell her." At this point I wasn't scared of Emmie Armstrong… Okay, I wasn't *as* scared of her. That fierce little redhead would always scare me a little. I'd rather face a raging Wroth than her stormy green eyes any day.

TERRI ANNE BROWNING

"Good luck with that," Natalie muttered half under her breath before her voice rose up a little louder. "Did you hear? Of course you did. You're out there with Annabelle...pregnancy brain... whatever." I didn't try to sort out what she was saying. In the last few weeks I'd realized that pregnant Natalie spoke to herself. A lot. It was better to just go with it. "Emmie and Annabelle are official partners as of an hour ago. Hopefully my life is about to get a whole hell of a lot easier."

I blinked, thinking I couldn't have just heard her right. I hadn't slept in more than twenty-four hours, so my mind must have been playing tricks on me. "What did you say?"

Natalie repeated herself and I dropped my bottle of beer on the table, hard. Annabelle hadn't breathed a word about going into business with Emmie. She hadn't mentioned anything about any partnership. Fuck, I hadn't even seen her since she'd made pancakes for Mieke and me that morning and then rushed out the door for a meeting she'd claimed was important.

The whole time I'd been making plans for my future, she'd been making some of her own. I gritted my teeth, knowing I had no right to be upset that she'd made a huge decision like that without talking to me first. Didn't mean it didn't sting like hell.

"I'll talk to you later, Nat."

"But—"

"I have to go." I tried not to snap at her, but it came out harsh anyway.

"Damn it, Z—" was the last thing I heard before I hit disconnect and stood.

"Problems?" Noah asked with a grin.

I shrugged, swallowed the rest of my second beer—*or was it my third?*—and headed for the door. "I'll see you later."

"Yeah, sure. If my sister keeps you around that long," Noah called after me, sounding way too amused with himself. I flipped him the finger without pausing as I left the man cave. I didn't go through the kitchen to say goodbye to Chelsea, just left through the back door and crossed the yard to Annabelle's back patio.

Inside the house, I called out for her, not even sure if she was home yet or not. "Just a sec," she called back from upstairs and I stomped my way up to her bedroom.

The door to her room wasn't completely closed and I pushed it open to find her standing by her open closet, pulling a baggy T-shirt over her head. Yoga pants replaced the skirt she'd been wearing the last time I'd seen her. Turning to face me, she put a smile on her face, but it didn't reach her eyes. "Chelsea texted me saying you've been hanging out with Noah."

190

I didn't respond, too busy taking in the sight of her in comfortable clothes and her face washed free of any makeup. Fuck, she was so damn beautiful—even more now than she had been seventeen years ago. How had I been so stupid as to walk away from her and the life we could have had together?

Pulling the shirt completely over her hips, Annabelle walked toward me. I didn't move as she tried to step around me. Lifting her brows at me, she started to push past me but I reached out, catching her wrist and pulling her against me. Hard.

Blue eyes widened as she lifted them to meet mine. "What are you—?"

I swallowed the rest of her question as I covered her lips with my own. For a second Annabelle went completely still against me, but I continued to kiss her, drinking in my fill of the sweet taste of her mouth. How had I forgotten how delicious she tasted?

My tongue slipped out, teasing her bottom lip and making her open her mouth for me. Taking advantage, I dove deep, exploring her mouth the way I'd been aching to from the moment I'd seen her again. With a small gasp, Annabelle melted against me. Her arms wrapped around my neck, her soft fingers thrusting into my hair and pulling my head down farther as she kissed me back.

Groaning at how amazing she tasted and felt in my arms, I wrapped my arms around her waist and lifted her several inches off the ground. Using my foot to close the door, I carried her to the bed and dropped her on the edge before pushing her back, never once breaking my lips away from her own. Lying on top of her, I could feel every shiver, every tremble of her body as she arched into me, wanting every caress of my seeking hands—as greedy for more of my touch as I was to relearn every angle of her amazing body.

Finding her breasts, I sucked in a deep breath through my nose when I realized that she was braless under that baggy T-shirt she wore. I kneaded each fleshy globe before finding her nipples, already diamond-hard and begging for my attention. Breaking the kiss, I pulled her shirt up to expose her full, tight tits with the puckered nipples. Unable to control the growl that escaped my throat, I sucked first one nipple into my mouth before turning the same attention to the other.

Annabelle's fingers tightened in my hair, holding me against her as her lower body pushed up against me. I could feel the heat of her scalding pussy even through her yoga pants and my jeans. My dick flexed against my zipper, pleading to be set free and allowed entrance into the hot little body withering under me.

Still sucking on one ripe nipple, my hands reached for the top of her yoga pants and started tugging them down. As soon as I'd exposed her pussy, the scent of her desire lifted, filling my nose and making my own desire burn hotter. Pulling away, I muttered a vicious curse as I trailed kisses down her flat stomach to her drenched pussy. Shoving the damn yoga pants out of my way, I heard a ripping noise as I finally got them completely off her just as my tongue found her delicious pussy lips.

The last time I'd tasted this pussy, it had been sweet as honey. Now, it was pure nirvana. I loved the taste of her on my tongue, her cream flooding down my throat and overflowing, washing my face in her essence.

Her hips came completely off the bed as she ground her pussy against my face, offering me all of her juices in a meal I was starving for. "Oh, God. Oh, God," she whimpered as I thrust two fingers into her tightness.

The extent of her tightness surprised me. It felt just as tight as it had when I'd first made love to her seventeen years ago. Mentally shaking my head, I knew she couldn't still be that tight. There must have been other men who had gotten to taste…

I quickly put up a mental wall to stop that particular thought from continuing. No way was I going to be able to handle thinking of her with some other jerk-off. The thought of some faceless man taking what I'd given up enraged me. Not wanting to go down that road, I laved my tongue over her pulsing clit before sucking it deep, nipping at the little bundle of nerves with my teeth as she convulsed under me. With her pussy walls contracting, trying to suck my two fingers deeper, I lifted my eyes to watch her come apart for me.

As she slowly came down from the rush of the release I'd given her, I stood and pushed my jeans down my hips. Too far gone to stop and think about protection, I thrust into her still convulsing pussy. Blue eyes snapped open and a mixture of pain and pleasure crossed her face, telling me that maybe I should have questioned her tightness after all.

Buried in her, balls deep, I realized something that made me grin down at the girl who still owned every inch of me. Heart and soul. The grin was smug, cocky even, and I sucked in a deep breath and fought for control over the need to start pounding into her even as I let a new contentment wash over me. "You okay, babe?"

A small mewling noise left her throat and she nodded her head quickly, letting me know that she wanted more. "You sure about that?" I didn't want to hurt her, but the way her walls were clenching around me, I knew I wasn't going to be able to control myself for much longer.

"Plea-please," she breathed and I pulled back until I was nearly free from her tightness before thrusting back into her, my balls bouncing against her perfect ass. Her eyes closed and she let out a small moan in pleasure. "Z," she whimpered. "More."

At that one word, I couldn't hold back a second longer. My body took over, vetoing my brain altogether as I thrust into her over and over again with the force of a speeding train. The bed groaned and squeaked as I pounded into her harder, faster. Her hands brushed up my back under my shirt and I realized I was still partially clothed. Stopping only long enough to pull my shirt over my head, I went back to work on sending us both into oblivion.

Annabelle's nails dug into my back, signaling to me that she was holding on by a thread. Thank fuck. I was seconds away from exploding inside her soaking wet, almost-as-tight-as-a-virgin pussy. No sooner did her walls start contracting around me than her back arched and she started begging God for more. My jaw clenched as my balls tightened, and I went still over her. Closing my eyes, I let her quivering pussy suck the release from me.

"Anna." I whispered as I fell on top of her, her body shivering from the force of the orgasm I'd just given her.

It felt like hours later before my heartrate started to return to normal, but it was only a few minutes. Finally able to breathe again, I lifted my head, unable to keep from grinning down at the beauty I was still buried deep inside of. "Tell me the name of the last man who tasted your pussy, Anna."

Pink filled her cheeks and she turned her head to the left, avoiding my eyes. "No," she whispered in a voice roughened from screaming as she had come all over my dick.

Lowering my head, I nuzzled her ear with my nose. "Tell me the name of the last guy who put his dick in you, Anna."

"Fuck you," she muttered, still refusing to meet my gaze.

I didn't need her confirmation. I already knew the answers to my questions. It had been me to last taste her. I was the last man to touch her, taste her. Make love to her. Maybe I shouldn't have been so happy about knowing that, but I was. Brushing a soft kiss over her cheek, I pulled out of her body, making us both moan as I left her tightness. Fuck, I wanted back in there already.

Reaching for the shirt I'd taken off earlier, I used it to first wipe off the rest of my come from my dick before gently wiping away the thick, hot, white fluid that was flooding out of her wet pussy. Seeing the evidence of what I'd done on the dark shirt I'd been wearing, I bit back a curse. "I didn't use anything," I told her, lifting my eyes to hers.

Blue eyes widened and she finally met my gaze. "What?" she cried and pushed against my chest as she looked from my bare dick to the cream that was on the shirt in my hand. "You…?" She shook her head as if she couldn't even form words before shoving me back a little more. "Are you clean, Z?"

"The one thing you'll learn from working with Emmie Armstrong is that she makes her clients do random drug screenings and STD tests. I had one six months ago, and it was clean. I haven't had sex since before then, so you're safe."

Her eyes turned skeptical. "You haven't had sex in more than six months?"

I shrugged. "It's probably closer to two years, but yeah." I didn't hook up with the groupies that hung around after shows, and only went looking for some action when I couldn't fight the need for some kind of release. Every girl I'd ever hooked up with never looked anything like Annabelle, though. I couldn't handle that shit. I didn't go looking for a type, just someone that didn't remind me of her in any way.

"Whatever," she muttered and stood. I was momentarily distracted from seeing her bare ass as she walked away from me, but her next words instantly caught my attention. "I think we're safe. My period is due any day now."

Why that disappointed me, I couldn't tell you, but it did. It stung like a hornet's nest was attacking my chest.

Grabbing my jeans, I pulled out my wallet and set it on the nightstand beside the bed as Annabelle went back to her closet, keeping protection within reach this time. She started to pull out another pair of pants, but I stopped her as I crossed the room and lifted her into my arms. She slapped at my chest as I carried her back to the bed, but once I had her flat on her back once again, I made sure she didn't want to go anywhere anytime soon.

"Mieke?" I growled our daughter's name, wondering where the kid was and when she would be home. I loved spending time with my kid, but right then I wanted her as far away from that house as possible.

"She's at her test-prep study group. She won't be home until late," Annabelle said, her voice coming out breathless because I was already sucking on her berry-ripe nipples again. "She might even spend the night over at…her…Z, that feels so good…Her friend's house."

"Good." I'd make every free minute we had that night count.

Chapter Twenty Five

Annabelle

My phone was ringing from somewhere close. I reached for it blindly, hoping it was on my nightstand. Finding the noisy thing, I half lifted one lid. I'd only answer if it was Mieke, or so I promised myself. Then I saw Emmie's name flashing across the screen. Groaning, I lifted the phone to my ear.

"Hello?"

"I'm looking for Zander," Emmie said in greeting, her tone a mixture of agitation and exasperation. Even in the few weeks I'd known the chick, I knew those weren't the emotions anyone wanted to deal with when facing Emmie. "Have you seen him?"

I lowered my phone and saw the time on the screen—11:34 p.m.—before glancing at the man on the bed behind me. He was lightly snoring and his arm was anchored around my waist tightly, not letting me get more than an inch away from him. Swallowing down my curse, I lifted the phone to my ear once again. "No, I haven't seen him."

"When you do, you tell that motherfucker that I want to talk to him. Immediately." Emmie's tone was full of ice but, before I could question why, she hung up on me.

Still trying to blink sleep from my eyes, I put the phone back on the nightstand and rolled over. I cuddled against Zander for a full minute, soaking up the feel of him all around me, his heartbeat under my ear. It felt good. Right. Just like it had all those years ago when I would sleep in his arms every night, safe from the outside world.

I allowed myself only that one minute, though. Breathing in deep, I lifted my head and pushed on Z's chest. "Hey," I muttered. "Z, wake up."

His eyes didn't move, but he turned on his side, strong arms wrapping even tighter around my waist as he pulled me closer. Zander buried his face in my hair and his breathing evened out even more. I bit my lip to keep it from trembling, enjoying this moment so much that I knew when he left again it would completely eviscerate my heart this time.

Shaking my head, I shoved against his chest, harder this time. "Z, wake up." I said the words loudly, right in his ear.

Grunting, he lifted his head and looked down at me through half-open eyes. "Babe, I'm exhausted. I want you again, but give me a few more minutes of sleep. Okay?" He brushed his lips over mine in a small but nonetheless passionate kiss before lowering his head again. I didn't doubt he was exhausted. We'd made love—*no*, I quickly chastised myself, *we'd fucked*—four times before falling asleep in each other's arms around eight thirty. "Just a few more minutes, Anna."

"No. Z, you have to get up. Emmie is looking for you. She wants you to call her."

His eyes lifted a little farther this time. Seeing the seriousness on my face, he blew out a frustrated breath and reached for the phone. My phone. Leaning over me, his weight pressing me into the softness of my mattress, he swiped his thumb over the screen of the phone and lifted it to his ear. It obviously didn't take long for her to answer because Zander spoke after only a few seconds.

"Nope, not Annabelle. It's me, Em." He paused, listening to whatever his manager had to say. I couldn't hear what she was saying and I had no clue what she was telling him. His face was still relaxed, his eyes still only half open as he listened. "Yeah, I know. I told Nat I'd tell you myself, but I got distracted... Well, you know now, don't you?" Another pause and this time I could hear that Emmie's voice had risen, but I couldn't make out anything she said. The look on Zander's face told me he was getting bored with the conversation. "I don't really give a shit what the other guys want. I'm over it. Over them. This isn't even about them, Em. It's about me. I'm out. Done.... Why?" Hazel eyes looked down at me then, a smile tilting at his lips. "I need something else. Trading one dream for another."

From the phone, I could hear Emmie saying something, but Zander didn't pay her any attention. He disconnected and dropped the phone back on the stand before lowering his head and kissing me again. I was confused by the one-sided conversation I'd just heard, but any questions I might have wanted answered were quickly forgotten as I surrendered to Zander once again.

The sound of the doorbell woke me. Moaning, I pulled the covers over my head and cuddled closer to the warm body wrapped around my own. A small smile teased at my lips as I inhaled the scent I remembered all too clearly as belonging to Zander Brockman. Mixed with that slightly spicy scent was the muskiness of our lovemaking. My entire room smelled of sex, and I loved it.

Another ring of the doorbell had the smile fading before it had completely formed. Zander jerked, his arms instinctively tightening around me. A rough sigh escaped him and his lips found mine. I didn't try to fight it or him as he deepened the kiss and our hands started seeking parts of each other's bodies that we knew would start the kind of burn that would take hours to extinguish.

The third ring of the doorbell lasted longer; whoever was at my front door was pressing down and not releasing it for several long seconds. Zander pulled back, a murderous look on his face. "Isn't Mieke home? Can't she answer that damn thing?"

Glancing at the clock on my nightstand, I saw that it was after ten in the morning. Even if Mieke had come home the night before, she was probably at school by now, given that it was a Friday. Another ring of the damn bell and I was pushing the covers aside and reaching for my robe.

"Where the fuck are you going?" Zander growled as he stood and pulled on his boxers. Grabbing his shirt, he got to the bedroom door before me and blocked my exit. "I'll handle this. You get some clothes on. No way are you answering the door with nothing on but that little silky thing." He dropped a quick, hard kiss on my lips and stomped away, closing the door behind him as he started pulling his shirt over his head.

A stupid smile lifted at my lips and I rushed to put on clothes. Grabbing the first things I came to, I pulled on a bra, tank top, and running shorts that I was sure belonged to Mieke but had been mistakenly put in my dresser rather than her own. I won't lie, it was a good feeling, being able to wear the same clothes as my teenaged daughter. My ass was a little curvier than hers, but it only made the shorts hug my hips better.

Dressed, I grabbed a hair tie and headed downstairs, pulling my long blond hair into a knot on top of my head as I descended the stairs. Raised male voices stopped me halfway down and I stopped, instantly recognizing them.

"You can't just quit on us, Z," Axton Cage's voice snapped.

"We've worked through tougher shit than this, man," Liam Bryant spoke up. "I've fucked-up the most in our little family here, but don't walk away because we were dicks. Look, we're sorry. Okay? Annabelle is a great chick and she didn't deserve the way we talked about her."

"Stop being a pussy, fucker," Wroth Niall's scary voice came next. "I'm not putting up with this shit. I'm tired and want to get home. So let's settle this shit now. You aren't quitting and we're all friends again."

I frowned, the happy fog evaporating from my brain as I listened to the rockers speak to Zander. What the hell was going on? He'd quit OtherWorld? No way. I didn't believe that shit for a single second. Hurrying down the last of the stairs, I walked into the living room where four scary-looking rockers stood over Zander who was sitting on my couch, looking bored. His arms were crossed over his chest, his feet propped up on my stone coffee table, and his eyes were hazel.

Still hazel? Even with those four looking at him like they were? Even with Wroth Niall hulking up? Something was seriously off and I didn't understand a single second of it.

As I entered the living room, they all turned their heads. Seeing me, Axton stepped forward. "Annabelle, I want to say I'm sorry for the things I might have said about you. You obviously had your reasons for not telling Z about his kid and I'm going to respect that. Now, will you tell him to get his head out of his ass and stop talking about quitting the band?"

My eyes moved from the rock god to the man sitting so quietly on my couch. "You quit?" I whispered, still not sure I'd heard Axton right. Still not sure I understood anything right then. After spending the entire night with Z, my emotions were raw and scattered everywhere.

"Yup."

That was it? I asked him a question that serious and all I got was a 'yup'? I wanted to smack his sinfully sexy face. Instead I felt tears stinging my eyes as I looked back at the four angry rockers. "I don't understand what's going on. Why are you here?"

Devlin took several steps forward, the slight smile on his handsome face flashing those killer dimples at me. His aquamarine eyes were considerably calmer than the other three but he still looked concerned. "Z emailed Natalie yesterday, officially quitting OtherWorld. Asked her to make a statement to the press and all that. Apparently he got distracted last night and forgot to tell Emmie. But we don't want him to leave, Annabelle. Together we've always made OtherWorld. Without even one of us,

OtherWorld isn't the band it should be. Maybe we're all a little fucked up and we don't like each other half the time, but we're still a family."

I understood what Devlin was saying. Knew that, although OtherWorld's members weren't as close as they could have been, they did make up a bizarre kind of family. A family that had worked, even through the hard times, like when Liam had been struggling with his drug addiction. Without all of them together, OtherWorld wasn't what it should be.

That still didn't answer the one question that was burning through my brain. Why had Zander quit?

"Z?" His name came out quietly, almost afraid of his answer.

Sighing, Zander got to his feet and crossed the living room until he was standing in front of me. Cupping my face in his hands, he forced me to meet his gaze. Still hazel. A smile lifted at the corners of his lips. "I'm doing what I should have done seventeen years ago, Anna. I'm picking the one thing I want more than anything else in the world. The thing I love beyond all else."

My heart stopped. Completely. I couldn't get it to beat again as the smile turned into a grin and he lowered his head to brush a soft kiss over the tip of my nose. "I love you, Anna. I always have and I always will. I choose you. Nothing else matters. Not the band or the outside world. All I want is to be with you. To be the man you deserve, the man who will pick you over everything else that could possibly matter."

"I…" I couldn't think, couldn't speak. Couldn't. Fucking. Breathe.

"I know I'm not going to be able to prove that to you overnight, but I'm never going to stop trying. I love you, and our daughter. I want to be here with you and her. Fuck, woman, I want the life we should have had all along. Maybe you don't want that yet, but I'll go to my grave fighting for us this time." A rough thumb skimmed up and down my neck, his smile dimming a little when I didn't say a word.

It wasn't that I didn't want to. It was that I couldn't. The tears stinging my eyes started to fall and I gasped for a lungful of air as I shook my head at the man I had loved my entire life. "Okay," I whispered, unable to get anything else out.

A choked laugh left him. "Okay?" I nodded and his fingers tightened at the base of my neck. "Well, thank fuck for that." He brushed a tender kiss over my lips and lifted his head, smirking at the four men standing behind him. "See you fuckers around."

I lifted my hands to cover his, somehow finding my voice. "But only if you stay with OtherWorld."

Hazel eyes shot back to mine, not looking nearly as hazel all of a sudden. The gold started to fade, leaving nearly green orbs staring back at me. "What?"

"I'm willing to see where this goes, if you stay with the band. As your new manager, I can't let you back out of your contract. Besides, when the band has to travel, don't you want to go with me?" I grinned up at him, loving the shocked look on his face.

"You... But... Okay, explain, woman."

I nodded at the other guys, Devlin in particular. "Natalie will have to go on maternity leave soon, and she isn't going to want to come back to work right away. One of the stipulations of the contract I signed with Emmie making us equal partners is that I take over OtherWorld." I'd known I'd been signing my heart's death wish when I'd told Emmie I wanted to have the OtherWorld account the day before, but I was a glutton for punishment. Or so I'd thought. Now it didn't seem that way.

Zander frowned down at me before closing his eyes and dropping his head. Muttering a curse, he opened his eyes again several moments later. "Only for you, Anna. You understand that right now. Only for you."

I nodded, feeling happier in that moment than I had in a long time. "Okay."

"So he's not quitting?" Wroth growled.

"No," I assured the beast of a man. "He's not going anywhere."

"I go where you go," Zander muttered, making my heart skip another beat. "Don't expect anything else."

"So we're okay?" Liam was looking between Zander and me, his blue eyes concerned. "Anna Banana?"

"I'm cool with you guys," I assured him. I had no idea what Axton, Liam and Wroth had said about me. Honestly, I didn't care. It was over. The past was done. I just wanted to concentrate on the present...and maybe the future.

"Z?"

Zander glared at Liam. "Ask me again in a few days. Until then, shouldn't you be with your little Italian rocker?"

"Alexis is staying with her until I get back." Liam stepped forward, offering his hand to us. When Zander didn't look like he was going to shake it, I put mine in the rocker's hand. He smiled with relief. "I'm glad you're taking over for Nat. That works well since you're Brie's manager too."

I grinned up at him. "Go home, Liam. Tell Gabriella I'll call her." I turned to the other men in my living room. "You should all go home. Your wives will be missing you. I've got this handled."

Strong arms wrapped around my waist and Zander buried his face in my neck. "You'd fucking better believe it," he growled, kissing my neck.

One by one the four rockers left my house. I stood at the front door watching as they climbed back into the big SUV that had some huge dude in a suit behind the wheel. I assumed it was one of Seller's men. As I watched, Noah appeared and walked over to the SUV. The grin on my brother's face told me he was glad to see his old friends.

I turned my attention back to the man who still had his arms locked around me. "What are we going to tell Mieke?"

Zander frowned in thought for a long moment. "I don't know. I don't want to upset her."

"I doubt she'll be upset if we're dating. I think that was her goal all along when she went to California to see you." I knew it was something that Mieke had always wanted —for her mother and father to be together. She'd mentioned it once and only once, but I'd never forgotten it and I knew she hadn't either.

"Dating?" The gold in his eyes started to fade again. "Baby, I want to do more than date you. I'm going to marry you."

Again my heart stopped and I couldn't breathe as I stared up at Zander. Shaking his head, he grabbed my hand and tugged me away from the door, shutting and locking it behind him. Quietly, he pulled me up the stairs and into my room. Leading me over to my bed, he sat down on the edge of the mattress and pulled me onto his lap.

There wasn't a single gold fleck in his green eyes when he looked at me this time. "One day, I'm going to ask you to marry me. Not today, probably not tomorrow. When you're ready. When I've proven to you that you mean more to me than anything—anything, Anna. Only then will I ask you to be my wife." He grimaced. "I wish I had Gram's old ring."

I felt the pink that filled my cheeks as I glanced toward the small jewelry box on my dresser. "You do," I whispered. I'd stopped wearing the promise ring when Michelle had died, had even contemplated burying it with my little girl. In the end I hadn't been able to completely let the little gold ring go.

Zander followed my gaze. "Then one day I'll put it on your finger—the finger it belongs on. But only when I know you're ready."

"Z…"

"Shh," he murmured, kissing my lips to keep anything I might have said locked away. "We still have a few hours before our daughter gets home, Anna. Let's not waste them."

Annabelle

If one more thing went wrong that day I was going to scream. Like, throw down everything in my arms, stomp my feet and scream. I could even imagine myself rolling on the floor in one of the tantrums Mieke had been known to give me on rare occasions when she was a toddler. Right then I felt like I had the emotional stability of a frigging toddler, so I felt like I was entitled to it.

From the time I'd woken up that morning I'd known it was going to be a shitty day. My alarm had gone off and when I'd turned over to snuggle into Zander for a few extra minutes, I'd realized he was gone and had been gone for a while since the bed was cool. Pouting, I'd gotten ready for the zillion and one things that needed my attention that day and went into the kitchen for some coffee and a slice of toast.

We were back in California for the holidays because both Emmie and I were busy as hell with all the new clients we were signing on, plus getting our staff trained and eleven million other things. It was nice staying in Zander's penthouse apartment, but the three of us were used to the room of my house back in Tennessee. Mieke and her father had been grumbling the night before over dinner about it and Zander had even hinted at looking at houses while we were still in California. I didn't know what to think. Why would we want to look at houses there when we spent most of our time back in Tennessee?

Not that I was against it or anything, I was just curious. Two houses seemed a little excessive to me.

After my first drink of coffee, I'd ended up pouring the rest of the mug's contents down the drain. It had tasted bitter to me and when I'd tried to eat the toast, my gag reflex had sent me rushing to the sink to empty the contents of my dinner from the previous evening. After cleaning myself up again, I'd felt better and had gone into work.

Emmie had found us some office space in L.A. and we had an entire floor to ourselves. She'd already set up my office for me while I'd been in Tennessee and I was really happy with how it had turned out. So far she'd added fifteen people to our staff while I'd recruited three to help me back in Nashville.

As soon as I'd sat down at my desk, my cell in one hand trying to find out where Zander and Mieke had run off to that morning, the phone on my desk had started ringing and hadn't stopped for over an hour. Emmie was in and out of my office and we had six different meetings in the conference room by lunchtime.

One particular meeting had set me off, because I was fed up with dealing with Tasha Vowel's diva attitude. I'd gone off on her and thankfully Emmie had backed me up when I'd point blank told the singer that we wouldn't be renewing her contract after all. The bitch had left in a huff, but not before she'd gotten a tongue lashing from Emmie. I'd taken a sick kind of pleasure in seeing the embarrassment on my ex-client's face as she'd stepped into the elevator.

Emmie ordered lunch, which brought back my queasy stomach and I locked myself in my office until the smells went away. After lunch, Emmie left me to the rest of the work that was piled up on my desk. She was having a Christmas party at her house that night and everyone was invited. Even Noah and Chelsea had brought their kids out to the West Coast so that Mieke and I wouldn't have to miss the holidays with them.

My queasiness stayed with me for most of the afternoon, making me short-tempered, and the fifteen or so people running around the floor learned real quick to steer clear of me. While I was glad that they avoided me, I didn't want them to think that one of their bosses was a tyrant to be afraid of.

Around four that afternoon I finally got a text from Mieke telling me she was out with her cousins as well as Jenna Stevenson and Lucy Thornton. She said she would meet me at Emmie's house at eight. Apparently she was doing some Christmas shopping. I didn't worry about her, knowing that Lucy Thornton's bodyguard would keep my baby girl safe.

There were still no messages from Zander though, and that bugged me more than I knew it should. It wasn't like I didn't know I'd see him that night, and since we'd gotten back together in September, we'd basically been inseparable. I saw him throughout the day, every day. Even when I didn't get to see him as often as I wanted, he texted me religiously and even sent me flowers at the small office I now had in Nashville every Friday.

I didn't know why I was feeling so hurt over not seeing him or hearing from him all day, though. It was stupid. Maybe it was just because I was feeling sick and emotional. Whatever. I wouldn't let it make me feel insecure. Our relationship was a strong one. He told me he loved me every day and he was always doing things to make me feel special, proving to me just as he had promised, that I meant more to him than anything else in the world.

It hadn't been easy, finding our way back to the place in our relationship where we were at now. I'd had some days where I was so happy that we were back together. Some days, however, I'd been full-on pissed at the world that it had taken us this long to have our happily ever after. I tried not to think about the past—the wasted years we'd been apart—and for the most part I succeeded. But those few days that I didn't—couldn't—put the years we spent apart behind me, those days had kind of made us stronger. Zander knew that on those days I needed some extra TLC, and he always gave it to me. He always did something that made me realize that the past didn't matter. All that mattered was right now.

We were happy, all three of us. Even Mieke seemed happier than I'd ever seen her and I was so glad that she was enjoying having her dad around. Then again, what girl wouldn't want their father around if all he did was spoil her rotten? It had only been a few months since Zander had been in Mieke's life, but from the way those two adored each other no one would ever know that.

Thinking of what an amazing father Z was turning into, I finally felt a smile teasing at my lips. Finally getting over my bitchy mood, I gathered my things and left the office. It was getting late and I still had to get back to the apartment and change before going out to Malibu for Emmie's party.

I was just getting out of the shower when another wave of queasiness washed over me and I felt slightly lightheaded. Alone in the apartment, I was momentarily scared as I sat down on the closed toilet seat and waited for the dizziness to pass. With a shaky hand, I reached for my cell where I'd left it on the sink. My fingers trembling, I pulled up Zander's name and hit connect.

It went straight to voicemail just as I was swallowing back another wave of nausea. Fuck, what was wrong with me? There wasn't a bug going around and even if there was I'd have been surprised if I'd caught it. I rarely got ill, but there was always a first for everything.

After several minutes the dizziness passed and I wondered if I should just call Emmie and tell her I couldn't make it. I didn't want to get anyone else sick if I really did have a bug, yet at the same time I didn't want to miss out on the fun. This Christmas party was important to Emmie and her family, and now that she considered me a part of her family, I wanted to be there.

The Rocker Who Betrays Me

Sighing, I reached for my hairdryer, determined to make it to the party.

With my hair done and a nice green dress on, I finished up my makeup. Putting on just a little gloss, I nearly jumped out of my skin when my cell buzzed. It was a text from Mieke and I smiled at the goofy picture of my daughter that was in my messages. She was standing with her new friends and cousins in front of a Christmas tree in Emmie's living room.

Shaking my head, I closed my texts and briefly saw the date on the screen along with the time. It didn't immediately hit me, but for some reason I glanced back down at the date…

Holy shit.

Zander

She was running late and I was running out of nerves. I knew if I'd looked in a mirror right then I'd see that my eyes were complete green. It was probably why most of my bandmates were sticking to the opposite sides of the room. Even Emmie was shooting me strange, questioning looks that I tried to ignore.

Stuffing my hands into the dress pants I'd decided to wear, instead of the usual jeans I preferred, I glared out the glass wall that looked at the Pacific Ocean. With all the lights on in the huge living room, I couldn't see the crashing waves as they hit the beach, but I knew they were there. They mimicked the feelings crashing through me right at that moment.

Was it too soon? Was I moving things too fast? Had I been suffocating her?

The questions kept coming, each one of them sending my fucked-up head into even deeper chaos. I was probably moving too fast, but Annabelle had seemed happy over the last several months. She smiled all the time, laughed like she was the happiest she'd ever been in her life. When I wrapped my arms around her at night and pulled her close, she would cuddle against me and breathe me in deeply as if she never wanted our connection to end.

I'd promised her I'd wait until I knew she was ready, until I'd proven to her fully that she was my world and nothing else except her mattered. I wasn't sure if I'd done that yet. Fuck, it had only been a few months. It could take years before she was truly ready for a bigger commitment with me. Yet there I was, stressing over what I wanted to do right at that second.

Soft, warm hands touched my arm and I relaxed a little as I wrapped my arm around Mieke's slender shoulders. "Any word from your mom?"

"I sent her a text about an hour ago, Daddy. Relax. She's just running a little late. Everything is going to be alright, okay?" She reached up and kissed my cheek, squeezing my hand as she did so.

Mieke was the only one who knew what was going on, the only one who knew why I was acting like the crazy man I'd always been accused of being. There were no smiles from me that night; no making others laugh. I was lost in my own head and I would stay lost until I had Annabelle in my arms again.

"There you are!" I heard Emmie call out with a laugh and turned to find her stepping away from a small group that included Nik, Axton, and Dallas.

She hugged the newcomer before stepping back and my breath froze in my lungs at the breathtaking sight of Annabelle in the green dress and black ballet slippers. She looked perfect, but there was something in her sky-blue eyes that told me she wasn't feeling well.

I dropped a kiss on top of Mieke's head without glancing at her and moved across the living room toward the only thing that brought me peace. She was talking in a quiet tone with Emmie but quickly closed her mouth when she saw me coming toward her.

The little redhead faded away, probably going back to her husband as I reached Annabelle and wrapped her tightly in my arms. Her hair was pulled back into a sexy little up-do thing and I buried my face in her neck, inhaling her clean, delicious scent like a dying man taking his last breath. I felt her shiver and couldn't help the way my body hardened for her.

"Hey, stranger," she murmured with a little sass in her tone.

I pulled back just enough to see her beautiful face. "Hey. Miss me today?"

"More than you will ever realize." She lifted a hand to cup the left side of my face and I was surprised to see her fingers trembling. "There's something I have to tell you."

Everything inside of me froze. The look in her eyes was full of a fear I didn't understand mixed with worry and maybe a little bit of excitement. "Tell me," I rasped out, terrified of what was going to leave that mouth I loved to kiss.

"I love you," she breathed, making my heart stop for two full seconds before it started pounding against my ribs once more.

In the time we'd been back together, I'd told this woman every day how much I loved her, but she hadn't once repeated those three little words. I'd been feeling the loss of them, but knew that I had to earn them back. Hearing them now, I felt like she was offering me the world on a silver platter. It was everything I've ever wanted wrapped up in her silky voice.

"I love you, too." My voice was choked with emotion and my eyes stung with tears that I didn't try to hold back. "I love you so damn much,

Anna." I pulled the little present I'd been playing with in my pocket all day out and offered it to her. "Merry Christmas, baby."

She started to say something else but then looked down at the little box I'd placed in her hand. Her mouth snapped shut and she carefully pulled the little silver ribbon free before opening it.

Around us, everyone went completely silent. I didn't even think the babies in the room were whining anymore as all eyes turned to Annabelle as she pulled the gold band from the little box. It wasn't the ring that Gram had given me for Annabelle's seventeenth birthday, but it would match it when I slipped that little wedding band on her finger the day I married her.

That is, if she accepted this particular gold band with the five-carat princess-cut diamond that Mieke had helped me pick out earlier that week.

I watched Annabelle closely, watching for her reaction, needing to know if I'd just fucked everything up or made us whole again. Tears filled her eyes and her chin trembled. One large tear spilled from first her left eye and another followed from her right. They came slowly at first but soon were pouring out of her gorgeous eyes. Lifting her tear-filled eyes from the ring in her hand, she turned them on me, questioningly.

I cleared my throat twice before I could get it to work so I could speak. "I've been losing my mind for the last month, baby. I don't mean to rush you. I've promised you I'll give you as long as you need and won't stop until I've proven to you how much you mean to me. None of that has changed, and if you say no now, I'm not going to give up. Fuck, babe, I don't ever want to let you go. Please, I love you so damn much. Will you marry me?"

"Z..." she breathed, shaking her head. It felt like a lead ball fell into the pit of my stomach, and I fought back a wave of despair and pain. Then she laughed, a happy almost bell-like sound that echoed throughout the room, and she threw her arms around me. "Yes, Z. Yes."

I didn't hear the cheers or the claps or even the congratulations as they filled the room from our friends and family. All I heard was her soft sob of yes as she buried her face in my chest and held onto me like I was her lifeline. I held onto her for several long minutes. No one dared to approach us as we soaked up that moment of pure joy.

After a while, Annabelle lifted her head and smiled shakily at me. "I still need to talk to you."

"So talk," I encouraged, wiping away her tears with my thumbs. Nothing she had to say could dim the high I had rushing through my veins right then. I had everything that I wanted, everything that I would cherish right there in my arms.

Annabelle bit her lip and looked down at the ring still sitting in the box for a moment before slowly lifting her eyes again. "I think I'm pregnant," she whispered so softly I nearly didn't hear her.

The words and their meaning hit me dead center in the chest, and for a moment I couldn't breathe. When at last I was able to suck in a deep breath, I wrapped my arms around the woman I loved and swung her around twice, kissing her tear-salted lips as I laughed with a happiness that went soul deep. If I'd thought I couldn't be any happier after having her say she would marry me, I was wrong.

If she was pregnant —and somehow I could almost feel that she was — I would be the happiest man who walked the Earth. I would get to watch her stomach grow with our child this time around. This time she wouldn't have to go through a single second without me beside her. I would love our baby more than any father had ever loved his child.

That didn't mean I would love Mieke any less. Nothing could ever make me love my daughter any less. She was the stars in my sky while her mother was my moon, both of them lighting up the darkness I'd been living in for most of my life. Another baby would only make our family complete.

"You're happy?" Annabelle murmured when I set her on her feet again.

I kissed the tip of her nose. "Happiest man in the world, Anna. I love you, baby."

Her face softened. "I love you too, Z."

Playlist

"Outcast" by Shinedown
"State of my Head" by Shinedown
"Broken" by Seether (ft. Amy Lee)
"Let Me Go" by Avril Lavigne (ft. Chad Kroeger)
"Breaking Inside" by Shinedown (ft. Lzzy Hale)
"If You Only Knew" by Shinedown
"Call Me" by Shinedown
"Like I'm Gonna Lose You" by Meghan Trainor (ft. John Legend)
"Ashes Of Eden" by Breaking Benjamin
"Burn With Me" by Amaranthe
"Let It Go" by James Bay
"Fire N Gold" by Bea Miller
"Poison" by Rita Ora
"Say You Love Me" by Jessie Ware
"Let Your Tears Fall" by Kelly Clarkson
"Sorry" by Art of Dying
"What Sober Couldn't Say" by Halestorm
"Last Regret" by Casey Donovan

MORE BY TERRI ANNE BROWNING

THE ROCKER SERIES
Book 1: The Rocker Who Holds Me
Book 2: The Rocker Who Savors Me
Book 3: The Rocker Who Needs Me
Book 4: The Rocker Who Loves Me
Book 5: The Rocker Who Holds Her
Book 6: The Rockers' Babies
Book 7: The Rocker Who Wants Me
Book 8: The Rocker Who Cherishes Me
Book 9: The Rocker Who Shatters Me
Book 10: The Rocker Who Hates Me
Book 11: The Rocker Who Betrays Me

THE ANGELS SERIES
Book 1: Angel's Halo
Book 2: Entangled
Book 3: Guardian Angel

THE LUCY AND HARRIS SERIES
Book 1: Catching Lucy

Reckless With Their Hearts
Reese: A Safe Haven Novella

You can follow Terri Anne Browning here:
www.facebook.com/writerchic27
www.twitter.com/AuthorTERRIANNE
www.terriannebrowning.com

Coming Soon!
The Rocker Series continues with its final book, **Forever Rockers**.

Now turn the page for exclusive sneak peeks into two awesome books.
Blood & Loyalties by Ryan Michele
Jag by Stevie J. Cole

BLOOD & LOYALTIES
By
Ryan Michele

CHAPTER 1—CATARINA

"You stupid fucking bitch!" Antonio seethed like a pussy as he looked up from the filthy-ass floor of the bar, holding his throbbing crotch.

I laughed, tossing my head back for good measure. Bitch was the worst he could come up with? I had been called worse than that at work when I lost a client's millions on a bum deal.

I lifted the pointed heel of my black, stiletto boot and plowed it hard into his windpipe, crushing it as he gasped for breath, his eyes wide with fear. He needed to be taught a lesson about fucking over a Lambardoni. It didn't come without repercussions, and I wanted to be the one to teach him.

Unfortunately, I knew my bodyguards had called my brother Val. They always did when shit with me happened, and if I didn't get on with it, Val would ruin all my fun. I was more than capable of handling this weak, pathetic asshole. Val should know that. He and my other brother D had trained me to fight and shoot a target with precision, but something about being "the sister" gave them the right to be overprotective and overbearing, even if I was older than both of them.

As I removed my foot, one of his hands wrapped around his throat as the other continued to grip his aching crotch. The stupid fucker didn't know whether to grab his balls or neck, his arms flailing in both directions as he rolled from side to side, trying to ease the pain. He gasped for breath, the look of confusion in his eyes laughable. I did pack one hell of a powerful knee thrust, though. No doubt his balls were shoved so deep inside he could taste them in his mouth.

Wicked thoughts crept in my head. Using my best weapon of the moment—the hot ass boots my cousin Kiera had insisted I wear for the night—I picked a spot on his rib cage and began kicking it over and over, plowing into him, hoping like hell the blows would crack the fuckers. It was the least he deserved.

I moved with him at each turn he tried to make, hitting him dead in the same spot. He grunted and attempted to bat my foot away with his hands as he tried to hold himself at the same time. His less than stealthy attempts only made him look like a bigger pansy-assed bitch. It was amazing how much actual joy I felt from watching him struggle.

He tried to curl up in the fetal position, the dirt from the floor coating his clothes and both sides of his face. He groaned, taking each hit, but it didn't feel like enough. The fucker didn't even have the balls to really fight back.

"Catarina, what the hell happened?" Kiera said loudly at my side, trying to compensate for the music blaring in the distance. She was my cousin, best friend, and pretty much sister in every way that counts. Regardless, my focus stayed on the fucker on the floor as I stepped farther back from his withering body.

When Kiera and I had decided to come out to the club to let off some steam from a brutal week at work, I hadn't realized I would be getting a hefty workout like this instead of on the dance floor.

I stared down at the man I'd thought loved me, who had said I was the one for him. The *only* one. Stupid. I should have known by now that the only reason men found any interest in me was because of my father and family. Each one seemed to want that pivotal "in" to the business, and for some reason, they thought I could get it for them.

I knew Antonio wanted to move up in the ranks with his family, but it wasn't in the cards for him. That right there should have been a huge red flag for me, but I had trusted him when he told me if he couldn't move up in his own family, he didn't want to move up at all.

Lies. All fucking lies. One would think I had learned this lesson after twenty-nine years on this earth, but I kept falling for it: hook, line, and sinker. The word sucker was plastered on my fucking forehead, and the life that I craved so much was completely unobtainable. Not anymore. This would be it. This fucker would be the absolute last.

Being the daughter of a very powerful man came with a stiff price, the biggest being whom to trust, which I had learned—mostly the hard way— wasn't many. Family was about the only ones I could, and damn if that didn't suck ass with finding a love life.

Even women had proved too scarce in the honesty department. Most wanting to fuck my brothers rather than actually get to know me. That was why Kiera and I had stuck together over the years. It was safer for everyone. No one else understood this life.

I wasn't and never had been a weak person. Growing up in the Lambardoni family, it wasn't an option. Between my father, uncle, brothers, and cousins, both Kiera and I had been taught with an iron fist—a loving iron fist—but still, a strong-gripping fist.

Glancing down at the floor, I couldn't believe I had wasted my time on this man. I would have to thank my brother Dominic—D—for teaching me kickboxing. It proved handy, even if my technique was shit at the moment, but it was kind of hard to really show technique when the guy was on the ground.

The asshole growling under my feet thought he could profess his undying love for me and then go fuck some blonde whore in the bathroom. Mistake. Big mistake.

When he told me he was going to get drinks then headed in the opposite way of the bar, every flag in my head stood to alert. Val had taught me how to observe one's surroundings, promising me it would come in handy one day, and that day was definitely one of them.

Throughout Val's teachings, my eyes became sharper in viewing my surroundings and noticing key things that were out of place: a car parked somewhere it shouldn't be or a person walking a bit to closely. I'd see it, and it would keep me on my toes.

Realizing Antonio turned down the hallway in his quest for drinks, I'd motioned for my full-time guard, Scraper—yes, that was his name—to follow him. He took off, only to report back minutes later that Antonio had a piece of ass in the women's bathroom.

The pained expression on Scraper's face sent me into action. I knew it was pained because of the betrayal to me, and I would be putting Antonio's ass on a stick.

I rushed through the crowd with Scraper on my heels, trying to get through the crush of people. I knew Scraper would stay out of the confrontation until or if he needed to intervene. He had been my guard for the past six years, and while at first we couldn't stand the sight of each other, he'd grown on me over the years. After growing up together, I even liked him, and he knew when to step back and let me take the lead so I could prove myself capable to my family, which was a must.

I'd caught a glimpse through the crack in the door of that piece of shit, confirming he was in fact balls deep in pussy that wasn't mine, and then I waited. I was exceptionally patient, one of my many redeeming qualities. As I stood back in the shadows of the darkened, narrow hallway that led to the bathroom, I tried reining in my anger. It would get me nowhere and cause me to make stupid mistakes. Having a clear head was the only way to go. Hurt had already gone out the damn window. There was no need for that or any other emotion.

Scraper had stayed on the other side as my back-up. He knew the fucker had to pay, exactly as I did. It would actually just be the start of his repercussions. Once my brothers, cousins, and—God help him—father and uncle heard, he would get a hell of a lot worse than what I was about to dish out. It was probably demented, but I was actually happy about that.

After the blonde whore left, swaying her fake ass down the hallway, Antonio came strutting out like the cat who got his mouse. There had been a wide smile across his face and even a bead of sweat on his brow. Before he could see me, I'd lifted my knee with every ounce of power I could muster in my five-foot-ten body and kneed him in his balls. He hunched over, and I helped him to the floor by kicking his legs out from under him. He plummeted to the ground hard, his shoulder taking the weight of the fall. Stupid fuck.

"Just handling some trash. Caught him fucking some blond in the bathroom," I said to Kiera, whose beautiful face turned glacial in seconds. The smooth skin around her eyes narrowed with lines as she released a heavy breath.

Kiera lifted the her heel of her beautiful, hot pink pumps and smashed them into Antonio's nose, causing blood to splatter at my feet and across the floor. I had been going for no blood, but shit happened.

"Dammit, I just got these boots, too." I pretended to whine, stomping my foot for added emphasis. In actuality, I couldn't give a shit. I would go buy new ones tomorrow.

Never in my life had I wanted for anything, but don't think for a moment that I hadn't worked for every penny of it. In my family, you learned very early on everything you got, you worked hard for. Your blood, sweat, and tears went into every dollar you spent; hence, why Kiera and I wanted a fun night out, hoping to get a reprieve from life. Life had other ideas, though.

"We'll shop tomorrow," Kiera spat down on Antonio as he started shrieking nasty names at us. Some in Italian, some in English. I ignored him as I hacked up a wad and spit it down on his worthless body.

Spitting on someone in my family was the formal yet disgusting sign of a person being dead to you. If someone was trash and unworthy of you, you spit. It was pretty damn gross, but people understood it and normally asked no questions once it was done. If they did, they were more than likely going to get the shit beat out of them again. In Antonio's case, I hoped he would, just for fun.

"All right, ladies. It's done." Scraper slid up to us and rested his hands on our shoulders, giving a slight, comforting squeeze.

I wasn't quite ready to give it up. The tension in my body was still wound tight and needed release, but I looked over to Kiera who nodded in agreement, deflating my plans.

Kiera was always my voice of reason. It was why we worked so well together. We complimented each other to a T.

"The boys will be here soon to clean up. Let's go get you ladies a drink," Scraper said with another squeeze as we stepped farther back, and I tried to pull out of my tension.

Antonio tried hard to stand, his feet and knees wobbling underneath him as he groaned in pain with each movement. He was able to partially get up, but he was bent at the waist and kept shifting from one foot to the other, like either one he chose hurt too much to put his full weight on.

"I'll fucking kill you for this bitch!" Antonio snapped at me. He didn't seem to understand the concept of '*you just got your ass handed to you, so shut the fuck up.*'

Scraper pulled both Kiera and I behind him then landed a hard punch to Antonio's jaw. The loud crack echoed through the hall, even over all the boisterous music playing. Antonio's eyes rolled into the back of his head as he fell onto the floor, his head landing with an audible thud on the tile. His body was unmoving from what I hoped was just being passed out. I didn't need to explain this man's death to my father or uncle.

"Come. Now," Scraper commanded, looking down at the piece of shit. "Or else a bullet goes through the fucker's head."

I rolled my eyes. While I knew he would totally do it, I also knew he would pick a more discreet location than right by the bathroom in a bar. Too many witnesses. Even though no one was around us at the moment, a gunshot would surely bring everyone running.

"Let me wash up." I didn't wait for a response from either of them, entering the bathroom to clean off Antonio once and for all. I hated having Antonio's blood on me in any way, even on my shoes.

Months of my life were wasted on that piece of shit, time I would never get back. I sighed, wishing things had been different. I thought he might have actually been *the one*. Who was I shitting? The one, my ass. He didn't exist for me.

After I was done, I stepped out of the bathroom to a waiting Kiera and Scraper.

"Come on, girl. I'm thirsty." I needed to get something inside of me to calm the hyped up feeling I had coursing through my veins. Love it or hate it, the crash from adrenaline usually sucked, and I wanted to be drunk when it happened. Forgetting seeing Antonio and that whore fucking was an added bonus.

"I bet you are," Kiera giggled, grabbing my arm and pulling me back up to the VIP section.

Scraper led the way up the side stairs, but I could feel Dune and Case behind us. They were Kiera's guards. She had two because of the whole being the daughter of the great Vino Lambardoni thing. We each had two other guards who we called Ghost One and Ghost Two. We had met them there, but they hid in the shadows, only coming out when necessary, which was seldom. They were there yet not there. It was eerie in a way, but we got used to it like everything else.

I couldn't remember a time in my life when she and I hadn't had guards of some sort tailing our every movement. Most would say it wasn't normal, but what the hell was normal, anyway? Our fathers did it for our safety, and we accepted that. Although I'm not saying back in the day we hadn't tried to ditch them and escape the confines of our fathers.

I laughed thinking about it. We had been so dumb and had no understanding of what kinds of threats were out there for us. We were honest to God lucky nothing had happened to us.

Music thumped through the large speakers while men and women shook their asses and everything else they had on the dance floor below us. All of them were oblivious to what just occurred in the back of the bar, which was perfect, easier to clean up. It was also a sure sign life went on even in the midst of someone's mistakes.

Scraper led us to the plush red velvet chairs with the white trim in our closed off room. We took a seat in the dimly lit space where glass mirrored walls lined the front, allowing a great view of the bar and dance floor.

The waitress with her tight red and white shirt and barely there black shorts approached hastily after we were seated. "What can I get ya, ladies?"

The perkiness of the woman's voice made me want to wretch. I had been a lot of things in my life, but perky was not one of them, and I was seriously not in the mood for a bubbly cheerleader. I let it go, however, ignoring it.

"Shots!" Both Kiera and I said together then smiled, looking at each other knowingly. I loved how we could always read each other's minds. Sometimes it was a bit scary when we could do it from across the room.

"Patrón, please. Just bring the bottle, glasses, and limes," I said.

She nodded, rushing off down the stairs with Dune's eyes latched on to her ass. Men.

Kiera leaned back in the chair, her eyes flickering around, surveying our surroundings. She had a radiant beauty about her. Her long, chestnut brown hair in a shade or two different than my own flowed down her back. She had brown eyes with golden specks flashing inside of them, so different than my bluish-green eyes. She drew in any man she wanted, but rarely did she take a guy up on his propositions. She was happy with herself just the way she was, and I loved her dearly.

With Scraper at the entrance of the VIP area, Dune and Case made themselves at home on the other side of the small space, leaning against the wall, mirroring each other with arms crossed over their chests.

The Rocker Who Betrays Me

We loved having our own area up here. It gave us the opportunity to dance when we wanted and then get away without anyone bothering us unless we wanted them to. It was no secret who we were—personally or professionally—but neither of us ever let that shit go to our heads.

"Antonio had the fucking balls to screw some chick while he was here with you?" Kiera broke the silence between us, obviously not done talking about what had happened. In truth, I wasn't done, either. I needed to get shit out and calm the hell down.

I chuckled even though I didn't find any part of it a bit funny; it was just what came out with an evil death twinge to it. "Stupid, huh? And he must have set it up ahead of time because he wanted to make it quick. There's no way he just picked this chick up tonight. He was in there less than five minutes. I should feel bad for the woman, but I don't. He never could keep it up long. Loser," I growled with the laughter. He always had been fast to the punch, but it was one of those things I'd overlooked.

"I thought you said he was good in bed?" She raised her eyebrow in question, staring at me. I had never lied to Kiera and never would.

I shrugged. "Define good. He made me come. Was it mind-blowing? Fuck no, but he made me feel good, told me I was beautiful, blah, blah, blah. He acted like he wasn't afraid of my dad or brothers beating the shit out him, but who the hell knows?" I wondered if all of that was a lie, too. More than likely, yes.

"Dumbass. He should have worried about you," Kiera said with another slight giggle.

She had seen my handiwork over the years. Some of it was a bit overdone, but I always had a purpose, like tonight. I wasn't one of those women who were lovers and not fighters. While I wanted to be, I was more the opposite. I always blamed it on my brothers because I sure as shit didn't want to blame myself.

"No shit there." I laughed for real this time. Everyone, including my family sometimes, underestimated me. It worked out in my favor, though. I was a snake—lethal when you pissed me off and would strike when you least expected it. "What a fucking pussy. Did you see him?" I rolled my eyes, waving my hand, unable to help myself. "I didn't realize how big of one he was until tonight." Antonio didn't come off to me like that for all the months I had known him. He had always been a standup guy, even to my father. It was like he did a one-eighty.

"Sorry, babe." Her arm snaked around my shoulders, and she pulled me to her side, giving me a squeeze as I leaned into her comforting touch. The compassion she gave me filled my heart.

If anything, I knew I would always have her by my side. We might grow old and grey together because no man had the balls to step up to either of our fathers, but we would have each other.

The waitress flounced back into the room, setting glasses full of clear liquid, the bottle, and a bowl of limes onto the small table in front of us. Kiera released me, leaned over, and handed me a shot while taking one for herself. Then she held it high in the air, and I followed. She was clearly in a toasting mood tonight. Fine by me.

"To one day finding Mr. Right who loves to eat pussy and not be one!"

I laughed hard at her words, clinking my glass to hers and watching the clear liquid sway around the glass. We tossed back the shot in unison, and I felt the burn race down my throat then splash into my stomach. I sucked on a lime and squinted at the sourness on my tongue, already thinking it was time for another.

If anything, Kiera's love life was worse than mine when it came to her family. With her dad—my Uncle Vino—being the head of the family, guys flocked to her, too, but their main goal was to be with the boss's daughter, marry her, and then take over the business. At least with my dad as second in command, it wasn't as bad.

Who was I fucking kidding? We were both doomed.

Several shots and some serious lime sucking later, our laughter billowed all around us. My body relaxed, and the tension from *the asshole* melted away.

I scanned the joint, seeing if there were any potential men in the crowd—hey, I was a free woman now—but none were calling to me. Maybe it was just me. Getting laid had never been the problem; it was all the other shit in my life that came into play. After the night I'd had, I wasn't feeling it all that much.

There might not be potential men, but that was a moot point as my brother Val, his best friend Ace, and a man I had never seen before—but holy hell would like to see more of—entered the VIP section. I breathed out deeply and quickly turned away from the handsome man, my body fluttering merely being in the same room as him.

What was wrong with me? Men didn't do this to me. Ever. My eyes connected with my brothers, whose tight brows, sky blue eyes glaring, and thin-lined mouth told me he was pissed as shit. Too damn bad. I was too drunk to care.

"What mess did you get yourself into this time?" Val asked in a clipped tone. Most people would probably fall at his feet and pray for mercy or cower in a corner at that tone. Me? Not so much.

The Rocker Who Betrays Me

Being my younger brother by two years, he thought it was his job to protect me. For some reason, he thought he was the older sibling and took the overprotective brother thing to another level. Too bad he was wrong.

Val and I were almost carbon copies of each other, with the same dark hair and golden-toned skin. The only difference was Val had blue eyes, while I had ones that were sometimes blue and sometimes green. It simply depended on the lighting. Even with his more rough and demanding features, no one would mistake that we were siblings.

I waved him off, flicking my hand in the air because nothing would tap down his anger. It was too raw in his eyes. Whenever something went badly that involved me, he had serious issues. God love him, but he needed to calm the hell down.

I leaned back in the chair and took a sip of the cranberry juice and patron I'd had the waitress bring a while ago. "Scraper's handling the cleanup. No big deal," I told him. It was over and done with, and Scraper had guys taking care of the rest.

"Bullshit. That asshole fucks some bitch in a bathroom while he's dating *my*"—he pointed his finger to his chest and pressed firmly for emphasis—"sister. I'll handle this shit," he growled deeply, the veins in his head throbbing and his face turning beet red. He was seriously going to have a heart attack before he reached thirty at this rate. He needed to relax and not let this shit get to him so bad.

"No need. He learned his lesson. If he didn't and comes after me, I'll take care of it." I took another drink, feeling maybe a little bit cocky, letting the liquid bounce to my stomach, but by then it didn't give me any aftereffects.

I had every bit of confidence in myself that I would be able to handle whatever situation came up. Even drunk, I could deal.

"Hey, Val," Kiera greeted, breaking up the thick tension that was spiraling out of control from my brother. "Take a breath, boy."

Kiera was my age, only younger by three months, but that didn't matter with her brothers, either. She dealt with this same shit, so she understood. She normally would have a calming effect on my brother, which she had on most people, but not so much this time.

Val turned to Kiera with the same fury, but he lightened up just a tad. "Kiera, your dad's gonna be pissed you're in this shit." He pointed at both of us with a hostile glare, his eyes darting between the two of us. "You know he's part of the Capella family."

Since rolling my eyes at him and yelling duh was way too immature, I decided against it. "No shit, Sherlock. I don't care." It was my turn to growl at my brother. Family was family. If the Capella's had a problem, they could deal with their own fuck-up of a member. Not my problem.

"There's a meeting in a few days with Remeo. This will not go well." Val shook his head, grabbing the back of his neck. Remeo was the head of Antonio's family.

"It's not my fault his dick didn't stay in his pants. He got what he deserved." He had, but I was sure I would hear from my father about this and maybe Uncle Vino. However, I wouldn't change what I had done to that sorry ass. I was only a little pissed at myself for allowing him to leave with his balls still intact.

"Dammit, you think I don't know that? I just hate this drama shit." I couldn't see any of the men in my life being pissed at me. If anything, they would rip Antonio apart, so I was in the clear for the most part. Business-wise, I didn't work alongside any of them to know what that outcome would be.

"Hi, Ace." I winked at the man who's been by my brother's side since we were kids.

"Hey, babe. How you been?" Ace's sexy voice fell over the room as he slowly walked closer to me.

I wouldn't deny for a second that I found Ace dreamy as shit. With his dark hair, deep chocolate eyes, and a body built like an Italian rock, I throbbed every time I saw the man. Problem was, he had a girl and had since high school—Beth.

"Great. Who's your friend?" I nodded toward him, sweeping my gaze over to the man with sharp denim eyes boring holes right through me, sending shivers down my spine.

Now Ace was hot, but this guy tipped the hot-o-meter by another twenty plus. Broad shoulders pulled his V-neck, black shirt tight, showing every ripple underneath of muscular perfection and giving a glimpse of a slight dusting of dark chest hair. Not the long kind, but the kind that looks like he cut it short, and it was sexy as hell. Tattoos lined his arms and snuck under the sleeves of his shirt, making my mouth water from wanting to lick up and down every muscle. His face was like something chiseled from a damn sculpture, and his beard and slight stash made my thighs quiver. I wouldn't mind a little rug burn.

"This is Jag."

Jag's eyes continued to set me on fire as they raked up and down my body, taking in every inch of me. I was not a small woman, but I had been told my curves were what set me apart from others. All ass and tits, one man had told me. Even better, I loved every one of them.

"You done eye-fucking me?" I boldly asked, smirking, before hearing my brother's exasperated sigh beside me.

"Not yet." His deep baritone voice glided over my skin like a silky glove just waiting to slide on. His terse words caused every sense in my body to come to full alert, and the hair rose on the back of my neck like a shock wave. My heart pounded in my chest, but I kept my breathing slow, not allowing any signs show.

"No, she's my sister. Off limits," my brother said.

I turned and glared at him, standing with my hip cocked and my hand resting on it. "Don't you dare, Val. No wonder the only men I hook up with are fucking douches."

My brother gave nothing except fury at my words that had never been truer. I could name five guys off the top of my head whom Val had played a role in making disappear from my life, and I'd had enough.

Val stepped in my space, getting close to my face, his hot breath bouncing off my nose. "What the hell is that supposed to mean? I told your ass to get rid of Antonio as soon as I heard you were dating him."

I stared, my nostrils flaring in rebellion, clenching my fists at my sides. Not the most attractive sight, but it got my don't-fuck-with-me vibe going. The sad thing was, it hadn't intimidated him since we were kids, but I refused to be walked over.

"I was hoping it would work. I was wrong. Better I learned that for my damn self instead of my overbearing brother getting in my damn business every time I turn around!" My voice rose, bringing more attention to our conversation as the guards took a step forward. "What the hell do you want from me? Just to live with Kiera for the rest of my life, have random fucks with men, and never find my one?" I had lost control by letting the last part slip out, but it was out there. Time to deal.

"First, no random fucks. Ever."

I blew out an exasperated breath, trying to calm myself as I ran my fingers through my hair, pulling it tersely.

"Second, living with Kiera keeps you both safe. Third, what the fuck is this 'one' bullshit. Don't tell me your little clock is ticking, and you need to find a man." He chuckled sardonically, actually making fun of me.

Blood boiled in my veins as I stepped closer. Even with my heels, I had to tilt my head to connect with his eyes. I needed to get my point across and have his full, undivided attention. Inside, I vibrated, pulsing with anger that fled through every cell of my body, eating away at me like a virus.

"This damn bubble you and Daddy have me in is about to burst. I am a grown-ass woman you all have taught well. I run a damn business with Kiera, so I am not fucking stupid. Antonio was a poor choice, but with your dictation, my choices are pretty damn limited. I'm sick of this shit. Done. You keep this up and you will not like the results." I stepped away.

Our close-knit group was quiet, waiting for his reaction, but I didn't wait for it, didn't care what it was.

"I'm leaving," I announced to the room, moving to the door, the alcohol no longer having a hold on me. Fights with Val always seemed to sober me.

"Scraper," I called to the man still standing at the entrance of the VIP, his arms crossed, looking mean.

He nodded yet said nothing as I grabbed my purse from the red velvet chair and looked into Kiera's glowing eyes filled with concern.

"Sorry, babe. I just can't do this anymore. You coming or you gonna stay?"

"I've gotta go meet with my brothers. I just got a text." She held up her phone, dangling it in front of me. "I'll be home in a bit." Compassion laced her eyes, but she knew I had been on the brink of my family's meddling for a while now. The breaking point had to come sometime.

She nodded, calling her guards over as she walked out of the small room with them.

"Wait." My brother scowled, grabbing my arm tightly and pulling on me.

I yanked it back as I seethed with anger. How dare his ass put his hands on me?

"Get. Your. Hands. Off. Me." I bit out with what was left of my self-control, but he didn't relent. Instead, he pulled me more firmly to him, making me gasp and no doubt leaving a mark on my body.

"You know we love you. We just want to protect you. If you'd listen to what we said about Antonio, I wouldn't be here, cleaning up your fucking mess."

A red, hazy film covered my eyes as I used every ounce of strength to rip my arm out of his firm grasp. He stood there in shock, looking at his hand like he couldn't believe I had actually been able to get away from him. Apparently, I was stronger than I looked. He'd do best to remember that.

"You go clean up my mess, brother," I snapped even though Scraper had said it was handled. I was just pissed he had made the comment in the first place. "That is your job, after all," I sassed, leaving quickly with Scraper and my Ghost—who had come into play during the altercation—on my heels.

I just caught the smirk that played on Jag's face as I breezed by him and Ace.

Outside, Scraper opened the car door for me, and I climbed into the passenger seat of the sleek, black automobile, feeling the coolness of the leather on my thighs. It did nothing to cool down the raging inferno inside of me, though. I only wanted to go home.

I replayed the night in my head on a loop, the alcohol simmering in my veins. My brother was at the forefront of the raging thoughts. He couldn't expect me to continue on like this, being under this thumb, crushing me. He had flat out told Jag I was off limits. What right did he have to do that? None. Before I could finish my thoughts, we were home.

Preorder Blood & Loyalties by Ryan Michele now!
Out October 26th
Amazon: http://amzn.to/1POwJfR
Barnes & Noble: http://tinyurl.com/BloodLoyB-N
Kobo: http://tinyurl.com/BloodLoyKOBO
iTunes: http://tinyurl.com/BloodLoy-iTunes

Follow Ryan Michele here:
www.authorryanmichele.net
www.facebook.com/authorryanmichele
http://tinyurl.com/RyanMicheleNewsletter

JAG
by
Stevie J. Cole

CHAPTER 1

My mouth was dry like someone had shoved a fistful of cheap off-brand cotton balls in it. I ran my tongue over my teeth to wipe the film of bourbon off. Yawning, I rolled onto my back and stretched out in the king-sized bed before lifting the sheets back over my body. The smell of detergent floated up to my nose, and my lips curled up. No matter how nice the suite was, the sheets always smelled like that damn hotel laundry detergent. I couldn't *stand* that smell.

I heard someone next to me pull in a deep breath, and then the covers shifted off my body. Seconds later, I felt warm skin against mine as a hand wrapped around my stiff-ass dick. Fingers skimmed along its length, stopping to play with the metal bar lodged through the head.

I slowly opened my eyes. The sun was beaming in through one of the windows, and all I could see out of it was an overly crowded skyline. The sun glinted from the windows of the concrete skyscrapers competing for space; only a few slivers of blue sky managed to peep between them. I'd almost forgotten that I was in New York City. I couldn't really recall how she'd ended up with me, and I certainly had no idea what her fucking name was. To the best of my knowledge, I guessed she'd been at the club the night before. It wasn't out of the usual at all for me to wake up with an unknown woman beside me. It was habitual. One day, I'd probably luck out and bring back a psycho that'd try to off me, but I'd worry about that when it happened. *Most* of the time the sex was worth that small risk—at least it usually was when I could remember it.

Do I want to look over and see what she looks like, or not? That's one of the pluses about not letting them stay with you— you don't have to look poor judgment in the face.

Her grip tightened, and she gently stroked me in her hand. "Good morning," she whispered.

I grunted and closed my eyes again. I hated when they ended up staying the night. That was never the plan because it was so fucking awkward the next morning when I was sober and trying to piece together what all we'd done. I hated having to talk to them, having to listen to them go on and on about what a big fan they were. They'd all say fucking me was the most amazing thing that'd ever happened to them. Worst of all, I hated having them ask me if they could post the pictures from the night before on Facebook, Twitter, and Instagram. Fangirls, they're just dying to brag about having been bent over backwards and rammed by me, and rightfully so. It was quite the achievement.

Peeping through one halfway-opened eye, I saw a woman. *Okay. Well, at least I got that right despite being completely wasted.* She looked to be about twenty-four. *And thank God. She's legal.* Her platinum blonde hair stuck up in all directions, and black rings of mascara were smudged underneath her eyes. This girl was an absolute mess. It was *obvious* I'd been there *and* had a good time marking my territory.

Don't get me wrong, she wasn't bad looking, but she was absolutely no different than the rest of the other privileged rich girls whose daddies bought their horny daughters' way into the VIP areas. When she smiled, nothing on her face moved. When she abruptly sat up and slid her way down to my dick, her unnaturally round tits didn't budge either. It was evident she'd already started with the plastic surgery addiction. This was the kind of girl I was used to: fake, horny, and willing to do anything for a brush with fame.

A slight giggle bounced from her lips as she tugged the covers off my naked body.Her warm, slimy tongue, coated with morning breath germs traced up my shaft. The sensation sent a small tingle shooting up from my groin. I looked down to find her staring up at me, her eyes locked intimately on mine as she sucked half of me back into her throat.

I let out a short sigh. Leaning back, I shut my eyes, no hint of a smile on my face. The way she wrapppped her tongue around me felt damn good. Even though I had no interest in her being there, I wasn't going to deprive her of the joy she'd get from watching me get off *one* more time. I tried not to be selfish with that privilege.

After just a few minutes of her head bobbing up and down, her hand twisting at just the right moments, and her choking on my length a few times, I felt my body relax. My legs stiffened up, and then my entire body heated from the overwhelming rush of endorphins coursing through me. It's amazing how quickly orgasms come when you're not strung out on coke, or a bottle of oxycodone, or speed. Quicker, but weak compared to the euphoria that drugs granted me.

When that initial warm and fuzzy feeling wore off, I was ready to get her the hell out of my hotel room. Sitting up, I said, "Thanks for the great blow job. Pretty sure the door's still unlocked," and I flung my naked ass back down across the bed.

I watched her blink a couple of times, shocked at how rude I was being. I mean, she *had* just given me the gift of oral pleasure, and who knows what I told her the night before. I may have promised her she could go on tour with us. She narrowed her eyes. *Here comes the 'OMG, I can't believe what a bastard he is' huff that chicks are so good at in 3, 2, 1...* A loud breath flew out of her collagen plumped lips, and the springs of the mattress bounced as she hopped up. She mumbled to herself while gathering her things. I just laid there, staring up at the ceiling.

I tapped my finger in beat with her heels as they clicked across the tiled floors, and then they stopped. Raising my head from the pillow, I glanced up at her, arching one brow in disinterest. The girl, whose name I'd never bothered to ask for, glared at me for a minute before a smile inched across her face.

"I can't believe this!" She fell silent and shook her head, then covered her mouth with her hand. "I'm," she paused. "Getting kicked out of *Jag Steele's* hotel room. OMG! This. Is. *Amazing!*" she squealed, and pulled her phone to her face, her fingers typing furiously and her grin growing wider by the second. My guess was she had to check in on Foursquare and let everyone know she'd just become the one-thousand, five hundred and sixty-seventh woman to have her tonsils rammed by me—or some number close to that. I sure as hell didn't try to keep count anymore.

Her eyes darted up to me, and I could tell she was considering something. I caught her pointer finger creeping down the side of her phone, and I cleared my throat. "If you take a photo of me like this and post it, my lawyers will be in touch with you." I shot the biggest, most asshole-ish smile I could shape over at her. "Got that, princess?"

Her excited expression relaxed. She managed to huff out a dejected, "Uh, yeah," as she lowered her phone and dropped it into her purse. And there she stood, frozen, by the door.

Still nude, I rose and brushed past her, opening the door and circling my finger in the air before pointing directly out into the hallway. "Enjoy the rest of your day," I said.

Ms. No-Name skirted through, taking one last glance at me over her shoulder before I shut the door.

Rubbing my hands over my face, I made my way to the bathroom. I flipped the light switch and gave my eyes a minute to adjust to the artificial light. Sometimes I felt guilty after I kicked a girl out like that. I didn't use to be such a jackass. And during my fleeting *moments* of sobriety, I could recall that at one time I was actually nice, sometimes even shy. Funny how well-rehearsed you can become at being who everyone *thinks* you should be. There was no doubt that I was a different guy.

At this point, life just annoyed the shit out of me.

A few hours later I was leaning against a doorway, watching the interns scamper around with lattes and double shot espressos. My eyes traced over the black cords running from the cameras, and then up at the canned lights hanging from the ceiling. The bustling New York City crowd was visible through the large window at the far end of the room, constant movement of people going through their mundane daily routines. Every so often someone would stop, cup their hands around their face, and peer into the studio.

Two more hours until I had to be in front of those cameras, and my nerves were already tightly bundled up, my stomach uneasy. All I could think about was running to the bathroom and snorting a few lines real quick. The only problem with that was I didn't have any coke—oh, and I was supposed to be clean.

I hated being interviewed, especially when it required me to rehash all the ridiculous shit that had happened over the past few years. Really, the biggest problem I had at that moment was my sobriety. I'd never done an interview sober, and I doubted that I could make it through this one.

"Excuse me, Jag." One of the hipster interns attempted to get my attention. Not saying a word, I turned to face him. The intern didn't glance up from his pad as he continued. "They need you to come back to the dressing room, do some makeup before they start."

I pushed myself away from the door frame, then followed him down the slender white hallway.

He glanced back at me, a slight grin shaping his lips. "Man. I know I'm supposed to act all chill and stuff, but I can't help it. Pandemic Sorrow is my favorite band. You're a legend."

Shoving my shades through my hair, I forced my lips to curve up. I'd been told in rehab that I needed to act more appreciative, but when you're as numb and arrogant as I am, sometimes it's hard to act thankful about anything.

I answered with what I'd been told was an appropriate response. "Thanks, man. Really appreciate that."

The guy stopped, dropping his clipboard down by his side and staring at me through his thick, black-rimmed Buddy Holly glasses. He shook his head and looked me dead in the eyes. "You guys aren't really done, are you? Those are just rumors?"

"Nah. We can't go nowhere. Music's all we know."

Pleased with that response, he turned and continued to the dressing room.

About seven months ago I'd almost made my heart explode, or almost overdosed, if you want to get technical with it. I think the exploding heart thing sounds much better, less accusing. I had been *forced* into rehab, kicking and screaming because I didn't have a fucking problem. I just got a little too excited, a little too carried away, and snorted one too many lines. That's not a problem, that's an accident. Right after I finished my treatment and was told I was "cured" from my "habit," I threatened and swore that I was going to leave Hollywood behind in an effort to stay clean. Of course, when that happened, people thought the band was done for. I hadn't threatened that because I wanted to stay clean—honestly, it all just sounded like a hassle—but more so that I wanted to get the fuck away and have some privacy. The idea of fading into the background, of having a life where each damn breath I drew wouldn't be scrutinized and slapped across the front page of every tabloid in existence, well, sometimes that just seemed abso-fucking-lutely amazing.

We stopped outside the dressing room, and I grabbed the intern's shoulder before he walked away. "What's your name?" I asked.

"Jay."

One side of my mouth flipped up in a halfhearted grin, and I said, "Why do you work here, Jay?"

A ridge formed on his brow as he stared at me, not exactly sure why the hell I was asking him that question.

"What do you want to get from this place? From working at MTV? Fame? Is that what you're running after?" I pointed back to the studio. "You want to eventually end up in front of that camera?"

Nodding, he said, "Well, yeah. I mean, who doesn't want to be famous?"

I shook my head in disgust and turned to enter the dressing room as I mumbled, "Yeah. Well, some people that are famous just wish they weren't."

You can get Jag now!

US: http://amzn.to/1JiudmF
UK: http://amzn.to/1Hg3XHg
CA: http://amzn.to/1GHy7BX
AU: http://amzn.to/1GHy7BX

Follow Stevie J. Cole here:
https://www.facebook.com/authorsteviejcole
Website: www.steviejcole.com
Twitter: @steviejcole

The Rocker Who Betrays Me

Newsletter:

http://steviejcole.us11.list-manage.com/subscribe?u=62a21494139bac948abba7821&id=7e33657abe

Amazon:

http://www.amazon.com/Stevie-J.-Cole/e/B00K9PK3EY/ref=sr_tc_2_0?qid=1411841741&sr=8-2-ent

CPSIA information can be obtained
at www.ICGtesting.com
Printed in the USA
LVOW10s1738230717
542320LV00021B/1766/P